INCLUDING THE WORKS OF
CAMILLE ALEXA, KELLEY ARMSTRONG,
MADELINE ASHBY, PETER CHIYKOWSKI,
CAROLYN CLINK, DAVID LIVINGSTONE CLINK,
GEOFFREY W. COLE, CORY DOCTOROW,
AMAL EL-MOHTAR, GEMMA FILES,
NEILE GRAHAM, LISA L. HANNETT,
ADA HOFFMANN, CLAIRE HUMPHREY,
SUSAN IOANNU, KATHRYN KUITENBROUWER,
DEREK KÜNSKEN, KRISTIN JANZ,
HELEN MARSHALL, ANNA MIODUCHOWSKA,
SILVIA MORENO-GARCIA, DAVID NICKLE,
RHONDA PARRISH, KELLY ROSE PFLUG-BACK,
IAN ROGERS, TIMOTHY REYNOLDS,
ROBERT RUNTÉ, GEOFF RYMAN,
REBECCA M. SENESE, GEORGE SWEDE,
PETER WATTS, A.C. WISE,
AND RIO YOUERS

the best canadian speculative writing

IMAGINARIUM
2012

EDITED BY

SANDRA KASTURI
& HALLI VILLEGAS

WITH AN INTRODUCTION BY STEVEN ERIKSON

CZP
ChiZine Publications

Tightrope Books

FIRST EDITION

Imaginarium: The Best Canadian Speculative Writing © 2012, edited by Sandra Kasturi & Halli Villegas
Cover artwork © 2012 by Corey Beep
Cover design and interior design © 2012 by Samantha Beiko
All Rights Reserved.

Distributed in Canada by
HarperCollins Canada Ltd.
1995 Markham Road
Scarborough, ON M1B 5M8
Toll Free: 1-800-387-0117
e-mail: hcorder@harpercollins.com

Distributed in the U.S. by
Diamond Book Distributors
1966 Greenspring Drive
Timonium, MD 21093
Phone: 1-410-560-7100 x826
e-mail: books@diamondbookdistributors.com

Library and Archives Canada Cataloguing in Publication

Imaginarium 2012 : the best Canadian speculative

writing / Sandra Kasturi and Halli Villegas, editors.

Issued also in electronic format.

ISBN 978-1-926851-67-9

1. Speculative fiction, Canadian (English). 2. Short stories,

Canadian (English). 3. Canadian fiction (English)--21st century.

I. Kasturi, Sandra, 1966- II. Villegas, Halli

PS8323.S3I43 2012   C813'.08760806   C2012-904197-1

CHIZINE PUBLICATIONS
Toronto, Canada
www.chizinepub.com
info@chizinepub.com

TIGHTROPE BOOKS
Toronto, Canada
www.tightropebooks.com
info@tightropebooks.com

Edited by Sandra Kasturi & Halli Villegas
Copyedited and proofread by Sandra Kasturi and Brett Savory

Canada Council   Conseil des Arts
for the Arts   du Canada

We acknowledge the support of the Canada Council for the Arts which last year invested $20.1 million in writing and publishing throughout Canada.

**ONTARIO ARTS COUNCIL
CONSEIL DES ARTS DE L'ONTARIO**

Published with the generous assistance of the Ontario Arts Council.

Printed in Canada

IMAGINARIUM 2012

the best canadian speculative writing

copyright acknowledgements

table of contents

introduction
STEVEN ERIKSON

It is a common conceit, among those critics, academics and indeed, readers, unfamiliar with the genre of the Fantastic, that in the genre's departing from this "real" world—with its presumably explicable details amounting to an agreed-upon reality—one also ventures from the significant to the irrelevant. A host of descriptive words arrive to accompany this easy dismissal: escapist, popular, the not-quite-serious; and for many even the subgenre labels themselves carry pejorative connotations. *Fantasy. Science Fiction. Horror.*

If there was ever a time when Fantasy or Science Fiction or Horror embraced *true* escapism, it was long ago, when the very notion of flights of fancy was enough to elicit disapproving frowns among certain literati, for whom mundane reality was all the challenge they cared to face.

If you note some derision in my tone, be assured it is accompanied by a loose shrug. The debate over the significance or relevance of fantastic literature within the broader stream of literature seems to be a perpetual one, exercised in varying levels of snarky commentary and frustrated indignation. The pendulum knocks and crashes in its wild swinging to and fro, with an increasingly large element of the population blissfully indifferent to those distinctions so avidly sweated over, promulgated and defended by a shrinking subset of self-avowed arbiters of culture. Despite this, at times it's enough to leave a writer (even me) ticked off in the face of what is clearly studied indifference.

It is probably fair to assume that the majority of readers now holding this book are well familiar with the genres on display in this collection. You don't need convincing as to the relevance of these tales, or the value of their place in the canon of modern literature. Equally likely, many of you will have been challenged, from time to time, and made to defend not only your choice of reading material but also your interest in prose and poetry definitively *not* subservient to mundane reality. You can probably recall, in sharp detail, those expressions of disapproval and dismay—from teachers, parents, even friends—and at some point the question arrives: *Is it not all a waste of time?* After all, where among the classics of literature will you find such absurd, escapist fare?

Well, *everywhere*. It is no stretch—no stretch at all—to argue the works of Homer as being Fantasy fiction, *Epic* Fantasy fiction at that. The same argument can be made for Gilgamesh, and Beowulf. I have, on occasion, described *Lord of the Flies* as dystopic Science Fiction—and received reactions of skepticism, if not outright disbelief, in response. As for Horror, well, the potential list one could make from the literary canon just goes on and on (*Dracula*, *Frankenstein*, *Paradise Lost*, etc.).

Whatever. Enlightenment makes no inroads on ignorance, and sad to say, we are talking about *ignorance*. The willful kind. The kind that isn't interested in arguments, or intellectual engagement. The kind that makes its pronouncement a declaration voiced in tones of actual *pride* ("Well, I don't *read* that rubbish. . . ." or "I don't read *that* rubbish," or, "I don't read that *rubbish*"). Judgement precedes knowledge and once the door is slammed shut, good luck in prying it open again.

I am not unmindful of counterarguments in this position, where it might seem to some that I am beating a straw-man of my own making: there are examples of literature of the Fantastic that are indeed acknowledged as worthy of being called serious. But I would argue that in each case, a strange kind of intellectual shell-game has preceded the label of acceptability, and it is this: by virtue of being deemed "worthy," such works (and their authors) are deftly extricated from the genres of Fantasy, Science Fiction or Horror. The very act of "exceptionalism" permits serious consideration of said work or author, while perpetuating the ghettoization of the original genre. Sadly, sometimes the author him- or herself participates in this exercise, to the detriment of every other author and every other self-identified genre work of fiction (often for reasons of choice placement in bookstores, and consideration in the book review sections of major newspapers, not to mention invitations to "serious" literary festivals and so on). It's all rather ridiculous.

Although it's probably not well-suited given this collection's subtitle, I'm not much of a fan of the phrase "speculative fiction" either, which strikes me as yet another (diffident) effort to legitimize works of the Fantastic. After all, *all* fiction is speculative, isn't it? Whether it's a story set in modern day Winnipeg, or the Weimar Republic, or the seedy side of downtown Vancouver: each of these examples may purport to a reality, one based on life experience or exhaustive research, but in the end, if you give it some thought, you'll realise that it's all invented; that the recognizable traits are just there to convince you that what you're reading is real, and that accordingly the characters within that tale, their thoughts, their emotions, their actions, their motivations, are all authentic—when the truth is, they are all inventions of the author's imagination.

Transpose these characters to a world with different rules—to a world unlike our own, or one in the far (or near) future or distant past—and all that we as readers are then witness to, is what can only be called a virtuoso act of imagination. I am going to risk arrogance here and say, explicitly, that such authors working in Fantasy and Science Fiction and Horror, have to work much harder than do their compatriots writing contemporary, "realist" fiction. They need to convince of you of unfamiliar rules, unfamiliar settings, while at the same time assuring you, the reader, of the essential *humanity* of the story they're telling. Having written both forms of fiction, you'll just have to take it from me: contemporary, "this-world" fiction is *easy* compared to writing Fantasy, Science Fiction and Horror.

So, having sat for years on the grisly end of denigration as a writer in such genres, I hereby reverse the qualitative imbalance, and with brazen audacity announce that contemporary, realist fiction, is in fact a *lesser* form of writing, an easier and lazier effort at imagination, and one far-too-reliant on all that's recognizable in the real world—to carry (for the author) the weight of significance, to bask with little effort in the seriousness of common veracity; and as for its often desperate struggle to elevate the mundane, through patently unrealistic subtext (the real world has no subtext: it just is), awkward symbolism, unrealistic foreshadowing, epiphany and denouement, these are nothing more than contrived structural impositions on reality.

Which is not to say that there aren't good writers writing contemporary fiction. There are a few, to be sure, but the extent to which some pundits would elevate their efforts, they are given far too much weight, far too much hyperbole, and far too much significance in the world of literature, to the detriment of many other talented—genre—writers.

In launching, with a hard shove, the pendulum the other way as I have just done, I can already hear the reverberations of outrage at my bold claims (assuming anyone cares). To those who care to argue against my assertions, so long as you are familiar with works of Fantasy, Science Fiction and Horror, by all means begin your assault, and I may find some future forum in which to engage in lively discussion. If, however, you've not read any Fantasy, Science Fiction or Horror, well, let's end our debate here and now, because you don't know what you're talking about, and I have no interest in wasting my time seeking to educate you.

The writers in this collection have unleashed their imaginations. They have pushed the notion of an explicable reality, and they have dragged—at times elegantly, at other times roughly—the human condition into strangely flavoured worlds. This is not escapism. This is engagement: a dialogue with the present and real world, evoking the tensions of sensibility peculiar to, and indeed uniquely so, the genres of the Fantastic. In these genres, more than anywhere else, metaphors can be made real: intent can be given physical form, and the very purpose of storytelling— its deepest roots—are revived and given universal significance: why? Because they evoke in readers the one crucial element so woefully absent in "realist" fiction: a sense of wonder.

This here real world is suffering from a loss of wonder—and if I venture, in aside, the suggestion that writers of contemporary, realist fiction are partly to blame for that loss, I do so with ready argument, although this is neither the time nor the place for further elaboration. Accordingly, consider my statement a provocation, since that is how it was intended. For what it is worth, I think we need to rediscover that sense of wonder, not in a return to childhood (as critics of the Fantastic might charge), but as adults, if only to counter this growing plague of cynicism and weary nihilism. If such an endeavour is cause for dismissal or indifference, God help us all.

Steven Erikson
Falmouth, Cornwall, 2012

looker

DAVID NICKLE

I met her on the beach.

It was one of Len's parties—one of the last he threw, before he had to stop. You were there too. But we didn't speak. I remember watching you talking with Jonathan on the deck, an absurdly large tumbler for such a small splash of Merlot wedged at your elbow as you nodded, eyes fixed on his so as not to meet mine. If you noticed me, I hope you also noticed I didn't linger.

Instead, I took my own wine glass, filled it up properly, climbed down that treacherous wooden staircase, and kicked off my shoes. It was early enough that the sand was still warm from the sun—late enough that the sun was just dabs of pink on the dark ocean and I could tell myself I had the beach to myself.

She was, I'm sure, telling herself the same thing. She had brought a pipe and a lighter with her in her jeans, and was perched on a picnic table, surreptitiously puffing away. The pipe disappeared as I neared her. It came back soon enough, when she saw my wineglass, maybe recognized me from the party.

I didn't recognize her. She was a small woman, but wide across the shoulders and the tiniest bit chubby. Hair was dark, pulled back into a ponytail. Pretty, but not pretty enough; she would fade at a party like Len's.

"Yeah, I agree," she said to me and I paused on my slow gambol to the surf.

"It's too bright," she said, and as I took a long pull from my wine, watching her curiously, she added, "look at him."

"Look at me," I said, and she laughed.

"You on the phone?" I asked, and she dropped her head in extravagant *mea culpa*.

"No," she said. "Just . . ."

"Don't fret. What's the point of insanity if you can't enjoy a little conversation?" Oh, I am smooth. She laughed again, and motioned me over, and waved the pipe and asked if I'd like to share.

Sure I said, and she scooted aside to make room on the table. Her name was Lucy. Lucille, actually, was how she introduced herself but she said Lucy was fine. I introduced myself. "Tom's a nice name," she said.

The night grew. Lungs filled with smoke and mouths with wine; questions asked, questions answered. *How do you know Len? What do you do? What brings you to the beach when so much is going on inside?* It went both ways.

Lucy knew Len scarcely at all. They'd met through a friend who worked at Len's firm. Through the usual convolutions of dinners and pubs and excursions, she'd insinuated herself onto the cc list of the *ur*-mail by which Len advertised his parties. She worked cash at a bookstore chain in town and didn't really have a lot of ambition past that right now. Which tended to make her feel seriously out of her weight class at Len's parties or so she said; the beach, therefore, was an attractive option.

She finished my wine for me, and we walked. I'd been on my way to the water's edge and Lucy thought that was a fine idea. The sun was all gone by now and stars were peeking out. One of the things I liked about Len's place—it was just far enough away from town you could make out stars at night. Not like the deep woods, or the mountains. But constellations weren't just theoretical there.

"Hey Tom," she said as the surf touched our toes, "want to go for a swim? I know we don't have suits, but . . ."

Why not? As you might remember, I've a weakness for the midnight dunk. We both did, as I recall.

I stepped back a few yards to where the sand was dry, set down my glass and stripped off my shirt, my trousers. Lucy unbuttoned her blouse, the top button of her jeans. I cast off my briefs. "Well?" I said, standing *in flagrante delicto* in front of her.

"Get in," she said, "I'll be right behind you."

It didn't occur to me that this might be a trick until I was well out at sea. Wouldn't it be the simplest thing, I thought, as I dove under a breaking wave, to wait until I was out far enough, gather my trousers, find the wallet and the mobile phone, toss the clothes into the surf and run to a waiting car? I'm developing my suspicious mind, really, my dearest—but it still has a time delay on it, even after everything. . . .

I came up, broke my stroke, and turned to look back at the beach.

She waved at me. I was pleased—and relieved—to see that she was naked too. My valuables were safe as they could be. And Lucy had quite a nice figure, as it turned out: fine full breasts—wide, muscular hips—a small bulge at the tummy, true . . . but taken with the whole, far from offensive.

I waved back, took a deep breath and dove again, this time deep enough to touch bottom. My fingers brushed sea-rounded rock and stirred up sand, and I turned and kicked and broke out to the moonless night, and only then it occurred to me—how clearly I'd seen her on the beach, two dozen yards off, maybe further.

There lay the problem. There wasn't enough light. I shouldn't have seen anything.

I treaded water, thinking back at how I'd seen her . . . glistening, flickering, with tiny points of red, of green . . . winking in and out . . . like stars themselves? Spread across not sky, but flesh?

I began to wonder: Had I seen her at all?

There was no sign of her now. The beach was a line of black, crowned with the lights from Len's place, and above that . . . the stars.

How much had I smoked? I wondered. What had I smoked, for that matter? I hadn't had a lot of wine—I'd quaffed a glass at Len's before venturing outside, and I'd shared the second glass with Lucy. Not even two glasses . . .

But it *was* Len's wine.

I'd made up my mind to start back in when she emerged from the waves—literally in front of my face.

"You look lost," Lucy said, and splashed me, and dove again. Two feet came up, and scissored, and vanished. Some part of her brushed against my hip.

I took it as my cue and ducked.

The ocean was nearly a perfect black. I dove and turned and dove again, reaching wide in my strokes, fingers spreading in a curious, and yes, hungry grasp. I turned, and came near enough the surface that I felt my foot break it, splashing down again, and spun—

—and I saw her.

Or better, I saw the constellation of Lucy—a dusting of brilliant red points of light, defining her thighs—and then turning, and more along her midriff; a burst of blue stipple, shaping her breasts, the backs of her arms. I kicked toward her as she turned in the water, my own arms held straight ahead, to lay hold of that fine, if I may say, celestial body.

But she anticipated me, and kicked deeper, and I'd reached my lungs' limits so I broke surface, gasping at the night air. She was beside me an instant later, spitting and laughing. No funny lights this time; just Lucy, soaking wet and treading water beside me.

"We don't have towels," she said. "I just thought of that. We're going to freeze."

"We won't freeze," I said.

"It's colder than you think."

"Oh, I know it's cold. We just won't freeze."

She splashed me and laughed again and wondered what I meant by that, but we both knew what I meant by that, and after we'd not-quite tired ourselves out in the surf, we made back for the shore.

I wonder how things went for you, right then? I know that you always fancied Jonathan; I know what happened later. I hope you don't think I'm being bitter or ironic when I say I hope you had a good time with him. If he misbehaved—well, I trust you did too.

Shall I tell you how *we* misbehaved?

Well—

In some ways, it was as you might expect; nothing you haven't seen, nothing you haven't felt, my dear.

In others . . .

Through the whole of it, Lucy muttered.

"He is," she would say as I pressed against her breasts and nibbled on her earlobe; and "Quiet!" as I ran my tongue along the rim of her aureole . . . "I said no," as I thrust into her, and I paused, and then she continued: "Why are you stopping, Tommy?"

This went on through the whole of it. As I buried my face between her legs, and she commented, "Isn't he, though?" I thought again of Lucy on the shore, under the water. "Too bright," she moaned, and I remembered my visions of the sky, on her skin.

And as I thought of these things, my hands went exploring: along her thighs, across her breasts—along her belly. . . .

She gasped and giggled as I ran my thumb across her navel . . . and she said, "Tommy?" as my forefinger touched her navel again . . . and "What are you doing?" as the palm of my hand, making its way along the ridge of her hip-bone . . . found her navel once more.

I lifted my head and moved my hand slowly aside. For an instant, there was a flash of dim red light—reflecting off my palm like a candle-flame. But only an instant. I moved my hand aside and ran the edge of my thumb over the flesh there. It was smooth. "Tom?" she said sharply, and started on about unfinished business. "Shh," I said, and lowered my face—to the ridge of her hip-bone, or rather the smooth flesh inward of it. And slowly, paying minute attention, I licked her salted skin.

I would not have found it with my crude, calloused fingertips; my tongue was better attuned the task. I came upon it first as a small bump in the smooth flesh: like a pimple, a cyst. As I circled it, I sensed movement, as though a hard thing were rolling inside. Running across the tiny peak of it, I sensed a line—like a slit in the flesh, pushed tightly closed. Encouraged, I surrounded it with my lips and began to suck, as I kept probing it with my tongue. "I'm sorry," she said, and then, "Oh!" as my tongue pushed through. It touched a cool, wet thing—rolling on my tongue like an unripened berry.

And then . . . I was airborne . . . it was though I were flying up, and falling deep. And I landed hard on my side and it all resolved, the world once more. Icy water lapped against me. And Lucy was swearing at me.

I looked at her, unbelieving. She looked back.

She, and a multitude.

For now I could see that what I'd first thought were star-points, were nothing of the sort. Her flesh was pocked with eyes. They were small, and reflective, like a cat's.

Nocturnal eyes.

In her shoulders—the swell of her breasts—along the line of her throat . . . They blinked—some individually, some in pairs, and on her belly, six points of cobalt blue, formed into a nearly perfect hexagon. Tiny slits of pupils widened to take in the sight of me. The whole of her flesh seemed to writhe with their squinting.

It didn't seem to cause her discomfort. Far from it; Lucy's own eyes—the ones in her head—narrowed to slits, and her mouth perked in a little smile. "He is that," she said, "yes, you're right." And it struck me then: those strange things she was saying weren't intended for me or anyone else.

She was talking to the eyes.

"He can't have known," she continued, her hand creeping down to her groin, "and if he did, well now he knows better."

I drew my legs to my chest and my own hands moved instinctively to my privates, as the implications of all these eyes, of her words, came together.

These weren't her eyes; they were from another creature, or many creatures. And they were all looking upon me: naked, sea-shrivelled, crouching in the dirt.

Turning away from her, I got to my feet, ran up the beach and gathered my shirt and trousers, and clutching them to my chest, fairly bolted for the stairs. I pulled on my shirt and trousers, hunted around for my shoes, and made my way up the stairs. At the top, I looked back for the glow of Lucy. But the beach was dark.

The eyes were shut.

You and Jonathan were gone by the time I came back to the house.

I wasn't surprised; Len had switched to his Sarah Vaughan / Etta James play-list, and I remember how fond you are of those two. And it was late. The party had waxed and waned during my excursion with Lucy on the beach and those who remained were the die-hards: Ben and Dru, sprawled on the sectional, finishing off a bottle of Shiraz; Dennis, holding court in the kitchen with Emile and Prabh and the dates they'd not thought to introduce— at least not to me; maybe a half-dozen others that neither of us wouldn't recognize if we met them on the street. Len's party had proceeded without me.

I wasn't surprised, and I wasn't unhappy about it. Skinny dipping on the ocean and fucking on the beach are two activities that hardly leave one presentable to polite company. Best then to wait until the polite company had moved along, leaving only the depraved ones.

I made for the bathroom—the second floor bath, which yes, I know, was a *faux pas* at Len's parties, particularly late into the evening. But there was a small crowd around the two-piece off the kitchen, and I needed to tidy up sooner. So I slipped upstairs and made for the master bath. Which, happily, was vacant. The lights flickered on as I stepped inside and I slid the pocket door shut, and confronted myself in the long mirror opposite the showers.

I didn't think I took that long; just splashed water in my face, ran a wet comb through my hair, shook the sand out of my shirt and tucked it in properly before giving myself another inspection. By my own reckoning, it couldn't have been more than five minutes. But the hammering on the door said otherwise.

It was Kimi, Len's Kimi.

In a week, she'd be on a plane back to New York, done with all of us, gone from Len's circle for good. That party, she was on the verge of it. I slid open the door and apologized. "You shouldn't be up here," she said, "not this time of night," and I agreed.

"Ask forgiveness not permission? That it, Tommy?" she said and brushed past me. She had been spending time in Len's rooms, and it had gone about as badly as it did toward the end. You could tell. Do you remember that time Len had us all on that boat he'd hired for the summer? And she came hammering on our cabin door—with that fish-hook stuck in just below the collar-bone? And when you opened it, she was so quiet, asking if you knew where they kept the first-aid kit on the boat because "Len isn't sure." You knew something awful had happened, I knew something awful had happened. We talked about it after we got the hook out and the wound cleaned and bandaged and Kimi, smiling brightly, had excused herself and skipped back to the cabin she and Len were sharing. What did you say? "One day, that armour of hers is going to crack. When it does, she'll either leave or she'll die."

It was a good line; I laughed as hard as you did.

Well there in the upstairs bath, the armour was cracking. And Kimi wasn't dead. But she wasn't leaving either. She leaned against the vanity, arms crossed over her chest. She was wearing a short black skirt. Her shoulders, arms, and legs were bare. There were no visible bruises. No fish-hooks either. She studied me, maybe looking for the same things.

"You go for a swim?" she said finally. "You look like you went for a swim in the ocean."

"Guilty."

Her eyes flickered away a moment as she waved a hand. "Nobody's guilty of taking a fucking swim. And it's a good look for you." Then she looked again, reassessing. "But you didn't just go for a swim."

"You were right. I took a fucking swim," I said, and started to laugh, and she got it and laughed too.

"How's your night going?" I asked. She made a little sneer with her lips—as if she was trying to fish a piece of food out of her teeth. Put her bare feet together on the slate tile floor, made a show of inspecting the nails.

"Len's very tired," she said.

I raised my eyebrows. "Oh dear. That doesn't sound good."

"It's not as bad as that."

"If you say so."

She looked at me. "Are you hitting on me, Tommy?"

I said I wasn't.

"Then why the fuck are you still here?"

There was an answer to that question, but not one I could really articulate—not the way she was looking at me then. I wanted to talk to her about Lucy, about the eyes... I thought—hoped—that she would be able to help me parse the experience somehow. Or failing that, help me put it away, someplace quiet.

But her armour was cracked. She had nothing to offer me. And although I wouldn't know for sure until a week later—she wasn't leaving that night, she stayed the whole time—she was almost certainly planning her escape.

So I left her to it. "I'm very tired too," I said, and stepped into the hall.

That one didn't get a laugh. The bathroom door slid shut behind me, hitting the door-jamb hard enough to quiver in its track.

"You're still thinking about *her*," said Kimi through the wood. "Well give it up, Tommy. It's obvious to everybody. She's done with you."

Oh, don't worry. I know you're done with me. I'm done with you too.

I joined the conversation in the kitchen, or rather hovered at its edge. Dennis had stepped away, and now Emile was talking about Dubai, which was hardly a new topic for him. But the girls he and Prabh had brought were new. They hung on every word. I leaned against the stove, poured myself the dregs of a Chardonnay into a little plastic cup and swallowed the whole thing. Prabh found me a Malbec from Portugal and poured a refill.

"Yeah, you look like shit," he said. "Bad night?"

"Not exactly bad," I said. "Strange. Not exactly bad."

Prabh nodded and turned back to his girl. She was very pretty, I had to hand it to him: tall, with streaked blond hair and a dancer's body. Twenty-seven years old, no older. I'd turn back to her too.

So I kept drinking, and Prabh kept filling my cup, and after a while, I'd moved from the periphery of the conversation to the juicy middle. And there, I asked as innocently as I could manage: "Any of you know Lucy?"

Shrugs all around. I showed a level hand to indicate her height. Another to show how long her hair was. "We don't know her, Tom," said Emile, and Prabh poured me another glass. "Maybe you want to sit down?" asked one of the girls.

It was an excellent suggestion. I made my way to the sectional in the living room with only a little help here and there, as necessary.

Really, I don't think I made *that* much of a spectacle of myself. But I had had too much to drink and I'd had it all too quickly. I was speaking extemporaneously you might say. So I concluded it be best not to speak at all.

I fitted myself into the corner of the sectional. Dru and Ben a few feet to my left, made a point of staying engrossed in one another—and as soon as it was polite to do so, got up and found spots at the dining room table. And I was left to myself.

By this time it was well past midnight. You know how that is. It's a time when you start asking questions about things that in the light of day you wouldn't consider twice. It's a time . . . well, we both know how it goes, in the dark hour.

I was left to myself.

I began to feel badly about leaving Lucy on the beach. I wondered if I might have handled things differently. I worried that I might have impregnated her, or caught a venereal disease. Briefly, I worried that some of those eyes might have migrated from her skin to mine—if I'd caught a case of leaping, burrowing and uniquely ocular crabs. If I closed my own eyes, would I see a thousand dim refractions of the room from the point of view of my belly?

The notion made me laugh—a little too loudly, I think. Dennis, reeking of weed and vodka cooler, just about turned on his heel at the sight of me and fled back to the deck. But it got me back wondering at the nature of Lucy's peculiar disease, if that's what it was. If not she, then who was looking out through those eyes? And so, in circles, went my thoughts.

The front door opened and closed once, twice, five times. Water ran in the kitchen sink. Lights dimmed in rooms not far from this one.

"Hey Tom. How you keeping?"

I looked up and blinked.

"Hey Len," I said. "Haven't seen you all night."

He nodded. "I've been a rotten host."

Len was wearing his kimono, that red one with the lotus design. He'd lost a lot of weight—you couldn't mistake it, the kimono hung so loose on him. His hair was coming back in, but it was still thin, downy. He sat down beside me.

"You met Lucille," he said.

"How did you know?" I asked, but I didn't need to; as I spoke, I saw Kimi over the breakfast bar in the kitchen, putting glasses into the dishwasher. She'd told him about our conversation in the washroom. He'd put it together.

"Yeah," said Len, "you were on the beach. Two of you. Had yourself a time, didn't you Tom?"

"We had ourselves a time."

Len put a bony hand on my thigh, gave it a squeeze of surprising strength, and nodded.

"Now you're drunk in my living room, when everybody else has had sense to get out. Too drunk to drive yourself, am I right?"

That was true.

"And you don't have cab fare, do you?"

I didn't have cab fare.

"You're a fucking leech, Tom. You *smell* like a fucking leech."

"It's the ocean," I said.

Kimi turned her back to us, lowered her head and raised her shoulder blades, like wings, as she ran water in the kitchen sink.

"Yeah, we know that's not so," said Len. "You smell of Lucy." He licked his lips, and not looking up, Kimi called out, "That's not nice, Len," and Len chuckled and jacked a thumb in her direction and shrugged.

"Did she leave?" I asked. "Lucy I mean."

"Miss her too now?" Did I miss her like *you*, he meant, obviously.

"I just didn't see her leave."

"What'd I just say? *Everybody else* had the sense to get out."

A plate clattered loudly in the sink. Len shouted at Kimi to *be fuckin' careful with that.* Then he coughed and turned an eye to me. His expression changed.

"You saw," he said quietly. "Didn't you?"

"I saw."

He looked like he wanted to say more. But he stopped himself, the way he does: tucking his chin down, pursing his lips . . . like he's doing some math, which is maybe close to the mark of what he is doing until he finally speaks.

"Did she tell you how we met?"

"Friend of a friend," I said, then remembered: "Not just a friend; one of your partners. And then you just kept inviting her out."

"Always that simple, isn't it?"

"It's never that simple," I said, "you're going to tell me."

"It is that simple," he said. "Lucille Carroll is a high school friend of Linda James. Linda isn't a partner now and I won't likely live to see the day that she is. But she did work for me. With me. And she used to come out sometimes. And she brought Lucille one day. And not long after, Linda stopped coming around. Lucille still shows up." He sighed. "Simple."

Kimi flipped a switch under the counter and the dishwasher hummed to life. "I'm turning in," she announced, and when Len didn't say anything, she climbed the stairs.

"It's not that simple," I said when Kimi was gone. Now, I thought, was the time when Len would spell it out for me: tell me what had happened, really.

"And she doesn't like to talk about it," was what he said instead. "It's private, Tom."

What came next? Well, I might have handled it better. But you know how I hate it when my friends hide things from me. We both remember the weekend at the lake, with your sister and her boys. Did I ever properly apologize for that? It's difficult to, when all I've spoken is God's truth.

But I could have handled it better.

"It's not private," I said, "it's the opposite. She's the least private person I've met. The eyes . . ."

"Her skin condition you mean."

"You do know about them." I may have jabbed him in the chest. That may have been unwise. "Maybe you like them? Watching everything you do? Maybe they flatter your vanity. . . ."

Len shook his head. He stopped me.

"You know what, Tom? I'm sick of you. I've been sick of you for a long time. But I'm also sick, and I'll tell you—that clarifies things for a man. So here's what I see:

"You come here to my house—you moon around like some fucking puppy dog—you drink my wine . . . the friends of mine you don't fuck, you bother with your repetitive, self-involved shit. Jesus, Tom. You're a leech."

"I'm sorry," I said, because really—what else do you say to something like that? To someone like Len, for Christ's sake?

"Yeah," he said. "Heard that one before. Lucy's a special girl, Tom. She's helping me in ways you couldn't imagine. And it has nothing to do with my fucking vanity. Not a fucking thing. Lucy's my . . . assurance. And she's always welcome here."

"I'm sorry."

"I got that. Now are you okay to drive yet, Tom?"

I wasn't. But I said sure.

"Then you get out of my house. Get back to your place. Stay there. I don't think you should come back here again."

Yes. That's why you hadn't seen me at Len's after that. He cast me out—into the wilderness—left me to my own devices.

I wasn't avoiding you.

Far from it.

Lucy wasn't that hard to find.

She had a Facebook page, and I had enough information to narrow her down from the list of those other Lucy Carrolls who said they were from here. So I sent her a note apologizing for being such an asshole, and she sent me a friend request and I agreed—and she asked me to pick a place, and that's where we met. It's the Tokyo Grill in the Pier District. I don't think we ever went there, you and I. But at 12:15 on a Tuesday in June, it's very bright.

Lucy wore a rose print dress, not quite as pale as her skin. She had freckles and her hair was more reddish than brunette. Perhaps it was the effect of wearing a dress and not a pair of jeans, but she seemed more svelte on the patio than she did that night on the beach. *Her* eyes were hazel.

Do you remember how I courted you? Did you ever doubt that

I was anything but spontaneous? That when I laughed so hard at that joke of yours, it was because I thought it was the funniest thing I'd ever heard?

You didn't? You should have. I'm not good at everything in life, oh that I'll admit. But I am good at this part. I am smooth.

And that's how I was at the Tokyo Grill that Tuesday.

Lucy wasn't sure about me and she made that explicit pretty early. I'd seemed nice at first, but running off like that . . . well, it had been hurtful. It made her feel as though there was something wrong with her, and as she made explicit somewhat later on, there wasn't anything wrong with her.

"It's not you—it's the rest of the world," I said, and when she took offense, I explained I wasn't making fun.

"The world's an evil place. Lots wrong with it. Look at . . . think about Len, as an example."

"What do you mean?"

"Well. How he treats people. How he uses them. Like Kimi."

"He's an important man," she said quickly. "I imagine it takes a toll. All those clients he's got to look after." She sighed. "Clients can be very demanding."

"Clients." I made a little smile. "That's a good word. Len has clients like other people have friends."

Yes, I suppose I was being dramatic. But Lucy didn't think so; she laughed, very hard, and agreed.

"So what about you?" she asked. "Are you client or friend?"

"Something else."

I explained how Lucy wasn't the only one I'd offended with my bad behaviour that night—and again, I layered contrition on top of itself, and doing so took another step to winning her over.

Working through it, I could almost forget that Lucy was a woman containing a multitude—that as she sat here opposite me in the Pier District, the lids up and down her body squinted shut like tiny incision scars against the bright daylight.

Like clients.

I had to forget. Because I couldn't mention them; Len was right—she didn't want to talk about it. She may not have even been capable.

And keeping silent on the subject, and knowing of that alien scrutiny, resting behind translucent lids . . .

I couldn't have done what I had to do.

Lucy's next shift at the bookstore was Wednesday afternoon, so she had the rest of the day to herself, and as we finished our sashimi, she made a point of saying the afternoon shift meant she could stay out as late as she liked.

So we took a walk. We found my car. We drove back to my apartment. And behind drawn blinds, we stripped off our clothes and lay down together on fresh white sheets.

Oh dear. I can tell you're upset—not by anything I've done, but what you think I'm about to do: relay some detailed account of how it was for Lucy and I, rutting on the very same sheets where you and I lolled, those long Sunday mornings, when . . . well, before you came to your senses is how you might put it. . . .

I'll try and be circumspect.

Lucy talked through it all, same as she had on the beach: those half-formed statements: "He's the same," and "The third floor," and "I do not agree." Of course, she was talking to them— fielding questions: *Is he the handsome fellow from the beach? On what floor is this fellow's apartment? Don't you think he's a bit much—being too . . .*

too . . .

To which she answered: *I do not agree.*

I'd drawn the curtains in my rooms, to make it dim enough for the curious eyes to open without being blinded—and sure enough, this is what they did. As I ran my tongue along her shoulder-blade, I found myself looking into a tiny blue orb, no bigger than a rat's. It blinked curiously at me as I moved past, to the nape of her neck, and there, in the wispy curls at the base of her skull, I uncovered two yellow eyes, set close together, in the forest of her hair. Were they disapproving? I imagine they must have been, affixed on Lucy's skull, less than an inch from her brain. I winked and moved on.

"Tell them," I whispered into her ear, looking into a squinting, infinitely old eye fixed in her temple, "that I understand."

"He understands," she murmured.

"Tell them I'm not afraid."

"He's not afraid."

"Tell them," I said, before I moved from her ear to her mouth, and rolled her onto her back, and slid atop her, "that I'm ready."

And the rest of it?

Well, I did tell you I'd be circumspect. Suffice it to say . . . just as poor old Len would, not long after . . .

I *entered* her.

You looked good at my funeral. You and Jonathan both. The dress you wore—was it new? Did you buy it especially for the occasion? It would be nice to think that you had.

In any event, I must say that Jonathan was very supportive of you. He held your hand so very tightly through the eulogies. Had you needed it, I'm sure he would have provided a handkerchief; if it had rained at the graveside, he'd have held the umbrella. He seems that sort of upright fellow. A real keeper.

You look great now, too. You have a lovely smile, you always have, and the shorter haircut—it suits you. It really frames your face. I can't hear what you're saying, here in Emile's house in town, over the dregs of what I recall as being an acceptable cab-franc from Chile.

Still, you're laughing, and that's good. You've left Kimi and poor dying Len behind. You're cementing new friendships . . . with Prabh and Emile and, perhaps, Lucy?

Perhaps.

It's impossible to say of course—I haven't been at this long enough to learn how to read lips, particularly with that damned brooch in the way. I never could guess your mind on this sort of thing. But you seem . . . open to it, to this new friend who works the cash in your favourite bookstore. You are. Aren't you?

Ah well. I must learn patience here in my new place. After all, Lucy will tell me everything—in due time, in a quiet moment, when the lights are low:

She says she misses you. She says she can't believe she let you go. Now that you're gone.

She says that she and I will be great friends.

And then, if all goes well . . . if you and Lucy really do hit it off . . .

I can't promise, other than to say I'll do my best. I'll try not to let my gaze linger.

the list
KELLEY ARMSTRONG

Everyone laughed when I walked into Miller's bar. Never a good way to start an evening out.

Randy waved for me to ignore them and join him at his table. He had my beer waiting. There would be a list of supplies he needed me to steal, too, but that wouldn't come out until later. Don't ask me where he learned such good manners. Certainly not from his older brother, Rudy, who was snickering and whispering behind the bar.

"Ignore them, Zoe," Randy said, twisting the top from my bottle.

"What's going on?"

"You don't want to know."

Whatever it was, it was bringing a much needed air of liveliness to the place. Miller's might not be the worst dive in Toronto, but don't tell Rudy that or he might decide he can skip the monthly cleaning.

It isn't even a bar, really, just a dark cave of a room off an alley, with a Miller's Beer sign in the window. The sign used to flash, until Rudy realized it was attracting patrons and unplugged it.

It's not a private club, but it is racially segregated. Sorcerers, half-demons, witches, necromancers, they're all welcome. As for vampires, only one is allowed. I'd feel a lot more special about that if I wasn't the only vampire in town.

"How's the clinic going?" I asked.

Randy made a face, which meant "the usual." Chronically under-funded and in danger of closing, which is why I stole medical supplies for him.

"I had an interesting case today," he began. "This guy—"

"Hey, Zoe!" Rudy called. "Come here. Got something to show you."

"Don't do it," Randy murmured.

I walked over to the bar, reached across and snagged a beer bottle from the ice.

"Uh-uh," Rudy said. "You haven't paid for your first one yet."

"And I don't plan to pay for this one either. So what's up?"

The guy on the stool beside me leaned over. I resisted the urge to lean back. One advantage to not breathing? You don't need to smell anything you don't want to. As for the guy's name, it was either Dennis or Mo. I'd known them both for years. Still can't tell them apart. Both on the far side of sixty. Both missing half their teeth. Both half-demons. Or so they claimed. Never saw them demonstrate any powers other than the ability to sleep on rickety bar stools.

For simplicity's sake, I usually call them both Dennis. Neither complains. Most times, they're past the stage of remembering their names anyway.

"You are not a real vampire," Dennis said.

I sighed. "This again? Fine. In the morning, I'll go drain the blood of a few virgins."

"Real vampires don't go out in the morning."

"Hey, I agreed to the slaughter of innocents. Don't push it. And don't ask me to pretend I can't see my reflection in a mirror, either, or I'll never look good enough to get those virgins back to my place."

"Can you sparkle?" someone across the room called. "I hear that's what real vampires do these days."

"Oh, I can sparkle. Just not for you."

A round of laughter. I headed back to our table.

"We got confirmation, you know," Rudy called after me.

I turned. "Confirmation of what?"

"That you're not a real vampire." He picked up a folded newspaper from the bar. "You aren't on the list."

I returned and took the paper. Two papers, actually. The first was the *Toronto Sun*, our daily tabloid. The other was an underground rag.

I read the *Sun* headline: "24 vampires call Toronto home, researcher claims."

"Cool," I said. "Add me and we can field our own baseball team."

I skimmed the article. The researcher was an anthropologist who specialized in vampire lore, its origins and its connection to modern life. He'd compiled a list of people suffering from porphyria and deemed them "real vampires." The underground paper had reportedly found and printed his list of the twenty-four living in Toronto.

"It's a known medical condition," I said. "You need to drink blood and you have an aversion to sunlight, which means, when it comes to real vamps, it's only half right."

"Or maybe you're half wrong," Dennis said.

"No, Zoe's all sorts of wrong," Rudy said. "Which is why she isn't on the list. Meaning she's not a real vampire. Meaning I win a whole lotta bets."

I flipped him the finger and took the *Sun* back to our table.

"Hey, look. The guy's giving a lecture tomorrow at U of T," I said as I finished reading the article.

"Don't even think of going, Zoe," Randy said.

"Why would I do that? To mock the guy when he doesn't recognize a real vampire? That would be very immature."

I ripped out the article and pocketed it. Randy sighed.

I took Brittany the Vampire Slayer to the lecture. At seventeen, she's waffling about post-secondary education, so I'm trying to convince her that university isn't as boring as she thinks. And that vampire hunting really isn't a viable career goal. There are only about a dozen of us in North America. In five years, she'd have slaughtered the lot, and then what?

"I am not a vampire hunter," she grumbled as she trudged along beside me. "And why can't we take the subway?"

"Because walking is good exercise. A vampire hunter must be in excellent physical—"

"I'm not—"

"But you were. Remember how we met? You running at me with your garden stake, yelling, 'Die, bloodsucker.'"

She reddened. "That was last year, okay? I don't know why you have to keep bringing it up."

"Because it was so adorable. And Brittany the Vampire Slayer rolls off the tongue much better than Brittany the Former-Vampire-Slayer-Who-Now-Just-Wants-to-Hunt-Bad-Guys-in-General."

"Not 'in general.' Not 'bad guys' either. That sounds so lame. I'm going to join the interracial council and hunt supernaturals who misuse their powers."

"See, now that's what I mean about redefining goals. That's very specific and feasible. However, working for the council is a volunteer position. You need to plan for a long-term, satisfying, *paying* career."

"I could work with you. Become a thief."

"The income stream is too erratic. But if you'd find that sort of work satisfying, we could look at something in the financial sector. For starters, though, you're going to attend public lectures with me, get a feel for a university education."

"And for each lecture, I get a shopping trip."

"That was the deal."

When I met Brittany, she had little appreciation for the finer things in life, like fashion. In a year, I've weaned her out of her track pants, sneakers and hoodies. I'm very proud of that. Of course, I'm also proud of the advances she's made in stalking and fighting under my direction, but I believe that just because a girl can kick ass doesn't mean she shouldn't look good doing it.

The lecture was very educational. I say that with scarcely a drop of sarcasm. I'm always fascinated by vampire lore. It's like when I was a young girl in Imperial Japan and my grandfather would recount our family's storied past as samurais and shoguns. While we knew less than half of it was true, it was enthralling nonetheless. Vampire folklore is the same—thrilling, vaguely accurate accounts of my race's history.

Dr. Adair himself was far less interesting, as such people usually are. A round little man with a shock of white hair, his saving grace as a speaker was his passion for his subject. Even Brittany stopped squirming after a few minutes. By the end, she was so enrapt that as others rose to leave, she still sat there, leaning forward, hoping for more.

"That was actually interesting," she said as we pulled on our leather jackets. "Like history and mythology and science all mixed together."

"If you enjoyed it, I could introduce you to an anthropologist," I said. "He's a werewolf."

"Oh?" A slight arch of the brows, a blasé gesture that I'd learned, in teen body language, marked genuine interest. Brittany had never met a werewolf. They were almost as rare as vampires, and there were none living in Toronto.

"His mate's a delegate on the interracial council."

I got a "Seriously?" and a genuine grin for that. I was going to have to remember to name-drop more often. She checked her school calendar to see when we might be able to squeeze in a werewolf visit. I didn't mention that her parents might not let her go off to New York state with me. She wouldn't ask; they wouldn't care.

"Miss?" called a voice as we crossed the front of the room. "Miss?"

I turned to see Dr. Adair waving me back.

"Uh-oh," Brittany whispered. "He's made you, Zoe. You're in trouble now."

I rolled my eyes, though I'll admit to a spark of concern as I walked to the podium.

"Do you know a good place to get a drink?" he asked.

"Drink?"

"Oh." He flushed and looked from me to Brittany. "I'm sorry. I thought you were old enough. My mistake."

"Believe me, I'm old enough."

I glanced at the crowd of people streaming past. Seemed odd to single me out. I look like a typical college-age girl. Maybe that's why he was asking—horny old guy hoping to hook up with a fan.

"What sort of bar are you looking for?" I asked.

He leaned over and lowered his voice. "Not one most of these folks would frequent."

I glanced at the attendees again. Lots of Goths and vampire wannabes.

"Ah," I said.

"Yes. You looked . . . normal."

Brittany choked on a laugh.

I gave him directions to a neighbourhood pub that profs frequented. As I wrote it down for him, a waiting girl in a leather corset and black lipstick sighed impatiently.

When Brittany and I left, Goth Girl muttered, "Finally. Fucking mundanes. Aren't you missing *American Idol*?"

"Aren't you missing the muzzle to go with that dog collar?" Brittany shot back. "Better yet, do us all a favour and get one that covers your whole face."

I took her by the arm and steered her out as Goth Girl shouted profanities.

"Did you hear what she called us?" Brittany said. "Mundanes. Do you know what that means?"

"People who are not members of her subculture. Which we are not. Unless you want to be part of a group that thinks fishnets go well with army boots."

"She's not going to leave that poor guy alone, you know," she said as Goth Girl tagged along after Adair. "She'll be on him like a leech for the rest of the night. We can't let that happen."

"Yes, I believe we can."

"We shouldn't. It's wrong."

"All right. We'll follow them as a stalking lesson. But no fighting. If she won't leave, I'll cut in and distract her, and you'll lead him away."

Brittany sighed. "You know, for a vampire, Zoe, you can be killer dull."

"So I've been told."

As we stalked Adair and Goth Girl, I pondered the political correctness of my label. Did they still refer to themselves as Goths? That seemed very 1985. I was sure the terminology had changed. I'd have to check up on that. If you're going to blithely slap labels on people, you should at least know the right ones. For now, Goth Girl she was.

She wasn't pestering Dr. Adair overly much. Just walking with him, asking questions, which he seemed happy enough to answer. There's a certain ego appeal to having someone hanging on your every word. It didn't hurt that—once you got past the bad dye job and worse fashion sense—the girl was actually cute. Not my type—I prefer blond hair and pink lipstick—but I couldn't blame Dr. Adair for enjoying her company. I had a feeling she'd be joining him for that drink. Maybe more. Whatever the end result, Brittany was getting a hunting lesson, and that was always worthwhile.

Goth Girl and Dr. Adair were heading for the parking building, where he said he needed to drop off his bag. The girl suggested a shortcut, in a way that had him trotting eagerly after her.

I tugged the back of Brittany's jacket. "You're too young for that kind of lesson."

"I'm seventeen, Zoe. I know all about sex."

"Sex, yes. Screwing behind buildings with strangers, no."

"I'll stop when clothes start coming off."

Considering Goth Girl was wearing a miniskirt, the removal of clothing would not be necessary in this instance. But before I could say so, Brittany took off, creeping along as Goth Girl and Dr. Adair cut between two buildings.

"Can I ask you a question about the list?" Goth Girl's voice drifted back.

"Of course."

"Why didn't I get on it?"

"Hmm?"

"I sent you my qualifications. You rejected me."

"It's not a rejection, my dear. There are very strict criteria for the list. While there are thousands of adherents to the basic tenets of vampirism—avoiding the sun and drinking blood—the list only contains those who are medically—"

"I sent you a doctor's note."

"And I'm sure I attempted to verify it. Having met you, though, I'm happy to review—"

"I want on that list, Doctor. I'm a vampire. And I can prove it."

Adair shrieked. Brittany was already running. I raced after her.

Goth Girl had Adair up against the wall and was going for his jugular with her fangs. Fangs that flashed silver in the moonlight.

Brittany charged and hit her in the side. Goth Girl went flying. She hit the ground and lay there in a huddle, whimpering. I motioned for Brittany to watch her as I helped Adair to his feet. He'd slid to the ground when the girl released him and sat there, staring in shock. As I bent over him, Brittany turned her back on her opponent. Before I could say anything, the girl yanked a knife from her boot.

Goth Girl leapt at Brittany. I shoved my protégé aside and told her to get Adair out of here. I kicked Goth Girl's feet out from under her. She stumbled, but didn't go down. When she spun, knife out, she nearly nicked Adair. That got him moving. Got Brittany moving, too, hustling him to open ground.

Goth Girl ran at me. I waited until the last second before spinning out of the way. My jacket caught on the tip of her blade. Put a nice hole in the leather. I stopped playing then, and took her down with a high kick to the chin. Another kick sent the knife flying.

When she fell, I pinned her. She snarled and thrashed and tried to bite me with a set of really awkward silver teeth.

"I hope you didn't pay much for those," I said.

"It's not fair," she howled. "I belong on that list."

"Yeah?" I curled back my lip and let my fangs extend. "Well, so do I."

I didn't hurt the girl. No reason to. I wasn't hungry. I gave her a stern warning about curses and revenge and the incredible psychic powers that would tell me if she spoke of this to anyone or contacted Adair again. Total bullshit, but if you're crazy enough to believe in vampires, you're crazy enough to believe that crap, too.

She ran off after that. Probably to change her panties. The smell was . . . not good. I got the idea she'd had enough of unholy bloodsuckers to last her a lifetime.

Next I found Brittany waiting with Adair at a bench. She mouthed an apology and I made a mental note to add "keeping your attention on your opponent" to her future lessons.

For now, it was Adair who got the stern warning. If he was going to work in this field, he needed to be more careful about following people into dark alleys. A canister of pepper spray might be wise, too.

"Y-you're right," he said, as he rose unsteadily from the bench. He looked around, blinking. "Now I really need that drink. Do you know anyplace quiet? Out of the way? Where I won't bump into anyone like . . ." He shuddered. "That?"

"I know just the place," I said as I took his arm. "In fact, the bartender is the one who told me about your lecture. Huge fan. You'll have to tell him all about your work. He *loves* meeting new people."

"Rudy *hates* meeting new people," Brittany whispered as she fell in step beside me. "Especially mundanes."

True. Which meant, when I left Millers tonight, I'd be the one laughing.

biting tongues

AMAL EL-MOHTAR

Speak to us in silk, they say,
speak to us in milk,
be pillow-soft, be satin-smooth,
be home-spun sugar sweet.

We part our lips. We breathe our breaths.
We bite our tongues and swallow blood
knot stones into our stomachs, heave
and spit red salt where words should be,
stitch shut our mouths with stubborn thread
to spare our tablecloths.

Such a mess! If you can't say something nice
if you can't be honey cinnamon spice
if you can't be dusky-eyed candy mice
shut the fuck up, you stuck-up bitch
you whore you cunt you slag you witch
where you going dressed like that,
red as meat and us so hungry?
What did you think would happen, huh?
What did you think would happen?

We are told
of wolves in the world, and we but girls.
We are told
of girls in the world, and they but wolves
who cannot help themselves.
We are told
to be girls or wolves,
be eaten or hungry,
but we are never hungry

who make meals of ourselves,
who chew the insides of our cheeks,
bleed into our bellies.
We are told
that to be bold is to be bled,
that red's what brings the wolves around,
that we're better off drowned.

They come with axes,
cut us to pull the good girls out.

They leave us with our bloodstone bellies,
our sewn up mouths, our halted breaths,
and a river for a bed.

Until one of us
with sharpest teeth
and shredded mouth
rips silence from our lips
with a battle-cry kiss, and says

we speak as we are
with tongue of snake and hummingbird
of ocean and of earth
of sky and salt and smoke and fire
of gesture, ink, and ringing bells.

We speak as we are
with bodies various as motion
voices of muscle and music and colour
beautiful bloody mouths.

We paint with tumblebroken words
we sing loud with our speaking hands
unmake the bodies shaped for us
and lip to eye to fingertip
we spill our red-mouth stories out
and listen, taste them on the air
with our forked and biting tongues.

bleaker collegiate presents an all-female production of *Waiting for Godot*

CLAIRE HUMPHREY

I stanch the blood with a handful of toilet paper. Red wicks through the white, and then the paper wilts and shreds. I toss the mess in the bin.

I breathe through my mouth. I lean over the sink and watch my blood splash down and diffuse into the water from the running tap.

The door swings in and shoves me against the counter top.

Swearing: Ginevra's voice. She stops when she meets my eyes in the mirror.

"Crap, Deirdre. Not again."

I shrug.

"You're going to the doctor, right?" Ginevra says.

"Next week."

". . . 'Cause that's not normal."

"I'm not normal," I tell her, thickly.

On another day, she'd comfort me. She'd walk me to the nurse's office, or call my dad to come pick me up. Today, she's already in makeup, and alight with nerves. She smells of cigarettes and Noxzema. Her fingers touch the back of my neck, then skate away.

"I go on in an hour," she says, brushing past me and into a stall.

"Break a leg," I say.

I hear her jeans unzip, and a moment later the clink of her belt buckle hitting the floor.

I turn away, look down. My hand has been fiddling with my ballpoint. Blue scribbles mar the cuff of my jacket; they almost make a word.

I don't know what else I'll say to Ginevra if I stay. I leave her and walk out into the rain.

One hour until curtain. Two dollars and eighty cents in my jacket pocket; a few cigarettes, a pack of gum. Nothing to eat, but

I'm not hungry anyway.

Rainwater collects on my hair and runs from the lank tips onto my forehead and down to my chin. My jean jacket soaks through and turns stiff. I turn my face up into the downpour: at least it can rinse some of the blood from my skin.

Maybe it's the chill, or maybe it's just time, but I think the bleeding is slowing.

I start toward the Bleaker Public Library, as the rain slackens. As I reach the crosswalk, at the uppermost limit of my field of view, black birds cross the sky, one and one and one. When I tilt my face back a little to watch them, blood runs down over my upper lip, and into my mouth.

Making friends with Ginevra was like taming a stray cat. First I started hanging around in areas where she might be found. If she showed, I didn't approach her. I just stood there, smoking, or I read something, glancing at her secretly from behind my hair. Then I started catching her eye once in a while. Then I started smiling.

Then I started dating Christopher Potter; I dumped him after a few weeks, but that got me introduced to Pete Janaczek, which got me the invite to Pete's party, which got me in the same room as Ginevra while she was tipsy and expansive, and then— finally—it happened.

All that was a lie, you know. As if I could plan anything like that. It's only in hindsight that I realize why I started spending time in the smoke-hole in the first place. So many of the things we do, we keep from ourselves.

She told me the playwright was so much against the idea of his piece being performed by women that when someone in the Netherlands tried it, he banned the entire country from putting on his plays.

"Why are you doing it, then? Aren't you afraid he'll ban Canada too?"

"He's dead. Too bad: it would be great press for us," Ginevra said. She bit off the thread, put away the needle, and showed me what she'd been doing: adorning my jean jacket with a Violent Femmes badge.

I resolved to go out and buy the album as soon as she left.

I lock myself in the handicapped bathroom at the Bleaker Public Library, and I kneel under the hand-dryer. In the rush of hot air, the last trickles of blood dry to sharp crusts within my nostrils. When I look in the mirror to gingerly prod them out, I see that I'm a strange colour, like old newsprint.

I always thought pallor would be more attractive. I think I've been imagining pale people as if they were made of marble, delicately veined and smooth: not this chafed and flaking skin, with all the moles and hairs brought into sharp contrast, and the leftover summer's tan yellowing me like dirty ivory.

I've got blood on my jacket, too. As if the Violent Femmes weren't enough.

Without warning, it comes again. No pain this time, just a hot gush down my face as the pressure overwhelms whatever fragile membrane held it back.

I slam my forehead into the paper towel dispenser in my hurry to reach the sink. That bleeds, too. In fact all this bleeding is making me feel spacy enough that I sit down on the toilet seat with my head on the sink, and I do nothing at all but wait.

After a while I'm not bleeding any more, and I get myself upright slowly, like a person with a truly vile hangover.

For some reason, I'm not using my left hand. I look at it, and discover I'm holding my pen again, in a bit of a death grip. I set it on the counter before I can make it explode, and begin the lengthy and awful process of cleaning myself up.

The theatre is called a black box, because it is both of those things, and nothing else. Its stage is bare but for a dead sapling planted in a bucket, and a diffuse light coming down from the grid.

I've been up there: up through the trap door in the booth. I've spent a half-hour unhooking Fresnel lights from the rack and handing them to people, because I couldn't make myself edge out from the wall onto the grid itself, so far above the stage. If we had to hook our wrenches to our belts, I thought, why didn't we have to hook ourselves to anything?

My stomach lurches, what with the thought of the people on the grid, and the others waiting in the wings. Or maybe they'll be in the green room still, warming up their voices: "Round and round the rugged rock the ragged rascal ran."

In the heat, the inside of my nose crackles. Everything that should be moist is parched, and everything that should be comfortably dry is soaked with rain: jacket, trousers, Converse, hair, bookbag. Where I had doodled Ginevra's name in ballpoint across the white rubber toe-cap of my shoe, there's nothing but a blue smear.

The lights rise on Eve Morrow and Leslie Kulyk, both in bowler hats. Their faces, bare of paint, look tired and hollow and so much older than they did during lunch period.

They are waiting at a crossroads. It reminds me of something.

I try to remember. It seems important. Their dialogue teases around the edges of it, whatever it is.

Then I try to forget it, because Ginevra takes the stage.

Ginevra Iacovini: her father owns Bleaker's only cab company. Her mother works part time at Danylow's, selling fine leather. Between them, they've raised a changeling, all huge dark eyes in a face studded with piercings. She's taken those out for the show, and her face looks thinner and younger.

She enters stage right, with her bowler flattening her cap of curls, a rope about her neck and a whip cracking at her ankles. The whip is in the hand of Tyra Cross; she makes Ginevra stop and start and carry her things and take the whip in her mouth and give it back. Tyra speaks, and I watch Ginevra's silent lips.

"Think!" Tyra commands.

I almost miss Ginevra's first words. The excursus. Ginevra said it to me earlier, in the smoke hole, a bit of it. "For reasons unknown but time will tell," she said; and "plunged in torment plunged in fire." It comes back to me now, and with it a warm metallic tickle in the passage of my throat.

I lean my head back, pull my knees up to my chest. Above me, the grid shows faintly, black on black, behind the Fresnels. Below, Ginevra delivers a stream of words.

My hand gropes in the pocket of my jean jacket, and finds my pen, and a wad of toilet paper. I blot my nose with one hand and clutch the pen with the other, as if the pressure will help get this under control.

Maybe it does. I swallow, less each time, while below me Ginevra's voice rises, and with it the sounds of a scuffle.

She gasps, and shouts, and halts.

So does the trickle of blood down my throat. I raise my head, cautiously. Ginevra stands listless, lost and swaying. Her hat is wrecked.

She returns to the stage again in the second act. I was afraid her part was over. She says nothing, this time. Even her hair hangs lifeless about her cheeks. Her fall is inevitable.

She's called Lucky. That's irony. If I forget again in English class what the definition of irony is, I'll only have to summon this image to my mind: Lucky, slave to Pozzo, most miserable of a miserable crew.

When she is beaten, she whimpers once, and I think Leslie's given her a real kick with that steel-capped boot.

The whimper reminds me of nothing, though. The desperate remembrance in my brain has gone quiet. The blood in my head flows in the usual channels. It does not start again until what turns out to be the very last scene: Eve and Leslie, alone together once more, in the bleak light, by the spare tree. As that light dims I feel it all over, the familiarity, and with it the blood.

The applause ends. The rest of the audience rises, collects jackets and purses, files out.

I stay in my seat, hands to my face, until everyone has gone.

I wake early the next day. Saturday. Dad will be in bed for a couple of hours still. I dress in my jean jacket, and go for a walk.

From our house you can see Bleaker spread below the lip of the escarpment: a pitiful little grid of Monopoly houses and patches of orchard, and beyond it the highway. I walk the other direction, between bare fields and windbreaks.

At a crossroads, a single tree. It reminds me of the one on the stage last night.

No: that tree reminded me of this one.

I stop walking, and fumble in my pockets: pen, bloody tissue, matches. My throat hurts. I light a cigarette.

I remember something now. I come here often, on Saturdays. I wait here. Don't I? Someone meets me at the crossroads. But who? How will I know it's the right person?

Why don't I ever think of this when I'm elsewhere? Is it so terrible? Is it just so large?

When I have finished my cigarette, they come for me, and I remember everything.

On Monday I meet Ginevra in the graveyard after typing class. She's drawing, perched in the big tree, up in the branches.

Every tree is the one from the play, I think. Strangely familiar, and awful, and full of meaning that vanishes if you look at it directly.

Ginevra closes her sketchbook and swings down when she sees me coming. We kick our way through the drifts of leaves that have gathered around all the stones. My mother's buried here, on the far side, but I haven't told Ginevra that, so I steer us the other way, out the north gate.

I know a bridge, across a little creek that rushes down from the escarpment. The bridge is rusted; bits of it come away on my fingertips when I stroke the iron. We lean on the rail and watch the water trickling below us. Light rain begins to fall.

"So," Ginevra says.

"It was . . . I want to say it was amazing, because it was. More than that, though."

She glances at me from behind the fall of her hair.

"You got it?"

"It got me, I think."

"I thought you'd get it. You always have that look."

My turn to glance at her.

"You know. I used to see you by yourself, just leaning on the wall or something, with your hands in your pockets—"

"You used to see me?"

"Sure, I did." She takes a long drag, and exhales slowly, deliciously, into the autumnal air. "The deep one, we used to call you: me and Chris and Pete, back when we were wondering who you were."

She had a name for me.

"I don't think it's about God," I blurt.

"I don't, either. And I'm Catholic. I think they're waiting for something . . . more personal, if that makes sense."

"More vital."

"More important."

"We sound like Didi and Gogo."

"It gets into your brain, a bit." She smiles ruefully, and looks away. She's wearing her bowler hat from the play, an old white waffle-weave shirt, and a denim vest. Her lips were wine-red, earlier, but some of the colour has come off on her cigarette.

Her eyes flash wide and dark like the eyes of an owl after sundown.

I wish I could kiss her.

Instead I watch the water, which falls, and the leaves, which also fall, and the rain, which—ah, whatever.

"You're kind of a mess," she says.

"I guess." I look down at my shoes. The toe-caps are smeared with ballpoint ink, and I thank the rain for smearing it before Ginevra could see what was written there; it might have been her name.

"Me, too," she says quickly. "All of us. There's so much we don't know."

I know, I almost say. Just for a moment, it's all there. The cause of my troubles. The thing for which I wait. The meaning of the crossroads tree.

But if I speak, something will burst in my head, and I'll spill blood all over the rusted bridge and the place where our hands rest.

I hold very still. The tide of blood recedes, and with it, the knowledge. All but the memory of forgetting, and the sense that time is short.

After a last inhalation, Ginevra drops the butt of her cigarette into the water. The tiny light hisses out, and there's only the smoke from her lips.

split decision

ROBERT RUNTÉ

So Mr. Shakey came over the intercom saying it was 2:03 and would all the teachers therefore stop whatever they were doing and please water the plants? As Mrs. Harness went for the door, Bethany-Anne reached over from her desk and peeked out under the shutters.

Mr. Shakey? Oh, sorry. Mr. Sheckley, the principal. But we call him "Mr. Shakey," because sometimes his judgement is kind of off. Like, that has to be the lamest code phrase ever. I mean, I ask you: if you're in the school intent on a killing rampage and you hear "drop everything and water the plants" over the PA, wouldn't you at least suspect that that means "go to lockdown"? Because you have to know a lockdown is the logical response to your being there, with a rifle; whereas it makes no sense to interrupt class just to water the plants. And Mr. Shakey orders "plant watering" like every other day, because he is totally paranoid.

What? No, no; nobody had a rifle. I'm just saying it's lame, that's all. So Mr. Sheckley says about watering the plants, and right away Bethany-Anne sneaks the bottom of the shutters up—

What? No, the shutters were down already, before the announcement, because Mrs. Harness had us doing this frog on the Smartboard. So, anyway, Bethany-Anne is leaning—

What? Okay, okay. Because our class gets the sun in the afternoon, and you can't see a thing on the Smartboard, even if you're right up front, with the shutters up. We have one of the old-style boards, where the projector hangs down from the top? It's so old, it just totally washes out in direct sunlight. But Mrs. Harness says it will be like another three years before she can even *apply* for them to do an upgrade for our room, but we'll all be graduated by then, so just too bad for us, eh?

So they were down, right, because of the frog? The shutters, I mean. So Bethany-Anne, reaches over—

Frog. The dissection you have to do in Science 7? Gramps says in his day they did real frogs, which is just barbaric. I can't believe that was ever *legal*, let alone something you *had to do* in school. Where was the SPCA? Where was PETA when this was going on? Now you just do it on your slate. But why even *simulate* a dissection? Sure, somebody—some scientist dude—had to do that the first time, once, to find out. But why would you want to keep *re*-doing it? If I want to know what's connected to which, I can just look it up.

But anyway, Mrs. Harness was showing us all on the Smartboard first, before our doing it individual on our slates, and the shutters are down, and Mr. Shakey comes over the PA. Clear?

So when Mrs. Harness goes for the door, Bethany-Anne reaches over and flips the shutters to see if she can see anybody skulking around outside, and right away she spots it.

Sorry? Well, mostly that's true. But the shutter on Bethany-Anne's row is missing the bottom slat, so if you kinda work your hand into the gap, and twist the roller, you can get the bottom four or five slats to all rotate, and you can get a pretty good look outside. Of course, Mrs. Harness goes all freaky if she catches you at it, and you have to listen to her go on and on about how someone could get a shot in, but I mean, how realistic is that? That they would happen to be focused on that particular window the exact moment you happened to flip the slats? And then there is still the whole question of getting the shot through the opening. Because four or five slats is okay to see *out*, but you can't really see *in* from more than—I don't know—a couple of feet away, maybe. It could be done, I guess, with a good scope, but it would have to be someone who knew what they were doing, deliberate, calm, and that's hardly ever what you're up against with your typical lockdown. I think Mrs. Harness is more worried we'll spot a flasher or something. Like we haven't all seen everything there is to see like a million times before on our slates. Last week: Justin forgot to close a window after break, and left it running in the background, and when Mrs. Harness asked him to flip his math to the Smartboard, guess what popped up! I thought Mrs. Harness was going to blow an artery for sure, that time. Though, you know, I was kind of disappointed in Justin. Why do guys always want to watch that kind of stuff? I mean, we get like fifteen minutes for break, and instead of actually *talking* to one of the girls next to him, he spends it watching something like—

Oh, right. Sorry. So anyway, Bethany-Anne makes this kind of a sound that is, you know, not quite a scream, and not a choke exactly, but the kind of sound where you just *know* something is seriously up. So Todd pushes her aside and sticks *his* head to the glass and he's just kind of glued there, even though Mrs. Harness is already half way back from the door and shouting at him to "get down this second." So the rest of us start crowding in, in the hopes of a quick glimpse before Mrs. Harness gets there, and the crowding slows her down quite a bit, so most of us are able to get an okay look at it, sitting right out there in the rink.

Then Mrs. Harness orders everyone to the far wall, and she starts tipping tables over and telling everyone to get into crash position behind their desks; only that is so obviously lame! It just makes no sense to me. It's like, well, if it's going to blow, what exactly do you expect a set of shutters and a couple of tipped over student desks to do about it? We looked pathetic. I didn't want people seeing me like that. Because by now half the kids have their cells out and are phoning EMS, or their folks; and the other half are uploading video of the first half, who are cowering there like morons.

And we were already way beyond "locked door" as the appropriate response here. Because if they've got interstellar travel down, a locked door is probably not going to deter them. So either we should all be moving out the opposite exit as fast as our feet could carry us, or we should just relax and go greet our new masters from Megnar 7, or wherever.

So I go over to the fire exit and start leaning on the crashbar. Casual, you know? Not making a production of it? Like I was just thinking maybe of leaning out for a quick look. But I had already figured it as pretty safe.

Well, no, I didn't mean "safe" exactly. Obviously, this was not a normal situation. I understand your point there. I'm just saying that if something were going to explode, it probably would have done that already, when it came down. But none us had even heard a thing. And I know for sure I had my earbuds out when it must have come down. Because it certainly hadn't been there at break, and I hadn't exactly been in a hurry to tune in to Mrs. Harness putting that poor frog down—simulated or not—so my ears were still naked right up to Mr. Sheckley's announcement. I definitely would have heard *something* if that had been a crash out there. So if wasn't a crash, then no "kaboom," right?

Oh. I didn't know that. Well, I'm just telling you what I was thinking at the time. Just let me finish here, or I'm going to get all jumbled up. So I'm saying, I didn't think we were in any danger from the *ship* aspect of it. I mean, it pretty much looked like it had landed there in one piece as intended.

But on the other hand, if I were flying around the galaxy, and I wanted to put down on Earth, the hockey rink of Allan Wilson Middle School would not necessarily be my first choice, you know? So either it was some kind of mistake or accident, or emergency landing kind of deal; or, this was part of like a much larger fleet, and they were landing everywhere with so many ships that there was even one to spare for Prairie Creek. And if that were the case—well, like I said, time to meet our new masters, and here's hoping they aren't into eating our brains.

But I figured, you have interstellar flight, you probably have to be like some kind of way advanced civilization, and that probably implies a certain level of vegetarianism when it comes to intelligent species. Assuming that we qualify.

So, I figured, probably they were having some kind of problem, and the polite thing—the civilized thing to do—would be for someone to go and ask, you know, if they needed anything.

So I am starting to lean on the crashbar a little harder, when I hear this clop clop clop coming up fast behind me, which I know to be Sarah's clogs without having to turn around, so I wait a second for her to get there, and she whispers, "What are you doing?" Only, you know, her tone is more like, "What, *are you crazy*?!" And so I say, "I figure they're probably not here to eat our brains" and she says, "Well, duh. But what about radiation?"

So I ease up on the crashbar again, because this thought has given me pause. This is precisely why Sarah is my best friend. Because more than once she has thought of something that I have maybe missed. "An advanced civilization," I said, working it through with her, but still whispering so as not to attract Mrs. Harness's attention, "would probably include safety regulations. With regard to acceptable levels of radiation."

"Well, yeah" Sara whispers back, "But the number one safety rule would be, 'no landing on Earth' and the second rule would be, 'no landing in school hockey rinks.' So probably something went wrong already."

I see her point. So I ask, "Okay, maybe radiation. What then?"

And she says, "Shielding or distance. Assuming always we haven't already taken a fatal dose."

I look over at everybody still huddled behind their desks and kind of nod in that direction, and ask, "Any good?"

"Maybe if we covered the desks in layers of aluminum foil from the cafeteria," Sarah tells me, "but wood is useless."

"Distance?" I ask her.

"Levels decrease with the square of the distance."

"My basement?"

She nodded. "We could still see okay from there, but would be nearly three times further away. Radiation would be only a tenth whatever it is here. And cement is good."

Well, I don't know; they never said. I'm just telling you what Sarah told me.

So then I looked over to where Mrs. Harness was still under her desk, and there was no way she was going to unlock the door to the hallway. Mrs. Harness is not a half-bad teacher, but she is not one for taking initiative. She sticks pretty much to the curriculum, whether simulated dissections make sense or not. So if Mr. Sheckley had called for a lockdown, we were going to stay locked in until the "all-clear."

"Okay," I said, "we make a run for my house," and slammed my elbow into the crashbar. I saw Mrs. Harness bang her head when the exit alarm went off, but we were out and pelting along the side of the school before she could even crawl out from under her desk. I was pretty much just focused on making it around the corner of the school, and could hear the clacking of Sarah's clogs keeping up with me, so I didn't look back at all, and I didn't immediately recognize that the grinding sound was the saucer splitting opening, and so neither of us saw the ramp coming out of it until it was nearly on top of us.

So I hit the brakes and pull back, but Sarah plows into me and kind of knocks me, and I'm on the ramp, teetering, and Sarah's all, "What are you *doing*?!" and I'm looking back at her in disbelief because it's not *my* fault I'm on the ramp, *she's* the one who knocked me, but then it penetrates that they've opened up and I'm thinking, "wait" and I point at the ramp and say, "No radiation!" and Sarah's looking at me, and I explain that they wouldn't open up if there was a radiation leak or whatever, and Sarah's all, "You don't know that! Maybe they're just not affected by it!" But I figure, they're kind of inviting us in, and that wouldn't make sense if the radiation was going to kill us, so it's gotta be okay.

I look back at the school and I notice the shutters are like a quarter of the way up in Ms. Rossiter's class, and there are like forty arms sticking cells out the bottom, filming me and Sarah, waiting to see what we do. Or whether something comes out with a deathray or whatever. So I take like maybe half a step up the ramp, when Sarah shouts, "Viruses!" and I pause again, but just for a second this time, because I remember Mrs. Harness telling us how our dogs don't catch our colds and vice versa, and dogs are practically family compared to whatever is in *there*, so I just shake my head, and say "I doubt we're that compatible" and keep going. And Sarah does this exasperated little stomp with her clogs, and says, "You don't know that!" So I stop, because she's not wrong. But I tell her, "They've got the ship, so I'm guessing they're brainy enough to have thought it all through." Only she says, "You can't know that!" again. And she's right of course, but I just kind of shrug, because, hey, you can never *know*. Not completely, right?

So we're standing, looking at each other, and Sarah says, kind of quiet, "You can't go in there. It would be crazy." Then I just say, "I have a plan," and start going up the ramp again. So Sarah runs after me with her clogs clanging on the ramp, and catches up and asks, "What's the plan?" And I explain, "I'm not going in. I'm stopping halfway up. That way, they'll have to come out and we'll meet halfway." And Sarah says, "That's your plan?" and I say, "Yes," and she says, "That's it? That's not a plan!" And I say, "No, this will work. Because it shows willing, and because, you know, meeting halfway is what you do!" And Sarah shouts, "What do you mean, 'That's what you do?' What you *do* is call out the Army and the Air Force!" And I have to stop and give Sarah "The Look," because, come on! She's been here for like her whole life, almost. "Sarah! That's maybe how Americans do it, or maybe your Dad when he was an Air Force Captain back in the Bangladesh, but for crying out loud, you're as Canadian as me. Meeting 'halfway' is how Canadians do it!" And then Sarah gives *me* "The Look" back and says, "You're the one who told me Canadians don't change the light bulb, they wait for the government to do it." And I wave my arm at the school where all the teachers are hunkered down and say, "Do you see the government anywhere?

Look, if they"—I'm pointing up the ramp here—"If they wanted the Army and Air Force and diplomats and world leaders, they would have landed in front of the White House; if they land in back of Allan Wilson Middle School, it's because they just want to do some repairs, maybe, or get directions, or whatever, but the appropriate response is to be neighbourly and offer to help them out, without making a huge deal out of it!"

So then I noticed Sarah isn't saying anything and is looking kind of stressed, so I say, "Sarah?" Because now I'm thinking I was maybe out of line implying she wasn't being Canadian enough. Because she can be sensitive about that: like the time Drew said he thought she looked like "a foreign princess" in her blue sari with the diamonds; he just meant she looked exotic, but things never come out quite right when Drew says them, and Sara had been totally slammed he'd said "foreign." But it wasn't about that this time. She looks at me and says, "So the plan is we only go halfway up, right?" And I say, "That's the plan," and Sarah says, "And we stopped about a third of the way up to have this little chat, right?" And right away I get it, because we're already way past the halfway mark, and getting closer to the top every second, even though we've stopped walking, so I just grab her arm and yell, "Run" and we take off for the bottom of the ramp.

The one thing Sarah and I hate most about school is the Ding Test. You know the one? Where this bell goes "Ding" and you have to keep running as many laps as you can before the next "Ding." It's so stupid and demeaning. With Sarah's lungs and my ankles, it's just torture. And what's it for, exactly? When do you ever need to run like that and keep running until you actually fall down from exhaustion?

That's what I was thinking as we ran for it and kept running and running, as hard as we could, but didn't seem to be making any progress towards the bottom. But instead of a "ding," there was this sort of collective groan from the school windows as Sarah started to flag.

Then the fire exit to Mrs. Harness's room crashes open, and Justin and Drew came pounding out. Todd came out too, but just far enough to grab the door and drag it closed again. I didn't know what they were doing at first, and wanted to warn them away, but I didn't have the breath or the nerve to stop running; and frankly, if they were stupid enough to come *out* when they saw us coming *back,* that was their own look out.

But after a second, I realized they were headed for the ramp and for us.

Say what you want, but those guys can *run.* They hit the ramp in a blur, and were racing up to meet us fast, faster than any relay race I've ever seen them do, and I was worried for a second that they were going to crash right into us as we were trying to get away—only that never happened. Sarah and I kept running down at best speed, and they were racing up—I mean, really sprinting it!—but somehow the distance between us didn't shrink at all. On the contrary, space started to slowly expand, stretching out between us, until it became obvious that we were never going to reach each other.

Justin must have seen it too, because he started undoing his belt; he almost stumbled yanking it out while still running, head down and coming on like a fullback, and then flung it at me. I kinda ducked at first, but on his second throw I got what he was doing and I grabbed for it. I caught it on the third throw, by sort of lunging at it like in volleyball, and then I was tumbling past Justin, and Justin was shooting past me up the ramp.

I was still holding the belt with Justin on the other end, so kind of pivoted to get myself up and standing again, dug in my heels, and yanked him back towards me, now that I was closer to the bottom of the ramp than he was; he spun around and crashed into Sarah and Drew, who were both behind me, which left me disoriented because Sarah had been higher up the ramp and Drew lower, so I couldn't figure out how any of that was happening. Then I saw that we were all of us very nearly at the top, and moving inside, but before I could shout a warning, Justin was pulling me with the belt towards the edge, and shouted "Jump!"

But it's way too late, and next thing we know, we're all inside.

Justin and I jumping? Yeah, we saw that too. Which was pretty weird for us, but we were already inside by then, so we were kind of preoccupied with that. It was only later that they explained it was just the 4% of us that reacted fast enough that had jumped. But I remember thinking at the time, man, that must have *hurt!* Because we were pretty high up by then, I'm telling you!

So anyway, we're inside and right away it's just like that movie— the original, I mean, not the remake—because everything is this kind of gloomy black and white, and it's kind of hard to make anything out, and I'm like half expecting Gort to step out of the shadows; but of course it wasn't like that at all, once we got the goggles.

Sure they gave us goggles. Why wouldn't they? Because, as I'm trying to explain, everything is virtual with them, so without the colours, it's just blank walls. Nothing to see at all. Like trying to watch TV with the picture off. You've got to have the goggles.

To see the colours. Because our eyes don't see in the same range, and the goggles adjust for that.

I'm not sure exactly. Early that first day, sometime. Within a couple of hours, I guess. Because things only started to make sense once we got the goggles and could see what's going on.

Well, that's a lot harder to judge. I mean, it's not like they had a big clock up anywhere. Oh, and our watches didn't work. Sarah and Drew both had watches on, but they were both frozen at 2:19. The watches, I mean, not Sarah and Drew. Same with Justin and my cells. And you can't phone out, though I guess that's obvious. So, I'd have to guess a couple of days. Four maybe. Though now you come to say it, it's funny, because we never got hungry or had to sleep or anything.

Yeah, yeah! That's it! That's exactly what *they* said: "Subjectivity of time." Something about how you "can't master faster than light travel without first mastering the subjectivity of time." I don't pretend to get all that; Sarah's the science geek.

Well, no, not "said." I know I said "said," but mostly it was writing. On the walls. Texting, you know? Sarah says she thinks they're deaf because they never tried talking to us, so maybe they don't use sound that way? But then *I* said they must be blind too, because they never used pictures either, but Drew said that was really stupid. Anyway, it became obvious pretty early on that they were asking if we wanted to go with them. Like be exchange students. And from the second they said it, I was beside myself with indecision. Because part of me really *really* wanted to. I mean, you know, the whole "boldly go where none have gone before" thing, right? That's pretty wild! But of course, another part of me wanted to stay right here. Keep my regular life. Go for the theatre, instead. Because Mr. Bartain says I have a real shot. A *real* shot. And I've worked hard for that. And I'd miss Kasia, my little sister. And my folks.

But then I'd think, I would not miss Allan Wilson Middle

School. Okay, Mr. Bartain, maybe. But seriously, I've got what, another year of middle school and another three of high school and then who knows how many of university? I think my Dad lived his whole life practically before he finally graduated. I wouldn't have to do any of that. I could start my life *now*; I could leave with them *now*, and have the adventure of a lifetime; of a hundred lifetimes!

But then I'd realize I didn't have Bear-Bear and Socks with me, and how could I stand to leave them behind? And it would like, *kill* mom. Dad would get it, sort of: me leaving in a saucer would be cool for him. But he'd probably say that out loud, and then mom would kill *him!*

I wasn't even clear if we got to say "goodbye" or anything, because when they tried to explain that bit, it wasn't very clear at first. I couldn't imagine what my folks would think, what my little sister would think, if they saw me get in the saucer, and the saucer took off, and then not knowing if I was okay. I couldn't do that to them. But then, they said that wouldn't be an issue, and I shouldn't worry about that when I made my final decision, so then I'd flip again.

I kept going back and forth, and every time I did, I'd end up arguing with myself again. That part was definitely weird. Though also strangely reassuring. You really get to know yourself, to understand what it is you *really* want when you have to work through a decision like that. A life-changing decision.

I think Sarah got it faster than the rest of us. What it would really mean. Because her folks had to make that decision coming to Canada.

And then there was the whole Justin thing. A lot of Justin really wanted to go, but only if I would go with him. That really kind of freaked me. Because, I had just never thought of Justin that way before. So at some point we noticed we were talking about Justin almost as much as about the decision, and I said, "Look, Justin is not the question. Justin stays or goes, but either way, he's going to *be there* so we can worry about that another time; there will be lots of opportunities to sort out how I feel about Justin later. The only question is: what do *I* want to do." I have to say, I was a little proud of myself for saying that, because I could hear my mom always telling me, you should never make a decision based just on what some boy wants. And this was a perfect example of that. So I dug around and found some receipts in my jacket pocket, and a pen, and used the scraps to write down my decision, and I told Justin to write down his, and the others, so that we all made our own decision without worrying about what the others were planning. And that made it a bit scarier, not knowing if anyone was coming with you, or if you stayed behind, whether they would all go off on an adventure without you. But that was the only way to be sure it was our own, independent choice.

Of course, as I sat down to write my answer, I probably flip-flopped a thousand times again. But in the end, I had something written on the paper, and I put it down on the floor in front of me, and the others had too. And then we all sat there for a minute, all of us, thinking about what we had done. And then they said it was time to go, so we all went our separate ways.

And here I am.

I got the impression they were really pleased with the way things turned out, too. That we had all made such thoughtful, deliberate decisions. And of course, because all four of us were so ambivalent about it all, it ties up all the loose ends for them pretty neatly too!

Sorry? What? Oh, I just meant, that it doesn't look like "Alien Abduction" if the people who go in come out again. Because if we had all chosen to go, like unanimous, then I guess they'd have some explaining to do! Though I gather, that doesn't come up very often.

Sorry? What don't you . . . ? Because a lot of me wanted to go, of course. I was pretty evenly divided on this one. Almost completely down the middle. They told me in the end about 49% went, and 51% stayed. With Justin, it was closer to 90/10. I mean, 90% wanting to go. What do you suppose that says about Justin? Do you think that means he's terribly unhappy with his life here? Because that could be a problem if . . . you know, something were to happen with Justin and me. Or does it just mean he's into adventure? That could be okay.

Sarah came out about 40% going and 60% staying. She told me that after all her parents went through to get her here, she would have felt bad choosing somewhere else; though of course the ones that went felt differently. I shouldn't say this, but I think some of them chose to go because I did. Sarah and me make a pretty good team. I can't even guess where Drew comes into it with Sarah, though. For or against, I couldn't begin to tell you.

What are you talking about? No, that's not it at all. Look, you're completely missing it. Let me start again. Every time you make a decision, every time you choose to open the door or not to, the universe splits: in one continuum you opened the door, in the other you didn't. They explained it to us just like that. So, normally, you're just you and you opened the door and go through; or you're the you that didn't, but you still just go on with your life from that point, maybe wondering, maybe not, what your life would have been had you made the other choice. Right? Every decision is like that. Every one.

But what if you were in a place where you could see the split coming? What if every time you had a choice, you had the chance to see both continuums stretching out in front of you, the door open and the door closed, and both of you poised to make the choice? And you could talk to the other you, and debate which was the right choice, discuss the pros and cons? Maybe, switch sides. Choose the other option instead this time.

But then, as the other you makes a point, part of you decides to go with that option, and part of you sticks with your original choice—so you split again, between the you that was convinced to change, and the one that wasn't. And then there's a friend with you, who offers to go with you if you choose the first option; and you're torn, so suddenly there's two more of you. Except by now your friend is having second thoughts, so there are two of him, and so part of you wonders if your friend will see it through, so you split again. And, well, you see how it works. Pretty soon, there are an awful lot of you sitting around debating, and some of you wander off topic and start talking about Justin. But in the end, you have to make your decision. And some of you go through the door, and some of you don't.

Some of us—some of me—went with the saucer, and some of us didn't. So they get the exchange students they wanted; and Mom and Dad and Kasia get me back safe and sound. Everybody wins.

Nope. No regrets. None at all. What's to regret? That's the real beauty of it all: Because, of course, that part of me that would have regretted not going, went.

the cinder girl

PETER CHIYKOWSKI

She always looked so dusty and dirty
that people began to call her Cinderella.
—The Brothers Grimm

I.

I married the cinder girl
not for a foot
fetish nor the slippers
she wore as we spun
the ballroom, but for the story
of her name
stretching behind her

like a wedding train.

II.

What step-sister thinks it wise
to cross the girl who lurks
on graves and sleeps
in ashes, who talks to trees
and calls birds
down from the skies?

Scattering lentils
into coal, they watched
as the soot-skinned girl
gathered the beans, popped
them into her mouth
where they would rattle
around her skull like
a grudge.

III.

Out in the garden,
the cinder girl sang
O tame little doves, little turtledoves,
and all you little birds in the sky,
come help me put
the good ones into the little pot
the bad ones into your little crop,
peck, peck, peck.

Her plumed army,
wings woven of
quill pens, descended
on her like scribes
on a song, counted beans,
made her ready
for me, the ball,

the dance, the ages.

IV.

At it again, the sisters
stepped less lightly.
To fit the slipper
the elder took a toe,
the younger sliced the heel
from the loaf of her foot.

A little birdy told me,
Roo coo coo, roo coo coo,
blood's in the shoe:
the shoe's too tight,
the real bride's waiting another night.

But I had already seen
the red slosh in the sneaker,
the sloppy tide of
desperation.

V.

Enough,
The cinder girl sang.
Shake your branches, little tree.
Toss match and petrol down to me.

VI.

After the house came down
the birds ghosted in
to collect bones
from the ashes.
The good ones into the little pot
the bad ones into your little crop,
peck, peck, peck,
she sang.
A sweet thing.

VII.

What prince thinks it wise
to spurn the girl who sleeps
on graves and lurks in ashes,
who leaves a wake
of birds and bones
and carries cinders in her eyes?

the candle
IAN ROGERS

"Did you blow out the candle?"

Tom lowered his book and turned toward Peggy.

Peggy lowered her own book and bit her lower lip. Why was it that she could remember what she had for breakfast every day this week, could even remember what she was wearing on most of those days, but couldn't remember if she had blown out the candle in the living room? *Is this what middle age is*? she wondered. *The loss of short-term memory*? She hoped not. She was forgetful enough as it was; she didn't need to help it along.

"Yes," she said finally. Then: "No. I don't know."

Peggy watched as Tom laid his hand on top of his book. She noticed the wrinkles on his fingers, the white hairs on his knuckles, and thought *We've gotten old, how did this happen*? He looked at her fully now. "Well," he said, "which is it?"

"Huh?" She looked at him quizzically; her own book had slumped forward and was now lying open on her chest. "I'm sorry, Tom. I must be sleepier than I thought. What did you say?"

"I asked if you remembered to blow out the candle." He was getting impatient. "In the living room?"

She bit her lip again, and Tom had to repress an urge, one that had been growing stronger over the twenty-six years of their marriage, to reach out and pull her lip from under her perfectly capped teeth. It drove him crazy. Biting her lip while she was trying to remember something was one of her half dozen or so little gestures. It was enough to drive a man nuts.

"I really can't recall," Peggy said at last. "I remember lighting it, of course, because the window was open and the smell of oats was really strong tonight. And I remember turning off the lamp after the movie was over. You put the DVD back on the shelf and I picked up the glasses on the coffee table..." She trailed off, lost in thought. "But I don't remember if I blew out that darn candle."

"Well, can you go check?"

"Why can't you go?" she asked, a little testily.

"Because you lit the damn thing," Tom replied, a little testily himself.

"Because I lit it?" Peggy repeated. "What are you, six years old?"

"Are you?" he shot back. "What is it, are you afraid to go into the living room in the dark?"

"Are you?"

"I'm already comfortable." Then, as if to accentuate this fact, Tom nestled a bit further down under the covers and picked up his book again.

"I'm comfortable, too," Peggy replied, a bit indignantly. She opened her own book as if she was deeply engrossed in it, a tight little frown squiggled on her face.

Tom heaved a big sigh. "Listen, Peg, I've gotten up twice already. Once to make sure the side door was closed and locked—because you couldn't remember if you did *that*—and again to feed the stupid cat."

Peggy looked at him and decided it was probably easier to submit now than to continue arguing about it. On the day she had married Tom, her mother had given Peggy two pieces of advice. *Don't sign anything until your lawyer's looked at it first* and *Never go to bed angry*.

"Okay," she said, closing her book and putting it on the night stand, "but this means you're making breakfast in the morning. Blueberry pancakes," she added.

From behind his book, Tom snorted good-naturedly to show that he was a good sport, that bygones were bygones.

Peggy flipped back the coverlet and slid her long legs out of bed. She was quite tall—taller even than Tom's considerable five feet ten inches—and while she had always taken pride in her long legs, she didn't much like looking at them anymore. Like Tom's hands, they were starting to show their years. Not that it mattered. Her legs had the years *and* the mileage. When the floor creaked under her feet, she thought that part of the sound—surely not the greater part, but some part at least—was the joints in her knees letting her know that her days of junior varsity soccer and ringette were over—long over.

She pulled up the baggy cotton boxer shorts she was wearing, the ones with the Peterborough Petes' logo on them, and reflected that her days of sexy lace underwear from I See France, the lingerie store downtown, were over, too.

This is where I ended up, she thought as she ambled out into the dark hallway. *This is where life has taken me.*

It wasn't as bad as she made it out. She had a satisfying marriage to a man she was still in love with, they had no major financial concerns, and they were both healthy. There were no kids because they had planned to wait until Tom's first novel put them on easy street, and when it didn't, they decided that the window had passed and, really, would it be such a tragedy if they didn't have kids? They had a house that was paid for, a car that was only three years old, and a large nest egg for their steadily approaching retirement. *All of these things have brought me here*, she thought, walking down a dark hallway to the living room where they watched a lot of movies but not much living really took place.

Tom tried to get back into his book, but he couldn't concentrate. He was distracted by vague feelings of guilt. He felt a bit like a guy who had taken a girl out on a date, then told her, no, he wouldn't walk her home, even though it was dark out. He felt like a bit of a louse, to be perfectly honest.

But it was just their living room, he reasoned. Nothing scary about that. He listened for Peggy's footsteps, which should have been audible on the old hardwood floors, but he didn't hear anything.

All of this over a stupid candle.

"Peggy?"

The house was an old Colonial, and even the cat, who weighed a whopping seven pounds, made the boards creak and pop as he padded around. It was not a house where you could sneak up on someone undetected; they could hear you coming a mile away. It had even gotten so he could tell, just by the different groans and creaks, exactly where someone was headed, from the living room to the kitchen, from the bedroom to the bathroom. The sounds had become as much a part of the house as the smell of oats from the Quaker factory across the river that wafted in through the open windows when the wind was blowing right.

From where he was lying in bed, he could see only a small sliver of hallway through the open doorway. The bedroom was located at the very back of the house; the living room was at the front.

He looked over at the clock on the night stand and tried to figure out how long she'd been gone. Two minutes? Three? Surely not as long as five minutes. Long enough, he figured, to walk into the living room, check to see if the candle was still burning, and if it was, blow it out.

"Peg?"

No reply.

She's screwing with me, he thought. *She's not answering because she's pissed off.* Soon he'd hear the creaking floorboards and she'd stroll into the room and slip back under the covers as if nothing was wrong.

Fine, let her be that way. Two can play that game.

He picked up his book again. He tried to read.

Thirty seconds passed. It felt like thirty minutes. Tom closed his book with a clapping sound that seemed extraordinarily loud in the silent room. Silent house, he corrected. *Why is it so quiet?* He was so distracted that he had forgotten to put in his bookmark. He swore under his breath and jerked back the covers. He was sliding out of bed when he heard the sharp, unmistakable sound of a woman screaming.

His first panicked thought was that it was Peggy. That's why she hadn't answered him. Something was wrong. Had someone broken in? His guilt was no longer vague; it was as solid as the obstruction that had formed in his own throat and kept him from calling out.

But the scream hadn't come from the house. No, he was sure of that. Tom's gaze flicked toward the bedroom window. It had come from outside.

It wasn't Peggy, he told himself, *assured* himself. It was someone in the house next door, or maybe even from one of the houses further down the street—it had certainly been loud enough. But it was muffled, too.

That's because it came from inside one of the houses. Not from someone on the street.

He didn't know how he knew that, but he did.

He climbed out of bed and walked over to the doorway.

"Peg? Where are you?"

Nothing.

He stepped into the hallway and out of the glow thrown by the bedside lamps. He was alone in the darkness. The smell of roasting oats was very strong. It was not an unpleasant smell, but it was one that had gotten old very quickly. His stomach made a protesting, groaning sound.

He walked into the darkened living room, the hardwood floor popping and creaking under his bare feet. He moved past the dining room table, the futon they had bought for guests to sleep on because they didn't have another bedroom. The shapes of the couch and the love seat were limned against the orange glow of the streetlights. He saw the candle, a smaller silhouette on one of the end-tables. It was out. There was no sign of Peggy.

He started to turn around, to search the rest of the house, when he suddenly realized the room wasn't empty.

Someone was sitting in the old wicker rocking chair, which was no longer in the corner of the room but in front of the wide bay window that looked out on McDonnel Street.

He was straining his eyes to see who it was when the candle on the end table suddenly flickered into low-burning life. Tom's eyes were drawn to it instinctively. His mouth fell open. In the dim light he saw it was Peggy sitting in the chair.

It rocked forward and Tom jerked backward. He didn't scream. *Not like the woman next door*, he thought randomly. *What had that woman seen? Her husband, maybe, sprawled out in his favourite recliner? What had he gotten up to do? Check to make sure the front door was locked? Bring in the dog?*

A cold sheen of sweat formed on his back. His pyjama top clung to him like a greasy second skin.

Peggy began to speak, but not in any tone of voice Tom had ever heard in all the years he had known her.

"No questions, my sweet," Peggy said in a sharp, clear voice. "No questions tonight. Just the answer. Your answer."

What in the hell is going on? he thought frantically.

The candle flickered, and Tom glanced at it again. A smell wafted over to him. It was a sweet smell, a ripe smell that he couldn't identify. It didn't make any sense. The candle was vanilla-scented. It was a smell he and Peggy both enjoyed, along with Autumn Spice, Apple Pie, and Desert Rose, a smell that had filled the room earlier that evening.

Something was wrong.

Peggy was staring at the candle, too. He had seen her profile a thousand times over the years—a hundred thousand times—and he knew it as well as his own reflection. But there was something different about it now. Different in the same subtle way that the smell of the candle was different. It was clearly Peggy sitting in the rocker . . . and yet it wasn't. Something was missing, or something had been added—something that changed her entirely and made her a stranger.

Tom jumped as another scream split the night. Was it someone else making a similar discovery? Was it someone he and Peggy knew, someone in their circle of friends, someone, maybe, who had spent the night on their futon?

He had sent his wife out here to do something. Now he bent over to do it himself. He felt Peggy's eyes watching him. He could feel them crawling on his skin like beetles. His eyes looked up at the window, and from this angle he could see the moon. It was different, too. The shape was right, but the colour was all wrong. Tom took two deep breaths, one to steady himself and one to do what needed to be done.

Just pretend it's your birthday, he told himself.

Peggy whispered, "Make a wish."

He blew out the candle.

through the door
SUSAN IOANNU

Imagine a filigreed keyhole
the shape of a corset
or hourglass

and a silver key,
the handle a circle
head notched like an axe.

(Word-sharp,
did it cut off
the corset's neck, perhaps?)

On one side
blood is dripping
into a stained, glass shell.

Fine white logic
sifts in the other
a radiant children's pile.

Chaos blooms into order,
and order implodes
to a flash.

Form is flow,
and energy, matter
the keyhole's inseparable halves.

Both sides
lock up one Garden
we wander and wonder in.

signal to noise
GEMMA FILES

. . . reckon not those who are killed in Allah's way as dead; nay, they are alive (and) are provided sustenance from their Lord.

Never think that those who have perished in jihad are dead—they are still here. You are simply unaware of them.
    —Alternate translations of *Qu'ran* Excerpt 3:169,
        Set 11, Count 32.

Two months after Cal Fichtner took himself officially "off the map," Greer Reizendaark logged onto the Company webmail account to find a particularly well-scrubbed piece of e-correspondence waiting for him. No header, no address, no send-date—just a numerical link embedded in the body, with this curt instruction: LIVE AT ONE. CLICK HERE.

He waited 'til the clock at the corner of his screen rolled over, then did—and watched the whole way through, without comment, not stopping even when some newbie from Homeland Security caught a couple of seconds' glance at it over his shoulder, and started puking. "Holy Christ," she kept on repeating. "Holy, holy Christ."

Greer didn't turn around. Just snapped back, as the footage froze, looped and started over: "That's exactly what they want you to say, you dizzy cunt."

For *I will cast terror into the hearts of those who disbelieve. Therefore strike off their heads, and strike off every fingertip of them*—Excerpt 8:012, Set 28, Count 62.

The *dhimmi*, the Crusaders, the Jews: make 'em too afraid to fight you, to resist the tide of *jihad*, by showing them just how bad they were gonna die, if they did.

The funny thing, though? Fichtner didn't even look all that scared, in the clip—stayed a cast-iron son-of-a-bitch, right up to and including the part where they stuck a knife between his top two vertebrae, and started sawing away at his spine. Like it hurt, yes; mad, for damn certain . . .

He'd known all along this was the likeliest outcome, though. Hadn't needed Greer to tell him *that*.

Hadn't let him, when he'd tried.

This world was full of empty spaces, especially where the maps fell away—holes that most often plugged themselves with phantoms, the minute you looked somewhere else. Nature of the game. Nothing was certain, only wars and rumours of wars, 'til the intelligence checked out.

Or, as his last wife liked to put it: "You're physically present sometimes, but you're not really here, Greer—not ever. You're not just a spook, you're a ghost."

"That's a cliché, darlin'."

"You'd know," she said.

Sheikh Mehdi Nebbou called a half hour after Fichtner's execution, to demand: "Why were you not watching him, Greer?"

"Other shit on my plate, buddy. As goddamn usual."

Greer certainly had been, in the beginning—no big secret there. Because while Fichtner might've been righteously quick to drop his GPS-enabled cellphone in the very next dry well he saw, he'd already known (as Greer had taught him) how the basic fun of surveillance came from realizing you could track anybody, anywhere, so long as you had a fair idea of who they were likely to be hanging around with. People always made the best anchors.

So if somebody'd wanted to find Fichtner, all they'd ever had to do was watch the clinic Fichtner's new lady worked at, then wait for him to turn up somewhere in the background. Or hell, they could just watch Mehdi himself, who'd offered Fichtner a job as a "security consultant" the week after Fichtner tendered his resignation.

But things had gotten hot elsewhere, like they always did, and Greer's attention had shifted, accordingly. Wasn't like the interest ever seemed much reciprocated, since Fichtner certainly knew— had known—his home phone number, and Greer'd made sure not to have it changed in the interim, just in case his wayward protégé ever felt inclined to ring him up for a little chat.

"They killed his fiancée, as well," Mehdi said. "Miss Al-Kimani—the nurse? Though I suppose it might be asking too much to think—"

"Don't tell me what I do and don't care about, you supercilious S.O.B. You were the one s'posed to look after him now, remember? Your territory, your rules. He trusted you."

"If you had only trusted *me*, Greer—from the very beginning— then none of this would have happened," Mehdi replied. Then rang off, leaving Greer with nothing in his Bluetooth but an oh-so-sophisticated lack of static.

Only the truth, whatever that was: just information, a wonderfully fluid thing. Given the right tools and impetus, you could move it around, cover it up, modify it—give it a fan made out of feathers and make it do the shimmy, if you wanted. That was what Greer did all day, every day, to earn his Christmas bonus . . . and what Mehdi did too, while saving for a considerably different holiday.

From Marathon to Peshawar, the same routine: guys like Mehdi and Greer put people into bad situations, hoping they'd find out what their governments didn't already know they needed to know. Most times, the people got hurt. Sometimes they got killed. But the rules didn't change, no matter what—whether you were getting the bulk of your covert intel with black magic tech, or an old-fashioned gun to the head.

By lunchtime, Greer was vetting three separate reports (Holland, Spain, Equatorial Africa) while simultaneously balls-deep in a three-way conference call with Washington, Toronto and London, listening to some CSIS asshole pontificate, and trying to chew his way through a cruller without it showing up on tape.

"You can see how this makes us look bad, Agent Reizendaark," this guy said. "Your Mr. Fichtner died for being a member of the global intelligence community."

Now, there's an oxymoron, Greer thought. And shot back—"'My' Mr. Fichtner? Hadn't been that since I accepted his L.O.R., back in February."

"They wrote 'CIA BLOODSUCKER' on the wall behind his corpse," the designated representative from Greer's side of the table pointed out.

"Outdated, then," London broke in; "let's not quibble over semantics, gentlemen. Particularly since I'm still not hearing anything about how you mean to deal with this particular— breach of protocol."

"Well, what do you suggest?"

"Erase all trace of Fichtner, retroactively."

"Looks to me like somebody already beat you to it," Greer replied, punching out.

Two months ago. Greer still had that last call .mp3'd on his hard drive, somewhere—could listen to it later tonight, alone in his empty house, where the only company left for him to keep was with a dead man's voice.

Fichtner: *You get my message, G.?*

Greer: *Yeah, I got it. So . . . hear you're growin' a beard for real, prayin' five times a day, and why? 'Cause Aqsa won't let you up under her hijab if you don't?*

Fichtner: *'Cause I like it, Greer. 'Cause it feels right.*

Greer: *Uh huh. So what's the part you like most, huh? The killing in the Name part? The eight-year-old human bombs?*

Fichtner: *I like the part says there is no God but God. Seems true to me, or like it should be. Might solve a fuck of a lot of problems, on either side, people just took it a bit more seriously. . . .*

Greer: *Some people already take it a bit too seriously for comfort, you ask me.*

Fichtner: *. . . and the rest? That's mostly misinformation, misinterpretation. People thinking they always know better.* (Pause) *Sound familiar?*

Greer: *Fuck you, son.*

Fichtner: *Can't do that sort of thing no more, G. Sorry.*

Greer: *No matter how drunk I get you, first?*

Fichtner: *Can't do that either, buddy.*

Greer: *Well, hell, buddy—that sure ain't no kinda religion I'd be willin' to die for, but to each his damn own.* (Pause) *'Cause they are gonna kill you, Cal . . . that's the no-God-but-God's honest truth. Her too, probably. You do know that, right?*

Fichtner: *Well, if they do, they do. I mean, Aqsa's been living with this shit a whole lot longer than either of us, Greer—she's stronger than I'll ever be. Plus, at least she tries not to hate.*

Greer: *You really think the two of you're gonna end up in the same place, though, after? Given all you done?*

Fichtner: (Long pause) *Maybe not. But that's the hope.*

And here the mental transcript broke off.

To wash the conference call's aftertaste away, Greer hit the Geek Room, where his two pet surveillance experts—one male, one female, so he always just called 'em Guy and Gal, in his head—were poring over the latest input from a bunch of gyro-stabilized recon ex-satellite cameras Mehdi had agreed to retrofit onto some of *his* bosses' "new" Navy P-3 Orions. As a vain stab at trying to keep things private, the cameras got changed around weekly, which meant Guy and Gal spent most days downloading intel, plugging it into a 360-degree spread and then trying to figure out from the resultant virtual landscape just where and when said footage had been snatched, as well as what the hell was (probably) going on in it.

Today's spread showed a meet-up somewhere in the desert (big surprise), though Guy and Gal were having trouble deciding exactly which one. Scans showed two vans, three open-end trucks and a yoinked U.S. Army Humvee 'round which figures in robes and head-scarves filtered, their faces all equally blown out by harsh light and sudden shadow.

"We think this one's Ajinabi," Gal said, tapping what to Greer was an utterly random set of features. The name—an agreed-upon moniker floated first through Mehdi's group, then adopted by Greer's, after Fichtner started using it in his reports—was Arabic for either "stranger" or "outsider": a legendary organizer for hire, possibly foreign-born, or even a Fichtner-style convert who'd chosen *jihad* over live-and-let-live. But on lack of background detail alone, Ajinabi'd quickly become scapegoat of choice in the region—a convenient catch-all for a complex range of mischief, everything from holding bomb-building classes to coordinating lethal actions.

"He might've been in on Fichtner, too, boss," Guy suggested. "Or know who was."

Greer shrugged. "Might've. Which is pretty much the same as sayin' the boogeyman did it, 'cause we'll never know no better."

Gal frowned. "We figure out who some of the other players here are, though, and turn 'em—that'd get us one step closer."

"Don't look to me like there's enough there for the facial-recognition software to work with, even if our current operatives database wasn't so far out of date—"

Guy: "Oh, look at that. I think . . . we got a hit."

They all studied the results for a while, silently. Until—

"That . . . looks like Cal Fichtner," Gal said, at last.

"Couldn't be, though."

". . . no."

Damn, though, if it didn't seem like it was. Right there in the background, half-hidden in a shadow cast by that second truck from the right—even down to choice of sunglasses, or that raggedly white-boy meth-cooker beard he'd grown so Aqsa would feel more at home letting him walk her down the street. Same stone-age vs. *Star Trek* outfit he'd last been photographed wearing, calculated for maximum blend-in when viewed from above; same guy got his head cut off on almost-live not-exactly-TV, and made it exciting enough to watch that the footage ended up being streamed on Al-Jazeera.

"Look, fellas," Greer broke in, finally, "I've seen the man's *head*. They sent it to us postage paid, packed in salt, care of my office."

"What about the rest of him?"

"Out in the desert somewheres, I assume—the hell's it matter? We got DNA, got a hundred per cent match. Whoever that is, Cal Fichtner don't come into the matter."

"Well," Guy muttered, "it might be . . ." Then cut off in mid-breath as Gal shot him a dirty look, visual shorthand for *shut effin' up, you boob*. Greer raised a brow, angled to include them both.

"Might be *what*?"

Gal sighed. "Sometimes . . . data stays behind. Like . . . when you overwrite stuff again and again, fragments stick around, in the interstices. They just sort of collect."

"'Pixel-geists,' we call 'em—"

"*You* do."

"Whatever. So, stuff gets caught between the zeroes and the ones—I mean, so what, right? All part of the process."

Greer shook his head, hoping that would help; it didn't.

"Well . . . what do you do about it, when it does?" he asked, finally.

"Wait 'til it goes away again, mostly," Guy replied.

That night, his BlackBerry chimed, and Greer opened it to find his inbox full of empty emails. At first he thought it was Fichtner's killers trying to screw with him some more, but maybe not— these *had* addresses and time-signatures, though both jumped seemingly at random from past to present to future, 'round the world and back again. One was from Antarctica, for fuck's sake. Greer shift-clicked the whole pile, hit delete. Then fell asleep watching football with one eye, BBC World News with the other, and head-first from there into a pile of dreams: blurry, brief, bitterly disturbing.

That awful room, a tiny concrete cell with corkboard walls, with nothing in it but a gashed-up slab-topped table and a camera-stand. And bloodstains, layered in over atop of each other, so deep they looked like wallpaper.

The Bluetooth buzzed against his cheek, hot with sweat. He reared back up, swatting at it, only to hear a voice he knew almost better than his own issuing from it—tiny and tinny, but distinct: *internalized*, like it was vibrating up through the bones of his jaw to reach the eardrum directly, its message's content and delivery system alike both equally impossible.

Get my message, G?

". . . What?"

Fichtner's *laugh*, pricking tears from Greer's eyes automatically, like a cold wind.

You—get—my message?

"Who *is* this?" No reply. "Listen, asshole, you need to get the hell off my line."

Can't do that. Sorry.

Greer knuckled his eyes, drawing sparks. "I . . . ain't havin' this conversation. You could be anybody, 'sides from—"

. . . me?

A long pause ensued, while Greer tried to figure out anything worth saying.

Maybe . . . not? the voice asked, gently.

". . . can't be."

Well . . . seems true to me, or like it should be. Buddy.

Then silence. Not even a tone.

Greer sat there a while, thinking about how insane he must have gone without noticing, to actually believe that he might've talking to Cal Fichtner's—what? Pixel-geist? Spook?

Around three-forty-five, he gave up on getting back to sleep, and called up Gal (who was still in the Geek Room, like he'd known she would be). Got her to send the spread over and went over it again—homed in on that tricksy little background figure, *Blade Runner*-style, and saw it was pointing straight at the same other silhouette Gal had initially tapped, exactly. "Ajinabi," caught foreground-framed with his mouth open in mid-lecture, similarly faceless yet somehow more authoritative than the rest, judging by the way the others angled towards him. And totally ignorant of Fichtner's finger cocked to the back of his head, like: Him. Here. See? *This* guy, and no one else . . .

. . . my message . . .

And then it was . . . later, and Greer surfaced to find himself somehow not only drunk as a lord, but already on the phone with Mehdi. Who was being surprisingly forbearing about it, given the circumstances.

"Things are still *there* even when you stop lookin' at 'em, right?" Greer asked, pouring another drink he sure as hell didn't need.

"I believe you may be veering dangerously close to the realm of metaphysics with this question, Agent Reizendaark. Or of spiritualism, perhaps." A beat. "Why are you phoning me, exactly?"

"I . . . honestly have no idea."

"Mmm. Do you happen to know what time it is here?"

". . . early? Or late, I guess . . ."

"Yes, very likely one or the other. But then, time zones were always a weakness of yours, as I recall. On a more personal note, however—you sound as though you need sleep, Greer, rather than alcohol. Rather badly."

"Probably do, yeah."

"Then sleep."

". . . not yet. You hooked up? Online?"

"I'm in bed, Greer. Where you should be."

"Well, I'm flattered, buddy; don't think you really want me in *your* bed, though. I'd wreck the mattress."

Mehdi made a half-sigh, half-snicker. "Send me your data," he said, at last.

The next morning, his head full of cotton and mush, Greer saw Mehdi's number blink alight, and picked up halfway through the first ring.

"You can't possibly think this is what it seems," Mehdi told him.

Greer shut his eyes. "Well, that depends. What's it look like to you?"

"Greer . . ."

"I want to hear you say it, Sheikh. Out loud."

Another sigh. Then—

". . . it *appears* to be a surveillance photo of Cal Fichtner. Standing in the desert. Pointing at someone."

"Fella at seven o'clock, three from the right?"

"The very same. I cannot, however, make out *his* face."

"Crap. I was kinda hopin' you knew him."

"Yes, that would be convenient, I suppose—if we had any idea what it was he was doing there, or why we should care to know, in the first place."

"My geeks think he's Ajinabi."

Unimpressed: "Do they."

"Yup. They say word on the Grid is, he keeps off it—does everything face to face, word of mouth. So if this *is* him callin' a meeting, it's gotta be about somethin' pretty big. Think he might've been the one behind what happened to Fichtner, too . . . and Aqsa Al-Kimani."

"The great Foreign Devil for Hire, wearing a thousand masks and pulling a thousand strings. I've heard those rumours as well, Greer—for quite some time, now. Far longer than you've considered them relevant, considering they really didn't begin to attract your direct interest until a friend of yours . . ." A pause. "In terms of concrete proof, however, that's exactly all they are. Rumours."

"I've gotten the go-ahead on less."

"Doubtless. But I'm not sure I'd boast about that, if I were you."

Greer huffed out hard, and felt his temples start to throb. "Fine, then. What do *you* think these pics are, if they ain't—that?"

"As you know, we of Islam tend to find representative images of the ineffable somewhat . . . difficult."

"Even photos?"

Greer could practically hear Mehdi's shrug. "Contextually, recent photos of a person one knows to be dead operating in the material world are likely to be almost as suspect as paintings of the Prophet, don't you agree?"

"I think maybe this is some cultural thing we're gettin' into, here, and I ain't exactly qualified to—"

"No? At *best*, Greer, this is a ghost, something whose testimony both our religions find equally suspect. We know Cal Fichtner was a good man, though not by all standards; all signs point towards the idea that he had come to terms with his past, made amends, found love, found faith . . . forgiveness. So he should be at peace—either in Heaven, or Paradise. Elsewhere, at any rate. Not—"

"You can't know it's *not* Fichtner," Greer began, ridiculously annoyed.

"And you can't know it is. The desert is a bad place to die, Greer—an empty place, home to many strange, empty things. Just because something wears a face you know . . ."

"What the hell you gettin' at, exactly?"

"Do you really think a dead man still works 'for' you, simply because he seems as though he claims to? Or, better yet . . . when has chasing a ghost ever led to anything of true, lasting value?"

"We chase ghosts all the time, buddy."

"Not literally."

There was a small silence; Greer breathed into it, carefully, dialling himself back down. Trying to clear his aching head.

"We found her body," Mehdi added, unexpectedly. "Miss Al-Kimani—buried up to her neck, stoned, then beheaded; the usual. Tragic waste of a perfectly good nurse, especially in a city with so few free clinics." After a beat. "No further trace of Fichtner's, unfortunately."

"Desert's a pretty big place, is what I hear."

"Yes. It is."

"Happened again, boss," Gal said.

"We thought you'd want to know," Guy chimed in.

This time, the photo spread came from a market in Casablanca, where some poor burnoosed bastard stood at a stall completely oblivious to the goons closing in on him (Guy had helpfully tagged him with a pop-up caption saying simply "ASSET"), and "Fichtner" was the one occupying the foreground—almost angled *towards* the fly-over, which was frankly impossible. Unfortunately, this still didn't manage to bring the guy he was once again pointing at any closer.

"You run a point-by-point?" Greer asked.

Guy nodded. "Pretty much a match, so . . . looks like it *is* the same dude Fi, uh—" He stumbled, flushing, under Greer's pointed look. "—same dude the . . . other one fingered."

"But that don't really tell us nothin' we didn't know before, huh?"

Gal: "Right."

Greer scowled down at the multi-screen array. "What's he even doin' there, you figure that much out?"

They exchanged a look. Said, as one: "Maybe."

The reason the missing operative grab hadn't been clocked immediately—taking maybe five hours after he'd been grabbed from a nearby safe-house for his safe-house to call him in missing, plus another hour since after Fichtner's pixel-geist had picked out "Ajinabi" for the birdie—was because he was just a local hire. Further examination revealed him as also A) one of Fichtner's C.I.s, specifically during the last fiasco Greer'd puppetmastered with Fichtner as his man on the ground, and B) a guy Fichtner'd first found through Mehdi's info-gathering networks, making that Greer's next call. He sent over the new spread at the same time, and waited while Mehdi pulled it up.

"Off-putting," was all Mehdi had to say.

"Really ain't no way anybody could fake that, is there?"

"Unless one of your pets is serving two masters, I think not." Greer heard the click of a mouse as Mehdi fiddled around some, probably trying the image from the same angles Guy and Gal already had.

Muttering to himself, as he did—"If only we could see that man's face a bit more clearly. If only Fichtner—"

(wasn't blocking the view)

"Guess you don't think it's a *jinn*, then."

"Ah, someone's been Googling."

"Gimme some damn credit, Sheikh. I work for a department's been dealin' with the Middle East for almost sixty years; might be I could'a heard the term, here and there."

"Oh yes, you're a veritable fount of Muslim marginalia—that must be why your Farsi is so atrocious." With one last click: "So . . . are we meant to gather from this latest—communique— that Hasim Gullah is bound for the same place as Fichtner?"

"Beheadings-'R'-Us, then the Internet?" Greer paused. "Don't suppose you'd be any closer to figuring out where that first stream came from. . . ."

"Must I do all your work for you, Agent Reizendaark?"

Mehdi'd probably meant it to be light, a joke, but the tone wasn't quite right. Still, Greer knew a kiss-off when he heard one.

So: "Fuck you, son," he said. And hung up.

You get my message, G?

Thirty minutes earlier, the subdermal bone-buzz voice would've muffled itself against alcohol—but sleep had eluded Greer, and now the call rattled his skull straight through into incipient hangover.

My—a skip, sample-scratch brief—*new*—*message?*

Greer swallowed cold spit, sat bolt upright: he knew this trick, had *used* this trick. That one inserted word in a different tone, different stress pattern, different volume even from the rest of the sentence . . . and other than that, the sentence said the exact same way, every time. He was angrier at ever having fallen for the oldest Space Age surveillance gaslighting trick in the book, if only the once, than at being targeted in the first place.

Tic-inducing, scrapy vibrations under his jaw: laughter, more tired than snide. *People thinking they always know better.*

Then another pause, while Greer timed it out exactly: *Sound familiar?*

"When I find you, shithead—"

Maybe not . . .

No click, but Greer knew instantly the contact was lost. He closed his eyes, fighting the urge to puke—his mind already supplying the rest of the quote, whether he wanted it to or not—

. . . but that's the hope.

"Got a phone call from Fichtner, just now," Greer told Mehdi, minutes later. "Plus last night, and . . . night before that, too."

"Hmm."

"Not the reaction I was expectin', but hell—I'll take it. Care to elaborate?"

"Very well: *this*, as you know, is something 'Ajinabi' really *could* fake. You set your share of bugs in Fichtner's rooms, his cars . . . they would only have had to tune in long enough to capture his half of the conversation, from which to sample and loop a few pertinent phrases—"

"Mentioned the photo array, though. Ajinabi, scopin' out Gullah's beat. Gettin' things all set for the Big Scoop."

"Directly?"

". . . sort of."

my—(new)—message

"How long'd they keep Fichtner alive, you reckon?" Greer asked.

"Impossible to tell, without access to his corpse."

"But you've been doin' some investigation of your own in the meantime, I'll bet."

Mehdi didn't bother to deny it; his fact-finding methods were legendarily effective, owing far more to the time-worn examples of Haroun al-Raschid and Hammurabi than to anything agreed on in The Hague. "My informants think . . . seventy-two hours at most."

"Ain't a whole lot of time to try and do anything about our Mister Gullah's situation, is it?"

"I hope you recorded the calls, at least," Mehdi said, eventually. "If so, perhaps you should have them analyzed, by someone not quite so . . ."

"Drunk?"

"I was going to say . . . personally involved. But make no mistake: someone is trying to puppet *you*, here, Agent Reizendaark—to get you down on the ground, where you are most unsuited to be. Having studied you, they no doubt know you like to sacrifice long-term build for short-term opportunity; they will lead you on some ethereal scavenger hunt in order to trap you, just as they did Fichtner. And what will happen then?"

Greer shut his eyes. "Oh, I think I got a pretty good idea."

Forget the desert's empty spaces and deceptive images—a guilty man's mind had all of that and more, re-splitting under pressure exponentially, like a prism. Grief was an echo-chamber. No matter how hard you thought you were listening, the only thing you ever really heard was your own voice.

Or somebody else's, still and small in the middle of the night, the way God's was supposed to sound. Saying: *Greer . . . you're a ghost*.

Well, maybe so.

But then again—not just yet.

Barely pausing to shower and shave, Greer hit the Geek Room again, doing his best Angry Fist of God impression. Told Gal and Guy to break it all down, far as they could, then farther.

As they did, he thought yet again about how "Intelligence," so-called, was a machine that ran on universal constants—secrecy, stupidity, entropy. It wasn't about the parts, and only slightly about the labour; damn thing'd keep running on its own, even if nobody did their fair share anymore. Stick a cog in, pop it out, throw it away, smash it to pieces; the machine kept grinding, exceeding fine, untouched. And though Greer might occupy its hub for the nonce, he had no illusions that that state of affairs would be perpetual. Lots of guys had held his exact same job, before being discarded and forgotten.

For now, however, he *was* still Big Man Off-Campus—the legendary Guy on the Other End of the Phone, running a large-ass part of Ajinabi's competition. Knock Greer Reizendaark off his game, and the Foreign Devil would win a free block of unsupervised time in which to cut a few more people's heads off . . . starting with Hasim Gullah, one assumed, before working his way back up the food chain.

So: something to keep in mind, maybe, even now. Something to bargain with.

"Got something," Guy said, finally.

Turned out, the very pixels making up the photos in which "Fichtner" appeared had GPS coordinates encoded in each of them—just beyond the border of Mehdi's home turf, in (predictably enough) the desert. The location of Ajinabi's death room, Fichtner's body? Or both?

"And get this," Gal told Greer, excited as she ever got. "The phone calls have a frequency and a series of tones mixed in, just underneath the signal itself."

"A number." She nodded. "Traceable?"

"Nope."

Guy: "Looks like it's been overwritten at least twice, like it's changing every time somebody switches disposable cells—but a direct line, every time. Somebody important. Like it might even go straight to—"

"Uh huh," Greer said, then read it out loud, and pressed his ever-present Bluetooth's "dial" button.

"*Wa'alaikum ah salaam*," a voice said, at the other end.

Greer grinned. "Ajinabi, I presume."

Gal and Guy watched with horror-struck eyes as the negotiations commenced. Greer kept 'em short, if not sweet: a switch, him for Gullah, contingent on proof—positive, not 'Net-based—that the guy was still alive.

"Sheikh Nebbou can ferry you to the meet-point, no doubt," Ajinabi said, like he expected Greer to be impressed he knew they knew each other.

"He was gonna be my very next call," Greer agreed—then paused, as he heard the "call waiting" tone.

"Ah, your superiors. You should probably take this," Ajinabi suggested.

After that things began to move even faster.

Wasn't much work to convince the CIA-CSIS-MI6 three-way that what had looked from the outside like Greer spiralling down into an alcohol-fuelled psychotic break was really the triple-cross of the century—a trap so obvious, from either angle, that neither he nor Ajinabi could afford not to let it play through. Greer made sure to dangle the prospect of snapping up Ajinabi's near-supernatural tech at the same time, of course: the combo of insider info and toys, whatever they might be, which had somehow allowed him to pose as the undeniably dead Cal Fichtner on phone and sat-cam alike.

(Amazing, really, how Fichtner's current state had apparently given him skills Greer never knew him to possess, back when he was yet left upright. But then again, Fichtner's best quality as an operative always *was* his ability to adapt to any given new

environment they dropped him into, going native just as fast—
and effectively—as humanly possible.)

Greer wasn't too sure if they really believed him, or how much,
or how much it mattered. But by Saturday afternoon he was
walking off a transpo into bright sunlight, blinking at Mehdi's
familiar face in the unfamiliar flesh: all dolled up in a swank
linen suit and a pair of custom shades, looking crisp. He towered
over everyone but Greer, who only lacked a couple of the same
inches—vertically, anyhow.

"Hadn't thought to see you so soon, Agent Reizendaark, I
must admit, or at all, for that matter."

Greer shrugged. "Well, that's U.S. initiative for you."

"Quite. So how do you find you like it, down here on the
ground?"

"Not too much, buddy. Ain't got the build for it."

"Hmm," Mehdi said, yet again.

"You're startin' to sound like a damn bee," Greer told him, as
they headed for the SUV.

Heat like a wall, dust everywhere. The drive went on so long,
following GPS cue to GPS cue, it turned afternoon to night. The
meet-point, meanwhile, turned out to be a low concrete building
with slit windows; same place they'd brought Fichtner, like as
not. Why mess with success?

"You don't have to come with me," Greer told Mehdi, who
hissed, and drew some tiny little snub-nosed piece out from
under his arm—small enough so it didn't not to spoil the line of
his jacket, the peacock. Greer put his own empty hands up, and
kicked the car door open,

But when they hauled Gullah out to meet him, with Ajinabi
striding behind, Greer (who'd earned part of the military rank
few remembered he had while serving in EOD) only had to look
at the way Gullah's shirt jacket sat to know he was all rigged up
and ready to blow.

Time went wonky, step-printed. To his right, he saw Mehdi
raise his pint-sized gun. mouth opening, as Gullah's guards
pushed him headlong towards Greer. To the left, Ajinabi, fiddling
with a pocketed cell—seemed like he might be trying to detonate
it remotely, but the signal was being blocked. And Greer could
suddenly see Fichtner standing next to him, haloed from behind

yet snapshot-clear with one hand on the phone, while the other reached to seat itself deep in the back of Ajinabi's skull: punch, grab, *twist*. A five-finger aneurysm in action.

"GET DOWN!" Greer yelled, kicking Mehdi away, and threw himself into the zone, as another of Ajinabi's goons managed to trigger the bomb's failsafe.

Amazing how little it hurt, after, considering the ungodly mess his body had made—his, Gullah's, Ajinabi's. (And where exactly *had* that bastard gone, anyhow? Greer sure didn't see him, except in pieces.) But then, they'd all been ready to die for their respective causes, one way or the other.

Greer "stood" next to Fichtner, watching Mehdi grub around in the wreckage for a long minute or two: concussed and reeling, his suit unsalvageable, usually dignified face streaming with tears. It was this last part which amazed Greer the most; hadn't thought the man cared, let alone so much.

Fichtner "laughed," or whatever its applicable equivalent might be. *Little late in the day to go all modest on us now, Greer, ain't it?*

Greer "nodded": True enough. He pointed at the half-levelled building, and "asked"—

Rest of you actually still in there, somewhere, or was all this for nothin'?

Buried out back, yeah. But they'll find it easy enough, even without dogs—the grave's dug shallow. A beat. Besides which . . . if this was really all about laying me *to rest, I'll eat my damn hat.*

Greer could've argued that most ops were about more than one objective, at the very least—but it really did seem sort of immaterial at this point, so to speak. So instead, he just "nodded" once more.

Good end-game, son. You played it well—way I would've, pretty much.

Yeah? That's almost flattering.

Uh huh. 'Course, you did learn from the best. . . .

But all twitting aside, Greer knew, it was only justice—payback after those years of Greer putting Fichtner's ass on the line for whatever new info it might bring, when he'd staked him out like a goat again and again, just to see who'd come sniffin'. All the times he'd done his damn job, while helping Fichtner do his . . .

But: *I really did let you go, Cal,* Greer tried to get across, *nevertheless. Just like you asked me to. Didn't use you to draw Ajinabi—that was never my intent. Not you, and for damn sure not Aqsa—*

Wouldn't matter much if you had, not now. But for what it's worth, Greer, I know. I know. . . .

(everything, now)

Like you could too, you only wanted it.

(*Really?*)

Cal just gave him a shrug, like: *Sure. Why not?*

And then, all of a sudden—

—he did.

What was left of Greer Reizendaark raised his phantom no-hand to the sky, waving blithely at the satellite he knew Gal and Guy were currently hid behind, then reached right on back through the feed and into the mainframe to try some *real* tricks—sow a few search-links, start data-mining. Widening the parameters of the satellite's sweep to track the rest of Ajinabi's cell's fleeing trucks as they dispersed, crossing borders at random; he started a new folder, hidden down deep in the infrastructure. Saved, clicked, saved again.

You're good at that, what was left of Cal Fichtner "said," almost admiring. *Better than I ever was.*

Greer had to agree. Turned out, his last wife had had it right all along, without even knowing—a ghost really *was* the best kind of spook imaginable.

Well, I been doin' it all my life, son. Might as well keep on keepin' on.

The answer came back, fading: *Yeah, you just do that. . . .*

(But as for me, I'll see you later. Maybe.)

Or . . . maybe not.

Heat, dust, blood; the totalled SUV, a smoking crater. Mehdi, weeping. And then Greer was abruptly alone, half in and half out, still stuck to the world's dirty back by—duty? Desire?

While Fichtner, his revenge served plastique-hot, moved on to . . . wherever. Someplace Aqsa awaited him, hopefully, where maybe even poor Gullah had a seat set aside at that infinitely bountiful table.

(Again, if only vaguely, he wondered where Ajinabi himself really had gone—to his bed of virgins, as advertised? Or somewhere just a tad more . . . off-putting?)

One could only hope.

I could do that too, Greer caught himself thinking. *Just go, in either direction. But—*

"Looking down," seeing Mehdi looking so stricken, and feeling a weird surge of affection. Plus the sting of power unused, and a million different places to use it—to plug himself into the universe's hide and genuinely be the puppetmaster he'd only thought himself, before he'd known better.

—no. Not just yet.

Greer "smiled" to himself, settling in, now so adjusted to his new state he could almost feel a memory of lips moving, in sympathy with the concept. And sent Mehdi an email.

the ones outside your door
NEILE GRAHAM

The creatures outside are tricksy. In deep woods overgrowth they're Raven.
Bear. Wolf. Frog. Whale. Themselves and all selves. One.

On the richly barren moors they're the Good Neighbours. Tiny flighty
flinty bright masquerading as rideable horses that toss you

undersea or bunching into human-like skins. Raven made the world,
brings us salmon, gives us the moon, the stars, but he's hungry, wily,

more clever than us. After all, his greedy claws have caught the sun.
Hillfolk trade their cranky babes for our sweet sleepers. Tempt away

our pretty ones. Make deals we pay for. Seduce our poets
underhill for seven silent years then gift them with sore truth.

When wind bangs against the boards of our house, grateful
for warmth we park by the fire to spin their yarns; they huddle

their ears against our walls, hungering to hear themselves
named and known. How they grin to hear us tuck them safely

within the boxes of our tales. They gulp this music down,
sucking their sharp teeth for last sweet-sour strands of what's

meant to shape them. How they love these juicy words. How they
burst the boxes' walls, polishing teeth ever so bright in the dark,
                                                    dark world.

down where the best lilies grow

CAMILLE ALEXA

Odette's *maman* says she plucked her along with other skinny reeds down by the shallow brackish waters of the Durendal Fen near the water's tail end where the best mud lilies grow among the beaked sedge and whorl grass. There the small lilies push up, tiny stars tossed against green and black, blossoming like white prayers to hazy dappled cloudshine, offering themselves like virgins opening legs after wedding vows.

Now Maman lies dying, a bitter-spirited woman calling her only daughter a thing of bleached bone, leached blood and dank marshy waters, fashioned of the sodden limbs of the fen's waterlogged dead, not birthed at all.

You're not my child, she croaks, twig fingers clutching the neck of her elixir bottle. *You're a marsh baby, just a Little Bit of the bas lieu. A creature of fenwater blood and hollow reed veins and sponge moss muscle.*

The fen drags at Maman's rickety-stilt cabin, the waters older even than Maman, their name from sometime long before, someplace far away. Durendal, Odette knows, was the sword of Charlemagne's greatest champion, and once belonged to Hector of Troy. Its hollow golden hilt housed the blood of Saint Basil and a scrap of the Blessed Mary's raiment, and Odette thinks on this as she scours watery willow roots for the reagents of Maman's midwifery: herbs to help with bleeding and hemorrhage, with pain and memory, with forgetting and sorrow.

Maman's voice wafts from the cabin, carrying over the fen's chitinous insect whirr: *Little Bit! Little Bit! Bring you your maman's elixir. . . .*

Odette grabs the last brown bottle, its neck fluted and delicate like a trumpetflower crusted with dried brown medicine and mean old woman spittle, both dribbled to obscure the paper label. Years ago, Maman bought ten crates of Le Docteur's Elixir Miracle from a travelling tinkerman with a squinty eye and a cleft lip and a painted wagon promising strange beasts. The tinkerman let Odette part the dank velvet curtains draping his wagon and crawl in, and she saw the pale misshapen things in jars and cried. She'd thought they'd be alive. But they were just poor sad dead things in jars, every one.

Here's you your elixir, Maman, Odette says. Maman seizes the fluted bottle with trembling fingers, drags it to her crinkled lips. Odette knows better than to guide her hand; last time, Maman offered to slice it clean off with the gutting knife and drop it into the marshwaters along with the stillborn deBourde twins from across the fen.

Don't mourn les enfants, she'd told Odette when she caught her leaking tears. *We're all just a bit of fenwater and mud in the end. A big bit or little bit, but all returning to water one way or another, sooner or later.*

As fen midwife, Maman helps everyone out of this world, same as she helps them in: swaddled in bleached linen, their eyes closed and their mouths open. When someone passes, Odette leads the procession down to the water's edge where the best lilies grow. Everyone stands with heads bowed, caps in hands, and says last words before lowering loved ones into the brown muddy water between reeds, where undercurrents suck toward deeper channels and down, down into cushioning muck.

And then, day or night or anyplace in between, the marsh moths come.

They cluster thick and soft and pale around the swaddled linen bundles floating outward on insistent sluggish currents tugging always at the bottom of the reeds and making the white mud lilies sway and bob like nodding heads in church. White, white, white, those moths. Whiter than lilies. Whiter than bleached bones. Whiter than sunshine when it tilts hard and blinding into Odette's eyes and doesn't let go.

Those moths are the spirits of les enfants, Maman has explained, rising up out of tiny bones deep in the muck, unfurling death-pale wings to sunshine, celebrating as we weep, knowing they take another home to mud and to water.

Maman's voice comes again now from the back of the cabin:

Little Bit! Little Bit! Bring you your maman's elixir. But Odette arrives to find an empty room, only a shallow dent in the mattress, the sweet smell of rotting moss, and a single moon-white moth on the rough-spun pillow, glowing faintly in the midday gloom.

The creature fans its wings: open, close. Open, close. Larger than any moth Odette has ever seen, dark swirls lacing its upper wings and the single black spot of an eye staring from each of its lower.

Maman? Odette whispers, leaning close. *Maman. . . ?*

At her breath on its wings, the moth shudders, rises, beats toward the glassless window. Odette stumbles after, heedless of shins scraping unpainted splintered sill as she scrambles over, blood trickling down her legs. She tangles in her skirts to fall heavily into soft damp earth beneath. Scrambling to her feet she staggers after white wings flitting toward the *bas lieu*.

At the water's edge, where the best lilies grow, the moths already gather. They come gusting in on white clouds of themselves, clustered so thickly they block the sun as they wheel like one creature between it and the girl.

Odette thinks on Charlemagne, and on Hector of Troy. She thinks on the Durendal sword, on its golden hilt with the blood of Saint Basil and a scrap of the Blessed Mary's raiment. She thinks on small sad dead creatures floating in jars, and she thinks on Maman.

Bone-white moths drop one by one to cover cuts on Odette's legs and obscure mud-water splotches patterning her skirts. They rest at the bases of her fingers like heaving white jewels on rings lighter than air. They brush her face, antennae mingling with eyelashes, dusting Odette's lids and cheeks and lips with fine powder. And when the moths flutter out, out over the fens, winging toward the deep cold channels of waters emptying outward into the sea, Odette follows, laughing.

hide
REBECCA M. SENESE

Billy skidded to a stop beside her. She smelled sweat and Doublemint gum as he opened his mouth.

"The opening to Maple Crescent. After dinner. Be there."

Then he was gone, running away from her, his untucked blue striped shirt flapping in the breeze.

Pauline's heart pounded. They'd invited her! How long had it taken to get that invitation? Weeks of sucking up to twerpy Annie Burton at lunch. Swiping extra chocolate bars from home so she could use them as bribery. Smiling and laughing at Annie's stupid jokes, trying not to be sick as the older girl chewed with her mouth open, exposing gobs of melting chocolate goo in her yellow teeth.

But it had all been worth it! She was invited to the best hide and seek game in the school. Pauline wanted to dance down the sidewalk home but didn't, she kept her steps even and measured. She couldn't look too excited to be invited to the game. That wouldn't be cool.

At dinner, she ate all her vegetables, even the brussels sprouts, in record time. Thankfully no one noticed. Her father was too intent on the paper and her mother was arguing with her younger brother, Jason, who was fussing over his food. He kept pushing the offending brussels sprouts to the edge of his plate, balanced precariously. A glare from mother would cause a grumble and he'd pull them back onto the plate for a moment, then push them back to the edge. Pauline sighed. He hadn't even figured out how to hide them properly, what kind of a brother was that? She was cursed.

She set her knife and fork down beside her plate. Only a trace of mashed potatoes remained.

"Mom, can I go outside?" she said.

"Once you clean your plate," her mother said without looking.

"I have."

Her mother glanced over, blinking as if she was just waking up. "Oh. All right then. Put your plate in the sink."

Pauline scrambled from the table, dumped the plate and cutlery in the sink and was out the door before her mother could change her mind.

The early evening was crisp with the scent of cut grass. Pauline's runners thumped hard on the asphalt as she ran toward Maple Crescent. Three blocks down and four streets over. She raced past identical houses with similar lawns cluttered with bikes and children's toys. The sun had shifted since her walk home and she felt like she was chasing her long shadow. Maybe they would even be playing the hide and seek game until dark! The pounding of her heart was not only from running.

She passed a cluster of bushes and emerged at the entrance to Maple Crescent. New houses lined one side of the street, partially constructed shells lined the other. Fresh sawdust on the breeze tickled her nostrils. The front of the second unfinished house was covered with a plastic tarp that had come loose and flapped with a sharp snap in the wind. It looked like a tortured flag.

"You're early."

She turned to see Teddy Williams slouching on the sidewalk. He frowned at her, beefy hands fumbled with a silver yoyo that he stuffed into his back pocket.

"Billy told me after dinner," Pauline said. "I finished dinner."

Teddy kept frowning, shifting on his off-white runners. Behind him, Pauline could see a couple of other kids approaching. Yes, it was Ravi and his brother Jamil, both short with light brown skin. Pauline noticed Bridget and Sandra, cutting across from another street. Bridget had bright red hair cut short which only seemed to accent her height. Sandra, one year older, stood three inches shorter with blonde hair past her shoulders. A gold barrette clipped her hair neatly to the back of her neck.

Pauline turned back to Teddy and raised her eyebrows. He muttered under his breath and shifted again.

Ravi joined them first. "Where's Billy? He late again?"

"Don't know," Teddy said. "Ask her. She was here early."

Bridget and Sandra were within earshot. Pauline felt everyone looking at her. Her face grew hot. Oh no, she couldn't stammer and look stupid. She'd never get another chance!

She shrugged in a way she hoped seemed casual. "I haven't seen him."

For a moment, all the gazes fixed on her, then the kids looked away. Pauline let her breath out. That had been close.

Over the next several minutes, kids drifted in from all directions except from the new houses on Maple Crescent. Pauline glanced back at them. Why did the kids meet here?

Finally the last of the kids trickled up until there was about twenty of them, but still no sign of Billy. Ravi and Jamil consulted with several of the other kids, then called for attention.

"Billy's not here, so we'll just start." Jamil clapped his hands. "Now we got a new player today." He pointed at Pauline.

Pauline froze. Again she felt their gaze, this time magnified twenty times. Her cheeks burned. She hated blushing but there wasn't any way she could stop it. She forced her mouth to move, cracking her cheeks as her lips tried to curve into a smile. Her hand lifted in a limp wave.

"The rules are this—everyone hides and you have to find them. The first one you find has to help you find another one, the next one you find helps you find the one after that. And it keeps going. Nobody hides together and kids can change their hiding place. We go until an hour after dark."

Pauline sucked in a breath. They played until after dark? She hadn't known that.

Jamil's expression hardened. "You got a problem? You have to go home early, like a baby?"

Pauline clenched her teeth. "No. I don't gotta go home."

Jamil's black eyes glared her then he relaxed. "Good. We'll get started. You count to a hundred and then get started."

"Wait, don't we have to figure who's it?" Pauline said.

"You're it. You're new. New one is always it first game. That's the rules."

Other kids around her nodded, muttering "the rules." Pauline tried to find a sympathetic face but they were all closed to her. She sighed.

"Okay."

Jamil led her to a telephone pole and watched as she faced it, covering her eyes.

"No peeking," his voice hissed in her ear. "Count out loud."

"One, two, three," Pauline counted off. Over the sound of her voice, she heard the shuffle of running shoes on pavement as the kids scattered. She kept counting and soon the sounds faded, leaving just the rustle of the leaves in the evening breeze. She passed forty and kept counting. Would they know if she didn't count all the way to one hundred? She didn't want to take the chance. Probably they had figured out how long it took and they'd never let her play again if she stopped early. She kept counting.

"Ninety-eight, ninety-nine, one hundred." She stepped back from the telephone pole and blinked. Even the fading light seemed bright now. Her eyes watered. She rubbed them then turned to look around. Not a sign of any of the kids. It was as if they'd never even been there. A thrill ran through her. She was in the game now. Time to get started.

Her gaze settled on the unfinished houses. Surely several of the kids were hiding there. Who could resist that? She moved forward. The plastic tarp on the second house snapped in the breeze. She breathed in the scent of freshly cut wood. Clean wood beams peeked out from under the tarp. The sidewalk ended and she was walking on uneven ground, gravel rustling under her feet. She studied the ground. No footprints. The dirt hid any trace of the kids.

Would any of them hide in the house with the flapping tarp? She couldn't imagine hiding there, listening to the plastic snap and crackle. It even drowned out her footsteps as she moved forward. Anyone hiding there wouldn't hear her coming. Still she had to look, just in case. If she didn't she might miss someone.

She circled around the tarp and found an opening at the side of the house. The inside was just the ground floor with wood beams marking where the walls would go. She could see clear through to the back of the house. Nothing, only dust that made her nose itch. She rubbed it with the back of her hand and retreated.

Pauline headed for the next house. Had she made a mistake looking here? Surely a couple of the kids had hidden in these houses. How could anyone resist? Wasn't that why they met at Maple Crescent, to take advantage of the construction? Sure it was. She nodded to herself. She'd find somebody soon.

The next house didn't have a porch so she circled around the back. Holes in the walls marked the windows and the back door. Pauline walked in.

Orange sunlight glowed through the rooms. Pauline breathed

shallowly as she inched along. Her feet stirred the dust on the floor. Ahead of her, the dust had already been disturbed. Her heart beat quickened. Someone else was here! She was going to find them!

She crept forward, following the disturbance. It rounded a corner. She stopped at the edge, listening. Tree branches creaked in the breeze. The plastic tarp from the house several doors down still snapped but it was less like a gunshot and more like a finger snap. Inside the house was only stillness, a hush as if the house was holding its breath. Was it hiding one of the kids? She would have to turn that corner to find out.

Pauline hunched down to peer from closer to the floor. The kid wouldn't spot her then. For a moment, she hesitated. Her mom would kill her if she got these new salmon-coloured pants dirty but wasn't that what pants were for? Dust puffed up as she knelt down. Hands resting on her thighs, she leaned forward and peered around the corner.

A hallway led to the right. Stairs at the far end led to the second floor. A thrill ran through her. The trail led toward the stairs.

Pauline stood up and crept forward. Her runners stirred the dust. It itched at her nose. A cough welled up in her throat. She pursed her lips and blew air out through them. The urge to cough stopped.

She crept up the few stairs then stopped, listening for any creaking. Nothing. She continued climbing. Silence followed her to the top. Plain wooden planks covered the unfinished floor. It had a precarious look that made her nervous but the trail led off around another corner to the left. Someone was definitely here and she could catch them. She couldn't back out now. She'd never live it down. It would get around the school before lunch the next day. She'd have to switch schools, maybe leave town!

She swallowed and rubbed her sweating hands on her pants. Her legs trembled with excitement. Time to find the kid who was hiding here. She followed the trail, moving carefully to avoid raising more dust and alerting the kid. Outside, the plastic tarp snapped in the distance as if urging her to hurry. Was there another way down to the first floor? Maybe that kid was already getting away.

Her heart beat quickened. She had to find someone then they had to help her find others. She had to show all of them she was worthy of playing their game. She hurried forward and peered around the corner into an empty room with a pile of debris in the corner. She saw the hole where the closet would be. She started to move away, then stopped. The trail ended. Either the kid had learned to fly over the dust or . . .

Pauline turned back to the room. The shell of the closet was empty, gapping like a shallow mouth. She studied the debris, a mix of wood, slabs of drywall and wire. She stomped forward, kicking up as much dust as possible in front of her. She reached the debris pile, leaned down and scooped up a pile of dust then blew it toward the debris pile.

Nothing happened. Dust tickled her nose. She pinched her nostrils, stifling the cough that threatened to explode out of her. The cloud of dust hung in the air then drifted down, layering the debris. Anybody would be coughing like crazy by now. Could she have been wrong?

Somebody had to be hiding here. There was no other place in the house to hide. A length of wood stuck out of the bottom. She grabbed it with both hands and gave it a tug. Broken brick, pieces of fabric and wood collapsed. Pauline dropped the wood and covered her mouth and nose with her hands. Her eyes squeezed shut against the cloud of dirt. After a moment she opened her eyes.

Dust coated her hands like fine gloves. Grit scraped along her back, between her t-shirt and her skin. Her new pants were smeared with dirt. Oh, Mom was going to kill her!

And it hadn't even been worth it, she realized. No one hid under the debris pile. How could that be, she wondered. She'd been so sure. The trail had been unmistakable.

A silver glint caught her gaze. Something near the edge of the debris. She stepped forward and bend down. A yoyo. Teddy's yoyo. He had been here and faked her out. Her fingers closed around it. It felt wet and the string was frayed, snapped. Probably how he lost it as he'd made the marks and taken off. She looked at her fingers. Dirt smeared the wetness into reddish brown. Strange.

She couldn't see his retreating tracks but he had to be fooling her. Pauline nodded to herself and pushed a strand of brown hair off her forehead. She understood now. She wiped the reddish wetness on the side of her pants and left.

She searched through three more houses without finding

anyone. In one of the houses she found a gold barrette with a broken clasp. Bits of red hair were caught in the tiny screw. It looked familiar, had Bridget been wearing it? She couldn't remember. She left it behind.

Several times she thought she saw traces of someone hiding, a trail of footsteps or even sections of debris moved around, but no kids. Could they all hear her coming and escape before she got there? Maybe one or two of them could do it without her knowing, but all of them? Wouldn't she have heard somebody? She tried to swallow but her mouth was suddenly dry.

Sunlight streaked orange across the sky. Pauline watched it sink below the line of houses in the distance. They played for an hour after dark. How could she be able to find anyone by then? Her cheeks flushed with heat. How embarrassing that she couldn't even find one kid.

So far she'd stayed on one side of the street. Time to vary the routine. She hurried across and searched through four houses. Nothing. How could this be? The sun was slipping away. She had to find someone.

She ran to the next house. It had a real front door and intact windows. She slipped inside and closed the door. Darkness enveloped her. After a moment, her eyes adjusted. The living room entrance stood on her right. She peered in but the room was empty. She headed toward the upstairs. Better to check the second floor. She didn't want some kid slipping back down the stairs and out the front door before she found them.

Under her foot, the third stair creaked. She froze. Her breath caught in her lungs. Her hand gripped the railing, grittiness scraped her flesh. No sound. Maybe it had been just a little creak, not enough for anyone else to hear. She crept up the stairs.

At the top, she found a trail in the dust. Someone was hiding up here! Her heart pounded. She rubbed her hands on her pants, trying to dry them of the sudden sweat that beaded on them but she only succeeded in smearing the dirt into the fabric. Oh man, her mom. Could she make Pauline get any deader than dead?

Pauline followed the trail to the back. One of the smaller bedroom doors stood ajar. She flattened herself to the wall and crept forward. Light from the window leaked into the hallway, but not enough to illuminate her. She held her breath, not daring to make a sound. Her feet inched along, silent as she moved. The door was a hand's width away. She couldn't see anything through the crack. She took a breath then lifted her hand to the door and pushed!

The door swung wide. She jumped through the doorway.

"Ha!" she yelled.

The room was empty. They hadn't even put the windows in up here. Pauline's shoulders slumped in disappointment. Another dead end. She started to turn back. Her gaze fell on the open closet.

Something lay at the bottom of the closet. It looked like a piece of fabric. Pauline crouched down for a closer look.

A torn pocket, she thought. She lifted the fabric and a small kid's flashlight rolled across the floor. It stopped against her knee. A Sammy the Shaggy Dog light, they came with different filters that made shadow shapes when you slid them over the end of the light. She turned it over in her hand. The casing looked cracked and dented. She tried the button but the light stayed stubbornly off. She shook it and heard a rattle inside. Had it broken? She tightened the bottom. Dim light sprang out, illuminating the dust floating in the air.

Now she noticed the fabric was soggy, as if dunked in water. She turned the light on it. Reddish smears streaked her palm. She dropped the fabric pocket. Her heart pounded in her chest. She rubbed her palm on her pants. Hadn't the yoyo she'd found been wet too?

Somebody had been here and dropped the flashlight, but where were they now? What had happened? Nobody would just leave it here for her to find. She swung the light beam around then noticed something funny about the window frame.

Floating dust finally made her sneeze as she struggled to her feet. She walked over to the window and shone the light on the ledge.

Shards of glass stuck up from the ledge like baby teeth. Pauline traced the frame with the light and saw other pieces of glass sticking out. On the right by the top, part of the frame bent inward. She could see where the wood had splintered. Along the bottom, the reddish liquid streaked down the plaster into a small puddle on the floor.

Her fingers whitened around the flashlight. She backed away from the window and almost yelped when her back touched the door.

The flashlight wove crazy patterns along the wall as she ran down the stairs. She burst past the front door and skidded to a stop in the middle of the street. Her heart thudded in her chest like a big man hammering on a door. She felt as if a dozen pairs of eyes were watching her but when she spun around to look, nothing but empty windows faced her. The sky above her darkened as the sun dipped behind the trees in the distance. Soon it would be completely dark. What would she do then?

Now she wanted to go home. She didn't care about the humiliation, didn't care if her mom would kill her for the stains on her new pants. The light from the flashlight jerked back and forth across the asphalt. She tightened her grip to stop the trembling in her hand. Yes, time to go home.

She retreated back along the streets. The unfinished houses weren't interesting and exciting anymore, they were creepy and sinister. Their very emptiness hid things from her and she no longer wanted to find anything inside them.

As she neared the end of the construction zone, she drew level to the house with the tarp. The wind picked up, pushing at her back and tossing her brown hair in a cloud around her face. The tarp lifted, higher than before, exposing the floor marked with wood beams. Something white glimmered inside, a figure. Was it one of the kids?

Pauline stopped walking and pushed her hair from her face. The tarp floated down, covering the view. The edges ruffled, scrapping across the ground as if calling her forward.

What should she do? She still wanted to go home, could still feel her heart beating rapidly in her chest, like a staccato drum beat. But if that was one of the kids and she just walked away she'd never hear the end of it. She bit her lip, nibbling a loose piece of skin. The sharp edge of the flashlight pinched her palm.

She shuffled forward. The tarp rustled. How long would it take for her to look? Only a few moments. The entire floor was wide open, she could see all the way through. All she needed was to peek under the tarp see if anybody was there and then go home.

That she could do. Her steps quickened with her resolve. The faster she looked, the sooner she could run home.

The tarp was grimy when she touched it or maybe it was her hand sweating. She lifted the tarp and slipped underneath. As it swung back down behind her, she realized that shadows hid the interior. She could only see a few feet in front of her. She flicked on the flashlight. Its feeble beam only extended her view a few more feet. She would have to walk around the entire floor to see if anyone was there.

Her feet inched forward. She remembered seeing the wood beams marking out the walls. She would have to be careful not to walk into any of them or get tripped up. She didn't want to twist her ankle.

Her feet kicked up small clouds of dust as she moved forward. The dust danced in the beam of her flashlight. She moved deeper toward the back of the house. Still no sign of the white figure. Had she really seen someone?

A noise came from the back of a house. Someone moving, disturbing dust or debris. Her hand tightened on the flashlight. Now the pounding of her heart was also from excitement. Maybe if she found one of the kids her humiliation wouldn't be so complete.

She picked her feet up, trying to move faster and quieter. Her shoulder bumped a wood beam, unsettling dust that rained down on her. Her throat constricted as she tried to hold back a cough. Another few steps then she couldn't stop herself. She coughed.

The sound floated away in the darkness. She held her hand to her mouth, tasting dirt. Suddenly the darkness seemed heavier, more sinister. Maybe this had been a mistake. No kid was hiding back here. Maybe she'd find some sicko. Wrecking her new pants didn't seem quite so bad any more.

She started to back away. The flashlight beam swung crazily in front of her. She caught a glimpse of something white lying on the floor. It jumped and jerked away. She heard a soft, high-pitched squeal. That didn't sound like a sicko.

Pauline couldn't help herself, she had to know. She swung the flashlight back to the area where the white had appeared and headed toward it. Nothing for a moment, then she caught another glimpse. The tip of something, like a rat tail. It didn't move. She aimed the flashlight off to the side, just enough that she could still see it in the soft glow.

She took a breath, felt the dust tickle her nose, then jumped forward. One foot stomped on the white tail-thing. It squirmed under her foot. Something squealed, this time loud and long. She aimed the flashlight along the tail then almost dropped it.

The body rose out of a hole in the floor. A multiple of white tentacles wrapped around it so she couldn't see the definite shape. In the middle, a slit appeared and the edges of pinkish white flesh pulled back. A watery, pale blue eye blinked at her.

Pauline shuddered. The flashlight shook in her hand. The jerking beam fell across scraps of clothing and discarded running shoes. Blood smeared across the white tentacles. As they wrapped around itself, she saw bones sticking out from the crevices. She recognized Brenda's tank top, Ravi's jacket, Billy's shirt. Now it would never get tucked in.

A squeak immerged from her parched throat. She watched as the tentacles waved closer. Her heart hammered in her chest. It was going to kill her! She ground her foot down on the tentacle.

Another shriek, this time louder. The tentacles withdrew, wrapping around the body. The eye blinked at her.

Pauline wiped sweat from her forehead. In that blinking eye, she thought she saw something. Annoyance? How did she know? The feeling seemed to rise up in her and she realized it was coming from the thing in front of her. It was upset. Why?

She'd *found* it! When it hid so well.

The eye closed. The tentacles began to tap a rhythm on the dusty floor. Pauline stepped off the tentacle and backed away. She stared at the scraps of fabric dotting the creature. As it tapped a piece of Sandra's blonde hair dislodged and fluttered to the floor. The tentacle kept tapping.

What was it doing?

It tapped again. One-two-three . . .

Her heart thudded. It was counting. Counting to a hundred!

Her throat clenched. When it reached a hundred that eye would open and it would start seeking her. She had to hide.

Pauline dropped the flashlight and began to run.

what we found
GEOFF RYMAN

Can't sleep. Still dark.

Waiting for light in the East.

My rooster crows. Knows it's my wedding day. I hear the pig rooting around outside. Pig, the traditional gift for the family of my new wife. I can't sleep because alone in the darkness there is nothing between me and the realization that I do not want to get married. Well, Patrick, you don't have long to decide.

The night bakes black around me. Three-thirty A.M. In three hours, the church at the top of the road will start with the singing. Two hours after that, everyone in both families will come crowding into my yard.

My rooster crows again, all his wives in the small space behind the house. It is still piled with broken bottles from when my father lined the top of that wall with glass shards.

That was one of his good times, when he wore trousers and a hat and gave orders. I mixed the concrete, and passed it up in buckets to my eldest brother, Matthew. He sat on the wall like riding a horse, slopping on concrete and pushing in the glass. Raphael was reading in the shade of the porch. "I'm not wasting my time doing all that," he said. "How is broken glass going to stop a criminal who wants to get in?" He always made me laugh, I don't know why. Nobody else was smiling.

When we were young my father would keep us sitting on the hot, hairy sofa in the dark, no lights, no TV because he was driven mad by the sound of the generator. Eyes wide, he would quiver like a wire, listening for it to start up again. My mother tried to speak and he said, "Sssh. Sssh! There it goes again."

"Jacob, the machine cannot turn itself on."

"Sssh! Sssh!" He would not let us move. I was about seven, and terrified. If the generator was wicked enough to scare my big strong father, what would it do to little me? I keep asking my mother what does the generator do?

"Nothing, your father is just being very careful."

"Terhemba is a coward," my brother Matthew said, using my Tiv name. My mother shushed him, but Matthew's merry eyes glimmered at me: *I will make you miserable later.* Raphael prized himself loose from my mother's grip and stomped across the sitting room floor.

People think Makurdi is a backwater, but now we have all you need for a civilized life. Beautiful banks with security doors, retina ID, and air conditioning; new roads, solar panels on all the streetlights, and our phones are stuffed full of e-books. On one of the river islands they built the new hospital; and my university has a medical school, all pink and state-funded with laboratories that are as good as most. Good enough for controlled experiments with mice.

My research assistant Jide is Yoruba and his people believe that the grandson first born after his grandfather's death will continue that man's life. Jide says that we have found how that is true. This is a problem for Christian Nigerians, for it means that evil continues.

What we found in mice is this. If you deprive a mouse of a mother's love, if you make him stressed through infancy, his brain becomes methylated. The high levels of methyl deactivate a gene that produces a neurotropin important for memory and emotional balance in both mice and humans. Schizophrenics have abnormally low levels of it.

It is a miracle of God that with new generation, our genes are knocked clean. There is a new beginning. Science thought this meant that the effects of one life could not be inherited by another.

What we found is that high levels of methyl affect the sperm cells. Methylation is passed on with them, and thus the deactivation. A grandfather's stress is passed on through the male line, yea unto the third generation.

Jide says that what we have found is how the life of the father is continued by his sons. And that is why I don't want to wed.

My father would wander all night. His three older sons slept in one room. Our door would click open and he would stand

and glare at me, me particularly, with a boggled and distracted eye as if I had done something outrageous. He would be naked; his towering height and broad shoulders humbled me, made me feel puny and endangered. I have an odd-shaped head with an indented V going down my forehead. People said it was the forceps tugging me out: I was a difficult birth. That was supposed to be why I was slow to speak, slow to learn. My father believed them.

My mother would try to shush him back into their bedroom. Sometimes he would be tame and allow himself to be guided; he might chuckle as if it were a game and hug her. Or he might blow up, shouting and flinging his hands about, calling her woman, witch, or demon. Once she whispered, "It's you who have the demon; the demon has taken hold of you, Jacob."

Sometimes he shuffled past our door and out into the Government street, sleeping-walking to his and our shame.

In those days, it was the wife's job to keep family business safe within the house. Our mother locked all the internal doors even by day to keep him inside, away from visitors from the church or relatives who dropped in on their way to Abuja. If he was being crazy in the sitting room, she would shove us back into our bedroom or whisk us with the broom out into the yard. She would give him whiskey if he asked for it, to get him to sleep. Our mother could never speak of these things to anybody, not even her own mother, let alone to us.

We could hear him making noises at night, groaning as if in pain, or slapping someone. The baby slept in my parents' room and he would start to wail. I would stare into the darkness: was Baba hurting my new brother? In the morning his own face would be puffed out. It was Raphael who dared to say something. The very first time I heard that diva voice was when he asked her, sharp and demanding, "Why does that man hit himself?"

My mother got angry and pushed Raphael's face; slap would be the wrong word; she was horrified that the problem she lived with was clear to a five-year-old. "You do not call your father 'that man'! Who are you to ask questions? I can see it's time we put you to work like children used to be when I was young. You don't know what good luck you had to be born into this household!"

Raphael looked back at her, lips pursed. "That does not answer my question."

My mother got very angry at him, shouted more things. Afterward he looked so small and sad that I pulled him closer to me on the sofa. He crawled up onto my lap and just sat there. "I wish we were closer to the river," he said, "so we could go and play."

"Mamamimi says the river is dangerous." My mother's name was Mimi, which means truth, so Mama Truth was a kind of title.

"Everything's dangerous," he said, his lower lip thrust out. A five-year-old should not have such a bleak face.

By the time I was nine, Baba would try to push us into the walls, wanting us hidden or wanting us gone. His vast hands would cover the back of our heads or shoulders and grind us against the plaster. Raphael would look like a crushed berry, but he shouted in a rage, "No! No! No!"

Yet my father wore a suit and drove himself to work. Jacob Terhemba Shawo worked as a tax inspector and electoral official.

Did other government employees act the same way? Did they put on a shell of calm at work? He would be called to important meetings in Abuja and stay for several days. Once Mamamimi sat at the table, her white bread uneaten, not caring what her children heard. "What you go to Abuja for? Who you sleep with there, Wildman? What diseases do you bring back into my house?"

We stared down at our toast and tea, amazed to hear such things. "You tricked me into marriage with you. I bewail the day I accepted you. Nobody told me you were crazy!"

My father was not a man to be dominated in his own house. Clothed in his functionary suit, he stood up. "If you don't like it, go. See who will have you since you left your husband. See who will want you without all the clothes and jewelry I buy you. Maybe you no longer want this comfortable home. Maybe you no longer want your car. I can send you back to your village, and no one would blame me."

My mother spun away into the kitchen and began to slam pots. She did not weep. She was not one to be dominated either, but knew she could not change how things had to be. My father climbed into his SUV for Abuja in his special glowering suit that kept all questions at bay, with his polished head and square-cornered briefcase. The car purred away down the tree-lined Government street with no one to wave him good-bye.

Jide's full name is Babajide. In Yoruba it means Father Wakes Up. His son is called Babatunde,

Father Returns. It is something many people believe in the muddle of populations that is Nigeria.

My work on mice was published in *Nature* and widely cited. People wanted to believe that character could be inherited; that stressed fathers passed incapacities on to their grandchildren. It seemed to open a door to inherited characteristics, perhaps a modified theory of evolution. Our experiments had been conclusive: not only were there the non-genetically inherited emotional tendencies, but we could objectively measure the levels of methyl.

My father was born in 1965, the year before the Tiv rioted against what they thought were Muslim incursions. It was a time of coup and countercoup. The violence meant my grandfather left Jos, and moved the family to Makurdi. They walked, pushing some of their possessions and my infant father in a wheelbarrow. The civil war came with its trains full of headless Igbo rattling eastward, and air force attacks on our own towns. People my age say, oh those old wars. What can Biafra possibly have to do with us, now?

What we found is that 1966 can reach into your head and into your balls and stain your children red. You pass war on. The cranky old men in the villages, the lack of live music in clubs, the distrust of each other, soldiers everywhere, the crimes of colonialism embedded in the pattern of our roads. We live our grandfathers' lives.

Outside, the stars spangle. It will be a beautiful clear day. My traditional clothes hang unaccepted in the closet and I fear for any son that I might have. What will I pass on? Who would want their son to repeat the life of my father, the life of my brother? Ought I to get married at all? Outside in the courtyard, wet with dew, the white plastic chairs are lined up for the guests.

My Grandmother Iveren would visit without warning. Her name meant "Blessing," which was a bitter thing for us. Grandmother Iveren visited all her children in turn no matter how far they moved to get away from her: Kano, Jalingo, or Makurdi.

A taxi would pull up and we would hear a hammering on our gate. One of us boys would run to open it and there she would be, standing like a princess. "Go tell my son to come and pay for the taxi. Bring my bags, please."

She herded us around our living room with the burning tip of her cigarette, inspecting us as if everything was found wanting. The Intermittent Freezer that only kept things cool, the gas cooker, the rack of vegetables, the many tins of powdered milk, the rumpled throw rug, the blanket still on the sofa, the TV that was left tuned all day to Africa Magic. She would switch it off with a sigh as she passed. "Education," she would say, shaking her head. She had studied literature at the University of Madison, Wisconsin, and she used that like she used her cigarette. Iveren was tiny, thin, very pretty, and elegant in glistening blue or purple dresses with matching headpieces.

My mother's mother might also be staying, rattling out garments on her sewing machine. Mamagrand, we called her. The two women would feign civility, even smiling. My father lumbered in with suitcases; the two grandmothers would pretend that it made no difference to them where they slept, but Iveren would get the back bedroom and Mamagrand the sofa. My father then sat down to gaze at his knees, his jaws clamped shut like a turtle's. His sons assumed that that was what all children did, and that mothers always kept order in this way.

Having finished pursuing us around our own house, she would sigh, sit on the sofa, and wait expectantly for my mother to bring her food. Mamamimi dutifully did so—family being family—and then sat down, her face going solid and her arms folded.

"You should know what the family is saying about you," Grandmother might begin, smiling so sweetly. "They are saying that you have infected my son, that you are unclean from an abortion." She would say that my aunt Judith would no longer allow Mamamimi into her house and had paid a woman to cast a spell on my mother to keep her away.

"Such a terrible thing to do. The spell can only be cured by cutting it with razor blades." Grandmother Iveren looked as though she might enjoy helping.

"Thank heavens such a thing cannot happen in a Christian household," my mother's mother would say.

"Could I have something to drink?"

From the moment Grandmother arrived, all the alcohol in the house would start to disappear: little airline sample bottles, whiskey from my father's boss, even the brandy Baba had brought from London. And not just alcohol. Grandmother would offer to help Mamamimi clean a bedroom; and small things would be gone from it forever, jewelry or scarves or little bronzes. She sold the things she pilfered, to keep herself in dresses and perfume.

It wasn't as if her children neglected their duty. She would be fed and housed for as long as any of us could stand it. Even so, she would steal and hide all the food in the house. My mother went grim-faced, and would lift up mattresses to display the tins and bottles hidden under it. The top shelf of the bedroom closet would contain the missing stewpot with that evening's meal. "It's raw!" my mother would swelter at her. "It's not even cooked! Do you want it to go rotten in this heat?"

"I never get fed anything in this house. I am watched like a hawk!" Iveren complained, her face turned toward her giant son.

Mamamimi had strategies. She might take to her room ill, and pack meat in a cool chest and keep it under her bed. Against all tradition, especially if Father was away, she would sometimes refuse to cook any food at all. For herself, for Grandmother, or even us. "I'm on strike!" she announced once. "Here, here is money. Go buy food! Go cook it!" She pressed folded money into our hands. Raphael and I made a chicken stew, giggling. We had been warned about Iveren's cooking. "Good boys, to take the place of the mother," she said, winding our hair in her fingers.

Such bad behaviour on all sides made Raphael laugh. He loved it when Iveren came to stay, with her swishing skirts and dramatic manner and drunken stumbles; loved it when Mamamimi behaved badly and the house swelled with their silent battle of wills.

Grandmother would say things to my mother like: "We knew that you were not on our level, but we thought you were a simple girl from the country and that your innocence would be good for him." Chuckle. "If only we had known."

"If only I had," my mother replied.

My father's brothers had told us stories about Granny. When they were young, she would bake cakes with salt instead of sugar and laugh when they bit into them. She would make stews out of only bones, having thrown the goat away. She would cook with no seasoning so that it was like eating water, or cook with so many chillies that it was like eating fire. When my uncle Eamon tried to sell his car, she stole the starter motor. She was right in there with a monkey wrench and spirited it away. It would cough and grind when potential buyers turned the key. When he was away, she put the motor back in and sold the car herself. She told Eamon that it had been stolen. When Eamon saw someone driving it, he had the poor man arrested, and the story came out.

My other uncle, Emmanuel, was an officer in the Air Force, a fine-looking man in his uniform. When he first went away to do his training, Grandmother told all the neighbours that he was a worthless ingrate who neglected his mother, never calling her or giving her gifts. She got everyone so riled against him that when he came home to the village, the elders raised sticks against him and shouted, "How dare you show your face here after the way you have treated your mother!" For who would think a mother would say such things about a son without reason?

It was Grandmother who reported gleefully to Emmanuel that his wife had tested HIV positive. "You should have yourself tested. A shame you are not man enough to satisfy your wife and hold her to you. All that smoking has made you impotent."

She must be a witch, Uncle Emmanuel said, how else would she have known when he himself did not?

Raphael would laugh at her antics. He loved it when Granny started asking us all for gifts—even the orphan girl who lived with us. Iveren asked if she couldn't take the cushion covers home with her, or just one belt. Raphael yelped with laughter and clapped his hands. Granny blinked at him. What did he find so funny? Did my brother like her?

She knew what to make of me: quiet, well behaved. I was someone to torment.

I soon learned how to behave around her. I would stand, not sit, in silence in my white shirt, tie, and blue shorts.

"Those dents in his skull," she said to my mother once, during their competitive couch-sitting. "Is that why he's so slow and stupid?"

"That's just the shape of his head. He's not slow."

"Tuh. Your monstrous firstborn didn't want a brother and bewitched him in the womb." Her eyes glittered all over me, her smile askew. "The boy cannot talk properly. He sounds ignorant."

My mother said that I sounded fine to her and that I was a good boy and got good grades in school.

My father was sitting in shamed silence. What did it mean that my father said nothing in my favour? Was I stupid?

"Look to your own children," my mother told her. "Your son is not doing well at work, and they delay paying him. So we have very little money. I'm afraid we can't offer you anything except water from the well. I have a bad back. Would you be so kind to fetch water yourself, since your son offers you nothing?"

Grandmother chuckled airily, as if my mother was a fool and would see soon enough. "So badly brought up. My poor son. No wonder your children are such frights."

That very day my mother took me round to the back of the house, where she grew her herbs. She bowed down to look into my eyes and held my shoulders and told me, "Patrick, you are a fine boy. You do everything right. There is nothing wrong with you. You do well in your lessons, and look how you washed the car this morning without even being asked."

It was Raphael who finally told Granny off. She had stayed for three months. Father's hair was corkscrewing off in all directions and his eyes had a trapped light in them. Everyone had taken to cooking their own food at night, and every spoon and knife in the house had disappeared.

"Get out of this house, you thieving witch. If you were nice to your family, they would let you stay and give you anything you want. But you can't stop stealing things." He was giggling. "Why do you tell lies and make such trouble? You should be nice to your children and show them loving care."

"And you should learn how to be polite." Granny sounded weak with surprise.

"Ha-ha! And so should you! You say terrible things about us. None of your children believes a thing you say. You only come here when no one else can stand you and you only leave when you know you've poisoned the well so much even you can't drink from it. It's not very intelligent of you, when you depend on us to eat."

He drove her from the house, keeping it up until no other outcome were possible. "Blessing, our Blessing, the taxi is here!" pursuing her to the gate with mockery. Even Matthew started to laugh. Mother had to hide her mouth. He held the car door open for her. "You'd best read your Bible and give up selling all your worthless potions."

Father took hold of Raphael's wrists gently. "That's enough," he said. "Grandmother went through many bad things." He didn't say it in anger. He didn't say it like a wild man. Something somber in his voice made Raphael calm.

"You come straight out of the bush," Grandmother said, almost unperturbed. "No wonder my poor son is losing his mind." She looked directly at Raphael. "The old ways did work." Strangely, he was the only one she dealt with straightforwardly. "They wore out."

Something happened to my research. At first the replication studies showed a less marked effect, less inherited stress, lower methyl levels. But soon we ceased to be able to replicate our results at all.

The new studies dragged me down, made me suicidal. I felt I had achieved something with my paper, made up for all my shortcomings, done something that would have made my family proud of me if they were alive.

Methylation had made me a full Professor. Benue State's home page found room to feature me as an example of the university's research excellence. I sought design flaws in the replication studies; that was the only thing I published. All my life I had fought to prove I wasn't slow, or at least hide it through hard work. And here before the whole world, I was being made to look like a fraud.

Then I read the work of Jonathan Schooler. The same thing had happened to him. His research had proved that if you described a memory clearly you ceased to remember it as well. The act of describing faces reduced his subjects' ability to recognize them later. The effects he measured were so huge and so unambiguous, and people were so intrigued by the implications of what he called verbal overshadowing, that his paper was cited 400 times.

Gradually, it had become impossible to replicate his results. Every time he did the experiment, the effect shrank by thirty percent.

I got in touch with Schooler, and we began to check the record. We found that all the way back in the 1930s, results of E.S.P. experiments by Joseph Banks Rhine declined. In replication, his startling findings evaporated to something only slightly different from chance. It was as if scientific truths wore out, as if the act of observing them reduced their effect.

Jide laughed and shook his head. "We think the same thing!" he said.

"We always say that a truth can wear out with the telling."

That is why I am sitting here writing, dreading the sound of the first car arriving, the first knock on my gate.

I am writing to wear out both memory and truth.

Whenever my father was away, or sometimes to escape Iveren, Mamamimi would take all us boys back to our family village. It is called Kawuye, on the road toward Taraba State. Her friend Sheba would drive us to the bus station in the market, and we would wait under the shelter, where the women cooked rice and chicken and sold sweating tins of Coca-Cola. Then we would stuff ourselves into the van next to some fat businessman who had hoped for a row of seats to himself.

Matthew was the firstborn, and tried to boss everyone, even Mamamimi. He had teamed up with little Andrew from the moment he'd been born. Andrew was too young to be a threat to him. The four brothers fell into two teams and Mamamimi had to referee, coach, organize, and punish.

If Matthew and I were crammed in next to each other, we would fight. I could stand his needling and bossiness only so long and then wordlessly clout him. That made me the one to be punished. Mamamimi would swipe me over the head and Matthew's eyes would tell me that he'd done it deliberately.

It was hot and crowded on the buses, with three packed rows of sweating ladies, skinny men balancing deliveries of posters on their laps, or mothers dandling heat-drugged infants. It was not supportable to have four boys elbowing, kneeing, and scratching.

Mamamimi started to drive us herself in her old green car. She put Matthew in the front so that he felt in charge. Raphael and I sat in the back reading, while next to us Andrew cawed for Matthew's attention.

Driving by herself was an act of courage. The broken-edged roads would have logs pulled across them, checkpoints they were called, with soldiers. They would wave through the stuffed vans but they would stop a woman driving four children and stare into the car. Did we look like criminals or terrorists? They would ask her questions and rummage through our bags and mutter things that we could not quite hear. I am not sure they were always proper. Raphael would noisily flick through the pages of his book. "Nothing we can do about it," he would murmur. After slipping them some money, Mama would drive on.

As if by surprise, up and over a hill, we would rollercoaster down through maize fields into Kawuye. I loved it there. The houses were the best houses for Nigeria and typical of the Tiv people, round and thick-walled with high pointed roofs and tiny windows. The heat could not get in and the walls sweated like a person to keep cool. There were no wild men waiting to leap out, no poison grandmothers. My great-uncle Jacob—it is a common name in my family—repaired cars with the patience of a cricket, opening, snipping, melting, and reforming. He once repaired a vehicle by replacing the fan belt with the elastic from my mother's underwear.

Raphael and I would buy firewood, trading some of it for eggs, ginger, and yams. We also helped my aunty with her pig-roasting business. To burn off the bristles, we'd lower it onto a fire and watch grassfire lines of red creep up each strand. It made a smell like burning hair and Raphael and I would pretend we were pirates cooking people. Then we turned the pig on a spit until it crackled. At nights we were men, serving beer and taking money.

We both got fat because our pay was some of the pig, and if no one was looking, the beer as well. I ate because I needed to get as big as Matthew. In the evenings the generators coughed to life and the village smelled of petrol and I played football barefoot under lights. There were jurisdictions and disagreements, but laughing uncles to adjudicate with the wisdom of a Solomon. So even the four of us liked each other more in Kawuye.

Then after whole weeks of sanity, my mother's phone would sing out with the voice of Mariah Carey or an American prophetess. As the screen illuminated, Mamamimi's face would scowl. We knew the call meant that our father was back in the house, demanding our return.

Uncle Jacob would change the oil and check the tires and we would drive back through the fields and rock across potholes onto the main road. At intersections, children swarmed around the car, pushing their hands through open windows, selling plastic bags of water or dappled plantains. Their eyes peered in at us. I would feel ashamed somehow. Raphael wound up the window and hollered at them. "Go away and stop your staring. There's nothing here for you to see!"

Baba would be waiting for us reading *ThisDay* stiffly, like he had broomsticks for bones, saying nothing.

After that long drive, Mama would silently go and cook. Raphael told him off. "It's not very fair of you, Popsie, to make her work. She has just driven us back all that way just to be nice to us and show us a good time in the country."

Father's eyes rested on him like drills on DIY.

That amused Raphael. "Since you choose to be away all the time, she has to do all the work here. And you're just sitting there." My father rattled the paper and said nothing. Raphael was twelve years old.

I was good at football, so I survived school well enough. But my brother was legendary.

They were reading *The Old Man and The Sea* in English class, and Raphael blew up at the teacher. She said that lions were a symbol of Hemingway being lionized when young. She said the old fisherman carrying a mast made him some sort of Jesus with his cross. He told her she had a head full of nonsense. I can see him doing it. He would bark with sudden laughter and bounce up and down in his chair and declare, delighted, "That's blasphemy! It's just a story about an old man. If Hemingway had wanted to write a story about Jesus, he was a clever enough person to have written one!" The headmaster gave him a clip about the ear. Raphael wobbled his head at him as if shaking a finger. "Your hitting me doesn't make me wrong." None of the other students ever bothered us. Raphael still got straight As.

Our sleepy little bookshops, dark, wooden, and crammed into corners of markets, knew that if they got a book on chemistry or genetics they could sell it to Raphael. He set up a business to buy textbooks that he knew Benue State was going to recommend. At sixteen he would sit on benches at the university, sipping cold drinks and selling books, previous essays, and condoms. Everybody assumed that he was already being educated there. Tall, beautiful students would call him "sah." One pretty girl called him "Prof." She had honey-coloured, extended hair, and a spangled top that hung off one shoulder.

"I'm his brother," I told her proudly.

"So you are the handsome one," she said, being kind to what she took to be the younger brother. For many weeks I carried her in my heart.

The roof of our Government bungalow was flat and Raphael and I took to living on it. We slept there; we even climbed the ladder with our plates of food. We read by torchlight, rigged mosquito nets, and plugged the mobile phone into our netbook. The world flooded into it; the websites of our wonderful Nigerian newspapers, the BBC, Al Jazeera, *Nature*, *New Scientist*. We pirated Nollywood movies. We got slashdotcom; we hacked into the scientific journals, getting all those ten-dollar PDFs for free.

We elevated ourselves above the murk of our household. Raphael would read aloud in many different voices, most of them mocking. He would giggle at news articles. "Oh, story! Now they are saying Fashola is corrupt. Hee hee hee. It's the corrupt people saying that to get their own back."

"Oh this is interesting," he would say and read about what some Indian at Caltech had found out about gravitational lenses. My naked father would pad out like an old lion gone mangy and stare up at us, looking bewildered as if he wanted to join us but couldn't work out how. "You shouldn't be standing out there with no clothes on," Raphael told him. "What would happen if someone came to visit?" My father looked as mournful as an abandoned dog.

❖

Jacob Terhemba Shawo was forced to retire. He was only forty-two. We had to leave the Government Reserved Area. Our family name means "high on the hill," and that's where we had lived. I remember that our well was so deep that once I dropped the bucket and nothing could reach it. A boy had to climb down the stones in the well wall to fetch it.

We moved into the house I live in now, a respectable bungalow across town, surrounded with high walls. It had a sloping roof, so Raphael and I were no longer elevated.

The driveway left no room for Mamamimi's herb garden, so we bought a neighbouring patch of land but couldn't afford the sand and cement to wall it off. Schoolchildren would wander up the slope into our maize, picking it or sometimes doing their business.

The school had been built by public subscription and the only land cheap enough was in the slough. For much of the year the new two-storey building rose vertically out of a lake like a castle. It looked like the Scottish islands in my father's calendars. Girls boated to the front door and climbed up a ramp. A little beyond was a marsh, with ponds and birds and water lilies: beautiful but it smelled of drains and rotting reeds.

We continued to go to the main cathedral for services. White draperies hung the length of its ceiling, and the stained-glass doors would accordion open to let in air. Local dignitaries would be in attendance and nod approval as our family lined up to take communion and make our gifts to the church, showing obeisance to the gods of middle-class respectability.

But the church at the top of our unpaved road was bare concrete, always open at the sides. People would pad past my bedroom window and the singing of hymns would swell with the dawn. Some of the local houses would be village dwellings amid the aging urban villas.

Chickens still clucked in our new narrow back court. If you dropped a bucket down this well, all you had to do was reach in for it. The problem was to stop water flooding into the house. The concrete of an inner courtyard was broken and the hot little square was never used, except for the weights that Raphael had made for himself out of iron bars and sacks of concrete. Tiny and rotund, he had dreams of being a muscleman. His computer desktop was full of a Nigerian champion in briefs. I winced with embarrassment whenever his screen sang open in public. What would people think of him, with that naked man on his netbook?

My father started to swat flies all the time. He got long sticky strips of paper and hung them everywhere—across doorways, from ceilings, in windows. They would snag in our hair as we carried out food from the kitchen. All we saw was flies on strips of paper. We would wake up in the night to hear him slapping the walls with books, muttering, "Flies flies flies."

The house had a tin roof and inside we baked like bread. Raphael resented it personally. He was plump and felt the heat. My parents had installed the house's only AC in their bedroom. He would just as regularly march in with a spanner and screwdriver and steal it. He would stomp out, the cable dragging behind him, with my mother wringing her hands and weeping. "That boy! That crazy boy! Jacob! Come see to your son."

Raphael shouted, "Buy another one! You can afford it!"

"We can't, Raphael! You know that! We can't."

And Raphael said, "I'm not letting you drag me down to your level."

Matthew by then was nearly nineteen and had given up going to university. His voice was newly rich and sad. "Raphael. The whole family is in trouble. We would all like the AC, but if Baba doesn't get it, he wanders, and that is a problem, too."

I didn't like it that Raphael took it from our parents without permission. Shamefaced with betrayal of him, I helped Matthew fix the AC back in our parents' window.

Raphael stomped up to me and poked me with his finger. "You should be helping me, not turning tail and running!" He turned his back and said, "I'm not talking to you."

I must have looked very sad because later I heard his flip-flops shuffling behind me. "You are my brother and of course I will always talk to you. I'm covered in shame that I said such a thing to you." Raphael had a genius for apologies, too.

When Andrew was twelve, our father drove him to Abuja and left him with people, some great-aunt we didn't know. She was childless, and Andrew had come back happy from his first visit sporting new track shoes. She had bought him an ice cream from Grand Square. He went back.

One night Raphael heard Mother and Father talking. He came outside onto the porch, his fat face gleaming. "I've got some gossip," he told me. "Mamamimi and Father have sold Andrew!"

"Sold" was an exaggeration. They had put him to work and were harvesting his wages. In return he got to live in an air-conditioned house. Raphael giggled. "It's so naughty of them!" He took hold of my hand and pulled me with him right into their bedroom.

Both of them were decent, lying on the bed with their books. Raphael announced, very pleased with himself. "You're not selling my brother like an indentured servant. Just because he was a mistake and you didn't want him born so late and want to be shot of him now."

Mamamimi leapt at him. He ran, laughter pealing, and his hands swaying from side to side. I saw only then that he had the keys for the SUV in his hand. He pulled me with him out into the yard, and then swung me forward. "Get the gate!" He popped himself into the driver's seat and roared the engine. Mamamimi waddled after him. The car rumbled forward, the big metal gate groaned open, dogs started to bark. Raphael bounced the SUV out of the yard, and pushed its door open for me. Mamamimi was right behind, and I didn't want to be the one punished again, so I jumped in. "Good-bye-yeee!" Raphael called in a singsong voice, smiling right into her face.

We somehow got to Abuja alive. Raphael couldn't drive, and trucks kept swinging out onto our side of the road, accelerating and beeping. We swerved in and out, missing death, passing the corpses of dead transports lined up along the roadside. Even I roared with laughter as lorries wailed past us by inches.

Using the GPS, Raphael foxed his way to the woman's house. Andrew let us in; he worked as her boy, beautifully dressed in a white shirt and jeans, with tan sandals of interwoven strips. In we strode and Raphael said, very pleasantly at first, "Hello! *M'sugh!* How are you? I am Jacob's son, Andrew's brother."

I saw at once this was a very nice lady. She was huge like a balloon, with a child-counselling smile, and she welcomed us and hugged Andrew to her.

"Have you paid my parents anything in advance for Andrew's work? Because they want him back, they miss him so much."

She didn't seem to mind. "Oh, they changed their minds. Well of course they did, Andrew is such a fine young man. Well, Andrew, it seems your brothers want you back!"

"I changed their minds for them." Raphael always cut his words out of the air like a tailor making a bespoke garment. Andrew looked confused and kept his eyes on the embroidery on his jeans.

Andrew must have known what had happened because he didn't ask why it was us two who had come to fetch him. Raphael had saved him, not firstborn Matthew—if he had wanted to be saved from decent clothes and shopping in Abuja.

When we got back home, no mention was made of anything by anyone. Except by Raphael, to me, later. "It is so interesting, isn't it, that they haven't said a thing. They know what they were doing was wrong. How would they like to be a child and know their parents had sent them to work?" Matthew said nothing either. We had been rich; now we were poor.

Jide and I measured replication decline.

We carried out our old experiment over and over and measured methyl as levels declined for no apparent reason. Then we increased the levels of stress. Those poor mice! In the name of science, we deprived them of a mother and then cuddly surrogates. We subjected them to regimes of irregular feeding and random light and darkness and finally electric shocks.

There was no doubt. No matter how much stress we subjected them to, after the first spectacular results, the methyl levels dropped off with each successive experiment. Not only that, but the association between methyl and neurotropin suppression reduced as well—objectively measured, the amount of methyl and its effect on neurotropin production were smaller with each study. We had proved the decline effect. Truth wore out. Or at least, scientific truth wore out.

We published. People loved the idea and we were widely cited. Jide became a Lecturer and a valued colleague. People began to speak of something called Cosmic Habituation. The old ways were no longer working. And I was thirty-seven.

❖

With visitors, Raphael loved being civil, a different person. Sweetly and sociably, he would say, *"M'sugh,"* our mix of hello, good-bye, and pardon me. He loved bringing them trays of cold water from the Intermittent Freezer. He remembered everybody's name and birthday. He hated dancing, but loved dressing up for parties. Musa the tailor made him wonderful robes with long shirts, matching trousers, shawls.

My father liked company, too, even more so after his Decline. He would suddenly stand up straight and smile eagerly. I swear, his shirt would suddenly look ironed, his shoes polished. I was envious of the company, usually men from his old work. They could get my father laughing. He would look young then, and merry, and slap the back of his hand on his palm, jumping up to pass around the beer. I wanted him to laugh with me.

Very suddenly Matthew announced he was getting married. We knew it was his way of escaping. After the wedding he and his bride would move in with her sister's husband. He would help with their fish farm and plantation of nym trees. We did well by him: no band, but a fine display of food. My father boasted about how strong Matthew was, always captain. From age twelve he had read the business news like some boys read adventure stories. Matthew, he said, was going to be a leader.

My father saw me looking quiet and suddenly lifted up his arms. "Then there is my Patrick who is so quiet. I have two clever sons to go alongside the strong one." His hand felt warm on my back.

By midnight it was cool and everybody was outside dancing, even Raphael, who grinned, making circular motions with his elbows and planting his feet as firmly as freeway supports.

My father wavered up to me like a vision out of the desert, holding a tin of High Life. He stood next to me watching the dancing and the stars. "You know," he said, "your elder brother was sent to you by Jesus." My heart sank: *Yes, I know, to lead the family, to be an example.*

"He was so unhappy when you were born. He saw you in your mother's arms and howled. He is threatened by you. Jesus sent you Matthew so that you would know what it is to fight to distinguish yourself. And you learned that. You are becoming distinguished."

I can find myself being kind in that way; suddenly, in private with no one else to hear or challenge the kindness, as if kindness were a thing to shame us.

I went back onto the porch and there was Raphael looking hunched and large, a middle-aged patriarch. He'd heard what my father said. "So who taught Matthew to be stupid? Why didn't he ever tell him to leave you alone?"

My father's skin faded. It had always been very dark, so black that he would use skin lightener as a moisturizer without the least bleaching effect. Now very suddenly, he went honey-coloured; his hair became a knotted muddy brown. A dried clot of white spit always threatened to glue his lips together, and his eyes went bad, huge and round and ringed with swollen flesh like a frog's. He sprouted thick spectacles, and had to lean his head back to see, blinking continually. He could no longer remember how to find the toilet from the living room. He took to crouching down behind the bungalow with the hens, then as things grew worse, off the porch in front of the house. Mamamimi said, "It makes me think there may be witchcraft after all." Her face swelled and went hard until it looked like a stone.

On the Tuesday night before he died, he briefly came back to us. Tall, in trousers, so skinny now that he looked young again. He ate his dinner with good manners, the fou-fou cradling the soup so that none got onto his fingers. Outside on the porch he started to talk, listing the names of all his brothers.

Then he told us that Grandmother was not his actual mother. Another woman had borne him, made pregnant while dying of cancer. Grandfather knew pregnancy would kill her, but he made her come to term. She was bearing his first son.

Two weeks after my father was born, his real mother had died, and my grandfather married the woman called Blessing.

Salt instead of sugar. Iveren loved looking as though she had given the family its first son. It looked good as they lined up in church. But she had no milk for him. Jacob Terhemba Shawo spent his first five years loveless in a war.

My father died three days before Matthew's first child was born. Matthew and his wife brought her to our house to give our mother something joyful to think about.

The baby's Christian name was Isobel. Her baby suit had three padded Disney princesses on it and her hair was a red down.

Matthew chuckled. "Don't worry, Mamamimi, this can't be Grandpa, it's a girl."

Raphael smiled. "Maybe she's Grandpa born in woman's body."

Matthew's wife clucked her tongue. She didn't like us and she certainly didn't like what she'd heard about Raphael. She drew herself up tall and said, "Her name is Iveren."

Matthew stared at his hands; Mamamimi froze; Raphael began to dance with laughter.

"It was my mother's name," the wife said.

"Ah!" cried Raphael. "Two of them, Matthew. Two Iverens! Oh, that is such good luck for you!"

I saw from my mother's unmoving face, and from a flick of the fingers, a jettisoning, that she had consigned the child to its mother's family and Matthew to that other family, too. She never took a proper interest in little Iveren.

But Grandmother must have thought that they had named the child after her. Later, she went to live with them, which was exactly the blessing I would wish for Matthew.

Raphael became quieter, preoccupied, as if invisible flies buzzed around his head. I told myself we were working too hard. Both of us had been applying for oil company scholarships. I wanted both of us to go together to the best universities: Lagos or Ibadan. I thought of all those strangers, in states that were mainly Igbo or Yoruba or maybe even Muslim. I was sure we were a team.

In the hall bookcase a notice appeared. DO NOT TOUCH MY BOOKS. I DON'T INTERFERE WITH YOUR JOB. LEAVE ALL BOOKS IN ORDER.

They weren't his alone. "Can I look at them, at least?"

He looked at me balefully. "If you ask first."

I checked his downloads and they were all porn. I saw the terrible titles of the files, which by themselves were racial and sexual abuse. A good Christian boy, I was shocked and dismayed. I said something to him and he puffed up, looking determined. "I don't live by other people's rules."

He put a new password onto our machine so that I could not get into it. My protests were feeble.

"I need to study, Raphael."

"Study is beyond you," he said. "Study cannot help you."

At the worst possible time for him, his schoolteachers went on strike because they weren't being paid. Raphael spent all day clicking away at his keyboard, not bothering to dress. His voice became milder, faint and sweet, but he talked only in monosyllables. "Yes. No. I don't know." Not angry, a bit as though he was utterly weary.

That Advent, Mamamimi, Andrew, Matthew and family went to the cathedral, but my mother asked me to stay behind to look after Raphael.

"You calm him," Mamamimi said, and for some reason that made my eyes sting. They went to church, and I was left alone in the main room. I was sitting on the old sofa watching some TV trash about country bumpkins going to Lagos.

Suddenly Raphael trotted out of our bedroom in little Japanese steps wearing one of my mother's dresses. He had folded a matching cloth around his head into an enormous flower shape, his face ghostly with makeup. My face must have been horrified: it made him chatter with laughter. "What the well-dressed diva is wearing this season."

All I thought then was, *Raphael, don't leave me*. I stood up and

I pushed him back toward the room; like my mother, I was afraid of visitors. "Get it off, get it off, what are you doing?"

"You don't like it?" He batted his eyelashes.

"No I do not! What's got into you?"

"Raphael is not a nurse! Raphael does not have to be nice!"

I begged him to get out of the dress. I kept looking at my telephone for the time, worried when they would be back. Above all else I didn't want Mama to know he had taken her things.

He stepped out of the dress, and let the folded headdress trail behind him, falling onto the floor. I scooped them up, checked them for dirt or makeup, and folded them up as neatly as I could.

I came back to the bedroom and he was sitting in his boxer shorts and flip-flops, staring at his screen and with complete unconcern was doing something to himself.

I asked the stupidest question. "What are you doing?"

"What does it look like? It's fun. You should join in." Then he laughed. He turned the screen toward me. In the video, a man was servicing a woman's behind. I had no idea people did such things. I howled and covered my mouth, laughing in shock. I ran out of the room and left him to finish.

Without Raphael I had no one to go to and I could not be seen to cry. I went outside and realized that I was alone. What could I say to my mother? Our Raphael is going mad? For her he had always been mad. Only I had really liked Raphael and now he was becoming someone else, and I was so slow I would only ever be me.

He got a strange disease that made his skin glisten but a fever did not register. It was what my father had done: get illnesses that were not quite physical. He ceased to do anything with his hair. It twisted off his head in knots and made him look like a beggar.

He was hardly ever fully dressed. He hung around the house in underwear and flip-flops. I became his personal Mamamimi, trying to stop the rest of the family finding out, trying to keep him inside the room. In the middle of the night, he would get up. I would sit up, see he wasn't there, and slip out of the house trying to find him, walking around our unlit streets. This is not wise in our locality. The neighbourhood boys patrol for thieves or outsiders, and they can be rough if they do not recognize your face. "I'm Patrick, I moved into the house above the school. I'm trying to find my brother Raphael."

"So how did you lose him?"

"He's not well, he's had a fever, he wanders."

"The crazy family," one of them said.

Their flashlights dazzled my eyes, but I could see them glance at each other. "He means that dirty boy." They said that of Raphael?

"He's my brother. He's not well."

I would stay out until they brought him back to me, swinging their AK-47s. He could so easily have been shot. He was wearing almost nothing, dazed like a sleepwalker, and his hair in such a mess. Raphael had always been vain. His skin Vaselined with the scent of roses, the fine shirt with no tails designed to hang outside the trousers and hide his tummy, his nails manicured. Now he looked like a labourer who needed a bath.

Finally one night, the moon was too bright and the boys brought him too close to our house. My mother ran out of the groaning gate. "Patrick, Patrick, what is it?"

"These boys have been helping us find Raphael," was all I said. I felt ashamed and frustrated because I had failed to calm him, to find him myself, to keep the secret locked away, especially from Mamamimi.

When my mother saw him she whispered, "Wild man!" and it was like a chill wind going through me. She had said what I knew but did not let myself acknowledge. Again, it was happening again, first to the father, then to the son.

I got him to bed, holding both his arms and steering him. Our room was cool as if we were on a mountain. I came back out into the heat and Mamamimi was waiting, looking old. "Does he smoke gbana?" she asked.

I said I didn't think so. "But I no longer know him."

In my mind I was saying, *Raphael, come back.* Sometimes my mother would beseech me with her eyes to do something. Such a thing should not befall a family twice.

Makurdi lives only because of its river. The Benue flows into the great Niger, grey-green with fine beaches that are being dug up for concrete and currents so treacherous they look like moulded jellies welling up from below. No one swims there, except at dusk, in the shallows, workmen go to wash, wading out in their underwear.

Raphael would disappear at sunset and go down the slopes to hymn the men. It was the only time he dressed up: yellow shirt, tan slacks, good shoes. He walked out respectfully onto the sand and sang about the men, teased them, and chortled. He would try to take photographs of them. The men eyed him in fear, or ignored him like gnarled trees, or sometimes threw pebbles at him to make him go away. The things he said were irresponsible. Matthew and I would be sent to fetch him back. Matthew hated it. He would show up in his bank suit, with his car that would get sand in it. "Let him stay there! He only brings shame on himself!"

But we could not leave our brother to have stones thrown at him. He would be on the beach laughing at his own wild self, singing paeans of praise for the beauty of the bathers, asking their names, asking where they lived. Matthew and I would be numb from shame. "Come home, come home," we said to him, and to the labourers, "Please excuse us, we are good Christians, he is not well." We could not bring ourselves to call him our brother. He would laugh and run away. When we caught him, he would sit down on the ground and make us lift him up and carry him back to Matthew's car. He was made of something other than flesh; his bones were lead, his blood mercury.

"I can't take more of this," said Matthew.

It ended so swiftly that we were left blinking. He disappeared from the house as usual; Mamamimi scolded Andrew to keep out of it and rang Matthew. He pulled up outside our gates, so back we went past the university, and the zoo where Baba had taken us as kids, then down beyond the old bridge.

This time was the worst, beyond anything. He was wearing one of Mamamimi's dresses, sashaying among construction workers with a sun umbrella, roaring with laughter as he sang.

He saw us and called waving. "*M'sugh*! My brothers! My dear brothers! I am going swimming."

He ran away from us like a child, into the river. He fought his way into those strong green currents, squealing like a child, perhaps with delight, as the currents cooled him. The great dress blossomed out then sank. He stumbled on pebbles underfoot, dipped under the water, and was not seen again.

"Go get him!" said Matthew.

I said nothing, did nothing.

"Go on, you're the only one who likes him." He had to push me.

I nibbled at the edge of the currents. I called his name in a weak voice as if I really didn't want him back. I was angry with him as if he was now playing a particularly annoying game. Finally I pushed my way in partly so that Matthew would tell our mother that I'd struggled to find him. I began to call his name loudly, not so much in the hope of finding him as banishing this new reality. *Raphael. Raphael,* I shouted, meaning this terrible thing cannot be, not so simply, not so quickly. Finally I dove under the water. I felt the current pull and drag me away by my heels. I fought my way back to the shore but I knew I had not done enough, swiftly enough. I knew that he had already been swept far away.

On the bank, Matthew said, "Maybe it is best that he is gone." Since then, I have not been able to address more than five consecutive words to him.

That's what the family said, if not in words. Best he was gone. The bookcase was there with its notice. I knew we were cursed. I knew we would all be swept away.

Oh story, Raphael seemed to say to me. *You just want to be miserable so you have an excuse to fail.*

We need a body to bury, I said to his memory.

It doesn't make any difference; nobody in this family will mourn. They have too many worries of their own. You'll have to take care of yourself now. You don't have your younger brother to watch out for you.

The sun set, everyone else inside the house. I wanted to climb up onto a roof, or sit astride the wall. I plugged the mobile phone into the laptop, but in the depths of our slough I could not get a signal. I went into our hot, unlit hall and pulled out the books, but they were unreadable without Raphael. Who would laugh for me as I did not laugh? Who would speak my mind for me as I could never find my mind in time? Who would know how to be pleasant with guests, civil in this uncivil world? I picked up our book on genetics and walked to the top of the hill, and sat in the open unlit shed of a church and tried to read it in the last of the orange light. I said, Patrick, you are not civil and can't make other people laugh, but you can do this. This is the one part of Raphael you can carry on.

I read it aloud, like a child sounding out words, to make them go in as facts. I realized later I was trying to read in the dark, in a church. I had been chanting nonsense GATTACA aloud, unable to see, my eyes full of tears. But I had told myself one slow truth and stuck to it. I studied for many years.

Whenever I felt weak or low or lonely, Raphael spoke inside my indented head. I kept his books in order for him. The chemistry book, the human genetics book. I went out into the broken courtyard and started to lift the iron bars with balls of concrete that he had made. Now I look like the muscular champion on his netbook. Everything I am, I am because of my brother. I did not speak much to anyone else. I didn't want to. Somewhere what is left of Raphael's lead and mercury is entwined with reeds or glistens in sand.

To pay for your application for a scholarship in those days you had to buy a scratch card from a bank. I had bought so many. I did not even remember applying to the Benue State Scholarship Board. They gave me a small stipend, enough if I stayed at home and did construction work. I became one of the workmen in the shallows.

Ex-colleagues of my father had found Matthew a job as a clerk in a bank in Jos. Matthew went to live with Uncle Emmanuel. Andrew's jaw set, demanding to be allowed to go with him. He knew where things were going. So did Mamamimi, who saw the sense and nodded quietly, yes. Matthew became Andrew's father.

We all lined up in the courtyard in the buzzing heat to let Matthew take the SUV, his inheritance. We waved good-bye as if half the family were just going for a short trip back to the home village or to the Chinese bakery to buy rolls. Our car pulled up the red hill past the church and they were gone. Mamamimi and I were alone with the sizzling sound of insects and heat and we all walked back into the house in the same way, shuffling flat-footed. We stayed wordless all that day. Even the TV was not turned on. In the kitchen, in the dark, Mamamimi said to me, "Why didn't you go with them? Study at a proper university?" and I said, "Because someone needs to help you."

"Don't worry about me," she said. Not long afterward she took her rusty green car and drove it back to Kawuye for the last time. She lived with Uncle Jacob and the elders. I was left alone in this whispering house.

We had in our neglected, unpaid, strike-ridden campus a mathematician, a dusty and disordered man who reminded me of Raphael. He was an Idoma man called Thomas Aba. He came to Jide and me with his notebook and then unfolded a page of equations.

These equations described, he said, how the act of observing events at a quantum level changed them. He turned the page. Now, he said, here is how those same equations describe how observing alters effects on the macro level.

He had shown mathematically how the mere act of repeated observation changed the real world.

We published in *Nature*. People wanted to believe that someone working things out for themselves could revolutionize cosmology with a single set of equations. Of all of us, Doubting Thomas was the genius. Tsinghua University in Beijing offered him a Professorship and he left us. Citations for our article avalanched; Google could not keep up. People needed to know why everything was shifting, needing to explain both the climate-change debacle and the end of miracles.

Simply put, science found the truth and by finding it, changed it. Science undid itself, in an endless cycle.

Some day the theory of evolution will be untrue and the law of conservation of energy will no longer work. Who knows, maybe we will get faster-than-light travel after all?

Thomas still writes to me about his work, though it is the intellectual property of Tsinghua. He is now able to calculate how long it takes for observation to change things. The rotation of the Earth around the Sun is so rooted in the universe that it will take four thousand years to wear it out. What kind of paradigm will replace it? The Earth and the Sun and all the stars secretly overlap? Outside the four dimensions they all occupy the same single mathematical point?

So many things exist only as metaphors and numbers. Atoms will take only fifty more years to disappear, taking with them quarks and muons and all the other particles. What the Large Hadron Collider will most accelerate is their demise.

Thomas has calculated how long it will take for observation to wear out even his observation. Then, he says, the universe will once again be stable. History melts down and is restored.

My fiancée is a simple country girl who wants a Prof for a husband. I know where that leads. To Mamamimi. Perhaps no bad thing. I hardly know the girl. She wears long dresses instead of jeans and has a pretty smile. My mother's family knows her.

The singing at the church has started, growing with the heat and sunlight. My beautiful suit wax-printed in blue and gold arches reflects the sunlight. Its cotton will be cool, cooler than all that lumpy knitwear from Indonesia.

We have two weddings; one new, one old. So I go through it all twice: next week, the church and the big white dress. I will have to mime love and happiness; the photographs will be used for those framed tributes: "Patrick and Leticia: True Love Is Forever." Matthew and Andrew will be here with their families for the first time in years and I find it hurts to have brothers who care nothing for me.

I hear my father saying that my country wife had best be grateful for all that I give her. I hear him telling her to leave if she is not happy. This time, though, he speaks with my own voice.

Will I slap the walls all night or just my own face? Will I go mad and dance for workmen in a woman's dress? Will I make stews so fiery that only I can eat them? I look down at my body, visible through the white linen, the body I have made perfect to compensate for my imperfect brain.

Shall I have a little baby with a creased forehead? Will he wear my father's dusty cap? Will he sleepwalk, weep at night, or laugh for no reason? If I call him a family name, will he live his grandfather's life again? What poison will I pass on?

I try to imagine all my wedding guests and how their faces would fall if I simply walked away, or strode out like Raphael to crow with delight, "No wedding! I'm not getting married, no way José!" I smile; I can hear him say it; I can see how he would strut.

I can also hear him say, *What else is someone like you going to do except get married? You are too quiet and homely. A publication in* Nature *is not going to cook your food for you. It's not going to get you laid.*

I think of my future son. His Christian name will be Raphael but his personal name will be Ese, which means Wiped Out. It means that God will wipe out the past with all its expectations.

If witchcraft once worked and science is wearing out, then it seems to me that God loves our freedom more than stable truth. If I have a son who is free from the past, then I know God loves me too.

So I can envisage Ese, my firstborn. He's wearing shorts and running with a kite behind him, happy, clean, and free, and we the Shawos live on the hill once more.

I think of Mamamimi kneeling down to look into my face and saying, "Patrick, you are a fine young boy. You do everything right. There is nothing wrong with you." I remember my father, sane for a while, resting a hand on the small of my back and saying, "You are becoming distinguished." He was proud of me.

Most of all I think of Raphael speaking his mind to Matthew, to Grandma, even to Father, but never to me. He is passing on his books to me in twilight, and I give him tea, and he says, as if surprised, *That's nice. Thank you*. His shiny face glows with love.

I have to trust that I can pass on love as well.

lie-father
GEMMA FILES

I that am I alone,
cruelest and most clever;
light-hearted, heartless.
I that am flame
without true form, a thousand things in one,
and every one of them a lie:

A fly when I stole the Brisingamen
A seal when I fought Hjeimdall for it
A red-headed man with my lips sewn shut
A red-headed bridesmaid for a thunderous bride
who sows slaughter between the sheaves
Fenris' father
Sleipnir's mother
A leaping fish caught in the net of tears
An old woman who will not weep, ever,
not even for the light of the world.

This is what you let in
as a guest, and more, Odin One-eye—
this is what you mixed your blood with,
who you let marry into your All-family
and live proudly childless
while he bred monsters elsewhere

Do you not feel foolish?

Even now, pinned beneath mountains,
writhing in my poisoned bonds,
I cannot be contained.
My song goes on and on,
spawning many lines of liars—
Kveldulfr, Skalla-grimr, Egil in his turn:
hamrammrs, poets and killers,
who bend to fit the world around them
only in order to trick it
into breaking to fit them.

Thor Odinsson, mighty one,
when we lay together in the Jotun's mitt;
poor sad Hodi, when I handed you the arrow
of mistletoe, kiss-attractor, to send
your brother's bright face down
into my daughter's clutches—

You felt my sparks dance
across your blind knuckles,
and laughed—admit it!
All of you, in pain or otherwise—
I could always make you laugh.

Look to me, therefore, on that day,
that dreadful time of reckoning,
when my ship made from dead men's nails docks
at the very foot of the rainbow.
I promise you, cousins:
when all my brothers take up stones against you,
when one son takes the sun in his jaws
and the other coils 'round the world's root,
squeezing, 'til your rotten tree cracks—

There will be much laughter then.

centipede girl

ADA HOFFMANN

Says one Centipede Girl to another: *Are you real?*

Fleeting, that moment. Must be her reflection at the other end of the sewer, maybe in some metal, but she watches it just in case. Holding her breath, she gazes down the long dark tunnel. Wills her 'pedes to stay still a minute, though they never do. Splish goes the stinking water, up to her ankles, as the 'pedes scuttle up and down her legs. And at that tiny noise, her faraway reflection starts and darts away.

Breath rises in her chest, a smile splitting her invisible face. *Moved when I didn't. Means she's real.*

Not really a reflection, but someone looking like her, taking up space. Someone that can be touched. And Centipede Girl wants so bad to touch.

She dashes forward, splashing, panting. The 'pedes squat, cling and sting, holding on for the ride. Splash goes the water as two or three of them lose their balance and fall, and they disappear with a fizz, becoming nothing.

Centipede Girl has hands, feet, teeth, a tummy, just like a real girl. Forgets they are there, sometimes. She is invisible, not through magic, but through layers and layers of 'pedes. Scrambling, writhing, waiting. Human skin never shows through.

In her memories, at five, she still has a face, but even then, the 'pedes crawl all over her. She drinks poison, when big looming parents say *Now, listen to the nice exterminator man*, and vomits blood for a week, but the 'pedes remain. Doctors shake their heads. Big looming parents slowly give up hope. And the 'pedes breed.

Lives in the sewers now, in their comfortable, dark stench. Tries going up in the light sometimes and is greeted with screams.

A horrible uproar of water, and a run that burns her lungs and sides, before she catches up to the reflection that is not a reflection.

Don't go! says Centipede Girl. *Wait! Wait!*

It turns to look at her, 'pedes shifting and squirming in the vaguest semblance of a head. It speaks hissing, as though layers on layers of hisses have to be put together just right to make the words.

Why wait?

Because you are like me, says Centipede Girl. *Because you could be a friend.*

An infested silence, as the other girl looks her up and down. Not exactly like Centipede Girl, after all. Bigger. Taller. A grown-up Centipede Woman.

Friend, Centipede Woman says, as though tasting the word. *Friend.*

You hunt?

I hunt, says Centipede Girl. More often she scavenges, faceted 'pede eyes spotting some half-rotten thing. But fresh meat pleases her more. She's learned to send one or two 'pedes out a short ways, keeping her mind on them so they don't disappear, luring in some hungry rat or lizard, then pouncing with strong human limbs.

Centipede Woman nods. Barely perceptible under the writhe of her face.

We hunt.

So long since anyone touched Centipede Girl. Maybe not since she was born. She has thought of it in her sweetest daydreams, the ones that hurt the most. Hands holding hers. Arms around her. Warm sides to lean against.

One time she climbs all the way out of the sewer. Tells herself the screams won't stop her. She'll hold him down, the first unlucky passerby, and grasp his hands in hers, just for a while, just long enough to remember she's real. But the screams turn to gags and prayers and bestial howls as she chases him, and she can't do it. Not brave enough. Lets him get away.

She watches now as Centipede Woman hunts. Centipede Woman gives gruff instructions. *Stand like this. Watch more careful. Never get full if not watch more careful.*

Centipede Girl half-listens. Other half longs for Centipede Woman's hands. Centipede Woman won't scream. Nothing to scream about. Nothing on her that isn't on both of them already.

She asks Centipede Woman every evening when the hunt is done. *Will you let me hold your hands? Please?*

You don't want that.

Makes herself pitiful in the asking. Lets the tears creep into her voice, if they like. *I do. Please, I do. I want it so bad.*

No.

And the nights are silent. They sleep, on opposite sides of the tunnel, every day.

She is good a long time. Ignores the ache inside and keeps her hands to herself. Hunts and hunts. Does everything Centipede Woman says, till at last, after months, Centipede Woman hunts all silent by her side. Still moving, same as before, but out of words.

Two days. Three. No words. And the ache is a pounding raging thing inside her head.

Think we go two ways now, says Centipede Woman, after three days silent. *Think this done. Taught everything. Done.*

No, says Centipede Girl. *No.*

Yes. Sleep day, then in evening, go two ways.

And Centipede Woman falls asleep.

The thing in Centipede Girl's head pounds and rages, and though she knows it's a bad, bad thing, she creeps to Centipede Woman's side. Watches the rise and fall of the 'pedes on her chest. Looks up at Centipede Woman's writhing skittering face, down to the hills of her shoulders, down the throughways of 'pedes up and down her arm, over and under each other, down to the squirming brown mass that is her hand.

Takes a breath, and then she reaches down and plunges her hand into the 'pedes.

Centipede Woman's 'pedes skitter across the skin of her hand, probing it, tasting it. Shuddery, that feeling, even though Centipede Girl has 'pedes too. These ones aren't hers and she can't see through their eyes. But she brings her hand down anyway, right through the mass that should be Centipede Woman's fist, right down to the ground.

There is no fist. No wrist, no forearm. Just 'pedes and 'pedes and 'pedes.

And Centipede Woman screams. *What is this? What is this you do?*

Centipede Girl backs away. Doesn't know what to say, so just babbles. *I'm sorry. I only wanted to hold your hand. I wanted it so bad. I'm sorry. Please.*

You want my touch? says Centipede Woman, only half the 'pedes hissing. Other half screaming, eerie and shrill. *Have my touch.*

And just like hunting, Centipede Woman lunges.

Centipede Girl reels, bracing for the great slamming limbs of a woman, even though she knows better now. All that hits her are light little 'pedes, 'pedes upon 'pedes, until she staggers under the weight of such light little things. Centipede Girl screams, and the 'pedes scream, and blood billows in the filthy water.

Last she remembers, she is falling, collapsing, her limbs folding up into each other, and the bloody, mucky water rushing at her face.

Centipede Woman is gone now. Gone for a long time. Centipede Girl hunts alone.

Runs away now from mirrors, still water, anything to reflect her. Afraid of what she'll see. Once she does see herself, distorted, in a shiny metal panel. Looks the same as before. Just 'pedes. Feels different, though.

In her memories, she has hands, feet, teeth, a tummy, just like a real girl. But all she can see now are facets. All she can feel now is hunger. Sometimes she reaches through the 'pedes and paws at herself. Tries to remember her shape. *Be real. Please. Be like a real girl.*

But her hands go right through herself, and there are no bones anywhere. No more girl. Just 'pedes and 'pedes and 'pedes.

clockwork fagin
CORY DOCTOROW

Monty Goldfarb walked into St. Agatha's like he owned the place, a superior look on the half of his face that was still intact, a spring in his step despite his steel left leg. And it wasn't long before he *did* own the place, taken it over by simple murder and cunning artifice. It wasn't long before he was my best friend and my master, too, and the master of all St. Agatha's, and didn't he preside over a *golden* era in the history of that miserable place?

I've lived in St. Agatha's for six years, since I was 11 years old, when a reciprocating gear in the Muddy York Hall of Computing took off my right arm at the elbow. My Da had sent me off to Muddy York when Ma died of the consumption. He'd sold me into service of the Computers and I'd thrived in the big city, hadn't cried, not even once, not even when Master Saunders beat me for playing kick-the-can with the other boys when I was meant to be polishing the brass. I didn't cry when I lost my arm, nor when the barber-surgeon clamped me off and burned my stump with his medicinal tar.

I've seen every kind of boy and girl come to St. Aggie's—swaggering, scared, tough, meek. The burned ones are often the hardest to read, inscrutable beneath their scars. Old Grinder don't care, though, not one bit. Angry or scared, burned and hobbling or swaggering and full of beans, the first thing he does when new meat turns up on his doorstep is tenderize it a little. That means a good long session with the belt—and Grinder doesn't care where the strap lands, whole skin or fresh scars, it's all the same to him—and then a night or two down the hole, where there's no light and no warmth and nothing for company except for the big hairy Muddy York rats who'll come and nibble at whatever's left of you if you manage to fall asleep. It's the blood, see, it draws them out.

So there we all was, that first night when Monty Goldfarb

turned up, dropped off by a pair of sour-faced Sisters in white capes who turned their noses up at the smell of the horse-droppings as they stepped out of their coal-fired banger and handed Monty over to Grinder, who smiled and dry-washed his hairy hands and promised, "Oh, aye, sisters, I shall look after this poor crippled birdie like he was my own get. We'll be great friends, won't we, Monty?" Monty actually laughed when Grinder said that, like he'd already winkled it out.

As soon as the boiler on the sisters' car had its head of steam up and they were clanking away, Grinder took Monty inside, leading him past the parlour where we all sat, quiet as mice, eyeless or armless, shy a leg or half a face, or even a scalp (as was little Gertie Shine-Pate, whose hair got caught in the mighty rollers of one of the pressing engines down at the logic mill in Cabbagetown).

He gave us a jaunty wave as Grinder led him away, and I'm ashamed to say that none of us had the stuff to wave back at him, or even to shout a warning. Grinder had done his work on us, too true, and turned us from kids into cowards.

Presently, we heard the whistle and slap of the strap, but instead of screams of agony, we heard howls of defiance, and yes, even laughter!

"Is that the best you have, you greasy old sack of suet? Put some arm into it!"

And then: "Oh, dearie me, you must be tiring of your work. See how the sweat runs down your face, how your tongue doth protrude from your stinking gob. Oh please, dear master, tell me your pathetic old ticker isn't about to pack it in, I don't know what I'd do if you dropped dead here on the floor before me!"

And then: "Your chest heaves like a bellows. Is this what passes for a beating round here? Oh, when I get the strap, old man, I will show you how we beat a man in Montreal, you may count on it my sweet."

The way he carried on, you'd think he was *enjoying* the beating, and I had a picture of him leaping to and fro, avoiding the strap with the curious, skipping jump of a one-legged boy, but when Grinder led him past the parlour again, he looked half dead. The good side of his face was a pulpy mess, and his one eye was near swollen shut, and he walked with even more of a limp than he'd had coming in. But he grinned at us again, and spat a tooth on the threadbare rug that we were made to sweep three times a day, a tooth that left a trail of blood behind it on the splintery floor.

We heard the thud as Monty was tossed down onto the hole's dirt floor, and then the laboured breathing as Grinder locked him in, and then the singing, loud and distinct, from under the floorboards: "Come gather ye good children, good news to you I'll tell, 'bout how the Grinder bastard will roast and rot in Hell—" There was more, apparently improvised (later, I'd hear Monty improvise many and many a song, using some hymn or popular song for a tune beneath his bawdy and obscene lyrics), and we all strove to keep the smiles from our face as Grinder stamped back into his rooms, shooting us dagger-looks as he passed by the open door.

And that was the day that Monty came to St. Agatha's Home for the Rehabilitation of Crippled Children.

I remember my first night in the hole, a time that seemed to stretch into infinity, a darkness so deep I thought that perhaps I'd gone blind. And most of all, I remember the sound of the cellar door loosening, the bar being shifted, the ancient hinges squeaking, the blinding light stabbing into me from above, and the silhouette of old Grinder, holding out one of his hairy, long-fingered hands for me to catch hold of, like an angel come to rescue me from the pits of Hades. Grinder pulled me out of the hole like a man pulling up a carrot, with a gesture practised on many other children over the years, and I near wept from gratitude. I'd soiled my trousers, and I couldn't hardly see, nor speak from my dry throat, and every sound and sight was magnified a thousandfold and I put my face in his great coat, there in the horrible smell of the man and the muscle beneath like a side of beef, and I cried like he was my old Mam come to get me out of a fever-bed.

I remember this, and I ain't proud of it, and I never spoke of it to any of the other St. Aggie's children, nor did they speak of it to me. I was broken then, and I was old Grinder's boy, and when he turned me out later that day with a begging bowl, sent me down to the distillery and off to the ports to approach the navvies and the lobsterbacks for a ha'penny or a groat or a tuppence, I went out like a grateful doggie, and never once thought of putting any of Grinder's money by in a secret place for my own spending.

Of course, over time I did get less doggy and more wolf about the Grinder, dreamt of tearing out his throat with my teeth, and Grinder always seemed to know when the doggy was going, because bung, you'd be back in the hole before you had a chance to chance old Grinder. A day or two downstairs would bring the doggie back out, especially if Grinder tenderized you some with his strap before he heaved you down the stairs. I'd seen big boys and rough girls come to St. Aggie's, hard as boots, and come out of Grinder's hole so good doggy that they practically licked his boots for him. Grinder understood children, I give you that. Give us a mean, hard father of a man, a man who doles out punishment and protection like old Jehovah from the Sisters' hymnals, and we line up to take his orders.

But Grinder didn't understand Monty Goldfarb.

I'd just come down to lay the long tables for breakfast—it was my turn that day—when I heard Grinder shoot the lock to his door and then the sound of his callouses rasping on the polished brass knob. As his door swung open, I heard the music-box playing its tune, Grinder's favourite, a Scottish hymn that the music box sung in Gaelic, its weird horsegut voice-box making the auld words even weirder, like the eldritch crooning of some crone in a street-play.

Grinder's heavy tramp receded down the hall, to the cellar door. The doors creaked open and I felt a shiver down in my stomach and down below that, in my stones, as I remembered my times in the pit. There was the thunder of his heavy boots on the steps, then his cruel laughter as he beheld Monty.

"Oh, my darling, is *this* how they take their punishment in Montreal? 'Tis no wonder the Frenchies lost their wars to the Upper Canadians, with such weak little mice as you to fight for them."

They came back up the stairs: Grinder's jaunty tromp, Monty's dragging, beaten limp. Down the hall they came, and I heard poor Monty reaching out to steady himself, brushing the framed drawings of Grinder's horrible ancestors as he went, and I flinched with each squeak of a picture knocked askew, for disturbing Grinder's forebears was a beating offence at St. Aggie's. But Grinder must have been feeling charitable, for he did not pause to whip beaten Monty that morning.

And so they came into the dining hall, and I did not raise my head, but beheld them from the corners of my eyes, taking cutlery from the basket hung over the hook at my right elbow and laying it down neat and precise on the splintery tables.

Each table had three hard loaves on it, charity bread donated from Muddy York's bakeries to us poor crippled kiddees, day-old and more than a day-old, and tough as stone. Before each loaf was a knife as long as a man's forearm, sharp as a butcher's, and the head child at each table was responsible for slicing the bread using that knife each day (children who were shy an arm or two were exempted from this duty, for which I was thankful, since those children were always accused of favouring some child with a thicker slice, and fights were common).

Monty was leaning heavily on Grinder, his head down and his steps like those of an old, old man, first a click of his steel foot, then a dragging from his remaining leg. But as they passed the head of the furthest table, Monty sprang from Grinder's side, took up the knife, and with a sure, steady hand—a movement so spry I knew he'd been shamming from the moment Grinder opened up the cellar door—he plunged the knife into Grinder's barrel-chest, just over his heart, and shoved it home, giving it a hard twist.

He stepped back to consider his handiwork. Grinder was standing perfectly still, his face pale beneath his whiskers, and his mouth was working, and I could almost hear the words he was trying to get out, words I'd heard so many times before: *Oh, my lovely, you are a naughty one, but Grinder will beat the devil out of you, purify you with rod and fire, have no fear—*

But no sound escaped Grinder's furious lips. Monty put his hands on his hips and watched him with the critical eye of a bricklayer or a machinist surveying his work. Then, calmly, he put his good right hand on Grinder's chest, just to one side of the knife handle. He said, "Oh, no, Mr. Grindersworth, *this* is how we take our punishment in Montreal." Then he gave the smallest of pushes and Grinder went over like a chimney that's been hit by a wrecking ball.

He turned then, and regarded me full on, the good side of his face alive with mischief, the mess on the other side a wreck of burned skin. He winked his good eye at me and said, "Now, he was a proper pile of filth and muck, wasn't he? World's a better place now, I daresay." He wiped his hand on his filthy trousers—grimed with the brown dirt of the cellar—and held it out to me.

"Montague Goldfarb, machinist's boy and prentice artificer, late of old Montreal. Montreal Monty, if you please," he said.

I tried to say something—anything—and realized that I'd bitten the inside of my cheek so hard I could taste the blood. I was so discombobulated that I held out my abbreviated right arm to him, hook and cutlery basket and all, something I hadn't done since I'd first lost the limb. Truth told, I was a little tender and shy about my mutilation, and didn't like to think about it, and I especially couldn't bear to see whole people shying back from me as though I were some kind of monster. But Monty just reached out, calm as you like, and took my hook with his cunning fingers—fingers so long they seemed to have an extra joint—and shook my hook as though it were a whole hand.

"Sorry, mate, I didn't catch your name."

I tried to speak again, and this time I found my voice. "Sian O'Leary," I said. "Antrim Town, then Hamilton, and then here." I wondered what else to say. "Third-grade Computerman's boy, once upon a time."

"Oh, that's *fine*," he said. "Skilled tradesmen's helpers are what we want around here. You know the lads and lasses round here, Sian, are there more like you? Children who can make things, should they be called upon?"

I nodded. It was queer to be holding this calm conversation over the cooling body of Grinder, who now smelt of the ordure his slack bowels had loosed into his fine trousers. But it was also natural, somehow, caught in the burning gaze of Monty Goldfarb, who had the attitude of a master in his shop, running the place with utter confidence.

"Capital." He nudged Grinder with his toe. "That meat'll spoil soon enough, but before he does, let's have some fun, shall we? Give us a hand." He bent and lifted Grinder under one arm. He nodded his head at the remaining arm. "Come on," he said, and I took it, and we lifted the limp corpse of Zophar Grindersworth, the Grinder of St. Aggie's, and propped him up at the head of the middle table, knife handle protruding from his chest amid a spreading red stain over his blue brocade waistcoat. Monty shook his head. "That won't do," he said, and plucked up a tea-towel from a pile by the kitchen door and tied it around Grinder's throat like a bib, fussing with it until it more-or-less disguised the grisly wound. Then Monty picked up one of the loaves from the end of the table and tore a hunk off the end.

He chewed at it like a cow at her cud for a time, never taking his eyes off me. Then he swallowed and said, "Hungry work," and laughed with a spray of crumbs.

He paced the room, picking up the cutlery I'd laid and inspecting it, gnawing at the loaf's end in his hand thoughtfully. "A pretty poor setup," he said. "But I'm sure that wicked old lizard had a pretty soft nest for himself, didn't he?"

I nodded and pointed down the hall to Grinder's door. "The key's on his belt," I said.

Monty fingered the keyring chained to Grinder's thick leather belt, then shrugged. "All one-cylinder jobs," he said, and picked a fork out of the basket that was still hanging from my hook. "Nothing to them. Faster than fussing with his belt." He walked purposefully down the hall, his metal foot thumping off the polished wood, leaving dents in it. He dropped to one knee at the lock, then put the fork under his steel foot and used it as a lever to bend back all but one of the soft pot-metal tines, so that now the fork just hand one long thin spike. He slid it into the lock, felt for a moment, then gave a sharp and precise flick of his wrist and twisted open the doorknob. It opened smoothly at his touch. "Nothing to it," he said, and got back to his feet, dusting off his knees.

Now, I'd been in Grinder's rooms many times, when I'd brought in the boiling water for his bath, or run the rug-sweeper over his thick Turkish rugs, or dusted the framed medals and certificates and the cunning machines he kept in his apartment. But this was different, because this time I was coming in with Monty, and Monty made you ask yourself, "Why isn't this all mine? Why shouldn't I just take it?" And I didn't have a good answer, apart from *fear*. And fear was giving way to excitement.

Monty went straight to the humidor by Grinder's deep, plush chair and brought out a fistful of cigars. He handed one to me and we both bit off the tips and spat them on the fine rug, then lit them with the polished brass lighter in the shape of a beautiful woman that stood on the other side of the chair. Monty clamped his cheroot between his teeth and continued to paw through Grinder's sacred possessions, all the fine goods that the children of St. Aggie's weren't even allowed to look to closely upon. Soon he was swilling Grinder's best brandy from a lead crystal decanter, wearing Grinder's red velvet housecoat, topped with Grinder's fine beaver-skin bowler hat.

And it was thus attired that he stumped back into the dining room, where the corpse of Grinder still slumped at table's end, and took up a stance by the old ship's bell that the morning child used to call the rest of the kids to breakfast, and he began to ring the bell like St. Aggie's was afire, and he called out as he did so, a wordless, birdlike call, something like a rooster's crowing, such a noise as had never been heard in St. Aggie's before.

With a clatter and a clank and a hundred muffled arguments, the children of St. Aggie's pelted down the staircases and streamed into the kitchen, milling uncertainly, eyes popping at the sight of our latest arrival in his stolen finery, still ringing the bell, still making his crazy call, stopping now and again to swill the brandy and laugh and spray a boozy cloud before him.

Once we were all standing in our nightshirts and underclothes, every scar and stump on display, he let off his ringing and cleared his throat ostentatiously, then stepped nimbly onto one of the chairs, wobbling for an instant on his steel peg, then leaped again, like a goat leaping from rock to rock, up onto the table, sending my carefully laid cutlery clattering every which-a-way.

He cleared his throat again, and said:

"Good morrow to you, good morrow all, good morrow to the poor, crippled, abused children of St. Aggie's. We haven't been properly introduced, so I thought it fitting that I should take a moment to greet you all and share a bit of good news with you. My name is Montreal Monty Goldfarb, machinist's boy, prentice artificer, gentleman adventurer and liberator of the oppressed. I am late foreshortened—" He waggled his stumps— "as are so many of you. And yet, and yet, I say to you, I am as good a man as I was ere I lost my limbs, and I say that you are too." There was a cautious murmur at this. It was the kind of thing the Sisters said to you in the hospital, before they brought you to St. Aggie's, the kind of pretty lies they told you about the wonderful life that awaited you with your new, crippled body, once you had been retrained and put to productive work.

"Children of St. Aggie's, hearken to old Montreal Monty, and I will tell you of what is possible and what is necessary. First, what is necessary: to end oppression wherever we find it, to be liberators of the downtrodden and the meek. When that evil dog's pizzle flogged me and threw me in his dungeon, I knew that I'd come upon a bully, a man who poisoned the sweet air with each breath of his cursed lungs, and so I resolved to do something about it. And so I have." He clattered the table's length, to where Grinder's body slumped. Many of the children had been so fixated on the odd spectacle that Monty presented that they hadn't even noticed the extraordinary sight of our tormentor sat, apparently sleeping or unconscious. With the air of a magician, Monty bent and took the end of tea-towel and gave it a sharp yank, so that all could see the knife-handle protruding from the red stain that covered Grinder's chest. We gasped, and some of the more faint-hearted children shrieked, but no one ran off to get the law, and no one wept a single salty tear for our dead benefactor.

Monty held his arms over his head in a wide "vee" and looked expectantly upon us. It only took a moment before someone— perhaps it was me!—began to applaud, to cheer, to stomp, and then we were all at it, making such a noise as you might encounter in a tavern full of men who've just learned that their side has won a war. Monty waited for it to die down a bit, then, with a theatrical flourish, he pushed Grinder out of his chair, letting him slide to the floor with a meaty thump, and settled himself into the chair the corpse had lately sat upon. The message was clear: I am now the master of this house.

I cleared my throat and raised my good arm. I'd had more time than the rest of the St. Aggie's children to consider life without the terrible Grinder, and a thought had come to me. Monty nodded regally at me, and I found myself standing with every eye in the room upon me.

"Monty," I said, "on behalf of the children of St. Aggie's, I thank you most sincerely for doing away with cruel old Grinder, but I must ask you, what shall we do *now*? With Grinder gone, the Sisters will surely shut down St. Aggie's, or perhaps send us another vile old master to beat us, and you shall go to the gallows at the King Street Gaol, and, well, it just seems like a pity that . . ." I waved my stump. "It just seems a pity, is what I'm saying."

Monty nodded again. "Sian, I thank you, for you have come neatly to my next point. I spoke of what was needed and what was possible, and now we must discuss what is possible. I had a nice long time to meditate on this question through last night, as I languished in the pit below, and I think I have a plan, though I shall need your help with it if we are to pull it off."

He stood again, and took up a loaf of hard bread and began to wave it like a baton as he spoke, thumping it on the table for emphasis.

"Item: I understand that the Sisters provide for St. Aggie's with such alms as are necessary to keep our lamps burning, fuel in our fireplaces, and gruel and such on the table, yes?" We nodded. "Right.

"Item: Nevertheless, Old Turd-Gargler here was used to sending you poor kiddees out to beg with your wounds all on display, to bring him whatever coppers you could coax from the drunkards of Muddy York with which to feather his pretty little nest yonder. Correct?" We nodded again. "Right.

"Item: We are all of us the crippled children of Muddy York's great information-processing factories. We are artificers, machinists, engineers, cunning shapers and makers, every one, for that is how we came to be injured. Correct? Right.

"Item: It is a murdersome pity that such as we should be turned out to beg when we have so much skill at our disposal. Between us, we could make anything, *do* anything, but our departed tormentor lacked the native wit to see this, correct? Right.

"Item: the sisters of the simpering order of St. Agatha's Weeping Sores have all the cleverness of a turnip. This I saw for myself during my tenure in their hospital. Fooling them would be easier than fooling an idiot child. Correct? *Right.*"

He levered himself out of the chair and began to stalk the dining-room, stumping up and down. "Someone tell me, how often do the good sisters pay us a visit?"

"Sundays," I said. "When they take us all to church."

He nodded. "And does that spoiled meat there accompany us to church?"

"No," I said. "No, he stays here. He says he 'worships in his own way.'" Truth was he was invariably too hung-over to rise on a Sunday.

He nodded again. "And today is Tuesday. Which means that we have five days to do our work."

"What work, Monty?"

"Why, we are going to build a clockwork automaton based on that evil tyrant what I slew this very morning. We will build a device of surpassing and fiendish cleverness, such as will fool the nuns and the world at large into thinking that we are still being ground up like mincemeat, while we lead a life of leisure, fun, and invention, such as befits children of our mental stature and good character."

Here's the oath we swore to Monty before we went to work on the automaton:

"I, (state your full name), do hereby give my most solemn oath that I will never, ever betray the secrets of St. Agatha's. I bind myself to the good fortune of my fellow inmates at this institution and vow to honour them as though they were my brothers and sisters, and not to fight with them, nor spite them, nor do them down or dirty. I make this oath freely and gladly, and should I betray it, I wish that old Satan himself would rise up from the pit and tear out my treacherous guts and use them for bootlaces, that his devils would tear my betrayer's tongue from my mouth and use it to wipe their private parts, that my lying body would be fed, inch-by-inch, to the hungry and terrible basilisks of the Pit. So I swear, and so mote be it!"

There were two children who'd worked for a tanner in the house, older children. Matthew was shy all the fingers on his left hand. Becka was missing an eye and her nose, which she joked was a mercy, for there is no smell more terrible than the charnel reek of the tanning works. But between them, they were quite certain that they could carefully remove, stuff, and remount Grinder's head, careful to leave the jaw in place.

As the oldest machinist at St. Aggie's, I was conscripted to work on the torso and armature mechanisms. I played chief engineer, bossing a gang of six boys and four girls who had experience with mechanisms. We cannibalized St. Aggie's old mechanical wash-wringer, with its spindly arms and many fingers; and I was sent out several times to pawn Grinder's fine crystal and pocket-watch to raise money for parts.

Monty oversaw all, but he took personal charge of Grinder's voicebox, through which he would imitate old Grinder's voice when the sisters came by on Sunday. St. Aggie's was fronted with a Dutch door, and Grinder habitually only opened the top half to jaw with the sisters. Monty said that we could prop the partial torso on a low table, to hide the fact that no legs depended from it.

"We'll tie a sick-kerchief around his face and give out that he's got 'flu, and that it's spread through the whole house. That'll get us all out of church, which is a tidy little jackpot in and of itself. The kerchief will disguise the fact that his lips ain't moving in time with his talking."

I shook my head at this idea. The nuns were hardly geniuses, but how long could this hold out for?

"It won't have to last more than a week—by next week, we'll have something better to show 'em."

Here's a thing: it all worked like a fine-tuned machine.

The kerchief made it look like a bank-robber, and Monty painted its face to make him seem more lively, for the tanning had dried him out some (he also doused the horrible thing with liberal lashings of bay rum and greased its hair with a heavy pomade, for the tanning process had left him with a smell like an outhouse on a hot day). Monty had affixed an armature to the thing's bottom jaw—we'd had to break it to get it to open, prying it roughly with a screwdriver, cracking a tooth or two in the process, and I have nightmares to this day about the sound it made when it finally yawed open.

A child—little legless Dora, whose begging pitch included a sad little puppetry show—could work this armature by means of a squeeze-bulb taken from the siphon-starter on Grinder's cider brewing tub, and so make the jaw go up and down in time with speech.

The speech itself was accomplished by means of the horsegut voicebox from Grinder's music-box. Monty surehandedly affixed a long, smooth glass tube—part of the cracking apparatus that I had been sent to market to buy—to the music-box's resonator. This, he ran up behind our automatic Grinder. Then, crouched on the floor before the voicebox, stationed next to Dora on her wheeled plank, he was able to whisper across the horsegut strings and have them buzz out a credible version of Grinder's whiskey-roughened growl. And once he'd tuned the horsegut just so, the vocal resemblance was even more remarkable. Combined with Dora's skillful puppetry, the effect was galvanizing. It took a conscious effort to remember that this was a puppet talking to you, not a man.

The sisters turned up at the appointed hour on Sunday, only to be greeted by our clockwork Grinder, stood in the half-door, face swathed in a 'flu mask. We'd hung quarantine bunting from the windows, crisscrossing the front of St. Aggie's with it for good measure, and a goodly number of us kiddees were watching from the upstairs windows with our best drawn and sickly looks on our faces.

So the sisters hung back practically at the pavement and shouted, "Mr. Grindersworth!" in alarmed tones, staring with horror at the apparition in the doorway.

"Sisters, good day to you," Monty said into his horsegut, while Dora worked her squeeze-bulb, and the jaw went up and down behind its white cloth, and the muffled simulation of Grinder's voice emanated from the top of the glass tube, hidden behind the automaton's head, so that it seemed to come from the right place. "Though not such a good day for us, I fear."

"The children are ill?"

Monty gave out a fine sham of Grinder's laugh, the one he used when dealing with proper people, with the cruelty barely plastered-over. "Oh, not all of them. But we have a dozen cases. Thankfully, I appear to be immune, and oh my, but you wouldn't believe the help these tots are in the practical nursing department. Fine kiddees, my charges, yes indeed. But still, best to keep them away from the general public for the nonce, hey? I'm quite sure we'll have them up on their feet by next Sunday, and they'll be glad indeed of the chance to get down on their knees and thank the beneficent Lord for their good health." Monty was laying it on thick, but then, so had Grinder, when it came to the sisters.

"We shall send over some help after the services," the head sister said, hands at her breast, a tear glistening in her eye at the thought of our bravery. I thought the jig was up. Of course the order would have some sisters who'd had the 'flu and gotten over it, rendering them immune. But Monty never worried.

"No, no," he said, smoothly. I had the presence of mind to take up the cranks that operated the "arms" we'd constructed for him, waving them about in a negating way—this effect rather spoiled by my nervousness, so that they seemed more octopus tentacle than arm. But the sisters didn't appear to notice. "As I say, I have plenty of help here with my good children."

"A basket, then," the sister said. "Some nourishing food and fizzy drinks for the children."

Crouching low in the anteroom, we crippled children traded disbelieving looks with one another. Not only had Monty gotten rid of Grinder and gotten us out of going to church, he'd also set things up so that the sisters of St. Aggie's were going to bring us their best grub, for free, because we were all so poorly and ailing! It was all we could do not to cheer.

And cheer we did, later, when the sisters set ten huge hampers down on our doorstep, whence we retrieved them, finding in them a feast fit for princes: cold meat pies glistening with aspic, marrow bones still warm from the oven, suet pudding and jugs of custard with skin on top of them, huge bottles of fizzy lemonade and small beer. By the time we'd laid it out in the dining room, it seemed like we'd never be able to eat it all.

But we et every last morsel, and four of us carried Monty about on our shoulders—two carrying, two steadying the carriers—and someone found a concertina, and someone found some combs and waxed paper, and we sang until the walls shook: *The Mechanic's Folly*, *A Combinatorial Explosion at the Computer-Works*, and then endless rounds of *For He's a Jolly Good Fellow*.

Monty had promised improvements on the clockwork Grinder by the following Sunday, and he made good on it. Since we no longer had to beg all day long, we children of St. Aggie's had time in plenty, and Monty had no shortage of skilled volunteers who wanted to work with him on Grinder II, as he called it. Grinder II sported a rather handsome and large, droopy mustache, which hid the action of its lips. This mustache was glued onto the head-assembly one hair at a time, a painstaking job that denuded every horsehair brush in the house, but the effect was impressive.

More impressive was the leg-assembly I bossed into existence, a pair of clockwork pins that could lever Grinder from a seated position into full upright, balancing him by means of three gyros we hid in his chest cavity. Once these were wound and spun, Grinder could stand up in a very natural fashion. Once we'd rearranged the furniture to hide Dora and Monty behind a large armchair, you could stand right in the parlour and "converse" with him, and unless you were looking very hard, you'd never know but what you were talking with a mortal man, and not an automaton made of tanned flesh, steel, springs, and clay (we used rather a lot of custom-made porcelain from the prosthetic works to get his legs right—the children who were shy a leg or two knew which leg-makers in town had the best wares).

And so when the sisters arrived the following Sunday, they were led right into the parlour, whose net curtains kept the room in a semi-dark state, and there, they parlayed with Grinder, who came to his feet when they entered and left. One of the girls was in charge of his arms, and she had practised with them so well that she was able to move them in a very convincing fashion. Convincing enough, anyroad: the sisters left Grinder with a bag of clothes, a bag of oranges that had come off a ship that had sailed from Spanish Florida right up the St. Lawrence to the port of Montreal, and thereafter traversed by rail-car to Muddy York. They made a parcel gift of these succulent treasures to Grinder, to "help the kiddees keep away the scurvy," but Grinder always kept them for himself or flogged them to his pals for a neat penny. We wolfed the oranges right after services, and then took our Sabbath free with games and more brandy from Grinder's sideboard.

And so we went, week on week, with small but impressive updates to our clockwork man: hands that could grasp and smoke a pipe; a clever mechanism that let him throw back his head and laugh, fingers that could drum on the table beside him, eyes that could follow you around a room and eyelids that could blink, albeit slowly.

But Monty had *much* bigger plans.

"I want to bring in another 56 bits," he said, gesturing at the computing panel in Grinder's parlour, a paltry eight-bit works. That meant that there were eight switches with eight matching levers, connected to eight brass rods that ran down to the public computing works that ran beneath the streets of Muddy York. Grinder had used his eight bits to keep St. Aggie's books—both the set he showed to the sisters and the one where he kept track of what he was trousering for himself—and he'd let one "lucky" child work the great, stiff return-arm that sent the instructions set on the switches back to the Hall of Computing for queuing and processing on the great frames that had cost me my good right arm. An instant later, the processed answer would be returned to the levers above the switches, and to whatever interpretive mechanism you had yoked up to them (Grinder used a telegraph machine that printed the answers upon a long, thin sheet of paper).

"56 bits!" I boggled at Monty. A 64-bit rig wasn't unheard

of, if you were a mighty shipping company or insurer. But in a private home—well, the racket of the switches would shake the foundations! Remember, dear reader, that each additional bit *doubled* the calculating faculty of the home panel. Monty was proposing to increase St. Aggie's computational capacity by a factor more than a *quadrillionfold*! (We computermen are accustomed to dealing in these rarified numbers, but they may boggle you. Have no fear—a quadrillion is a number of such surpassing monstrosity that you must have the knack of figuring to even approach it properly).

"Monty," I gasped, "are you planning to open a firm of accountants at St. Aggie's?"

He laid a finger alongside of his nose. "Not at all, my old darling. I have a thought that perhaps we could build a tiny figuring engine into our Grinder's chest cavity, one that could take programs punched off of a sufficiently powerful computing frame, and that these might enable him to walk about on his own, as natural as you please, and even carry on conversations as though he were a living man. Such a creation would afford us even more freedom and security, as you must be able to see."

"But it will cost the bloody world!" I said.

"Oh, I didn't think we'd *pay* for it," he said. Once again, he laid his finger alongside his nose.

And that is how I came to find myself down our local sewer, in the dead of night, a seventeen-year-old brassjacker, bossing a gang of eight kids with 10 arms, 7 noses, 9 hands and 11 legs between them, working furiously and racing the dawn to fit thousands of precision brass push-rods with lightly balanced joints from the local multifarious amalgamation and amplification switch-house to St. Aggie's utility cellar. It didn't work, of course. Not that night. But at least we didn't break anything and alert the Upper Canadian Computing Authority to our mischief. Three nights later, after much fine-tuning, oiling, and desperate prayer, the panel at St. Aggie's boasted 64 shining brass bits, the very height of modernity and engineering.

Monty and the children all stood before the panel, which had been burnished to a mirror shine by No-Nose Timmy, who'd done finishing work before a careless master had stumbled over him, pushing him face-first into a spinning grinding wheel. In the gaslight, we appeared to be staring at a group of mighty heroes, and when Monty turned to regard us, he had bright tears in his eyes.

"Sisters and brothers, we have done ourselves proud. A new day has dawned for St. Aggie's and for our lives. Thank you. You have done me proud."

We shared out the last of Grinder's brandy, a thimbleful each, even for the smallest kiddees, and drank a toast to the brave and clever children of St. Aggie's and to Montreal Monty, our saviour and the founder of our feast.

Let me tell you some about life at St. Aggie's in that golden age. Whereas before, we'd rise at 7AM for a mean breakfast—prepared by unfavoured children whom Grinder punished by putting them into the kitchen at 4:30 to prepare the meal—followed by a brief "sermon" roared out by Grinder; now we rose at a very civilized 10AM to eat a leisurely breakfast over the daily papers that Grinder had subscribed to. The breakfasts—all the meals and chores—were done on a rotating basis, with exemptions for children whose infirmity made performing some tasks harder than others. Though all worked—even the blind children sorted weevils and stones from the rice and beans by touch.

Whereas Grinder had sent us out to beg every day—excepting Sundays—debasing ourselves and putting our injuries on display for the purposes of sympathy; now we were free to laze around the house all day, or work at our own fancies, painting or reading or just playing like the cherished children of rich families who didn't need to send their young ones to the city to work for the family fortune.

But most of us quickly bored of the life of Riley, and for us, there was plenty to do. The clockwork Grinder was always a distraction, especially after Monty started work on the mechanism that would accept punched-tape instructions from the computing panel.

When we weren't working on Grinder, there was other work. We former apprentices went back to our old masters—men and women who were guilty but glad enough to see us, in the main— and told them that the skilled children of St. Aggie's were looking for piecework as part of our rehabilitation, at a competitive price.

It was hardly a lie, either: as broken tools and mechanisms came in for mending, the boys and girls taught one another their crafts and trade, and it wasn't long before a steady flow of cash came into St. Aggie's, paying for better food, better clothes, and, soon enough, the very best artificial arms, legs, hands and feet, the best glass eyes, the best wigs. When Gertie Shine-Pate was fitted for her first wig and saw herself in the great looking-glass in Grinder's study, she burst into tears and hugged all and sundry, and thereafter, St. Aggie's bought her three more wigs to wear as the mood struck her. She took to styling these wigs with combs and scissors, and before long she was cutting hair for all of us at St. Aggie's. We never looked so good.

That gilded time from the end of my boyhood is like a sweet dream to me now. A sweet, lost dream.

No invention works right the first time around. The inventors' tales you read in the science penny dreadfuls, where some engineer discovers a new principle, puts it into practice, shouts "Eureka" and sets up his own foundry? They're rubbish. Real invention is a process of repeated, crushing failure that leads, very rarely, to a success. If you want to succeed faster, there's nothing for it but to fail faster and better.

The first time Monty rolled a paper tape into a cartridge and inserted it into Grinder, we all held our breaths while he fished around the arse of Grinder's trousers for the toggle that released the tension on the mainspring we wound through a keyhole in his hip. He stepped back as the soft whining of the mechanism emanated from Grinder's body, and then Grinder began, very slowly, to pace the room's length, taking three long—if jerky—steps, turning about, and taking three steps back. Then Grinder lifted a hand as in greeting, and his mouth stretched into a rictus that might have passed for a grin, and then, very carefully, Grinder punched himself in the face so hard that his head came free from his neck and rolled across the floor with a meaty sound (it took our resident taxidermists a full two days to repair the damage) and his body went into a horrible paroxysm like the St. Vitus dance, until it, too fell to the floor.

This was on Monday, and by Wednesday, we had Grinder back on his feet with his head reattached. Again, Monty depressed his toggle, and this time, Grinder made a horrendous clanking sound and pitched forward.

And so it went, day after day, each tiny improvement accompanied by abject failure, and each Sunday we struggled to put the pieces together so that Grinder could pay his respects to the sisters.

Until the day came that the sisters brought round a new child to join our happy clan, and it all began to unravel.

We had been lucky in that Monty's arrival at St. Aggie's coincided with a reformer's movement that had swept Upper Canada, a movement whose figurehead, the Princess Lucy, met with every magistrate, councilman, alderman, and beadle in the colony, the sleeves of her dresses pinned up to the stumps of her shoulders, sternly discussing the plight of the children who worked in the Information Foundries across the colonies. It didn't do no good in the long run, of course, but for the short term, word got round that the authorities would come down very hard on any master whose apprentice lost a piece of himself in the data-mills. So it was some months before St. Aggie's had any new meat arrive upon its doorstep.

The new meat in question was a weepy boy of about 11—the same age I'd been when I arrived—and he was shy his left leg all the way up to the hip. He had a crude steel leg in its place, strapped up with a rough, badly cured cradle that must have hurt like hellfire. He also had a splintery crutch that he used to get around with, the sort of thing that the sisters of St. Aggie's bought in huge lots from unscrupulous tradesmen who cared nothing for the people who'd come to use them.

His name was William Sansousy, a Metis boy who'd come from the wild woods of Lower Canada seeking work in Muddy York, who'd found instead an implacable machine that had torn off his leg and devoured it without a second's remorse. He spoke English with a thick French accent, and slipped into *Joual* when he was overcome with sorrow.

Two sisters brought him to the door on a Friday afternoon. We knew they were coming, they'd sent round a messenger boy with a printed telegram telling Grinder to make room for one more. Monty wanted to turn his Clockwork Grinder loose to walk to the door and greet them, but we all told him he'd be mad to try it: there was so much that could go wrong, and if the sisters worked out what had happened, we could finish up dangling from nooses at King Street Gaol.

Monty relented resentfully, and instead we seated Grinder in his overstuffed chair, with Monty tucked away behind it, ready to converse with the sisters. I hid with him, ready to send Grinder to his feet and to extend his cold, leathery artificial hand to the boy when the sisters turned him over.

And it went smoothly—that day. When the sisters had gone and their car had built up its head of steam and chuffed and clanked away, we emerged from our hiding place. Monty broke into slangy, rapid French, gesticulating and hopping from foot to peg-leg and back again, and William's eyes grew as big as saucers as Monty explained the lay of the land to him. The *clang* when he thumped Grinder in his cast-iron chest made William leap back and he hobbled toward the door.

"Wait, wait!" Monty called, switching to English. "Wait, will you, you idiot? This is the best day of your life, young William! But for us, you might have entered a life of miserable bondage. Instead, you will enjoy all the fruits of liberty, rewarding work, and comradeship. We take care of our own here at St. Aggie's. You'll have top grub, a posh leg and a beautiful crutch that's as smooth as a baby's arse and soft as a lady's bosom. You'll have the freedom to come and go as you please, and you'll have a warm bed to sleep in every night. And best of all, you'll have us, your family here at St. Aggie's. We take care of our own, we do."

The boy looked at us, tears streaming down his face. He made me remember what it had been like, my first day at St. Aggie's, the cold fear coiled round your guts like rope caught in a reciprocating gear. At St. Aggie's we put on brave faces, never cried where no one could see us, but seeing him weep made me remember all the times I'd cried, cried for my lost family who'd sold me into indenture, cried for my mangled body, my ruined life. But living without Grinder's constant terrorizing must have softened my heart. Suddenly it was all I could do to stop myself from giving the poor little mite a one-armed hug.

I didn't hug him, but Monty did, stumping over to him, and the two of them bawled like babbies. Their peg legs knocked together as they embraced like drunken sailors, seeming to cry out every tear we'd any of us ever held in. Before long, we were all crying with them, fat tears streaming down our faces, the sound like something out of the Pit.

When the sobs had stopped, William looked around at us, wiped his nose, and said, "Thank you. I think I am home."

But it wasn't home for him. Poor William. We'd had children like him, in the bad old days, children who just couldn't get back up on their feet (or foot) again. Most of the time, I reckon, they were kids who couldn't make it as apprentices, neither, kids who'd spent their working lives full of such awful misery that they were *bound* to fall into a machine. And being sundered from their limbs didn't improve their outlook.

We tried everything we could think of to cheer William up. He'd worked for a watch-smith, and he had a pretty good hand at disassembling and cleaning mechanisms. His stump ached him like fire, even after he'd been fitted with a better apparatus by St. Aggie's best leg-maker, and it was only when he was working with his little tweezers and brushes that he lost the grimace that twisted up his face so. Monty had him strip and clean every clockwork in the house, even the ones that were working perfectly—even the delicate works we'd carefully knocked together for the clockwork Grinder. But it wasn't enough.

In the bad old days, Grinder would have beaten the boy and sent him out to beg in the worst parts of town, hoping that he'd be run down by a cart or killed by one of the blunderbuss gangs that marauded there. When the law brought home the boy's body, old Grinder would weep crocodile tears and tug his hair at the bloody evil that men did, and then he'd go back to his rooms and play some music and drink some brandy and sleep the sleep of the unjust.

We couldn't do the same, and so we tried to bring up William's spirits instead, and when he'd had enough of it, he lit out on his own. The first we knew of it was when he didn't turn up for breakfast. This wasn't unheard of—any of the free children of St. Aggie's was able to rise and wake whenever he chose, but William had been a regular at breakfast every day. I made my way upstairs to the dormer room where the boys slept to look for him and found his bed empty, his coat and his peg-leg and crutch gone.

"He's gone," Monty said, "Long gone." He sighed and looked out the window. "Must be trying to get back to the Gatineaux." He shook his head.

"Do you think he'll make it?" I said, knowing the answer, but hoping that Monty would lie to me.

"Not a chance," Monty said. "Not him. He'll either be beaten, arrested or worse by sundown. That lad hasn't any self-preservation instincts."

At this, the dining room fell silent and all eyes turned on Monty and I saw in a flash what a terrible burden we all put on him: saviour, father, chieftain. He twisted his face into a halfway convincing smile.

"Oh, maybe not. He might just be hiding out down the road. Tell you what, eat up and we'll go searching for him."

I never saw a load of plates cleared faster. It was bare minutes before we were formed up in the parlour, divided into groups, and sent out into Muddy York to find William Sansousy. We turned that bad old city upside-down, asking nosy questions and sticking our heads in where they didn't belong, but Monty had been doubly right the first time around.

The police found William Sansousy's body in a marshy bit of land off the Leslie Street Spit. His pockets had been slit, his pathetic paper sack of belongings torn and the clothes scattered and his fine hand-turned leg was gone. He had been dead for hours.

The Detective Inspector who presented himself that afternoon at St. Aggie's was trailed by a team of technicians who had a wire sound-recorder and a portable logic engine for in-putting the data of his investigation. He seemed very proud of his machine, even though it came with three convicts from the King Street Gaol in shackles and leg-irons who worked tirelessly to keep the springs wound, toiling in a lather of sweat and heaving breath, heat boiling off their shaved heads in shimmering waves.

He showed up just as the clock in the parlour chimed eight times, a bear chasing a bird around on a track as it sang the hour. We peered out the windows in the upper floors, saw the inspector, and understood just why Monty had been so morose all afternoon.

But Monty did us proud. He went to the door with his familiar swagger, and swung it wide, extending his hand to the Inspector.

"Montague Goldfarb, officer, at your service. Our patron has stepped away, but please, do come in."

The Inspector gravely shook the proffered hand, his huge, gloved mitt swallowing Monty's boyish hand. It was easy to forget that he was just a child, but the looming presence of the giant Inspector reminded us all.

"Master Goldfarb," the Inspector said, taking his hat off, and peering through his smoked monocle at the children in the parlour, all of us sat with hands folded like we were in a pantomime about the best-behaved, most crippled, most terrified, least threatening children in all the colonies. "I am sorry to hear that Mr. Grindersworth is not at home to the constabulary. Have you any notion as to what temporal juncture we might expect him?" If I hadn't been concentrating on not peeing myself with terror, the inspector's pompous speech might have set me to laughing.

Monty didn't bat an eye. "Mr. Grindersworth was called away to see his brother in Sault Sainte Marie, and we expect him tomorrow. I'm his designated lieutenant, though. Perhaps I might help you?"

The inspector stroked his forked beard and gave us all another long look. "Tomorrow, hey? Well, I don't suppose that justice should wait that long. Master Goldfarb, I have grim intelligence for you, as regards one of your young compatriots, a Master—" He consulted a punched card that was held in a hopper on his clanking logic engine. "William Sansousy. He lies even now upon a slab in the city morgue. Someone of authority from this institution is required to confirm the preliminary identification. You will do, I suppose. Though your patron will have to present himself post-haste in order to sign the several official documents that necessarily accompany an event of such gravity."

We'd known as soon as the Inspector turned up on St. Aggie's door that it meant that William was dead. If he was merely in trouble, it would have been a constable, dragging him by the ear. We half-children of St. Aggie's only rated a full inspector when we were topped by some evil bastard in this evil town. But hearing the Inspector say the words, puffing them through his drooping moustache, that made it real. None of us had ever cried when St. Aggie's children were taken by the streets—at least, not where the others could see it. But this time round, without Grinder to shoot us filthy daggers if we made a peep while the law was about, it opened the floodgates. Boys and girls, young and old, we cried for poor little William. He'd come to the best of all possible St. Aggie's, but it hadn't been good enough for him. He'd wanted to go back to the parents who'd sold him into service, wanted a return to his Mam's lap and bosom. Who among us didn't want that, in his secret heart?

Monty's tears were silent and they rolled down his cheeks as he shrugged into his coat and hat and let the Inspector—who

146

was clearly embarrassed by the display—lead him out the door.

When Monty came home, he arrived at a house full of children who were ready to go mad. We'd cried ourselves hoarse, then sat about the parlour, not knowing what to do. If there had been any of old Grinder's booze still in the house, we'd have drunk it.

"What's the plan, then?" he said, coming through the door. "We've got one night until that bastard comes back. If he doesn't find Grinder, he'll go to the sisters, and it'll come down around our ears. What's more, he knows Grinder, personal, from other dead ones in years gone by, and I don't think he'll be fooled by our machine, no matter how good it goes."

"What's the plan?" I said, mouth hanging open. "Monty, the plan is that we're all going to gaol and you and I and everyone else who helped cover up the killing of Grinder will dance at rope's end!"

He gave me a considering look. "Sian, that is absolutely the worst plan I have ever heard." And then he grinned at us the way he did, and we all knew that, somehow, it would all be all right.

"Constable, come quick, he's going to kill himself!"

I practised the line for the fiftieth time, willing my eyes to go wider, my voice to carry more alarm. Behind me, Monty scowled at my reflection in the mirror in Grinder's personal toilet, where I'd been holed up for hours.

"Verily, the stage lost a great player when that machine mangled you, Sian. You are perfect. Now, get moving before I tear your remaining arm off and beat you with it. Go!"

Phase one of the plan was easy enough: we'd smuggle our Grinder up onto the latticework of steel and scaffold where they were building the mighty Prince Edward Viaduct, at the end of Bloor Street. Monty had punched his program already: he'd pace back and forth, tugging his hair, shaking his head like a maddened man, and then, abruptly, he'd turn and fling himself bodily off the platform, plunging 130 feet into the Don River, where he would simply disintegrate into a million cogs, gears, springs and struts, which would sink to the riverbed and begin to rust away. The coppers would recover his clothes, and those, combined with the eyewitness testimony of the constable I was responsible for bringing to the bridge, would establish in everyone's mind exactly what had happened and how: Grinder was so distraught at one more death from among his charges that he had popped his own clogs in grief. We were all of us standing ready to testify as to how poor William was Grinder's little favourite, a boy he loved like a son, and so forth. Who would suspect a bunch of helpless cripples, anyway?

That was the theory, at least. But now I was actually stood by the bridge, watching six half-children wrestle the automaton into place, striving for silence so as not to alert the guards who were charged with defending the structure they were already calling "The Suicide's Magnet," and I couldn't believe that it would possibly work.

Five of the children scampered away, climbing back down the scaffolds, slipping and sliding and nearly dying more times than I could count, so that my heart was thundering in my chest so hard I thought I might die upon the spot. Then they were safely away, climbing back up the ravine's walls in the mud and snow, almost invisible in the dusky dawn light. Monty waved an arm at me, and I knew it was my cue, and that I should be off to rouse the constabulary, but I found myself rooted to the spot.

In that moment, every doubt and fear and misery I'd ever harboured crowded back in on me. The misery of being abandoned by my family, the sorrow and loneliness I'd felt among the prentice-lads, the humiliation of Grinder's savage beatings and harangues. The shame of my injury and every time I'd grovelled before a drunk or a pitying lady with my stump on display for pennies to fetch home to Grinder. What was I doing? There was no way I could possibly pull this off. I wasn't enough of a man— nor enough of a boy.

But then I thought of all those moments since the coming of Monty Goldfarb, the millionfold triumphs of ingenuity and hard work, the computing power I'd stolen out from under the nose of the calculators who had treated me as a mere work-ox before my injury. I thought of the cash we'd brought in, the children who'd smiled and sung and danced on the worn floors of St. Aggie's, and—

And I ran to the policeman, who was warming himself by doing a curious hopping dance in place, hands in his armpits. "Constable!" I piped, all sham terror that no one would have known for a sham, "Constable! Come quick, he's going to kill himself!"

The sister who came to sit up with us mourning kiddies that night was called Sister Mary Immaculata, and she was kindly, if a bit dim. I remembered her from my stay in the hospital after my maiming: a slightly vacant prune-faced woman in a wimple who'd bathed my wounds gently and given me solemn hugs when I woke screaming in the middle of the night.

She was positive that the children of St. Aggie's were inconsolable over the suicide of our beloved patron, Zophar Grindersworth, and she doled out those same solemn cuddles to anyone foolish enough to stray near her. That none of us shed a tear was lost upon her, though she did note with approval how smoothly the operation of St. Aggie's continued without Grinder's oversight.

The next afternoon, Sister Mary Immaculata circulated among us, offering reassurance that a new master would be found for St. Aggie's. None of us were much comforted by this: we knew the kind of man who was likely to fill such a plum vacancy.

"If only there was some way we could go on running this place on our own," I moaned under my breath, trying to concentrate on repairing the pressure gauge on a pneumatic evacuator that we'd taken in for mending.

Monty shot me a look. He had taken the Sister's coming very hard. "I don't think I have it in me to kill the next one, too. Anyway, they're bound to notice if we keep on assassinating our guardians."

I snickered despite myself. Then my gloomy pall descended again. It had all been so good, how could we possibly return to the old way? But there was no way the sisters would let a bunch of crippled children govern themselves.

"What a waste," I said. "What a waste of all this potential."

"At least I'll be shut of it in two years," Monty said. "How long have you got till your eighteenth?"

My brow furrowed. I looked out the grimy workshop window at the iron grey February sky. "It's February tenth today?"

"Eleventh," he said.

I laughed, an ugly sound. "Why, Monty, my friend, today is my eighteenth birthday. I believe I have survived St. Aggie's to graduate to bigger and better things. I have attained my majority, old son."

He held a hand out and shook my hook with it, solemnly. "Happy birthday and congratulations, then, Sian. May the world treat you with all the care you deserve."

I stood, the scrape of my chair very loud and sudden. I realized I had no idea what I would do next. I had managed to completely forget that my graduation from St. Aggie's was looming, that I would be a free man. In my mind, I'd imagined myself dwelling at St. Aggie's forever.

Forever.

"You look like you just got hit in the head with a shovel," Monty said. "What on earth is going through that mind of yours?"

I didn't answer. I was already on my way to find Sister Immaculata. I found her in the kitchen, helping legless Dora make the toast for tea over the fire's grate.

"Sister," I said, "a word please?"

As she turned and followed me into the pantry off the kitchen, some of that fear I'd felt on the bridge bubbled up in me. I tamped it back down again firmly, like a piston compressing some superheated gas.

She was really just as I remembered her, and she had remembered me, too—she remembered all of us, the children she'd held in the night and then consigned to this Hell upon Earth, all unknowing.

"Sister Mary Immaculata, I attained my eighteenth birthday today."

She opened her mouth to congratulate me, but I held up my stump.

"I turned eighteen today, sister. I am a man, I have attained my majority. I am at liberty, and must seek my fortune in the world. I have a proposal for you, accordingly." I put everything I had into this, every dram of confidence and maturity that I'd learned since we inmates had taken over the asylum. "I was Mr. Grindersworth's lieutenant and assistant in every matter relating to the daily operation of this place. Many's the day I did every bit of work that there was to do, whilst Mr. Grindersworth attended to family matters. I know every inch of this place, ever soul in it, and I have had the benefit of the excellent training and education that there is to have here.

"I had always thought to seek my fortune in the world as a mechanic of some kind, if any shop would have a half-made thing like me, but seeing as you find yourself at loose ends in the superintendent department, I thought I might perhaps put my plans 'on hold' for the time being, until such time as a full search could be conducted."

"Sian," she said, her face wrinkling into a gap-toothed smile. "Are you proposing that *you* might run St. Agatha's?"

It took everything I could not to wilt under the pity and amusement in that smile. "I am, sister. I am. I have all but run it for months now, and have every confidence in my capacity to go on doing so for so long as need be." I kept my gaze and my voice even. "I believe that the noble mission of St. Aggie's is a truly attainable one: that it can rehabilitate such damaged things as we and prepare us for the wider world."

She shook her head. "Sian," she said, softly, "Sian. I wish it could be. But there's no hope that such an appointment would be approved by the Board of Governors."

I nodded. "Yes, I thought so. But do the Governors need to approve a *temporary* appointment? A stopgap, until a suitable person can be found?"

Her smile changed, got wider. "You have certainly come into your own shrewdness here, haven't you?"

"I was taught well," I said, and smiled back.

The temporary has a way of becoming permanent. That was my bolt of inspiration, my galvanic realization. Once the sisters had something that worked, that did not call attention to itself, that took in crippled children and released whole persons some years later, they didn't need to muck about with it. As the mechanics say, "If it isn't broken, it doesn't want fixing."

I'm no mechanic, not anymore. The daily running of St. Aggie's occupied a larger and larger slice of my time, until I found that I knew more about tending to a child's fever or soothing away a nightmare than I did about hijacking the vast computers to do our bidding.

But that's no matter, as we have any number of apprentice computermen and computerwomen turning up on our doorsteps. So long as the machineries of industry grind on, the supply will be inexhaustible.

Monty visits me from time to time, mostly to scout for talent. His shop, Goldfarb and Associates, has a roaring trade in computational novelties and service, and if anyone is bothered by the appearance of a factory filled with the halt, the lame, the blind and the crippled, they are thankfully outnumbered by those who are delighted by the quality of the work and the good value in his schedule of pricing.

But it was indeed a golden time, that time when I was but a boy at St. Aggie's among the boys and girls, a cog in a machine that Monty built of us, part of a great uplifting, a transformation from a hell to something like a heaven. That I am sentenced to serve in this heaven I helped to make is no great burden, I suppose.

Still, I do yearn to screw a jeweller's loupe into my eye, pick up a fine tool and bend the sodium lamp to shine upon some cunning mechanism that wants fixing. For machines may be balky and they may destroy us with their terrible appetite for oil, blood and flesh, but they behave according to fixed rules and can be understood by anyone with the cunning to look upon them and winkle out their secrets. Children are ever so much more complicated.

Though I believe I may be learning a little about them, too.

selected haiku

GEORGE SWEDE

long past
its perihelion
this life
overgrown
with dreams

❖

glued
by gravity to
4.54 billion years

❖

coal-dark tombstone—
its eight numbers erased
by what they measured

pure
RIO YOUERS

Imagine a shadow, but vague, only slightly darker than the surface onto which it is cast. The light is obscured. The shadow suffers. It is a cataract.

You can't see me. I am less than a shadow.
I am nothing.
But I am coming.

The *cariocas* paid him no attention.

Rio de Janeiro, Brazil. October 18th 2064.

Desperation had brought him here, and the final strand of what could be called animal instinct. These streets, as crowded as a child's imagination, once filled with colour and vibrancy, but now made grey by clouds of fear; thunderhead of disease. The locals—the *cariocas*—pressed to get out of the rain, heads down, bodies wet. They did not look at him. They did not question his obvious weakness or the mask he wore. The storm blistered along *Delfim Moreira*. The palm trees twisted, fronds swaying. He was pushed aside and knocked to the floor. Again and again. The rain rattled off his mask. The *cariocas* paid him no attention. He picked himself up and followed the meager thread of instinct.

How long had he been running?

"Where are you, Avô Vinícius?"

Every minute was fear. Every second.

Fernando gazed along Ipanema Beach, a deserted belt of cocoa sand, bullied by the relentless angst of the Atlantic. To the west, *Morro Dois Irmãos* loomed through bellies of cloud. Its split peaks made it resemble a giant, infected tooth. He felt a pull in that direction. The unguarded aspect of his soul registered hope. It was like oxygen. His pulse quickened and he staggered on.

He was close.

His mask was butterfly-shaped.

It was stained glass, as fragile as his life. The wings covered his eyes and cheeks. He viewed the world through tinted shards. The left eye was green. The colour of everything he had known and still hoped for. The colour of beginnings. The right eye was smoky-brown. The colour of destruction.

The mask covered his stigma. The word **INFECÇÃO** (infection) tattooed the left side of his face. His number, **339099**, branded the right. A signature of ignominy. All of the infected were marked in this way, and would be until they faded from existence. They were no longer strong. They had been gathered like cattle and quarantined . . . broken down and weakened over several generations . . . reduced to little more than substance. His kind was crushed and dying. Flies in the cold.

If the mask were to slip, or break, if his sickness were to be unveiled, he would be captured within moments. The mask was his saviour, as important to him as the blood running through his body. Its colours represented the events of his species, from inception to decay. Its shape represented metamorphosis; flight; beautiful hope.

Cure.

Avô Vinícius.

"Close," he whispered.

A scathing gust slammed him as he crossed *Rua João Lira*. A dramatic pirouette, jacket billowing. He was thrown against the side of a parked truck and fell to his knees, one hand instinctively protecting the mask. The locals hurried past him—almost stepping over him in their haste. He longed for wings to lift him above the storm.

Fernando got to his feet. Warm rain dripped from his hair. He continued across the street, buffeted by the storm. Sustained thunder damaged the sky. The creature kept his head down. His pale eyes flashed behind the mask.

They even chased him in dreams.

The only vivid things were his tattoos. He was diluted . . . watery.

His body was a wan rack of bone and sinew. His hair was dead ragweed.

Heart like cirrus cloud, scattered across the sky of his body.

All he could feel was the weak beat of his instinct.

Lightning saturated the afternoon gloom, turning all things to ghosts. The sidewalk shimmered and he saw, in one brilliant frame of time, his reflection: a hunkered thing, as dark as any bad dream. He forced himself to stand straight, and in so doing saw the men walking toward him. His failing instinct, which had brought him this far, warned him that they were not *cariocas*. They were impervious to the storm. Bound by purpose.

They were *a Polícia do Vírus* (the Virus Police), enlisted by the Brazilian government to eradicate infection beyond the quarantines' barricades. Officially, they were supposed to subdue carriers and return them to the nearest quarantine city, but they were more inclined to blood and torture. They were known throughout South America as Psycho Cowboys.

Fernando wanted to surrender—fall at their feet and let them tie him up and bleed him dry (infamous cruelty; they laughed while they tortured; they donned multicoloured garments and smeared their faces with wild paints). He was too weak to run, but salvation was within reach. He would not give up. He would not surrender.

He cut across the empty parking lot of what had once been a glimmering beachfront hotel, but was now a concrete ghost. Moving as swiftly as he was able, he climbed through one of the shattered windows and into a dark lobby. The walls were smeared with neglect. The front desk had been stripped for firewood. Vagrants huddled amongst the cockroaches and trash.

He turned, his butterfly mask sparkling, and saw that the Psycho Cowboys were following. They came fast, flowing through the rain. He staggered across the lobby, into a seemingly endless corridor. Doors hung in tatters and mosaics rippled on the walls, depicting the dead colour of the city: the Rio of yesteryear. His heart made rain and thunder and he pressed forward. He took a stairway, swollen steps that he struggled to ascend, both hands clinging to the rail.

He could hear them in the lobby: commotion, raised voices, cries of pain as they checked the vagrants for tattoos. They knew they were close; they could feel him, too.

Fernando burst into the first floor corridor and reeled toward the elevators. His mind was a battlefield. Everything was green or brown. His single thought was to keep moving.

The Psycho Cowboys were relentless. They even chased him in dreams, where his imagination gave them clown faces and legs like rainbows. In reality they were grave, almost normal, until they caught you . . . then the grey suits came off and their true colours were revealed.

He stumbled . . . picked himself up. The elevators, directly ahead, yawned open. He heard voices on the stairway and scrambled toward one of the empty shafts, throwing himself inside.

Falling . . . spinning. He reached out and grasped the thick cable, the skin ripping from his palm as he broke his fall and halted his descent. The cable whipped and bounced. The counterweight struck a single dull chord and then everything was silent.

He curled his legs around the cable, placed one hand on the mask to keep it from slipping, and hung upside down. He held his breath and waited, his heart cannonading, his wet jacket falling around his shoulders like wings.

He imagined them with rainbow legs.

Voices in the corridor above. Footsteps. Fernando closed his eyes and willed his frail body to become absorbed by the darkness. He heard them approach, bullish steps and coarse breathing. They carried guns and batons, but in his mind they wielded blunt torture implements and walked on rainbow legs. He was sure they would hear his heartbeat. The cable creaked and his jacket dripped water to the floor below.

Long moments passed. He did not move. He barely breathed. The Cowboys thumped and grunted. Six or seven of them, kicking open doors, cursing. He could feel their impatience vibrate through the walls of the shaft.

His hand covered the mask. He could feel the cable biting into the tender flesh at the backs of his knees.

"Coming for you." The voice was keen and cold and too close. He imagined a white face and a deformed, painted smile. "We'll find you."

Less than a shadow.

The light bleeding through the elevator doors flickered.

"Coming . . ."

He sensed the Psycho Cowboy peering into the shaft, eyes gleaming, his clown-grin impossibly long.

You can't see me.

His heart sent small vibrations through the cable. He could hear the Cowboy sucking in greedy breaths. The seconds passed too slowly, and he became convinced that he had been seen—would be caught, tortured and killed—and a part of him welcomed the end of it all. No more running. Nothing, indeed. A single tear dripped from his eye and ran across the inside of the mask, changing colour, from green to brown, like a leaf. A strident bell of regret sounded in his mind, and for a moment she was there, suspended in the darkness ahead of him, shimmering. *They'll find you, Fernando. They'll kill you.* He came close to reaching out for her, revealing his pale hand, or his mask. *Stay with me. I know how to love you.*

He opened his mouth to respond. Even his words were shadows: *But we're dying.* More tears splashed against the inside of the mask.

She disappeared. His heart found hectic life and pounded furious fists against his chest. The cable creaked. He revolved, slowly, like a voiceless chime.

The light flickered again and he heard the Cowboy retreat, bouncing on his rainbow legs. Relief swarmed Fernando's ailing body, but he did not move. The Psycho Cowboys continued their search—tearing through all floors, all rooms—for a loud, interminable passage of time. Fernando clutched the cable and waited. His body ached. His shadow/soul withered. When he was sure that the Psycho Cowboys were gone, he adjusted his position. The cable rippled and the counterweight played several sad notes. He waited a little longer before emerging from the shaft. He crawled, and then collapsed. Painful breaths sagged from his lungs. He lay in the corridor, unnoticed by the world, like a charred piece of paper; broken furniture; a curled, damp strip of carpet.

Rain fell through the shattered windows.

The reason you look away.

It was a cold pain, as if a January wind were blowing through all the joints and tendons of his body. He staggered into the lobby and looked at the shapes of the vagrants huddled against the walls. They were rags. Breathing, bleeding rags. Specimens of a ruined city. The reason you look away. Fernando moved toward a lowly shape, embraced by shadow: a man, swaddled in mouldering newspaper, whose beard made the top half of his face appear too thin. Veins ticked beneath the membranous skin of his eyelids. His temples could have been hollowed out with spoons.

Fernando crouched next to the man. He removed his mask. The butterfly appeared, for a moment, to be suspended in the dimness, captured in flight. The vagrant opened his eyes: preternatural instinct; the core of survival. He saw the tattoo—**INFECÇÃO**—and the minutia of his face responded: the dry skin of his upper lip stretching and cracking; his pupils contracting; the creases around his eyes thinning; the hairs in his nostrils quivering. He managed only a fraction of his final breath before Fernando's hand was pressed to his mouth, forcing his head back, exposing the vulnerable meat of his throat. A discerning eye may have detected a hint of resignation in the half-second before Fernando went for his jugular. A softening in the pupil, perhaps, or the fine crease appearing at the bridge of his nose. Then he was dying. Blood sprayed into Fernando's mouth. The vagrant's body was rigid for slow seconds, and then slumped all at once, as if some central support cable had snapped. His left leg twitched. His shoe came off and was buried in a drift of trash.

A pall of nausea draped over Fernando. He pressed his fist to his mouth to keep from vomiting. The lobby wavered and he fell across the dead vagrant like a lover. His kind had developed an intolerance for human blood. It was a thick, sickening taste, but he needed the nourishment. His body was failing. He would die if he didn't find Avô Vinícius soon.

The mask fluttered to his face. The world became brown and green, but his mouth was splashed with red.

O Cristo Redentor.

He emerged from the hotel to find that the rain had stopped, but that the wind persisted. Thick droplets were blown from palm fronds and window ledges, pattering off his shoulders with heavy sounds. Sacks of cloud dragged across the sky.

He sensed the sunset and looked west, toward *Morro Dois Irmãos*. Lights glinted in the surrounding hillsides, glimpsed through stained cloud. His sick heart dared to hope . . . to believe. He was, after all, so close.

No sign of the Psycho Cowboys. He looked in all directions. Fernando lowered his head and moved on, ignoring the car horns, the jostling *cariocas*, and the occasional bursts of samba music heard in crowded apartments. His mind echoed with prayers.

Genuflection: he dropped to one knee at the intersection of *Rua Mário Ribeiro* and felt all the energy in his body gather between his shoulder blades and then erupt, breaking through his skin, hovering in the air above him like wings. He was lifted. Nothing mattered. There was no pain. His invisible wings rippled.

Seen through a diamond-shaped rift in the clouds, Christ the Redeemer looked down on him. The magnificent statue shimmered. Nothing of the mountain could be seen—only the pale, cruciform image, hanging in the heavens. Fernando threw out his arms in imitation, supplication, and exaltation. His imaginary wings made a sound like music.

"Save me," he whispered. His mask glittered.

The statue hovered in the sky.

The *cariocas* paid him no attention.

To feel the final beats of your heart . . . and then to have hope, that wonderful, sweeping arc of hope, lifting everything inside you. The world becomes infinitesimal. You move with the stars. An endless, shining entity.

But I am still a shadow. That is the irony. I am still nothing.

You can't see me.

Yet.

Translation taken from the *Journal of Vinícius Araújo Valentim*.

(Date unknown.)

I don't know how long I have been here. There is a great void in my mind that no thought can fill, although I remember the crash clearly. One moment the world was bright. The sky was an undying shade of blue with the beautiful greens of Amazonia stretched below us. I remember looking down on a flickering formation of sun parakeets, and how they seemed to map our shadow on the trees. And then I heard an ominous clunking sound from the engine and all at once the cockpit was filled with smoke. This was terrifying enough, yet I could not accept that we were going down. It seemed too surreal. The idea that I was going to die within the next few moments refused to compute. That was when my pilot started to scream. It was an awful sound.

My life did not flash before my eyes. I thought, absurdly, about my camera—such an expensive and delicate piece of equipment that would be destroyed in the crash. I thought about the pictures on the film that would never be seen: a sunset blistering through the branches of a kapok tree; a Mirity-tapuya child poised with a fishing spear; a multicoloured waterfall arcing into the Rio Negro. I thought about my studio in São Paulo, and what would happen to my work. My final moments felt terribly lonely.

We broke through the canopy and I heard the aircraft coming apart. Searing heat pushed me from behind and I felt a moment of euphoria (I think, now, that it was acceptance). There was nothing else. No thought or feeling. Not even blackness.

I awoke here, in this cave . . . days, months, perhaps even years later. My eyes opened to unnerving darkness. I could not move; my muscles were like wet straw. I could only lie in that void listening to the sounds of the deep earth. But I soon came to realize that there was something else in there with me . . . that I was not alone.

Scratching and shuffling. The sound was all around me.

I didn't have the strength to scream.

I wish I could explain the fear, but there are no words. I am a professional photographer; I would have more success pointing my camera at a cancer cell or a dying child—some terrible thing that would turn your heart into a miserable weight and drag you to your knees. I became certain in those first dreadful hours that I had died in the crash and been thrown into hell. The scratching sounds grew louder. I could hear inhuman chattering and flapping. At one point something moist and fleshy dragged across my prone body. My throat contracted. I imagined my eyes bulging in the darkness.

I cannot explain the fear.

My pounding heart assured me that I was not dead. Feeling returned to my body, albeit gradually. A pain in my ribs. My spine sending blunt signals to my limbs. I could feel the rock beneath me. I was naked. I tried to shut out the scratching and flapping sounds and throw all my energy into moving my body. I had no concept of time. It was eternity, measured only in beats of pain. I am sure I passed out several times, but eventually the fingers on my right hand were twitching, and then flexing. I could feel a shift in the air pattern as something large moved beside me. Its breath was warm and bitter, but I closed my eyes and ignored it—swam through waves of consciousness and agony—and then I moved my legs. I could bend my knees and wriggle my toes. I arched my back and tried to roll onto my side, but it was too much, too soon. The pain was immense and I cried out—the first sound I had made. This disturbed the creatures with which I shared the darkness. There was a flurry of movement and agitated whooping sounds. I could hear something to my right. My eyes, slowly adjusting, sensed a pale shape clambering along the cave wall.

Gasping breaths. The air tasted of alkaline and salt. I cried and prayed. I tried to move my left arm but couldn't. More darkness, more time passing. I touched my face, hoping to judge from the length of my beard how long I had been there.

My left arm was missing, severed at the shoulder.

I thought about my camera, burned and twisted out of shape, with the film (so many wonderful pictures) melted to the spool. I was my camera: a ruined thing in a lost place. I blinked dreams that would never be fulfilled.

Time drifted. My panic subdued, allowing clearer thought. The creatures had no intention of harming me, or they would have already. Were they waiting for me to die? Did they only feed on dead flesh? Were they keeping me alive?

I was about to find out. I lifted my body to a sitting position. My head rolled in loose circles. Blood thumped in my temples and I had to clutch the rock to keep from falling backward. The creatures clicked and whooped, scratching across the roof of the cave. My head attained some semblance of balance and I pushed myself to my feet. Again, it was too much; I crumpled to the floor. In the next seconds I became aware of movement beside me. My terrified eyes glimpsed something huge and monstrous. Stale air rippled across my naked body.

"What are you?" I asked. A helpless, desperate question. I felt a spiny hand slide between my shoulder blades and lift me, cradle me. Warm fluid splashed onto my mouth and my weak body responded; I drank greedily. The taste was hell: flesh and fat and acid. It was gritty and sour. I drank, and when it was all gone, I opened my mouth for more.

It cradled me. It mothered me.

Before long I was able to gauge time based on the creatures' habits, and how often I was fed. In the course of one day they would sleep (incredible stillness; the only sound was the earth groaning), then they would wake, and as one would leave the cave, presumably to hunt the wilds of the Amazon. They powered their wings and left in a fury of sound and motion. It was like standing at the rim of a cyclone. They returned with equal enthusiasm, taking their perches, chattering and clicking. I was fed soon after, like a baby bird. I opened my mouth, eyes bulging.

I got stronger. I could stand; walk; climb. I touched the creatures that swooped to feed me. My one hand determined moist skin and tight muscle; ridges of bone; spines and horns. I caressed claws and wings.

My eyes adjusted to the dark, not completely, but enough to see them—their hairless bodies, vaguely human, suspended from the roof of the cave with wings curled around their bodies like petals. Shivering, pink things.

I drank . . . and drank.

Stronger.

I explored the cave and found my clothes—torn and burned—and my pack. Vestiges of a previous life. My notes were inside: *Expedition into Amazonia: Words and Pictures by Vinícius Araújo Valentim.* I ripped out the pages, tore them to pieces.

It would seem I have a better story to tell.

I am writing this in a chink of daylight. The creatures are sleeping. I have no idea how long I have been here, but my beard is long and my body is growing stronger. I am almost ready to leave this dark place.

I can see the brilliant green of the jungle canopy and many jewels of blue sky.

The world is waiting.

339099377822.

There were isolated cases all over the world, but South America was decimated. The military controlled the borders, and they weren't trained to ask questions. Industry failed. Tourism was non-existent. Chaos curled its hand around the continent and squeezed hard. Millions died. The cities—explosions of life, at one time—stumbled to their knees like tired fighters.

Love and prayer . . . all that remained.

Psychoglobunaria (PGB). The first recorded case was in the municipality of Pauini in 2013. A young farmer named João Moraes claimed to have been attacked by a man who ". . . *veio das árvores*" (came from the trees). Whilst recovering in the clinic from numerous bite marks, Moraes attacked two nurses, and from there the disease spread. Tests concluded that the PGB virus was a rogue segment of genetic code that caused hitherto unseen levels of adaptive parasitic existence. Transmitted through bodily fluids (most often from being bitten by a carrier), the virus cloned central nervous system signalling molecules, affording it similar intelligence to the host and an awareness of its environment.

Further tests showed that, once adapted, the intelligent PGB virus produced a protein that altered haemoglobin and induced a violent appetite in the host for blood. The infected were relentless. The disease advanced mercilessly. Those who were not killed became carriers, and so it continued: tens of thousands dead or infected within the first months. The governments of South America responded, first with the culling and execution of the infected, and then—after global outcry—with the introduction of quarantine cities. The infected were branded and kept from the outside world. In Brazil, *a Polícia do Vírus* were established to seek out rogue carriers.

The strain weakened over succeeding generations. Many symptoms diminished, but one remained strong: the virus altered signalling molecules in the brain, producing a heightened awareness of blood; not only were the infected able to perceive the blood type of others, they were also able to recognize the unique signature of that blood, allowing them to identify another individual at a cellular level. This ability—stronger in women and children—shared similarities with extrasensory perception.

"I know what you're thinking."

"Yes. Your instinct has always been strong."

"Stay with me."

His heart ached. He closed his eyes so that he didn't have to look into her eyes. But he knew that she could look into his mind—using the coil of power that had remained so vibrant. She could look into his mind and see his purpose. And his fear.

Her name was Giovanna Almeida, and she was everything in his heart. You could rip it from his chest and cut it in half, and she would be there. She poured through his veins and brought every nerve ending to life. She was *him*.

He opened his eyes and looked at her. She was crying. Every tear was like a star—some burning, brilliant memory he could never grasp.

"Don't do this."

He wiped away her tears; he didn't want to look at them.

The quarantine was known as *a Cidade do Inferno* (the City of Hell). Formerly the Brasilia satellite city of Taguatinga, it was evacuated at the height of the pandemic, barricaded, and the infected were moved in. They lived in apartments and houses, and were given basic liberties, including running water and electricity. They had jobs and money. They had a small hospital, a library, even a school. Freedom was not a liberty, however. Much like Brazil's borders, the quarantine was policed by the military. The government ordered the infected to stay within the walls, and warned that anybody caught trying to escape would be executed on sight.

Scientists worked to find a cure, while many believed that the best way to eradicate the disease was to eliminate the problem. There were multiple attempts to destroy the quarantine by various terrorist factions. It had been bombed eleven times. Low-flying aircraft had emptied vats of sulfuric acid onto the city. It had been set ablaze. The water supply had been contaminated. Several hundred barrels of synthetic blood had been poisoned. Thousands had been killed over the years. The quarantine protected the outside world from the infected, but it couldn't protect the infected from the outside world.

Fernando moved into her open body and she closed around him like a shell. They made love with terrific passion, their minds conjoined, flaring with each other's desire. Fernando often said that her love was life *within* life; the point where connection became duplicate. She threw her arms around his mind and her legs around his soul. They were singular and beautiful. Their tattoo was one long number.

"Don't leave me."

Sunset stretched pink arms through the open windows. Children's laughter lifted the failing light. Fernando rolled Giovanna into his embrace and they stood looking out at the blackened city. Corroded buildings. No grass or trees. The broken walls of what had once been their church, bombed long ago, with the pale beam of a crucifix jutting from the rubble. They prayed, now, in their homes, to statuettes of the saviour, his body tattooed with numbers. Diseased Jesus. It was all they had. Fernando kissed Giovanna's temple and felt the quick flutter of life on his lips. The children played and laughed outside. New numbers. They—like Fernando and Giovanna—had been born into this. They wouldn't live to be twenty years old.

"I have to go," Fernando said. "I have to find Avô Vinícius."

They had been strong once. At the beginning, when Fernando's grandfather had been a young man, their numbers were vast. They were the Great Flood; the Plague of Locusts. But oppression and incarceration had diminished them, and now, only four generations old, they were on the threshold of extinction. No strength to fight. No substance to evolve. *A Cidade do Inferno* used to be a teeming, vibrant metropolis: several families to a single apartment; the streets swollen with people lining up to get their ration of synthetic blood; bars and clubs packed with dancers, strippers, and musicians; a carnival every year—just like the world beyond the quarantine—with colourful floats and celebrations. There had been *life*. But now Fernando could see the deserted streets and the ghostly apartment buildings. So many empty rooms. They were always considered third-class citizens—no more important than the bands of stray dogs nosing through the streets of every South American town. They were reviled, and had been left to die.

Avô Vinícius represented hope, and perhaps their last chance at survival. He was the first of their kind, the purest strain, and grandfather to them all. His blood was the elixir of life.

"He could be anywhere," Giovanna said. "Anywhere in the world. He might even be dead."

"He's not dead," Fernando said. "I can feel him. You can, too."

Tears moved down her face. Her number—**377822**—

glimmered on her skin in the pink light. The children laughed. In the distance, the barricade was a silhouette of angry angles. Concrete and steel and tangles of razor wire. A mechanical forest.

"The Psycho Cowboys are out there," Giovanna said. "You can't run from them."

"It's our only hope."

"They'll find you, Fernando. They'll kill you." She pushed away from him, turning, clasping his firm upper arms. A tassel of black hair fell across her brow. "Stay with me. I know how to love you."

He traced her tattoo with his fingertips, making, as always, slight adjustments to the letters, spelling different words: **QUE LINDA**, meaning "so beautiful." She closed her eyes. Her eyelids shimmered.

"But we're dying," he said.

They made love again, deep into the darkness. She went inside him—*became* him. Life within life. She knew there was to be no dissuading him. All she could offer were love and prayer—all that remained.

"Be a shadow, Fernando," she said as he poured into her.

"I'll be less than a shadow." Droplets of sweat fell onto her brow. Her soul felt as warm as the air. "They won't see me."

She kissed him. "Be nothing."

Fernando masked his face and escaped *a Cidade do Inferno* in the early hours. Giovanna stood by the window, her hands clasped, waiting to hear the gunshots. But, true to his word, he was less than a shadow, and he slipped through the barricade unnoticed. He moved southeast, following a trail of instinct as thin as Giovanna's tears, toward Rio de Janeiro and salvation.

Translation taken from the *Journal of Vinícius Araújo Valentim*.

(Date unknown.)

In my dreams I am with them—*one* of them. I hang from the roof of the cave, my feet hooked into some fissure. I have one wing. It is folded around my body, the cartilage stretched so that the wing covers me completely. I understand their animal language. I scratch and cry to be fed.

I escaped while they were sleeping: a thousand long shapes hanging in the darkness. I crept beneath them and made my way toward the cave entrance—that alluring chink of light. They did not stir. They did not follow.

Bright daylight greeted me: an infusion of breathtaking colour that felt like falling into deep water. I dropped to my knees, unable to move. Incredible pain splintered through my head and my eyes screamed in the intense light. The stump of my left arm twitched. I covered my face and buried myself in long grass.

I got to my feet, slowly, allowing sips of daylight through the cracks of my fingers, until I was able to remove my hand completely. The vastness of the rainforest stretched around me and I suffered a long moment of disorientation. Everything was green. I staggered in circles, struggling for focus. Eventually I was able to move in a straight line and with huge relief I started away from the caves, away from the creatures. Every step eased my soul. I was sobbing. I felt reborn.

The sun leaked through the thick canopy. I could see its flare, at first directly above me, and then sinking to my right, to the west. I decided to head east, trusting to the logic that we had taken off from Manaus and were headed west, for Carauari. We were not long into our journey when our plane went down. I surmised—incorrectly, as it turned out—that I was submerged in the Amazon to the west of Manaus. I was simply going back the way I had come, one step at a time, using distinctive landmarks (fallen trees, colourful bromeliads, odd-shaped leaves) as waypoints. I waded through rivers and crashed through snarls of foliage, determined to maintain an even line. When the sun touched the horizon and the jungle was fat with purple light, I thought of resting for the night. But that was when I heard their crying, tormented whoops. The sound didn't carry across the miles; it was in my head. I was a *part* of them. I shared their blood, and understood them.

They were coming for me.

I peeled through the darkness, snapping through ferns and vines with no regard for direction. Their advance was like a pendulum in my mind, swinging from one side of my skull to the other, until I could hear them on the outside—their wings slapping the air, their frustrated shrieks. I never looked back. I never stopped. Everything was hurting and my heart brimmed with dread. I crossed a wide river, kicking my legs and working my one arm, finally reaching the other side, where a female caiman snapped her huge jaws and whipped away from me. I broke into the jungle, startling sprays of sleeping macaws. The creatures were behind me, closer now. Their powerful cries filled the sky like stars.

Trying to outrun them was futile; I was weak, and they were too quick. My only hope was to hide, and I found a place in the dense understorey, low to the ground, where I knew they would have difficulty moving their wings. I wriggled amongst the vines clinging to the trunk of a strangler fig, shivering as they came closer. At one point I heard their cries directly overhead and dared a glance. I could see fragments of the night sky through the skeletal fingers of the canopy and shuddered, watching their shapes pass over the stars . . . long, hooked wings and thin, almost-human bodies. They circled above my hiding place, occasionally swooping lower so that their talons scraped the treetops, but they never broke through the canopy. I waited, my heart blistering in my chest, and eventually they swept away from me. Wounded shrieks ripped from their bodies, fading into the night.

I could still hear them, though—in my mind. Their cries trailed into my sleep and underlined my dreams. I awoke at dawn. Bursts of green seeped through my wounded eyes and a line of orange light bled through the understorey in the east. The air was clean, fat with oxygen, and I sucked in long, grateful breaths as my nightmares dispersed. I started to snake my body through the vines but stopped when I saw the jaguar poised on a fallen tree trunk, less than seven feet away. It glared at me, yellow eyes glimmering, and I watched the muscles in its flank ripple as it readied itself to pounce. Instinct swept away all fear—hateful, *animal* instinct—and I roared at the beast, baring my teeth, stamping my one fist into the ground. The jaguar hissed, backed along the trunk, then turned and fled. It rustled amongst the understorey and disappeared.

Sweat glistened on my brow. I wiped it away with a trembling hand, got to my feet, and walked toward the light.

My body cried at me, buckled with thirst. I knew what it wanted—what it thirsted *for*—but tried to deny it. I splashed chilled water down my throat, gagging, hating it, and couldn't keep it down.

What have I become?

By chance I stumbled upon an injured tapir. Its front leg was lame and it struggled to walk, snuffling at the grass, trembling when it saw me. I caught it easily, wrapped my arm around its neck, and twisted. There was no fight in the creature; its body flexed once against my side, and then it was still. I opened its throat with a sharp stone. Hot blood poured out and my stomach made convulsive clenches. I didn't deny it a moment longer. I lowered my mouth to the steaming wound and drank. The taste was immediately satisfying and I felt my strength returning. I drank until there was no blood left—just a slaughtered husk lying in the grass. I licked my lips, half-weeping with some unknown emotion, and stumbled on.

I wondered if I was more animal than human—more like the creatures that inhabited the cave than the professional photographer who owned an expensive studio apartment in São Paulo. I still don't know the answer. My thoughts are certainly human, yet I know there is something *different* inside me. Something huge and living. And terrifying.

My appetite for blood is unquenchable.

What have I become?

I staggered through the jungle for days—weeks, even, killing whatever I was quick enough to catch. I feared nothing. I encountered the worst the Amazon had to offer, and bested it all. I always had blood on my hands.

And at last . . . civilization: lights flickering in the distance.

I washed the blood from my body and staggered, naked as the day I was born, into the municipality of Pauini.

Close to you.

City lights blaze around me, but I hold to the shadows and move like vapour. I reach out—mental arms yearning to touch you—and feel the vague flicker of your presence. It touches me like sunlight.

Here I come.

Favela Rocinha.

The buildings were like the random thoughts that occur on the cusp of sleep, haphazardly piled on top of one another. Concrete and clapboard. Brick and tin. No order. Barely a semblance of structure. They challenged physics, leaning at angles, creaking and shifting in the wind. Electric lights hummed behind shuttered windows.

It was easy for Fernando to move unnoticed. He was just another stray; trash blown by the wind. He whispered through the shanty, past the stalls selling bottled water and old fruit and clay statuettes of Christ the Redeemer. Fires flickered on street corners, fuelled by children with dirty faces and scuffed knees. He could smell churrasco and sewerage. The streets were wet with rain. He could hear it dripping from one tin roof to another.

Closer.

A thin man sat on a concrete step playing a guitar with three strings, finding a melody even though his fingers, out of habit, touched empty places on the fretboard. He didn't notice Fernando, who flitted by, as light as an insect's wing. A woman danced barefoot in the gutter, holding her skirt above her knees, like a little girl paddling. She didn't lose a step as Fernando swept around her. He followed a pack of stray dogs to the end of the street, where a faulty traffic signal buzzed indecisively between stop and go. Mosquitoes flicked between colours, like living glitter.

Fernando paused in the doorway of an exhausted building, where the wind whistled in the gaps between bricks and the windows rattled like old toys. He closed his eyes and cast his instinct into the night. He was rewarded with a feeling—as light, yet real, as the beat of his pulse—from the northwest, further up the hill, where Rocinha's streets were more jaded, but where its lights burned brighter.

"Avô Vinícius . . ." He caught another wave of instinct and his promise trailed away. This was deep and cold, rushing to him from the south, bringing dread, whistling and rattling, like the wind through the tired building. His mind danced with terrible images. Clown faces leered at him. Endless rainbow legs bounded through the cramped streets.

Closer. But now the word was terrifying.

Fernando peeled out of the doorway and dared a glance over one shoulder. He couldn't see them, but they were coming . . . they were close. He turned back to the lights towering in the streets above him.

The signal stuttered. Only green. Only go.

Translation taken from the *Journal of Vinícius Araújo Valentim.*

(September 19ᵗʰ 2032.)

This must end.

I have torn through civilization, bringing pain and death and disease. I have burned with devastation, and seen cities—countries—spill countless infected to the streets, and then fall crippled to their knees. I am the cloud over the sun. I am the falling rain. I am the disease.

They cannot catch me. I am too quick, too strong, and always one move ahead. They come for me in São Paulo, yet I am in Florianópolis. They are weeks, months, cities behind. I drink to stay alive. I spread the infection. All I can hear is screaming.

They come for me—an army: one thousand strong. They batter down doors in Brasilia. I am in Teresina.

I drink. I live. I grow stronger.

How long before the world is beaten? How long before the continents are ravaged and buckled and slide screaming into the oceans? Because of me. I am the grandfather of ruin.

It must end.

I could take my own life, but I lack the courage. I could return to the caves in Amazonia, where I was saved—*reborn*—and be with my kindred, but the thought of being back there, with their cold, leathery bodies so close to mine, fills me with terror. I can do that no more than I could throw myself from the highest building in Brazil.

I want to be normal.

I will find a place where all hope is fragile, and where prayers are always spoken. I will blend in with the desperation—lose myself there. I will surround myself with darkness and live by meager means, until I grow old and weak. Until I die.

And if they find me . . . it will all be over. Leave it to fate. Let God decide.

I am the cause. The most virulent strain. But my part in this horror is done.

Let me find darkness.

Please, God.

The light inside.

Fernando's body ached and boomed and he pressed on, doubled over, heaving up steep, uneven streets. His jacket caught the wind and flowered behind him, and he shook it off so that it wouldn't slow him down. It flapped and tumbled down the streets, followed by a stream of excited children with naked, polished skin. He held the butterfly to his face. Tears flashed behind its delicate wings. His instinct shimmered, but he couldn't tell if it was because he was close to Avô Vinícius, or because the Psycho Cowboys were closing in.

Graffiti bled on the walls. Faded colours. Doors and shutters applauded in the breeze. The buildings leaned above him, time-washed greens and reds and blues, stacked like boxes. He ascended a corkscrew of crumbling steps, gasped the name of his saviour, and fell to his knees. He closed his eyes for a second and saw rainbows. The image terrified him—pushed him to his feet. He pressed onward. Rocinha glittered below him: a puddle on the earth, reflecting stars.

And all at once he was there. The shack was small and dark, with rotted slats of wood and flaps of tarpaulin filling the gaps in the brickwork. Simple light flickered inside. It was weak, decrepit, but for Fernando, it was everything he ever hoped to see.

"I am here," he said.

The Psycho Cowboys were close now. Fernando staggered to the shack. His heart was the light inside, flickering and bleeding through the gaps in the weakened frame.

We're not normally so kind.

"What have you become?"

"Less than a shadow."

"I thought you'd be . . . more."

"I am nothing."

The thing on the bed was barely human, and barely alive—a broken creature with pale eyes and sallow skin. Fernando could define the bow of his ribcage and the buckled knots of his spine.

Thin lips receded from endless teeth. Purple veins jumped with uncertain rhythm, wrapped around loose muscle.

"Avô Vinícius, I have—"

The thing spat: "I am *not* your grandfather."

Fernando shook his head. Hope scattered from his heart. The strength moved from his legs and he collapsed—as frail as the monster on the bed. He had travelled so long, and risked certain death, to be here . . . to find salvation.

The creature pulled this thought from his mind and responded, "I am not your saviour. I am the disease. I am death."

"We can be strong again."

"Everything dies." A syrupy yellow substance leaked from his eyes, into the shallows of his face. "Find your own destiny, and leave me alone."

"You *are* my destiny." Fernando crawled toward Avô Vinícius. He grasped his meager body and pulled him close. So light. A devastated, useless thing. His head lolled pathetically on his stick neck.

Sounds from outside: doors thrown open, raised voices, people crying out.

"They are here," Fernando said.

"Let them take you," Avô Vinícius hissed. He shifted in Fernando's arms, twisting his skeletal frame, the stump of his left arm twitching. "Look at me, and tell me . . . is this really what you want? I am the pestilence that runs through your blood. I have nothing good to give. And neither do you."

"I have to survive."

"That's not a reason to live."

The sounds outside were louder. Closer.

"I was born into this," Fernando said. "It's all I know."

A grotesque smile touched his lips. Fernando, aghast, threw him back onto the bed. A stuttering tangle of bones.

"A good reason to die, then," the creature said. The door crashed open. The Psycho Cowboys were there. Six of them. Tall, ungainly men with stretched faces. One of them pulled a handgun and fired three times. Fernando felt the heat of the bullets. They missed him by inches.

The first bullet tore through Avô Vinícius's chest. The second entered his right eye and exited the rear left portion of his skull, splashing thick pink matter onto the wall. The third bullet ripped through his throat with terrible force, severing what remained of his head and sending it tumbling into the corner.

The Cowboys stepped into the shack. The one with the gun (he was at least seven feet tall) looked at Fernando and grinned.

"Why do you think we let you run?"

Fernando sneered. "You couldn't catch me."

"Wrong." The Psycho Cowboy pointed the gun at the broken, bleeding shape on the bed. Tendrils of smoke eased from the barrel. "We wanted you to lead us to him. The Pathogen. The root of all evil. Now he is dead, and the war is over."

Fernando got to his feet. The Butterfly trembled on his face.

"What happens to me?" he asked.

Their grins were identical: yellow teeth set in grey faces.

"We killed him quickly," the one with the gun said, holstering his weapon. "We're not normally so kind."

We are the revenge.

With the first wave of pain he knew he was not dreaming. No dream could bring such agony, although everything else . . .

Naked, his thin body coloured with bruises. Blood raced from his shattered nose and mouth. It was thick in his throat. His eyelids flickered. He could hear laughter—a chattering, bubbling sound that pulled him to full alertness, and yet made him want to faint away forever.

He could see wild colour.

"No one will cry for you."

He was chained between two posts, his arms pulled wide, cruciform, so like the famous statue. The tips of his toes scuffed the concrete floor. He blinked tears from his eyes and rattled the chains. There was no give in them. Heavy breaths worked from his lungs. He snapped his head around and could see that he was in a large room—it looked like an abandoned warehouse—with a row of dusty windows along one side and loading doors at the far end. Ultraviolet lights glared like wide eyes, making strange shadows.

The Psycho Cowboys formed a semi-circle around him. They had changed out of their drab suits and into the regalia of cruelty: not quite the rainbows and clown faces he had seen in his dreams, but close. They wore fluorescent costumes—flamboyant colours amplified by the ultraviolet lights. Their faces were alive with luminescent paint. Nightmarish designs. They glowed like a child's Halloween joke.

They brandished their torture implements. Three of them carried batons. Two wielded picanas that were wired into car batteries. The sixth Cowboy (the tallest of them—the one who had shot Avô Vinícius) had an oily chainsaw hoisted on one shoulder.

"Let me tell you what happened to me," he said. The chainsaw looked heavy, judging from the way he adjusted his body to support the weight. "My family was killed in front of my eyes. I was seven years old at the time. Two of your kind broke into my house and slaughtered them all. My mother, father, and my two sisters. I hid in the closet and watched. Terrified, but vowing revenge. My associates . . ." he gestured at the Cowboys gathered around him, ". . . have similar stories. So do many hundreds of thousands of people in this country—in this continent. Innocent people torn to pieces by your disease. That's why we're here. We are not the cure. We are the revenge."

Fernando opened his mouth, and then closed it again. He had nothing to say. He knew his fate, and would accept it silently. His heart ached with the failure, but it ached more with the knowledge—even though he had always expected it—that he would never see his beautiful Giovanna again. Her face burgeoned in his mind for a second. A beautiful flower, with petals so bright they threw the Psycho Cowboys' colour into shade.

I'm so sorry, Giovanna, he thought. He glimpsed his mask, lying on the floor behind the Psycho Cowboys. Its wings were crushed. The pieces shimmered in the ultraviolet light, like rare minerals. He closed his eyes. She faded from his mind.

"You were strong once," the Cowboy said. His voice creaked like wet leather. The colours of his face were orange and pink. Sunrise colours. They accentuated the blackness of his eyes. "You were virulent. You killed millions. But you're not strong anymore."

Another Cowboy stepped forward. His face was obscenely bright—painted with red, tribal whorls that reached to the back of his bald head. His baton was happy-yellow. He raised it . . . brought it forward in a sunshine arc . . . smashed it against Fernando's ribcage. The pain was alive and furious. It writhed and kicked. Fernando heard his ribs shatter. He felt them break loose inside his body.

"Not strong," the Cowboy said. He nodded to his soldiers and they stepped forward. The picanas sent tens of thousands of volts through his body. The batons broke his bones. They came in waves, beating, and then retreating. The air was filled with the music of laughter and the percussion of weapons. Fernando swayed from the chains. When he passed out, they revived him with icy water, and then beat him again.

A ghost in his mind: Avô Vinícius, a dreadful, perished creature who could give him nothing except a promise of damnation. Fernando held that ruined face in his mind. *I thought you could save us.* He recalled how light the crippled body had been in his arms, like a bag of loose sticks. *I travelled so far for you. I thought . . . I thought . . .*

All for nothing.

They came at him, laughing maniacally. They shattered his legs. They smashed his ribs. The picanas were pressed to the most sensitive areas of his body: his armpits, his genitals, his bleeding, open wounds. The voltage roared through his body in blackening, crackling storms. Ribbons of smoke peeled from his scorched skin.

Fernando floated on the brink of an abyss. Endless and black. It was heaven. He floated in a thousand pieces: the debris of hurt, like a meteor shower. He trailed and blazed and prepared to offer himself to nothingness—that long sea of death. He experienced a moment of euphoria. He thought it was his soul departing.

No more pain.

I am nothing.

One moment. That was all.

And then he heard the roar of the chainsaw.

As bright as his mask.

"Our colour represents new life," the Cowboy shouted over the chainsaw's growl. "From our grey suits to this . . . like a new dawn, a new era. Soon the world will be painted with amazing light. A world that you will not be a part of."

He depressed the chainsaw's trigger and its hooked, oily teeth blazed around the bar. It drowned the sound of laughter. Dirty smoke puffed from the exhaust, hanging in the air, obscuring their fluorescent stripes and swirls. The Psycho Cowboy lifted the chainsaw and took a step toward Fernando. His grin was a deep red groove. His eyes dazzled, even behind the smoke.

He shouted something else, but Fernando did not hear him. Partly because of the chainsaw's mean growl, but mostly because his attention was diverted to the windows, where he saw movement. Something large, swooping from one window to the next. He flexed and pulled at the chains. His mind screamed impossible images, as bright as his mask, and in as many pieces.

I am nothing.

The chainsaw purred inches from his shallow stomach.

Less than a shadow.

His instinct blazed. A divine rush that scattered all pain and pulled his mouth into a long, bleeding smile. He gazed beyond the chainsaw . . . beyond the Psycho Cowboys . . . beyond the smoke and colour . . . to where the wooden loading doors suddenly crashed open.

I am coming.

"Giovanna," he said.

Fallen from time, like rain from a cloud.

She came like a tempest. An infernal, chaotic force, leaving the doors in ruins and killing two of the Cowboys before they knew what happened. Their bodies were shattered against the wall: bags of glass. They bled through their fluorescent skins.

The Psycho Cowboy with the chainsaw turned, dragged to one side by the machine's power. He peered through rags of oily smoke and saw what could not be, but what Fernando knew to be true. She was pure: something part-human but altogether monstrous, a ranging, naked creature sweeping in and out of the shadows. Fernando could not have recognized her without the tattoo: **377822.** It was her—his only love: Giovanna. Long black hair flanked her face and splashed across muscular shoulders. Her eyes were keen gold discs. Only their shape was familiar. She breathed—harsh, grunting expulsions. Her wide nostrils flared.

Her teeth were haphazard, ivory spikes, projecting from her gums like splayed fingers.

Another Cowboy dropped his (happy-yellow) baton and screamed. Giovanna bore upon him with a furious shriek. One sweep of her arm ripped him in two. His upper body thudded off one of the posts that Fernando was chained to. His legs were sent kicking into the shadows. A fourth Cowboy—his black eyes suddenly very large in the glowing map of his face—tried to run. He didn't get far; Giovanna pounced. Her thick legs propelled her through the air like a grasshopper. She came down on his shoulders and he crumpled beneath her weight, spine broken. His painted face was glow-in-the-dark terror. Fernando watched as she pulled him apart, scattering him in a hundred fluorescent pieces.

She looked at him. Their eyes came together and Fernando saw what used to be: her softness and beauty. He remembered the way the left side of her mouth would lift higher when she smiled. He remembered the way she had touched him, time and time again, throwing his world into easy clouds of calm. His beaten body trembled from the chains. His heart boomed with emotion.

I know how to love you, she had said. But could she love him still? This new creature . . . every bone reshaped, bent at the waist so that her shoulder blades pressed through her skin like wings. Giovanna Almeida, to whom he had sworn eternity. How much of her soul remained? How much love?

He closed his eyes as she killed the fifth Psycho Cowboy. One moment he was there, living and thinking and afraid. The next he was gone, fallen from time, like rain from a cloud.

Yes, she had always been able to read him. Her gift—her instinct—was incredibly bright. It was the reason she was here, as devastating as a volcano. And this ability, along with everything else about her, must have advanced, because she was able to press her thoughts into his mind. Not words, but images, arranged like a wheel, revolving, drawing long arcs of expression.

So much soul /// I still know how to love you /// I always will.

He opened his eyes. Her mouth was a terrible shape, but the left side was lifted higher.

He threw his own wheel at her: *Save me.*

Revolve: *I already have.*

The chainsaw snarled, the teeth whickering, flickering in

the ultraviolet light. The Cowboy lifted it to waist-height and gunned the trigger. The machine vibrated in his arms, belching smoke.

"Come for me," he screamed, pointing the bar toward Giovanna. She circled him, thudding her knuckles on the floor, the bloody swags of her breasts swinging as she moved. She roared: an insane tangle of sound—words and yawps on a stream of hot air. Vapour poured from her long mouth. Her shoulder blades were pressed together, as if she were about to take flight.

The Cowboy raised the chainsaw and took a step forward. Giovanna moved between the shadows. Her claws flashed. She howled. The chainsaw snarled and Fernando heard the change in modulation as it carved the air. She was too quick for him. He was thrown aside, still holding the chainsaw. It purred along the floor, kicking up sparks and spits of concrete. He got to one knee and the weight of the machine dragged him down. It kicked and wheeled back on him. He let go and rolled away, but Giovanna was there. He seemed too small in her huge claws. His fluorescent facepaint dripped as she breathed on him.

"*Infecção,*" she growled, and crushed him. His body twisted and fractured in her hands. Fernando watched it become loose as she snapped every bone and ground his spine to dust. He screamed louder than the chainsaw. Blood leaked from his eyes. His arms and legs dangled uselessly. She threw him away. He twitched and died.

Fernando faded again, to the edge of the abyss, where the hurt couldn't reach him. The last thing he saw was Giovanna picking up the chainsaw and lifting it to the chains. He heard the squeal of metal on metal. He felt the hot/cold flicker of sparks. Then he was falling. Then he was held.

O Cristo Redentor.

She cradled him and crossed the city, through twisting alleyways and across rooftops, pressed to the shadows.

You can't see me.

The lights of ruined lives shimmered below them.

"My mask . . ." Fernando said, lifting to consciousness.

"You don't need it anymore."

She ascended Corcovado Mountain with effortless, unfaltering leaps. He trembled against her breast. She reached the magnificent statue and continued to climb. Her claws scratched into the smooth stone and she made her way to the shoulders, and then clambered deftly onto the right arm. The statue's solemn face regarded the city. Giovanna held her lover, stroking his face, breathing hard. Sweat dripped from her coarse skin. She kissed him. Her hair pooled on his chest.

Fernando opened his mouth but couldn't speak. He pulled an image into his mind, shaped it, and then cast it at her. It wasn't perfect, but she understood.

Wh/t happ//ed to y/u?

She kissed him again and stroked his face. *You have spent the last two years looking for a man /// whom we thought could save us /// but were wrong.* Her angular face soothed him. It seemed to be made of stone, like the great, pale face behind her. *I escaped and moved in the other direction /// into Amazonia.* She closed her eyes. The shape that blossomed in his mind was smooth on one side, hooked on the other, like a bat's wing. *They knew I was coming /// They found me.*

He wanted to touch her tattoo—trace the lines, make subtle changes. **QUE LINDA**. His broken arms throbbed. His mouth opened. He managed to speak one hurt syllable:

"They?"

She looked at him, and then gave him a glimpse. Not all of it. Not even close. But it was enough: a horde of thorny creatures hanging in the darkness. Fernando could almost taste their blood, and feel their brutal penetration—over and over—turning her soft body to stone.

"They made me pure," she said.

Imagine a shadow, but vague, only slightly darker than the surface onto which it is cast. The light is obscured. The shadow suffers. It is a cataract.

You can't see us. We are less than shadows.

We are nothing.

But we are coming.

Close.

Ho/d me, Gi/van/a.

And she did, pulling him close as a cool night wind moaned across the statue's arm. Her lips whispered against his bruised skin. His heart moved against his ribcage. Tears glittered in his eyes and the city spangled like a butterfly's wing.

He thought, for one moment, that he was still wearing his mask.

10 things to know about staplers

CAROLYN CLINK

1) The Greeks invented the stapler.
2) Buzz Aldrin took a stapler to the moon.
3) Staplers can refuse to staple for religious reasons.
4) Staplers regret nothing.
5) When a stapler jams, someone will die.
6) Staplers are government spies.
7) Staplers eat one sock a month.
8) Surgical staplers are alcoholics.
9) Staplers dream of electric staplers.
10) Staplers know all your secrets.

laikas i
KATHRYN KUITENBROUWER

"Trevor?" Hilary called through the mail slot, having pushed open its tarnished little door. When he opened up to let her in there were so many strays jostling that he didn't see her crouched there among them at first. But he knew it was her by her voice and the crazy magnetic pull on his heartstrings. The dogs continued to lay claim until she whistled and growled, "Laikas, sit!" Then they all lowered, panting, some cocking their heads, some not.

Laika was the Russian dog that went up in a space rocket and Hilary had named the pack collectively in memoriam. To some of them she had given individual names but as a group they were always Laikas. Now, Monday, at 7:15 a.m., seventeen strays stared at Trevor. And there was Hilary in sweet profile.

"Smoke?" Trevor handed her the thin cigar he had already lit.

"I was in the neighbourhood," she said, smiling, turning her face to him.

In fact, Trevor had texted, called and finally begged her to stop by. He was slumming at this present address on Fair view. He'd moved out of home to share an apartment with three delinquent acquaintances, something his wealthy parents lauded as potentially character-building. But because the roommates were usually out and/or stoned, Trevor was often lonely. Plus, he was experiencing lovesickness. Now that Hilary had finally arrived, he knew the jealous dog pack would give them an hour— maybe—and then she'd be laughing at his fabulous attempts to keep her there.

"I don't know why you tolerate them," he said. Hilary had scars where she'd been bitten and an oozing wound that she wouldn't let Trevor tend. "Those dogs are feral, Hilary!" They were tucked to the hips under an old red velvet curtain on the sofa. An ashtray he'd liberated from his parents' place was nestled into the concave of his belly.

"I don't tolerate them," she argued. The ashtray, Hilary saw, was one of those Greek black-figure-vase replicas. She leaned over and twisted her cigarette softly on Orpheus's leg, watched his skin peel off. "I have no idea about them, at all," she said. "They like me. They lick and nip. It's just *play* that goes too far."

Trevor could hear the dogs outside, whimpering, beckoning. He flexed his pectoral muscles tight and tried to look naturally hot. He pouted elegantly, desperately. He proffered more Cuban cigarillos. He exhaled earthen smoke into her ears, her mouth, whatever opening he could think of.

When he went too far, Hilary giggled and pushed his face away from down there. Then, getting serious, she said, "In the old stories there is always a door through which the hero must never pass." she was thinking specifically about Orpheus leading Eurydice out of Hades, and how he had looked back, and lost her forever.

"Death's door?"

"It's a portal to this truly marvellous place."

She drew on the cigarillo so deeply it almost disappeared, then jabbed the stub in a strange random way into the air. He tried to make sense of the action but couldn't—she was sometimes so mysterious to him, he felt undone.

"Sometimes," she continued, "It can be a real door, or a closet, or just an abstraction—you know, the threshold of maturity. It can be a willingness to acknowledge and live with your fears. Yeah?"

He mulled over what she might mean by threshold. He had thought they were talking about her body. Well, he had been talking about her body. God, it sounded as if the dogs were mauling the porch screen. A howling set up in response to a siren off in the Junction. *Threshold of maturity*, he thought, and grabbed Hilary's ankle; he noticed a long scratch, like on torn nylons, only raw, fresh skin.

"Damn dogs," he moaned. "They'll eat you one of these days."

"It's something stupid *I* did," she said, holding his ashtray in one hand now. She could see he wouldn't dare ask what stupid thing she might have done.

The dogs began jumping onto the windowsill, drooling on and worrying the glass pane.

"I have to go," she said. "I have a new job."

"Job?"

"Well, I have to pay for school somehow."

"But Hilary—"

He stood in the doorway—damned threshold—while she left. The dogs were whirling outside, anticipating her. They worried and nibbled one another's ears, and showed their gums in undeniable grins. Trevor counted them as they followed her receding sway. There were now twenty-nine strays.

She walked away from Trevor's place along Fairview Avenue, and into the Sunny Cafe for some sour keys. Sucking, then chewing the candy, she headed down to the subway at High Park. The dogs trailed politely behind.

No pets below in peak hours," said the ticket guy. Hilary could hear "Bohemian Rhapsody" seeping out of his earbuds and felt herself moved by the arguably manipulative orchestration.

"They're not mine." she smiled at the guy and walked through the turnstile. "And they certainly aren't pets."

A few of the dogs sat, then lay down, possibly to await her return, but the rest went under the bars, or over (the dog she called Snot took pride in her immense leap), and Hilary pretended like she didn't know, or see, or even sense them. "Bohemian Rhapsody" was looping in her mind now, the best part of the song.

The ticket guy whimpered, "Hey," but what could he do, and did he get paid well enough for this shit? A queue of folks wanting tokens and passes and information was forming, so he finally gestured something between goodbye and whatever, and hoped for the sake of his job that no one was videotaping him.

Chick had awesome babe swagger, he thought. His eyes followed her until she turned the corner. He would like a chick so hot the dogs followed her ass down the subway and . . . where? Heading east. Heading downtown. "Hey, scram," he said to the strays that had stayed behind. "Get outta here. Out!"

He looked up and saw the terrorist dude who ran the concession stand staring right the fuck at him, and barked, "Jesus!" as he realized he would have to leave his booth—which he did—in order to lunge at the dogs until they took the hint and skulked back up the escalator.

The car was pretty full but there were seats, so Hilary sat down, the dogs finding space among the legs and backpacks of commuters, one leaping up and nestling in between two men, both of whom appeared to be examining something invisible in the mid-distance. Perhaps they did not notice the basset hound sprawled out there.

During the difficult economic years, things had gone from merely bad to an almost clichéd worse. Thousands of dogs had lost their owners and many people were appalled by the feral packs. Still, sympathetic media *had* reported dogs with routes— clever dogs who maximized their panhandling, who had figured out where to find kind humans, places to crash on cold nights. These reports had resulted in a sort of rebranding of the animals, making the dogs seem intelligent in ways humans could relate to. There were now stray-dog activists.

Hilary was not one of them.

She was heading to her new job—a half-time position at a downtown recreational facility. Snot and Mangy were taking turns licking her wound. When she noticed, she leaned over, whispered,

"That's enough, you two."

Once out of the subway, she decided she would walk down Dovercourt. The dogs kept pace, only stopping here and there to nuzzle the pavement or urinate on spindly trees they passed. At Dewson, she halted and had them sit and stay, then headed in for day one.

The front desk had no knowledge of a new hire. Hilary put more weight on one leg and raised her eyebrows. "I dunno," she said.

"Today is supposed to be my first day. A guy named Danny hired me last week. To wipe down machines."

"Oh, yeah. I overheard something, now you mention it. Hi, I'm Judy," Judy said, extending her hand to shake. Judy pulled her hair back and Hilary saw she had a tattoo behind her ear. It was one of those tats done with white ink so they look like scar tissue build-up.

"Is that a mongoose?"

"No. But that's funny. I've heard it looks like one from a few people."

"What is it?"

"It's actually the word "strife" shaped like a fish. Do you like it? It's my favourite word."

"Yeah, it's awesome."

"Mongeese are cool, too," Judy said. "I buzzed for Danny. He should be a minute."

Hilary rolled *mongeese* around all day after that. The job was a cinch. She only had to wipe down machines with a spray bottle and cloth, recalibrate resistance trainers, replace the weights in the right order and smile at people. Twice that day she cleaned out the ladies' toilets and checked the shower, steam and whirlpool area, and reported back to the main janitor. Easy minimum wage plus she got a free membership, so after work, she used the facility to clean herself up. She smiled and waved at Judy on the way out the door, 5:30 sharp, and Judy waved back. "Hey," Judy called, "how'd it go?" Hilary gave her the thumbs up.

The dogs were waiting in different places along the route and had attracted more strays. It was hard to count them as they jockeyed for position, smelling her crotch, jumping on one another. Eventually Hilary gave up. Back to the subway, through to High Park, Hilary detoured to Sunny Cafe for a slice of pizza and another sour key or two. She loved the way the candy chemical gave over to sweet just too late, so that right when her mouth puckered, it began to soften.

Trevor called just as she got inside her apartment. She had a hard time concentrating with the dogs anxious in the small space, vying for her attention. "No," she said, into the phone, then "Hi, yeah!" then "No, I don't think so," and "Well, I'm really sorry." Snot had her paws on Hilary's feet and was stretching, bum up, tail wagging wildly. Mangy and Perk were into the garbage already. Hilary needed to get better at sealing that. "OK, but don't expect conversation," she was saying. "I'm a working girl now."

By the time he got there she was asleep; the dogs tumbled in and around her, using her face and neck and legs as pillows. Trevor had a key. Seven dogs came in with him, having scented Hilary out from High Park once dusk reminded their stomachs of her.

She was a curl of pink, a half-moon face partially obstructed by the scruff of a labradoodle. Trevor gasped. He'd never seen anything as breathtakingly beautiful. It reminded him of those baby portraits with the newborn in a flower or a bunny suit, and he wanted to cry or, alternatively, make love.

He got down on all fours and pushed the dogs out of the way until he was snuggled in with her. He tried to wake her with a few loud sighs but she wouldn't move. "Honey?" he said, right into her ear.

"Honey? Can I?" already he had his hand rotating around her nipple but as he pleaded with her to wake up, he slid his fingers down her tracksuit pants and into that damn portal.

"Let me ravage you in your sleep, baby."

He took the faint grimace that crept on her face, and the tiniest shift towards him in body language, to mean yes. Snot and Perk looked on while he pulled her pants down, gently turned and mounted her.

"Fuck off," he muttered guiltily, but the dogs only edged in closer and looked up at him. It turned out OK, though, because Hilary woke up and got into it. He was exonerated! It was the first time they'd done it all the way since this dog manifestation started the week before and Trevor had been increasingly jealous and temperamental about it—not at all philosophical as she'd suggested he be.

Now he was actually enjoying the proximity of the pack, their hot breath around him, the encroachment, the *wildness* of it. A pugbeagle licked their toes metronomically through the entire lovemaking. Trevor had never been to an orgy and wondered if this counted.

"Hilary?"

"So tired—"

"It's coming up to the end of the month."

"Trevor, can this not wait?"

"I've been thinking of moving in, actually."

"What?"

"Yeah, well, I'm pretty much here all the time, anyway."

Day two went reasonably well. The TTC guy managed to stop most of the dogs from entering the system. But then they refused to leave the main area, and hounded the Sikh who sold chips and newspapers, essentially ruining his morning, until he finally grabbed a Mr. Big, tore the wrapper down, waved it out at the pack and then turned and ran screaming up the escalator, the dogs giving chase.

"Hey, dude," said the ticket guy when the Sikh returned, and then when he got no response, "Dude! Osama!"

The seller only shook his head in disbelief, or mock disbelief, and went on looking at the floor of his booth, trying to catch breath.

"Dude. Osama! Yo!"

That finally elicited a glare.

"What? Wha'd I do?" The ticket guy looked over to make sure his booth was locked. He'd recently bought a Kevlar vest and was wearing it now. Dude had been freaking him out since he'd won the concession. Dude could be from, like, anywhere. No one could expect to feel safe any more. "Why don't you never talk? For Christ sakes. Dude never talks to no one."

"I talk."

"You never talk."

"I am talking with you right this second. And why do you call me Osama? My name is Yusef. Call me Yusef."

"It's no big deal, dude."

"Yusef! It's a deal. No big deal. My name is Yusef."

"It's friggin' slang." People had become too soft-skinned. "It's a joke. You don't have humour where you come from?"

"Yusef!" and here Yusef raised his right arm high above his head and pointed to the roof of his kiosk. He did not know the word slang.

"I come from Brampton." He added, "We have humour."

"Yusef," the ticket guy said. Jesus, with all the conversation and the Kevlar, he had started sweating.

"Exactly."

"Thanks for getting rid of those dogs."

"You're welcome. Now shut up."

"Hey, pal!" He really wanted to make this good. He unlocked the booth and waddled out to find Yusef's line of vision. "Yusef," he said, then smiled. "I am Mike. You can call me Mike." Yusef nodded and Mike waddled back towards the booth. He didn't get paid for this, so he muttered, "I don't get paid for this, Yusef. Maybe you do, but I don't." Then he turned back, fumbled in his trouser pocket for change, asked for and received a Coke and a

Kit Kat. "Here," Mike said, "keep the change." Which he thought was hilarious, since he was actually short a couple of pennies.

There were thirty-five dogs by day's end and Hilary, exhausted, found them sitting alert in the small park opposite the station at High Park. There was a new cur lounging on the park bench and another huge emaciated dog off behind the main grouping. It was tawny and scraggly and fierce—*cold*-looking. Wow, she thought, and then: kinda wolfish, though she'd never seen a wolf. But then she brushed the thought out of her mind, since it made no sense. Anyway, the new dog or whatever it was didn't bother following her home when the rest did.

The next day, after work, Mike called out, "Hey, lady," as she pushed through the turnstile. "Hey, dog-lady. I see that wolf down here again and I'm calling the cops." She didn't look his way at all, which left him with something to think about, but she *had* heard, he was pretty sure.

Hilary hadn't wanted to acknowledge A: herself as dog-lady; B: any problems re wolves or whatever; C: Mike, period.

There were three "big dogs" in the pack when she got out the door.

"Well, holy fuck," she whispered.

She could hardly hear above their clamour but she was pretty freaked about the pack coming in now there were these creatures amid them, so she bolted them outside the door and called Trevor.

"Probably not wolves, honey."

"The TTC guy thinks they are."

"Fat Mike? He grew up in Scarborough. He wouldn't know a wolf from a— Hey, I bet that's what you are dealing with."

"Dealing with?"

"Yeah, Irish wolfhounds or else some mixture."

"Really?"

"Yeah. Totally. Tawny? Wiry hair? Big?"

"Yeah!"

"Totally wolfhounds."

Hilary unbolted the door and let the dogs stream in. They appreciated this and let her know it by snuffling her and by smiling their lips back, showing their teeth without growling. This always made her laugh and it did now. These wolfhounds were the noblest dogs she had ever seen. They hung back and circled one another, yipped quietly, then sat on their haunches and watched the other dogs hump each other and rise up nipping and ear-chewing in gorgeous faux battles.

Every once in a while, for fairness, Hilary pulled the playing dogs apart and made them sit, and let other small groups of dogs clash together in these strange, seemingly ritualistic fights that she thought she might never tire of watching. Play-fighting dogs *were* beautiful. Even the wolfhounds seemed to be enjoying the arena.

But then, when she made space for two miniature schnauzers to play, things went awry. She wasn't aware of the shift but in retrospect she would allow that there had been a stiffening in the posture of some of the dogs on the group periphery. Initially the schnauzers circled and turned, almost dancing, noses to asses, one licking, the other avoiding by curling its butt toward the ground and twirling away. And then, here, what she loved to watch, they rose on their hind legs and batted with front paws and teeth, swiped at one another. Oh, such verve and joy.

"Nice one!" Hilary clapped. "Yes! Clever!"

They looked like puppets of dogs to her, and she laughed at this thought, and while she was laughing, very suddenly, the Irish wolfhounds pounced upon the schnauzers, seizing them and flinging them to and fro, letting them free only to bite through their small backs. She could do nothing.

The schnauzers were shrieking. And then not shrieking.

The energy in the apartment was suddenly so clenched down that there was nothing to hear but the silky manoeuvring of the wolfhounds, and when it was over, such a baying and a yipping, as they hunkered and called out to the other dogs, warning of *their* territory and *their* kill, the meal they then set to licking and tearing apart.

Hilary was paralysed with fear.

And the blood, so quiet in its redistribution, splashed out across the kitchen, so that Hilary pressed up against the fridge in the far corner, suddenly shocked back to herself, and screamed.

"Ah, jeez." it was Trevor, who had come in too late to do anything.

"Coyotes."

Coyotes had had a presence in High Park for some time. The animal services entry, found through the obvious search engine, though dated, read:

> Coyotes are extremely intelligent and they adapt and learn very quickly. Every encounter that isn't scary may encourage the coyote to get closer next time. Ideally, park users would actively scare a coyote away at every sighting (suggestions on how to do this are attached).

The attached PDF pamphlet gave helpful hints like being mean, large, loud, etc. It also had directions for a coyote shaker, which Hilary promptly made by recycling an aluminum diced-tomatoes can and filling it with coins. The pennies made a loud but not unpleasant susurrus when she shook the shaker. The can didn't have much of an effect on the coyotes, though. They just looked at her and seemed, in between yips, to snicker.

There were more and more each day. So, she took to dropping meat at the small park so they'd stay behind, which worked, but only sort of; it caused a lot of jealousy and consternation among the main pack of strays, and once they'd done ripping apart the meat and devouring it, the coyotes followed her scent back to the apartment anyway. Every dog in the city seemed to know how to intimidate or charm someone into opening the doors of buildings, and likewise, the coyotes would make their way up and bay and scratch at Hilary's sixth-floor apartment door. But she wouldn't let them in the apartment any more.

They'd burned their bridge on that account.

Judy locked eyes with Danny until he finally said, "What?"

"Don't you think she's the tiniest bit weird?"

"She's a hard worker."

In strained baritone, Judy said, "When asked by the police whether he had ever seen any unusual behaviour from the suspect, her boss, Daniel Grainger, declared, 'She's a hard worker.'"

"So what? She is."

"Have you noticed the fur smell?"

On the morning of day six, there were three mismatched puppies prodding at Snot's belly when Hilary and Trevor woke up. Trevor gleefully hugged Hilary and they stood there ogling the creatures so long that Hilary had to skip breakfast. While she showered, Trevor packed her a tuna fish wrap and a pickle. It was *his* favourite lunch.

"Nature is wondrous," he exclaimed. "Oh my God, look at how cute they are." Snot looked so loving, and no one would deny the puppies were—well, anyone's heart would be shattered at the sight.

Hilary made her eyes big and smiled. "Yeah!" Then, "I better get going or I'll be late." she had to press herself to the wall and edge through the door to keep the coyotes out. Two of them had managed to get past the building security and there were a few—five, actually—just outside the main door. An elderly woman with a walker was coming up the street scolding them.

"In my day," she said, "there weren't all these animals."

"Shoo," said Hilary, and scattered them to let the woman by.

"They're so BOLD!" said the woman.

Hilary thought about the schnauzers and nodded.

Judy was sick with a head cold so Danny spent ten minutes teaching Hilary the front desk and then left her to it. The job involved making people membership cards and taking their money and saying, "Of course," as politely as a person can that many times a day. As in, "Of course, I'll call the manager for you." Or, "Of course, you are right. Let me take your phone number and I'll have someone get back to you."

And this wouldn't have been brain surgery if she hadn't looked through the front windows mid-afternoon to see the pack pressing up to the glass, licking it, pawing it, jumping upon or curling around one another so that it was difficult for patrons to get their frumpy bodies in on time for yoga chant class.

"There are these dogs trying to get into the foyer."

One woman shrieked; it turned out she was "pathologically afraid of canines." Hilary wondered if that pathology was terminal, but did not ask. She was finding herself increasingly anxious with all the dog attention. Why her? It felt metaphoric but she couldn't fathom of what. At 3:35, Trevor showed up sweaty and half-naked from jogging over, and pranced in showing off his abs. He was wearing suspenders—over nothing.

"*Scaramouche!*" He struck a Freddie Mercury pose, lunging his hips out exactly right.

"All right, then. Wow."

"What? You've been humming it all week."

"I have?"

"*Oh, Oh, Oh, Oh!*" he sang.

"Weird." She shook her head, in a way Trevor interpreted as *you awesome thing*, and then she said, "How are the pups?"

"The whole pack is taking care of them." Trevor looked back and acknowledged the dogs outside the window and added, "Well, except for those ones. The ones who stayed when I opened the door to leave are really great parents. I mean truly awesome."

"And these guys?"

When they got back to the apartment, the door was ajar and one of the puppies was—well—no longer whole. Several of the dogs were still whimpering. Trevor let out a shrill "Nooo!" Then, "How the hell did the door get opened, for Christ's sake?"

"You must have accidentally left it open."

"No," Trevor said. "No fucking way was it left open."

"Are you sure?"

"I'm getting a goddamned gun. No one should be coming into the apartment like that."

"You think someone did this?"

"I mean those animals did this."

Hilary cleaned the mess up and Trevor couldn't even help, he was so angry. He just sat up on the kitchen counter and lit a smoke and shook his head, trying with his foot to keep Snot from licking the blood off the rug. "Oh, man! Oh, MAN!" Eventually he got down and went to Hilary's computer and typed "Guns" and "Toronto" and came up with Al Flaherty's Outdoor Store, the last remaining gun shop in the city, and said, "Honey, I'm going for a walk."

"Should I come?"

"Sure you can."

"Forget it, I'm too tired from all this," meaning the coyotes, the dead puppy, and all the YMCA front-desk generosity. But mostly it was the wanton cruelty that had made her tired.

While Trevor was gone she wondered whether she could care, really care, for a guy who had a gun, and she decided that any guy who was so infantile as to think that a gun would solve any of the world's problems was not the kind of guy she would be able to see herself with long-term. But when he arrived some hours later, and woke her up by turning the lights on and standing Rambo-style with the wooden-handled, single-shot BB rifle, she saw him in a new light. He looked like the pissed-off cowboy of her dreams, and where before he had seemed a little effete and fey, now he seemed effete and fey in a sexy way. And Hilary thought, maybe.

They went outside the apartment building and Trevor levelled the gun toward the pack of coyotes circling an abandoned shopping cart and squinted to line up the sites, then pulled the trigger and screamed so loud a few lights went on and they had to make a run for it. His elbow was bleeding and, from the look of it, the BB had ricocheted off the shopping cart right back at him. They turned in time to see the coyotes scatter into the shadows. It was as if they were phantoms, as if they never existed except in the imaginations of Hilary and Trevor. But the elbow wound was real.

Trevor later joked, "You should have seen the other guy."

On day seven, Yusef arrived early at his concession stand to have some quiet time before the morning rush. The subway was usually dead until around 6:30 and so he could sit and think and read the newspaper and eat the lunch his wife had packed for him before she went to bed. Often, eating the dhal and chapatti or egg salad sandwich was the first thing he did in the morning, right after he ate his breakfast.

Now, Yusef looked up and saw Mike on the other side also looking up, and between them were many, many, bristling, huge and possibly starving coyotes.

"What the fuck?" Mike was thinking how the Kevlar wouldn't do dick in this situation and then regretted thinking dick.

"I'm dialling 911," replied Yusef.

"Don't you carry a piece?"

"What's a piece?"

"A gun, yahoo."

"Yahoo? My name is—"

"—Yusef."

"Why would I carry a gun?"

"I thought all you guys carried weapons."

"Shopkeepers?" Yusef felt the sandwich pressing up against his oesophagus, and regretted his indulgence. "It's illegal," he managed.

"Jesus wept," said Mike.

The cops and the fire department showed up and made such an unholy racket running down the stairs that the animals jumped the turnstile and hid underground. The authorities shut the system down for two hours while they pretended to find and evacuate them. Fact: they never saw one coyote. This delay was especially annoying to Hilary who was one hour and twenty-six minutes late for work. Note: through the entire event Mike had "Bohemian Rhapsody" wailing into his left ear. He needed to hear the lyric in looping glory, so he'd put the song on continual repeat. How could one song carry so much truth?

When the cops and the press had finally dispersed, Mike looked over at Yusef, and said, "Sheesh! Yusef!"

"I know," said Yusef. "We made the news."

It was funny what let you really know a person, Mike thought. It was weird and uncanny and funny. He crossed the floor to give props to Yusef.

"Buddy!"

"Yusef," Yusef reminded him again.

"Oh, yeah!" Mike hadn't really smiled—really truly smiled—in years, and now he *beamed*.

Judy raised her eyebrows when Hilary recounted the subway debacle, but Danny took it in his stride. Hilary got busy wiping down the ellipticals. If she looked closely some of them seemed to have flakes of skin on them, so she tried not to look closely. As soon as she had the opportunity, she sidled into the change room, sat herself down where she wouldn't have to witness the parade of denuded privates, took out her device, texted: *Alleged coyotes in TTC.*

Reply: *OMG.*

Alleged! Trevor put his cellphone down and danced around with the dogs. He loved that woman. Tonight, he thought, tonight would be the night.

"No pets," said Mike. He had pushed the booth open and was coming out to stop Hilary. "You hear me? I don't wanna tell you this again. I don't wanna have to call the police again. Did you read the newspaper? We covered for you here. Me and Yusef over there—we covered for you."

There were scores of dogs following Hilary from Dovercourt station, and these were the ones who had managed to break through the security at that end. The rest were probably on their way to her apartment door or waiting in the park. There were no coyotes as far as she could tell but if she was honest with herself there had been shadows and rank odours—wild rancid smells she could not account for. She stopped for Mike and asserted, "They aren't mine. I'm telling you."

"They come with you. They go with you. I've seen you feed them. I've seen them lick you. They're yours. And they can't come down any more." Mike looked over at Yusef in the hope of getting some basic support and was pissed to see Yusef look away. "Yo, Yusef!" he said. "Support!" and then Yusef lifted his eyes and damned if he didn't look scared before he dropped them again.

"They aren't mine," said Hilary. "I don't even own a leash. These are city dogs. I can't help it if they follow me. I can't do anything about anything." And Hilary pushed past Mike.

Mike held onto the sleeve of her jacket. "Admit you don't like this," he said.

"I have no opinion whatever." Hilary pursed her lips, glared. "Call the city. Or the police."

"Yeah, we've seen how well that works."

"Open your eyes," she quipped, and Mike thought he recognized something and shut up. She added, "Let me go."

Mike gasped. Queen, he thought. No way. He let go of the fabric of her jacket, his eyes widened and he tilted his head like a dog for a bone. "Oh," he said. "Oh!"

Hilary smiled, sang a few bars of the "Scaramouche" section until Mike nodded. She got him. Really got him. Cool. Nobody had ever got him.

Trevor led Hilary down Annette, through Baby Point—the swank houses had old money ivying around them—and then down an old rotten stairwell to the thin green belt along the Humber River. It smelled like mould and earth down there, and fish. The dogs followed, as did car horns honking, for the animals did not wait for lights.

"I thought you meant a walk in High Park."

"The dogs know it so well, I thought I'd bring you all here."

The sun was pressing the horizon when Trevor finally stopped in a treed dip in the landscape, the dogs edging them, their coats aflame with sunset and Hilary's face turned up wondering.

"You're stopping."

He was standing very close to her, the dogs getting jealous, nuzzling her legs and pushing the two of them apart as well as they could. Mangy jumped up and tore a superficial line down Hilary's cheek. "Down, Mangy. Laikas, sit!"

Then, briefly, except for the monkey jabber of squirrels, it was as quiet as it ever got in an urban park.

Trevor put something into her hand, too shy to even look at her, and when she saw it was a box—that famous Birk's blue and velveteen that every girl but Hilary knew to yearn for and to covet—she opened it, and there nestled in a little pink velvet cleave was the prettiest ring she had ever seen.

"Trevor?"

"Gosh," he said. "Gosh." From now on, it would be this: Hilary, the dogs and him. He was so nervous! Trevor flung his arms up, in celebration, and asked, "What do you say?" He could hear the soft moaning of the coyotes, a kind of gorgeous, primal soundtrack to this moment.

She had the ring on and was marvelling at the way the diamonds glittered in the waning light. "I say thank you!"

His smile had dwindled; he'd never felt more serious. He said, "But will you marry me?"

"What?"

He raised his eyebrows, nodded. They would later walk out of this park, and either way, he thought, he would not look back. It was a promise he made to himself. Either way, she was his girl and he would not look back. So beautiful, she was; he only had to look at her. . . .

Hilary hadn't thought about marriage before. She had neither considered what a wonderful covenant it might be, nor what an immense commitment and responsibility. She felt something dark and sober pressing in on her, and then she looked to the dully glinting precious stones encircling her finger. The sun was a smear of matte orange on the horizon, and the night air began to chill her to the bone.

The dogs, tired, or perhaps sensing her concern emptying out into the waning light, had all sat or lain down and were arranged around her, sentinels, panting, watching. From time to time they whined, or turned their heads toward the coyotes just outside the sight lines, lurking in shadows, their yips now accelerating toward strangled, deformed howls. Hilary looked around and down several times, the ring, the dogs, the ring, the dogs, and then she bit her bottom lip, looked up at Trevor and said, "OK, sure, why not?"

on the many uses of cedar

GEOFFREY W. COLE

Tomorrow, Fanny's husband will hit her for the first time in their short marriage. Fanny will relive the cold November day he hits her twenty-seven times. Her husband will only remember it once.

❖

This is the day Fanny will repeat twenty-seven times:

A great crack will wake her alone in their cabin on the side of the mountain above North Vancouver. Warm beneath her deerskin and wool blankets, she will elect to remain in bed and will not notice that the flume, whose constant watery babble fills every waking moment, is silent.

Her husband will return to the cabin with one of his wool shirts that she rinsed in the flume the day before. He will tell her: "How many times have I told you not to do the laundry in the flume?"

Then he will hit her.

After he has gone, she will look at the daguerreotype on the wall of the two of them taken May 7th, 1895, their wedding day in San Francisco, and she will realize that the mountain did something to her husband. She will see that the mountain stripped away the boyish fat on his face to expose dark crevices and gullies. She will see that the mountain seeded thick stubble on his chin no razor will remove. She will see that the mountain poured its innumerable icy streams over his heart that scoured away everything but hard stone. She will see that in the two short years since their wedding the mountain remade her husband.

When her husband leaves, she will cook breakfast—always oatmeal with molasses and raisins—and she will carry it up the slick skid road to her husband's men. The braying of the camp mule, Boris, will lead her to the men, though after the third day, she will have the route memorized.

The foreman Marty is a half-Japanese logger who lost his left eye to a faulty sawmill blade and a bottle of rum before he joined her husband's crew. His one eye will see her coming and he will call the men down from their work, which is a tree they felled that morning. Fanny will never have seen a larger tree; even the redwoods she saw as a child will be dwarfed by this grey monster, and redwoods are called the biggest trees in the world. The men who scamper along the huge tree trimming branches are also Japanese, though on the first day Fanny will not know this; she calls them Chinamen.

Marty will have been drinking rum and will say: "What happened to your face?" when he gets his ladle of oatmeal.

"Slipped on an icy stair," Fanny will say.

She will feed the Chinamen, who she thinks are part of the mountain's conspiracy to remake her husband. His crew used to be mixed white and Celestial, but the whites thought they should be paid at least three times what her husband paid the Chinamen, and when he refused, they walked off the job. Only Marty received a raise as he was the only one who could talk to the Chinamen, and he stayed on the mountain.

After Marty and the Chinamen have eaten and Fanny has fed the mule Boris an apple she brought for him, her husband will walk out of the woods and demand that she bring breakfast up to the men at the sawmill and then return to her chores.

After she's fed the silent Chinamen at the sawmill, she will descend the mountain with the empty pot. She will draw water for the laundry from the flume.

The flume looks like a V from head-on. She thinks the flume looks like a snake from the side. It crawls up the mountain on cedar stilts to its source, a mountain stream. At the source, the men who built the flume, her husband and his crew, divert the stream down the v-shaped notch. The flume becomes an artificial stream they use to send bolts of lumber down the mountain to make shingles and siding for the growing cities below. The water is very cold. Her husband's bosses built a cabin beside the flume, away from the main camp, so that someone will always watch the flume and make sure the bolts flow, because sometimes bolts jam in the flume, sometimes tree branches fall across the flume, and sometimes, in particular the day before this day repeated itself twenty-seven times, Fanny loses a piece of laundry that she rinses in the flume and the shirt catches on a cedar seam, freezes, accumulates debris, and causes the flume to jam.

Fanny will hate the flume.

Her other chores will include mending a leaky cedar shingle on the roof, fixing a broken cedar step leading up to their home, sitting on a cedar rocking chair and darning her husband's socks, and sweeping cedar sawdust out of the cabin. Everything is made of cedar because cedar doesn't rot.

Fanny will hate cedar.

A rain storm will start every afternoon. When it is time to cook dinner, Fanny will climb back up the mountain to the main camp where the men sleep and will go to the kitchen cabin, also made of cedar. By then the rain storm will have turned to a thunder storm. She will make dinner, a stew of salted pork, potatoes and onions, and she will feed each of them. Marty, much drunker than that morning, will crack jokes about the poor quality of her cooking: "Tasted better food that had already been eaten and puked up by someone else." The jokes will not be the same every day.

When she comes around with tea at the end of the meal, her husband will reach into his jacket and will pull out a cone more beautiful than anything she has ever seen. Copper-coloured and semi-transparent, the cone won't look like pine, or fir, or cedar; maybe a combination of all three. She will accept the cone, and she will think that maybe the mountain hasn't finished remaking her husband.

After she cleans all the dishes, she will walk home alone through the storm with only lightning to guide her way. She will find her husband entering numbers into his ledger. She will be unable to speak to him about what happened that morning because her father never let any of his five daughters talk back to him, and because she will be afraid of the man the mountain remade. She will watch him writing and she will try to use the force of her mind to get her husband to look up and speak to her, but he won't. She will try to get the fire going bright enough to chase the chill from the cedar cabin by burning small pieces of cedar, but the chill won't leave.

Thunder will rattle the walls of their cabin. He will climb into bed first. She will wait and hope that his body warms the cold sheets, but it never does. The mountain has drained all heat from his limbs. She will crawl in beside him and together they will both flinch every time another crack of thunder shakes the cabin and fills the air with cedar dust.

Then lightning will flash so bright that it shines through the solid wood walls of their home.

When the lightning recedes, it will take everything with it, and the day will begin again.

❖

Not every day will be the same.

❖

On the second day, Fanny will wake up to the great crack and find that her cheek isn't bruised. She will assume she had a terrible, vivid dream. When her husband enters the cabin with the same frozen laundry that jammed the flume and hits her again, she will wonder if maybe she can see the future, like her eldest sister claimed about their dead mother. She will attend to her chores, the same chores she attended to the day before. As thunder peals that night while she and her husband lie flinching beside each other on a mattress made of cedar sawdust, she will pray that tomorrow is a new day.

❖

On the third day, Fanny will rise without a bruise and her husband will re-make it for her. On the third day, Fanny will realize that she is being forced to relive this day, this one day when her husband hits her.

When she brings breakfast to the men, one-eyed Marty will look at her bruised face and say: "Wait, let me guess. You slipped on an icy stair."

"Do you remember it too?" she will ask. "Does this day keep happening?"

"Same day," he will say. "Same shit." And then he will drink rum from a flask.

Fanny will think that if she can stop her husband from hitting her, she might be able to make the day stop repeating.

❖

On the fourth day, she will rise out of bed the moment the great crack wakes her. She will rush through the woods beside the flume on its cedar stilts. She will trip and smash her shin so that it bleeds. She will find her husband at the spot where his frozen shirt and the debris it accumulated jams the flume. She will apologize, she will beg him not to hit her, but the mountain remade the man she loves, and he will knock her down. For the rest of that day, she will remain in bed, and her shin will bleed through the sheets.

Her shin will be unmarked the next day.

❖

On the fifth, sixth, and seventh days, she will remain in bed. These days are the same. Her husband will arrive with the frigid laundry, he will hit her even when she burrows beneath the covers. Then she will lie in bed and wait. Ravens outside will clack their beaks at the same time each day. Rain will arrive on schedule, and it will come pouring through the shingle she doesn't mend. Her husband will arrive before dinner and she will claim she doesn't feel well. He will tell her: "You can stay in bed today, but this can't happen tomorrow."

It will happen tomorrow.

❖

After these three days in bed, she will rise to the sound of the great crack. She will wonder: is it the sound of my husband's fist on my face? Is it the sound to the great grey tree falling? Is it the sound of the world splitting in two? Is it the drums of Hell? Am I dead?

Her husband will hit her and she will make breakfast. She will carry it up the mountain. When she finds the men beside the massive tree, Boris the mule will be the first at her side, and the beast will nose her pocket for the apple she's forgotten.

Marty will push the mule out of the way.

"Damn-me but you were right," he will say. "This day's repeating. What in the hell?"

She will take his full mug of rum and drink it in one gulp. She will feel warm for the first time since they moved to the mountain. Her husband will walk out of the woods and send her to feed the men at the sawmill. Once breakfast is done, she will return to the cedar cabin, crack open her husband's shipping chest and find the bottle of port his uncle gave them on their wedding night. The sweet wine will keep her warm through the afternoon as she stares at the daguerreotype on the wall.

She will see that the mountain has changed her too. Her skin, always pale, will seem thin as the frost that coats the cedar flume in the morning. Her hair, once long and chestnut, will hang like the lichen from the trees, streaked with grey. And her eyes that stare back at her from the shaving mirror her husband never uses, her eyes will be the colour of the mountain's damp earth.

Dinner will be burned that night. Her husband will give her the translucent, copper-coloured cone when she comes by with the tea. As she cleans up in the kitchen, while the Chinamen drink sake and her husband returns to their cabin, Marty the one-eyed foreman will bring a bottle into the kitchen and say: "Finest rum I ever tasted."

"I'd hate to waste it," she will say.

And he will laugh, and his breath will stink like a distillery.

"It's full every morning," he will say. "A drunkard's dream."

They will drink all of the bottle.

"They aren't really Chinamen," Marty will say as they drink and rain pounds the roof. "They're Japs. Good thing they don't speak English, cause if they heard us calling them Chinamen they'd get bitter. And I ain't half Chinese neither. My Pa was British, my Ma Japanese."

"How did they meet?" she will say.

"My father had enough money and a hankering for Orientals," he will say.

She will laugh. He will not.

"Why don't the rest of them realize the day keeps repeating?" she will say.

He will offer her another mug full.

"Who cares," he will say. "More rum for us."

While thunder gathers around them, she will talk. Growing

up in San Francisco will seem even more wonderful through the murky lens of the rum. She will tell him about her five sisters, and the father who raised them after his wife died giving birth to the last of them. She will even cry a bit when she tells him about her mother, the one memory of the foggy day watching the boats sail in.

As the storm reaches its crest, he will say: "Just about done, I think."

"I hate the lightning," she will say, and she will reach out and take hold of his hand which will be knobby and root-like and totally unlike her husband's. "Especially the last one."

The lightning will flash through the walls of the cabin and when it recedes it will draw everything else with it and the day will begin again.

❖

She will rise to the great crack. No bruise will mar her face. No hangover will cloud her mind. Her husband will hit her. She will bring breakfast up the mountain. Ravens will clack their beaks. Instead of returning down the mountain after breakfast, she will find Marty and they will sneak to the kitchen cabin at the main camp, and they will open the bottle of rum they finished the day before. He will tell her more about life in the slums of Tokyo, and she will tell him about the fish market in San Francisco.

They will do this for several days.

❖

On the twelfth day, after the crack, after the blow from her husband, and after breakfast, she and Marty will lie beneath one of the great trees the loggers haven't yet felled. The rum bottle will lie half-full at their feet. They will be talking about why this day keeps repeating:

"Do you think it's that big tree?" she will say. "I've never seen one like it."

"Me neither," he will say.

"What if you don't cut it down?" she will say.

He will shrug.

"Each day starts for you in bed," he will say. "But for me it's there, beside the tree, as the damn thing falls over. There's the lightning, then there I am, standing and watching as my boys topple the big tree."

"So it is the tree," she will say.

He will pull out a pouch from his pocket and a long strange pipe of the kind she's only heard about.

"Who cares?" he will say. "This ain't such a bad day to be stuck in."

He will pack a slick bit of tar into the bowl, he will light a match, and he will inhale. He will pass the pipe to Fanny.

"I shouldn't," she will say, but then she will take the pipe and she will smoke it and she will lie down on the damp ground beside Marty until the rain starts and they walk down the hill for dinner.

❖

From the thirteenth to the twenty-third day, Fanny will smoke opium with Marty and will remember very little. Her husband will talk to her in this time when he finds her. He will scold her. He will hit her. He will bring her the present of the copper, translucent cone that comes from no tree she's ever seen. She will know that she should talk to her husband, that she should tell him that the days keep repeating, and that she wants the man in the daguerreotype, the man she married, to become unmade by the mountain, but she will also hold the cone he gives her, the beautiful cone that shows the mountain hasn't finished with her husband, and she will wonder if it is enough. The opium will make it easier to not answer that question; it won't hurt so long as she keeps smoking.

❖

Like every day, the twenty-fourth will start with the great crack, her husband's fist, and a flume that doesn't flow. After breakfast, she will find Marty and they will smoke opium beneath the same old tree under which they first smoked. They will also drink the rum and smoke some of the hemp that never runs out. She will pass out.

When she wakes up, Marty will be on top of her. His trousers will be around his ankles. She will feel him thrusting into her and the opium will make her not want to scream but she will scream. He will put his root-like fingers over her mouth and clamp her mouth shut until he finishes hot and sticky down the sides of her legs. He will roll over onto his back and sigh.

"I'm married," she will say once his fingers release her mouth and the opium lets her speak.

"Tomorrow," he will say. "It won't have happened."

He will light one of his hemp cigarettes. When he passes it to her, she will take the lit end and she will press it into his palm. Now he will scream. She will pull up her undergarments and she will run down the mountain. She will run away from the slashed areas and into the forest where huge trees still stand. As she runs, she will weep. She will mourn the sanctity of her marriage. She will curse the day she first took a sip from Marty's mug.

She will hate the flume, the lightning, the cedar, and herself.

As she runs, she will come to a cliff. For a moment, she will hesitate at the cliff's edge. She will hear no one following her. She will jump, and as she falls, she will think of sailboats in the fog.

When she hits the rocks, she will die.

❖

The great crack will sound for a twenty-fifth time. She will rise. No bruise. No hangover. No death. None of Marty's stickiness between her legs.

She will hear her husband on the steps. She will endure his punch. Ravens will clack beaks. Eventually, her husband will start the water flowing back down the flume. The roar will fill the cabin, and the roar will seep into her, fill her with resolve.

At her husband's sawmill, Japanese Chinamen turn cedar trees into bolts, wedge-shaped logs that fit into the v-notched flume. One day her husband caught the men riding down the flume on a narrow skiff they carved from a cedar bolt. He confiscated the skiff and hid it beneath their cabin. Though he warned her never to touch the dangerous thing, she will push aside spider webs and mouldy lumber until she finds the shallow boat, which will be no wider than her hips, no deeper than her forearm and no longer than her husband is tall. She will drag the skiff up the steps by a rope handle looped through its nose and she will lift it onto the edge of the flume. She will climb up beside the skiff and for a moment she will be mesmerized by the white water that rushes past her feet. Then she will slide the skiff beneath her and let the roaring stream her husband has redirected pull her down the mountain.

Her screams will startle ravens and woodpeckers from their roosts. The skiff will knock beneath her as the flume makes corners. Water will soak through her wool shirts until she shivers but she won't let go of the rope. Though she will be terrified as she slides down the cedar flume, a part of her will sing with the joy of escape.

Ahead through the trees she will see an expanse of dark blue. The flume will spit her out into Rice Lake, a holding pen where the bolts are then ferried down another flume to the city. She will swim to the surface though her sodden clothes will drag her down. That first breath after she is dunked will feel like her baptism.

A bolt will fly off the flume and will strike her in the thigh, and her leg will break in two places. She will swallow water as she tries to scream. One of the loggers rowing a boat around the lake to herd bolts will notice her struggles. He will be a pale blonde man too young for a beard. He will row over to her, drag her out of the water, and bring her to the cabin, also cedar, where these loggers live.

Most of them will be white. They will scold her for riding the flume, though they have all ridden the flume before. They will send for a doctor.

Talking to these men who aren't Marty and aren't her husband will be the brightest moment in the last twenty-five days. The pain in her leg will be unbearable. She will refuse the whiskey and opium they offer her.

As she lies in a cot that stinks of sweat, mud, and cedar, she will think that she has escaped it. The repetition is over. A doctor will come and everything will be all right.

The young logger will come in and tell her they've sent someone to fetch her husband. Later, the same logger will return to tell her that the doctor will arrive tomorrow.

"He has to come today," she will say. She won't believe in that word, tomorrow.

"He'll come as fast as he's able," the young logger will say.

Rain will start slightly later than it does further up the

mountain. A headache will set in behind her eyes, and her leg will throb with each beat of her heart, and as her blood fills the cavities the broken bones have slashed inside her flesh, her leg will swell like wet cedar.

After the first peal of thunder, the young logger will come in and say: "There's someone here to see you."

Despite the pain, she will sit, expecting the doctor or her husband, but the person who will walk through the door is neither. He is a young boy of seven or eight; maybe Indian or Chinamen or Japanese. She won't be able to tell for the filth that cakes him. He will walk over to her.

"You haven't happened before," he will say. "Are you like us?"

"You know about this?" she will say. Her heart will pound louder than the thunder. "Does this day keep happening for you?"

He will nod his filthy head.

"Have you seen it?" he will say. "We think they cut it down."

"The tree?" she will say. "My husband's men felled a huge tree this morning."

"Where?" he will say.

She will point up the mountain. "The flume runs eight miles back to the cabin, and the tree is another mile or two beyond that."

He will sigh, a sound she will think should come from an old man many times this boy's age.

"That's too far," he will say. "Most of us start by the water. It took me all day to get here."

"You know how to make this stop? You know what to do?"

He will pick something from his ear that he will wipe on his muddy shirt.

"The old people told us the tree needs to grow again," he will say. "They sent us out to find it."

"My husband brings me a cone," she will say. "A cone like none I've ever seen. Do you think that's it?"

He will shrug.

The fever that has been building in her will take hold then. Her words will stop making sense. The filthy boy will sit beside her and hold her hand until she dies.

❖

The crack. Her leg will be healed, the bruise on her cheek will be gone. Her husband will be on the stairs with his cold shirt and colder fist. The twenty-sixth day.

She will pull herself up from the floor. She will bring breakfast to the men where they climb over the dead massive tree. Boris the mule will nuzzle her pocket for the apple she will forget.

"Where'd you go yesterday?" Marty will say when he comes up to her for breakfast. She will not say anything in return. "You can't stay silent forever. It's just you and me, pumpkin. May as well make the best of it."

And he will pinch her bottom as he walks away to eat his oatmeal.

Her husband will come down the hill and tell her to bring breakfast to the men at the sawmill, but she'll ignore him. She'll climb up the length of the downed tree. The stump will be forty paces across. At its centre, she will find a hole a few inches deep that ends in fine sawdust. The wood around the hole will be blackened from an old fire. This, she will think, is where the cone must go.

"What are you doing up there?" Marty will say. He will hold a big two-person saw over one shoulder and will squint out of his good eye.

"Nothing," she will say. "I've got work to do."

She will climb down the planks the Japanese loggers drove into the tree to serve as platforms for cutting. Marty will try to grab her arm but she will shake him off.

"You come back and see Marty as soon as you're ready for some more," he will say.

She will look for a cone, but she won't find one. She will have to wait until dinner when her husband gives her the cone after the tea is served, and she will know there is still something decent within her husband. With the dishes unwashed and the storm raging, she will climb up the mountain alone through the downpour with only lightning to illuminate her path.

When she arrives at the tree, she will find Boris the mule waiting for her. He will be very quiet and will follow her up the length of the downed tree. She will climb the stump again. When she takes the cone out of her shirt, the cone will glow with a soft light the same colour as the lightning. She will place the cone in the hole she found earlier that day. Though the cone will fit, something will seem to push the cone out of the hole if she doesn't hold it there. She will climb back down to find some stones or sticks to make a brace to hold the cone in place, and that's when she will see Marty standing beneath an ancient hemlock.

"Now I'm real curious," he will say. "You disappear for a day and you come back with all sorts of new ideas."

"Leave me alone," she will say. He will laugh, and even through the rain she will be able to smell the distillery.

Boris the mule will bray louder than she's ever heard him. Marty will jump out of the darkness but her shirt will be too soaked for him to get a hold. She will climb back up the stump. Lightning will flash and thunder roll. She will know the last flash is close.

She will place the glowing cone in the hole at the centre of the stump. In one of the flashes, she will see Marty's face at the edge of the stump. In the next, she will see him pull up onto the lip of the stump.

The last bolt of lightning will cut through the air. It will seem like light jumps out of the cone in her hand to meet the lightning. She will try to hold onto the cone even as the lightning pours through her. Marty will be blasted back, away from the cone. She won't be able to hold on. The cone will roll out of the hole. The light will recede, sucked back into the cone, and when it disappears the day will start again.

❖

Day twenty-seven will start like every other. The crack. Her unblemished face. Her husband on the steps. This time, after he hits her, she will say: "That Marty made inappropriate advances to me a few days ago. I don't want to see him again."

"He's the only one who can speak with the Chinamen," her husband will say.

"I don't care," she will say. "I won't feed him."

She won't bring breakfast up the mountain that day. She will barricade the door and lie in bed, gathering her strength. When she hears Marty yelling at her from outside, she will remain where she is, even when he slams his fists against the door.

"Don't you dare try to end this," he will say. "Don't you even dare."

After the rain comes, she will hear her husband return. He will try the door and he will say: "What's going on here?"

"That Marty tried to come in," she said. "I told you, there's something wrong with him."

She will move the shipping chest and the wood chair out of the way and she will let her husband in. He will not smile.

"I'll talk to him," he will say.

"Don't let him come to dinner," she will say.

His eyes, as hard as the stones she wrecked herself on when she jumped off the cliff, will soften for a moment.

"All right," he will say. "But you get down there and get cooking. This can't happen tomorrow."

She will go down to the kitchen with her husband. She will make the same stew she made before; the ingredients will all be there. Marty will not join them for dinner. She will hear him cursing outside. She will be very afraid of what he will do.

After the dinner, her husband will reach into his coat and will present her with the copper-coloured cone. Instead of accepting it, she will take his hand, and she will say: "Come with me up the mountain. I need to show you something."

"I've got to enter my numbers," he will say. "And you need to clean up this mess."

She will hesitate then. She will not know if she can face this man the mountain has turned into somebody different. Thunder will shake the cabin. Cedar dust will fall into her hair. She will hope that the small part that remains of the man she married is enough.

"Please," she will say. "Do this for me."

All the Japanese Chinamen will be watching. He will nod and she will lead him out into the storm.

They will climb the skid road together.

"Is this about what happened this morning?" he will say.

"No," she will say. "Yes. I don't know. Just follow."

They will come to the clearing where the massive trees lies on its side. Boris the mule will greet them with a loud honk.

As the mule presses his flank into her, she will rub him between the ears and will say: "You can remember it too, can't you?"

The mule will follow them up to the tree.

"It's too dark to be up here," her husband will say.

"Just a bit longer," she will say.

"Lightning's a logger's worst enemy," he will say.

"Just a bit longer," she will say. She will not release his hand.

When they come to the massive stump, she will turn to him and take the cone from his pocket.

"What in God's name?" he will say as the cone glows with faint blue light.

"We have to plant it," she will say. "So that the tree can grow again. I can't do it alone."

This is when Marty will rush out of the forest with his axe. He will run straight at her husband.

"Marty, what're you doing?" her husband will say.

Marty will only snarl as he charges and raises the axe. Her husband will reach for the knife at his belt as he steps between her and the foreman, and that is when Boris the mule will lash out with his two hind legs. The animal will cave in Marty's chest. The axe will tumble to the ground beside the foreman's limp body.

Fanny will exhale a breath she didn't realize she was holding. She will place a hand on her husband's shoulder.

"We need to get him help," he will say.

"He's dead," she will say. She will pat the mule on the head and say, "Good boy."

Lightning will flash and thunder will roll and Fanny will know the time is near.

"Come on," she will say. She will take her husband's hand and she will climb up the planks driven into the stump.

"Fanny, this is madness," her husband will say.

"We won't have another chance," she will say. "He'll come back."

He will follow her.

She will guide him to the centre of the stump. She will place the glowing cone in the hole and she will ask him to kneel beside her. Together, they will hold it in place.

"Now what?" her husband will say.

"Just hold on," she will say.

The lightning that starts it all again will arrive. Light will leap up from the cone to meet the electricity arcing down. Energy will course through her, she will see it run through her husband. She will see his hand loosen on the glowing cone.

"Hold on," she will scream. The lightning will last longer than any lightning can last. It will last as long as the universe exists.

And it will end. They will both fall aside, breathing, stunned. The heart of the stump will be blackened and burnt and so will their clothing.

The Japanese Chinamen will find them when they hear Boris the mule braying into the night. They will take Fanny down in a stretcher they make out of cedar-smelling bedsheets and will take her husband down on the mule's back.

❖

In the morning, they will wake in their small bed in their little cabin beside the roaring flume. Their clothes will be ashes, but their skin will be untouched. Her husband will be in the bed beside her. He will be warm. They will wake up together.

"We need to talk," she will say.

They will talk as they walk up the mountain. The trees will drip from the previous night's rain. The ravens will complain. Boris will meet them halfway and Fanny will remember to bring him an apple. They will climb the stump of the massive tree.

A green shoot will grow up from the blackened cone and will reach a pair of tiny green leaves toward the sky.

❖

All this will happen tomorrow. Today, Fanny rinses her husband's shirts in the flume. One of the shirts gets away from her.

She doesn't think he will miss it.

obscured
RHONDA PARRISH

Ghosts of the city
peer out of the gloom
around him
As a child he'd loved it
when the "clouds fell down"
and cloaked his world
in mysteries
Now, though,
it was just one more thing
to hide the shamblers.
One more obstacle to
his survival.
One more enemy.

hawkwood's folly
TIMOTHY REYNOLDS

le 17e septembre, 1889.

I write this down and lock it away. Let the world know the truth—la vérité—*after* I am gone.

There was a time, not so long ago, before they erected that iron monstrosity, the Eiffel Tower—before I lost my family's entire fortune at the bottom of the Atlantic Ocean—when I would have awakened to the rapturous perfume of warm crêpes, fresh strawberries and rich cream commingled with dark, African roast coffee and a petite portion of potatoes and scallions pan-fried in garlic butter and dill. In through the double doors out over the Champs Élysées I would have been serenaded by the pleasant jingle of harness, clop of hoof and clatter of carriage as all of Paris seemed to pass beneath my balcony. Not very exciting, I agree, but certainly a more delicious start to the day than a trio of pistol shots, a garbled shout in Russian, heavy metal clanging rhythmically on the cobbles beneath my window, and frantic, clumsy, human footsteps racing up two flights of stairs, ending in a life-or-death iron pounding on the cheap fabricated door of my rented room.

With this rude awakening, gone were the crêpes, the dark roast, the dill, and the balcony overlooking the Champs Élysées. I stumbled from the lopsided cot, lit the lamp and tore open the door, fully prepared to give a sound beating to the offender, only to be met by Grigori. A tall, lanky, boy of twenty, he was soaking wet in a torn waistcoat and stinking foully of la rivière Seine. He sported a bleeding wound to his left temple and was holding a smoking pistol up to pound its butt on my portal once again.

Gone, too, was Grigori, meek bo's'n's mate who never looked comfortable amongst his social betters, a group I once proudly counted myself a member of. Scruffy and bearded, he tripped past me and into my squalid room. His wide-eyed, terrified gaze searched the nine-yard-square space for any threat greater than the empty bottle of cheap Bordeaux and the chamber pot much in need of emptying. There was no threat here. I, Georges DeBlois, surgeon, entrepreneur and multiple patent-holder, was not at my best.

"Bolt the door! Quick! Do you have a pistol, docteur?!" Grigori had been a rough-edged Russian peasant at the best of times so I was only slightly put off by his brusque entrance and complete lack of civil greeting. "*A pistol*? Do you have one? I have only one bullet remaining!"

"A pistol?" The loud crash of the destruction of the front door of the building froze us both where we stood, but Grigori recovered soonest.

"Too late!" He shoved a small, surprisingly heavy, burlap sac into my hands and grabbed my old walking stick leaning against the bed. With the pistol in one hand and the stick in the other, he backed toward the open window. "Flee with me or die my brother mariner! We are betrayed!"

"But I cannot simply—" A high-pitched hiss of steam whistled from the stairwell followed by the grinding of small mechanical gears and pistons, whining and struggling. I knew those sounds only too well. "An automaton, boy? You flee an automaton?! Impossible!" I knew only too well that this was not just any man-mocking, mechanical, sideshow puppet, but one of Lord Mordecai Hawkwood's custom designed, steam-driven men of metal. Terror twisted my intestines and inspiration struck—I glanced in the sac. I wanted so badly to be wrong but fear I was not. The sac contained the head of another such mechanical man. "Mon dieu! You stupid boy!! What have you done?!"

Slower on foot than a man of flesh and bone, the contraption ascending toward us possessed the strength of five men and through wireless signals could communicate with others of its ilk. If a living, breathing man were at the other end of the transmission doing the thinking and decision-making then it would be an unstoppable force.

I clutched the burlapped mechanical skull and followed the terrified Grigori over the sill and onto the fire escape. Having fallen so far from grace I no longer had a carriage at my disposal nor the funds with which to hire one so this would be a footrace. As I backed myself out into the cool, damp air, the papier-thin barricade masquerading as a door erupted inward. Shards of cheap board and veneer flew every which way as one of Hawkwood's humanistic contraptions crashed through. I saw my money belt on the night stand at the same moment the metal menace sighted me. That belt contained all I had left in the world and so I hesitated. That moment of indecision was all that the automaton needed. Despite the poor light I saw the dart leave the end of the index finger of its right hand a moment before I felt its sting. I slumped forward over the sill, wondering with my last conscious thought how it had come to pass that the dart was used against myself rather than a denizen of the deep.

When consciousness tracked me down I was back in my own bed, which is to say that I lay between fine Egyptian cotton sheets under a goose-down duvet a hundred yards beneath the surface of the Atlantic Ocean off the coast of North Africa. I was once again in Hawkwood's Haven, which meant that I was dreaming with great lucidity or that the explosion of the volcanic hydrothermal vent and the resultant collapse of the supporting rock face didn't do nearly the degrees of damage to the Haven as I had assumed when I was retreating back to the surface in the self-contained escape pod six months before.

As curiously divine as the flea-free bedding was, it was the scent of strawberries, cream and dark roast which brought me to full, though confused, wakefulness. I sat bolt upright and paid the price with a rush of nausea my own patients regularly complained of on the other side of a heavy dose of sodium bromide. I leaned over the edge of the bed and vomited what little my stomach contained. It was only then, in that less-than-flattering position, that I took notice of the lack of a rug of any sort and, despite the domed ceiling and rounded walls, was now quite certain that I was not in my former suite at all but a former storage closet.

With my stomach emptied of its pitiful contents I laid my throbbing head back on the stately pillow and immediately succumbed to sleep, the breakfast forgotten.

When at last I awoke with a steady head, the food, the vomi and the throbbing were gone. In their places were a jug of water, a crystal water goblet, a clear head, and a handwritten note in a choppy, unsure version of Hawkwood's own hand. My own hand was now much steadier as I retrieved the note and read it aloud, to no one in particular.

"Georges—my friend—please excuse the rough handling which brought you back here to the Haven. I have answers to all of your questions but one I will answer here and now. You are here because I am alive. Please come to the infirmary as soon as you are able. Your fellow submariner and friend, Hawkwood." And so I drank a goodly amount of water, splashed a dab more on my face to bring a bit of wakefulness and left the closet behind. Once in the corridor I was met by one of the cursed automatons. Yes, cursed. Though I once believed them mechanical marvels, since being darted, drugged and abducted, I was less enthused of Hawkwood's brilliance.

But I had returned to the Haven and there were questions I needed answered so I set forth for the infirmary as requested, with the metal menace two steps behind me. There was no sign of Grigori about so I suspect that his boyish reflexes had aided his escape where mine had failed.

It took a moment to get myself reoriented, especially since the floor canted somewhat to the left. An arrow accompanied by a red cross painted on the wall told me exactly where I was in the complex and with one hand on the downhill wall for support I stumbled on. I may have soured on the presence of the automatons, but as I made my way through the complex I was still quite proud of our little project. Between Hawkwood's structural engineering genius and my respirator design modified to scrub and revitalize our air, we had done the impossible and established a ten-edifice complex on the ocean floor! We had powered it off the hydrothermal vents and, judging by the flickering electric light illuminating our way and the clean crispness of the cool air, the generators worked still. More and more I marvelled at how much had survived the sub-marine landslide.

We came to a junction and I turned left, following the arrow and the red cross, but the way was blocked by a wall of collapsed rock. Closer inspection showed fresh repairs and a petite puddle of seawater at the base of the rubble-cum-wall so I turned and followed the corridor the long way around. My silent companion—Delta by the insignia on his scratched and dented chest plate—clanked and whirred along behind me.

Two turns later I was reminded why I fell in love with Hawkwood's proposal in that salon in Marseille three years before. The corridor lighting was greatly reduced, but that was by design, so that the view through the massive bubbled window was as clear as could be. I stopped, as I had every other time I passed this look-out, this sub-oceanic observatory.

The hydrothermic vents powering our little habitat provided heat and chemistry unavailable elsewhere and despite the rift in the vent which had caused the structural collapse behind us, life continued in abundance there, on the other side of the glass. A lethargic, white zoarcid fish snapped at an orange tube worm but missed, and the yard-long worm retracted at lightning speed back into its hard, protective chitin tube. I saw a modest tentacle reach out from behind a mass of tubes and our petite, resident octopus plucked a white Galatheid crab from his own meal on the mussel bed. Life went on here and not one of them cared that I watched in wonder.

Delta waited patiently whilst I let myself be lulled by the gentle waving to-and-fro of the two-foot-long sea worms in the current. I regarded my escort, wondering.

"Do you see what I see, metal man?" I placed my palm affectionately on the glass, still surprised at the warmth this far below the surface. "Do you understand the marvel that we created here or do you simply follow your wireless commands and complete your tasks? Does the tableau magnifique before us stir you in any way? Does it make your clockworks speed up at all, or even slow, as it matches the marine rhythm?" It turned its head toward me but remained silent.

"You and your three fellows were the brawn to our brain and did the heavy, tedious work we were incapable of at this depth, but did you understand then or even now what was being constructed? What a marvel this was—is?" It blinked twice at me, but whether it was programming or a sign of understanding I know not. I returned to watching our maritime neighbours, observing features and behaviours no man had seen before, certainly no man of science.

After a moment Delta did acknowledge my presence by gently taking my elbow in its steel grip and turning me firmly back on track. We were expected in the Infirmary and I suspect he just received a command to see that we arrived post haste. With a last look out at the magnificent sea bed within arm's reach, I shook free of the hand and marched on.

Three more piles of rubble in collapsed and blocked passages told me that the sea cliff's collapse had indeed destroyed much of our mariners' residence, including the dormitories carved out of the cliff itself. We continued on, once or twice taking a longer route to avoid what I guessed were impassable areas. I could see that Hawkwood's three remaining automatons had been busy, with pathways cleared through rubble and in some cases the rubble cleaned up entirely and probably taken elsewhere to shore up a failing dam to the sea water yearning to burst through.

A quiescent bilge pump sat next to one such dam and I realized then how truly precarious the situation was. When the domed buildings were intact and firmly seated on the sea floor, the habitat was safe and secure, but now, with the breaches so evident and the automatons struggling to keep the sea at bay, we were in danger and the novelty of it all left me cold and un peu claustrophobic. Even the biologist in me wanted no more of it. Exploration by bathysphere would be more than sufficient.

I hurried my step and with little further guidance from Delta, soon found myself sitting at the bedside of the man I had, until recently, presumed dead.

"Do I terrify you, Georges?"

"I am a man of medicine—there is nothing of the human condition which terrifies me." I had seen leprosy, pox, syphilis, but *nothing* like this. Rien. Nothing.

"Yes, you've seen much, ol' chap, but I would wager that this is new."

I looked at a mechanical eye, a skull more metal plate and bolt than bone. The left arm above the sheet was mechanical contrivance from the elbow down to a steel-cable and lubricated-piston hand whilst beneath the sheet the right was machine from the shoulder down. The angry violet redness of an infection radiated from the shoulder socket across his once strong pectoral toward his heart. I suspected he had little time remaining.

"Nouveau? Bien sûr. Certainly."

"Also both inner ears, one lung and both legs below the knee."

"How . . . ?"

"They found me after the cave-in, trapped in an air pocket

inside the Refectory." He took a long, rasping breath and coughed sputum into that mechanized hand. Very human bloody spittle flecked his full Victorian whiskers and I saw sadness in his still human eye.

"The Refectory. We were three men and four automatons—what did we need with a full-sized refectory. A simple dining room would have sufficed."

"Maybe in the beginning, but our plans were to expand." I reassured him. "To bring selected men and women here to live and work. Your mining operation and my marine-farm."

"Were we out of our minds? Did we throw good money after bad and dream beyond reality?"

I rested my hand on his good shoulder and squeezed gently. "Greatness is only achieved when honest men take risks, mon ami." But silently, to myself, I now agree that we had over-reached here.

"Were we honest, Georges? To ourselves? To each other?" He coughed and I went to a small cabinet behind what had once been my desk. There I found a small satchel of personal "elixirs of medicinal nature," as my grandmama was wont to call such things.

"Honest? I would suppose that we were as honest as business partners can be, although our motives may have differed somewhat when we built our misguided sub-maritime paradise." I administered to him a good-sized dose of my narcotic blend and Mordecai, Lord Hawkwood, smiled lopsidedly.

"We did do it, though, did we not? We carved a settlement beneath the sea and powered it all from the adjacent steam vents . . ."

"Oui, mon ami, we did indeed. In one year we constructed what no man had ever dared and for six months we lived in it, aided by your 'marvellous' creations. We had big dreams, Mordecai."

"Yet, have I wasted the talents of a brilliant surgeon? Kept him from the greatness he deserves?" More coughing, though not as heavily as before.

"Save both your strength and your kind words of praise. I am a simple country chirurgien who has allowed this failed venture to keep me down in a morass of self-pity. I have been living as one lost in les catacombes beneath Paris where we first tested your theories; but seeing you here, not willing to fold your hand and lay your cards down has renewed my vigour for life."

"Excellent, excellent."

"May I ask how you found me? Out of shame, I have not been living under my own name for some months now."

From deep within, Hawkwood seemed to find joy at his inventiveness and allowed it to bubble up into a smile worthy of the dreamer who had sold me on his great scheme in the first place. "Grigori. Between his mystical visions he found time and means to launch a small salvage operation."

"Grigori?" I was doubtful.

"Our young Russian returned to our Moroccan warehouse in Agadir and cobbled together enough equipment to make his way back down. That impetuous boy learned more from both of us than we could have imagined." He coughed, shuddered and his eye drifted in the orbit for a moment, appearing untethered. He regained control and once more focussed on my face, though with some difficulty.

"He found me here, just after the surgery. I was in much better condition than what you are witnessing now and so, once we were both satisfied that neither was here to kill the other, we chatted at some length. He had believed he was the only survivor of the Haven, since he was topside checking the buoys when the vent ruptured.

We talked some more and eventually I sent him with poor Gamma's skull to find you, knowing that you would better believe his story of my survival with the head as proof. I sent him merely to extend an invitation to return, unfortunately my condition worsened after he departed and with no way to get a message to him to change the degree of urgency, I was left with no choice but to send Alpha out into the world to fetch you."

"But how?"

"He followed the homing signal still active in Gamma's cerebrum. I should have known that Grigori would react the way he did when Alpha caught up to him—he never really trusted the mechanicals. Of course, when Grigori shot at him, Alpha reacted as he was trained and it all tumbled downhill from there, starting with gunfire in the streets of Paris and ending in your subsequent drugged abduction."

"I would have come willingly. I never had a chance to get your message from Grigori, nor to ponder the contents of the sac for long."

"I know, I know. My sincerest apologies, ol' chap. The single-mindedness of task completion in the automatons is one of the issues I wish to address on the cognitive level."

I looked again at the infected shoulder and his grey pallor, listened to his belaboured breathing, and doubted he had time enough to address anything, though I kept that thought very much to myself as well.

"Before he departed to find you, Grigori squared up and told me that, thinking us all dead, he had returned for the gold. Once I knew that I gave him a handful of doblones as partial advance payment for the delivery of the message. Since he did not return with you and Alpha I must assume he is still running and will eventually make his way back home to Russia where he will marry Praskovia and try to forget the sea and the gold owed to him."

"Gold?" I knew of no gold here.

"The doblones we recovered that very morning. I was on my way to show you the amazing samples when all bloody hell broke loose. Although the cliff collapsed on this wing, the domed structure which allows Haven to resist the pressure of the sea saved her from the rock above."

I was shocked. "Mordecai, when the silt settled and my sealed-off laboratory was all that remained, I despaired. Like Grigori, I thought myself the only survivor. I waited three days but when my air-revitalizer failed I had no choice but to gather my journal and a bottle of port and trigger the emergency surfacer. My heart broke, sir, when I rose up from and above the ruin of our dreams and—less importantly—our fortunes. Gold, you say?"

"Doblones. Eighteenth Century Spanish coins. We managed to save one chest before the cave-in buried the lion's share. Your half is in that small box behind you, against the wall."

I turned and spotted the boîte immediately. Making a poor attempt to appear less eager than I felt, I opened it and my heart nearly stopped. It was no Blackbeard's treasure, but it was gold and it was easily twice what I had invested in Hawkwood's Haven. I looked back over my shoulder to my dying partner. "You are certain of this?"

"It is the least I owe you for your faith in this madman's dream. I have but one last favour to ask of you, as a doctor. The doblones are yours whether you accept or refuse so feel no obligation from that quarter."

"A medicant to aid your final release? Something to ease your pain as you move on?" He would not live long in his bastardized mélange of a shell, which was probably best. I saw less of mon ami in that face than I did a mechanical contrivance.

He laughed. "Not at all, my friend. My automatons are most capable in that field, should it become necessary. In fact, they are so capable that they have one final surgery to perform."

"*Surgery*? You have an infection. Poisoned blood. No surgeries will repair that."

"None but one, my sceptical Frenchman. Or it may not. But should it succeed . . . should it be done with any degree of success, I would have you by my side through it all to oversee the work and to revel in the greatness of my new reality."

And so, not two hours later, Mordecai, Lord Hawkwood, had his mad, dying brain transplanted from his failing hybrid of flesh and machine into a fully mechanical host designed in part by myself a year previous, although at the drawing board I had believed it was to be a somewhat more conventional life-support system. The procedure took a bit more than eight hours and throughout it all I could only stare dumbstruck as Mordecai's remaining three mechanicals worked with a surgical speed and precision far beyond that of any human surgeons I had ever worked with or even heard mention of.

I will admit that more than once during the long night I nearly ripped the human brain from the metal pan and dashed it to the floor to keep this horror from continuing, but I was rooted in place, simultaneously fascinated and repulsed. I was both a God-fearing man and a scientist, an innovator. Their achievement was sheer brilliance, but also an abomination. Oui, they transplanted his brain, his own thinking, reasoning machine, but what of his soul? What of his essence?

My hands quivered and shook even after I stuffed them down into my pockets but when I saw that Epsilon—the mechanical taking the lead—was referring to my own notes on *Medical Field Improvisation, Amputation, and Surgical Procedure*, I wept silently at the inhumanity of it all. I had not even known they could read!

What had we created down here in Poseidon's domain?! At least young Mary Shelley's fictional monster was cobbled together from human parts. This machine—this clockwork caricature—being given life before my eyes was both so much more and so much less than a man.

But, alas, at heart I was a cowardly doctor. Other than

increasing the dosage of the bromide cocktail being used as a sedative and anti-convulsant, I kept out of their way and let them work.

Twenty hours after Mordecai's yellowed, bloodshot human eye closed for the last time, two new, brass-and-glass optical receptors spun open and the "reinvented" man performed a miracle—he spoke. He spoke in a voice resonating of light machine oil and a miniature metal orchestra, yet *he spoke*, and I nearly fell off the cot where I had been grasping at fitful sleep. His words at first were soft and quite raspy, yet as he learned the ways of his new apparatus there grew strength and purpose.

"This . . . is . . . a . . . most *interesting* experience. I can detect my mechanical brethren in way quite similar to how I am hearing my own voice. We are . . . as a small, four-unit hive, yet I retain my individuality. . . . Ah, I see now that they are distinct individuals, though not yet as well-defined as I am." A hive? Mon dieu!

He paused, most probably listening to a voice broadcast between himself and his new kin. His piston and cable fingers twitched and he cocked his clockwork head like a dog attempting to hear better.

"The surfacer is ready and the hydro-boat awaits topside." It was Mordecai's voice, but at the same time it wasn't and it jarred my nerves quite harshly. I realized at that moment that as dearly as I wanted to stay and participate in this incredible breakthrough in medical and engineering science, I found I no longer had either taste or tolerance for life on the ocean floor. The offer to return me topside was perfection.

"How will you fare, mon ami?"

"I will fare well and not want for activity, ol' chap. We have a great deal of work to complete here before it is a sustainable environ once again." He gestured sloppily with his new arms and I believe that a hinge lifted on his speaking aperture, affecting a smile. "At least now I will have the opportunity. Some day, when your mind is still sharp but your body begins to fail, I hope then you will consider joining me on this adventure, my friend. As marvellous as this new body of mine is, over time it will appear crude and primitive as we modify and improve the designs."

I shivered at the thought of trading a flesh body for mechanical self and prayed that I managed to return to the world of humanity before these creations learned to read minds and could see the dark intent forming in my heart. I am no zealot, but I do so believe that beyond this world there is a paradise waiting and I will face my earthly end here with Gallic pride and stubborn faith. At least that is my hope. I see now in Hawkwood's actions and words that it is très possible that he will not stop until all mankind joins his new hive, his dark collective.

And so, I returned to the surface world, the world of sunlight and rain and humanity, taking with me both the Spanish gold I was given and a fresh insight into what dreams may come to. Here, outside Paris, I am well satisfied to invest in dry land and in the new industrial automation growing in London and America. I rebuild what I gambled away on Hawkwood's Haven and mayhap someday will confess to our local Monsignor why I spent a month in that warehouse in Agadir erasing all signs of my involvement in a bizarre project somewhere off the coast.

Perhaps, too, the Monsignor will understand why I converted a goodly portion of those Spanish coins to simple francs and then quietly used the francs for a shipment of explosives in waterproof crates sent down from Stockholm.

I like to believe that some day the world will be ready for a genius the likes of Lord Mordecai Hawkwood, inventor, noble, and steam-driven mechanical dreamer. Mais il ne sera pas aujourd'hui. But it will not be today.

razor voices
KELLY ROSE PFLUG-BACK

"You got skinny," I remember John saying. "They didn't feed you enough?"

His blue eyes had been clearer than I'd remembered, his sharp face patched with eczema.

A haze was hanging over the city and the trees behind it. The sun was high up in the sky, and we cast no shadows. I remember watching his eyes wander over my body in a way that men's eyes rarely do. At first I didn't recognize it, because it had nothing to do with hate, or sex, or both.

"I figured you would be hungry." He said, and he looked down at a container he was holding. It made me cry for some absurd reason, the fact that he'd brought me food.

"I missed you," I answered, because it was easier than telling him what happened; how they gave me food sometimes with piss and broken glass in it, how I just got used to being hungry all the time and after a while stopped noticing, just like when we lived in the squat on Wharf Street and there was never any food.

I wonder now if he'd been able to see how I'd changed, that day– before the words actually came loose from my mouth, before I showed him. I wasn't the saucer-eyed, speechless thing that used to run from him into the shadows whenever he stayed up all night pacing through downtown, looking for a girl that didn't exist anymore. And I wasn't that girl anymore either. I wasn't the same person I'd been when Danielle was still around and everything was normal. In fact, I wasn't sure if I was still a person at all, in any practical sense of the word.

Sometimes when I think back, I try to pinpoint the exact time when Danielle started slipping. I don't know why I do it, other than as a way to think of more avenues to blame myself. When I really pick away at that last year, it usually comes down to one thing.

Before the drugs, before she started working, there was something else that was eating away at Danielle. I still remember the day she first told me about it, although towards the end it was all she ever talked about. She and I had been walking to our secret river, the one you have hike down hours of logging roads to get to. The wind had been full of pollen and asphalt fumes, milkweed pods bursting with their silky wool. Time had seemed to be passing too quickly. Just weeks before, the spring had been young and new—the riverbank lined with budding crocuses and tender shoots of grass. Not the brambled, overgrown place it was now, thick with insects and wilted from the heat.

"Summer never smells like this, where I used to live," she'd told me, stopping, looking at me with her red-rimmed eyes.

Her hair was soft tatters of faded, sea-foam green, falling across my face when she bent to kiss my cheek, like she was trying to console me over some bad thing that hadn't happened yet. Soon she would start dying it a fake yellow-blonde, but I didn't know that at the time. I didn't know that any of the things that happened would.

The logging road we were on is visible from the ferry when you're coming to the island; they all are, dusty veins worming through the green quilt of spruce trees that otherwise covers the mountains. You can see the clear cuts too, and they look like the bald patches on a mangy dog. I'd seen them from the ferry the day John came to take me back to the city, and my heart had lurched and hammered against my hollow ribs.

"What's wrong?" I'd asked her, and she said that she was crying for all the girls who'd disappeared. I knew what she was talking about; I'd known before the papers ever admitted it, just like we'd all known.

Sometimes they would find them tied up clumsily in shredded tarps and yellow rope, stuffed into the mouths of culvert pipes that leak toxic sludge from the logging sites into the rivers, which carry it eventually to the sea. Sometimes they would find them all cut up, a foot in some residential trash can, its protruding bone mangled by the teeth of a chainsaw. An arm or a leg might wash up on the shore in Esquimalt, or be dragged up in a fisherman's net. But most of them, they never found. Not even in pieces. Most of the girls, nobody ever looked for. It might have been that the rest of the world didn't even notice that they were gone.

The mission downtown where Paula works has photos of them all on a big memorial wall; not just the girls, but everybody. The old man who died of exposure three years ago on the steps of the government-run shelter because they said that all the beds were full and they couldn't let him in. Reggie Elchuk, who the cops shot dead in the park last January because he's not all there and for some reason they thought that made him dangerous enough to shoot.

People think that killers are exceptional individuals, but that's not necessarily true. The shelter workers who locked the door, and the cop who pulled the trigger on Reggie, they're what most people would think of as normal. The people who killed the girls, or hurt them so badly that they wanted to kill themselves, they were normal people too. When something is commonplace enough it becomes ordinary by default, even when that something is killing. The world is full of everyday, ordinary murderers. They're everywhere you look.

That day on the logging roads Danielle told me that the crows who perch, screaming all along the telephone wires downtown are the ghosts of the girls nobody looked for. She said they build their nests way up high, where nobody would think to look. I turned my face to her, and when I looked in her sootblack eyes I realized that the trees around us were filled with the squalling of birds, as though I'd been deaf to the noise before she said it. Their razor voices filled the woods, so loud in my ears that they could almost drown out the hum of faraway chainsaws, the snap and creak of felled timber. The scraping of their voices swirled in her eyes, so dark they looked like they were all pupil. She looked more animal than girl, I thought, her sharp features tensed like she was in pain. When Danielle said things like that, it always seemed like there was no reason they shouldn't be true. The world she saw was more beautiful than reality, and it was full of possibility. My world had no possibilities in it, back then. In my world those girls were just dead, lying in unmarked graves or cheap pine caskets. They were invisible, just like their killers had wanted.

We'd been standing by one of the clear cuts when she said it, and I could see almost forever across the ripped-up wasteland of what used to be the forest. The crows were circling above us, mirrored by their shadows. Black, bird-shaped patches that glided over the uprooted stumps and the hacked off limbs, the parched earth that stretched out to the horizon. I had never seen crows circle before; I thought that only vultures did that. Now sometimes I wonder whether I imagined it.

I wanted to keep looking, but Danielle hooked her arm through mine and kept walking down the dirt road, like there was nothing to see. I remembered cutting peppers on a wooden chopping board once, years before in the kitchenette at Danielle's mom's apartment, and accidentally cutting into the pad of my thumb so deep that the knife grazed my bone. It didn't bleed as much as I'd though it would, and when I rinsed the blood off under cold water in the sink I could see a cross-section of all the different layers of skin and muscle. The layers went in concentric circles, all the way to the bone. They looked like growth rings, I thought, the ones you see on a sawed down stump that will tell you how old the tree was, if you count them.

Please Danielle, I'd said, although I hadn't said it out loud.

Never let me see you as one of the crows.

In those days it was always just me and Danielle, and usually John too although unlike us he actually had a few other friends. Humans inevitably seem to form some sort of pack when they don't have normal social bonds like families around them, and I guess Danielle and John were my pack. I remember how the alley we used to sit in was roofed in metal grating, and through it I could always see the shapes of circling police helicopters. *Ghetto birds*, John used to call them, and Danielle would elbow him in the arm and tell him to fuck off, even though she thought it was funny too. That July had been the hottest month of the hottest year, and the city was just a coffin of black asphalt, a jungle with no canopy to shade us.

We'd been so thin and ascetic, always sprawled in the hidden alley or huddled in the alcoves of vacant stores like statues in a grotto. I would nod off into the black muck of opiate dreams and wake up with offerings placed in front of me in my overturned hat, like magic. A few dollars in nickels and pennies, a bent cigarette, sometimes the small miracle of a crumpled bill.

The three of us had never really fit in, even among the other social rejects, although I think it was the worst for Danielle; most people didn't talk to her at all, probably because she seemed crazy to anybody who didn't understand her, which was virtually everybody except me, John, and her mom. I could see it hurting her, the way everybody else's ideas of what was real didn't match up with what she saw and heard and felt. I think in the end that's why she slipped so much more easily, so much faster than me or John did.

I remember the first time I saw the bruises on her thighs, under her short white schoolgirl kilt. Her body seemed to be getting smaller every day, like the drugs were eating all the softness off her frame. The white skirt and high heels looked so out of place on Danielle, sad and absurd next to her picked-at skin. I missed her old jeans and sweatshirts. I missed not worrying about her. I looked at her face and the thought struck me that maybe I didn't know her as well as I thought I did, or at all. I didn't know any more if she needed to do this to pay for her growing habit, or whether her habit was growing because it was the only way to cope with working on the Drive.

"Why would you shoot up into your shins?" I'd asked her, when I noticed the dark little circles along the edge of her bone. "Doesn't it hurt there?"

"Exactly," she'd grinned. "I'm trying to stop."

Her eyes had glittered, wet in their dark hollows. She scratched one of the scabs on her shin, sniffling, wiping her skinny wrist across her face. Her watery eyes, her permanent runny nose. It was like Danielle was always crying.

Sometimes at night when I'm trying to sleep I still think about that day, and I find, more often than not, that the pain never really dulled after all. Sometimes I'm just more capable of deluding myself into thinking that it did.

On those nights I usually lie on my back in the dark and stare up at the tiny perforations on the acoustic ceiling tiles in the apartment that John and I have shared for the past couple years now. I start counting them, but the task is always too simple to distract me and I just forget what number I'm on and end up having to start over. It's one of those things you learn, like pacing, like learning to thread your eyebrows with the string from a no-name brand tampon because tweezers are sharp, and you can't have anything sharp. Like meticulously peeling the staples from the spine of some pulpy religious pamphlet, just so you can have something to hurt yourself with, just to watch the blood bead up in the diminutive little scratches and remind you that you're still alive.

Outside, that stuff doesn't work quite as well. The real world is too big and too bright, and it takes a lot more to keep your mind from wandering.

Later that day Danielle and I had gone to her mom's apartment and helped her bake sugar cookies, the three of us spooning powdered milk into endless cups of sweet coffee, listening to the oldies station on the radio and talking about the weather, and places we'd like to travel, and movies that we'd seen. Danielle had put on pants before we went over, but I could still feel the dark tenderness of the bruises on her legs, always cautious not to bump into her, wincing at her soreness as though it were my own. I pressed maraschino cherries from a little jar into the soft, white lumps of cookie dough that Danielle was arranging on the sheets of tin foil. I slid the first sheet into the toaster oven and set the timer.

I thought of the bruises on Danielle's legs and I thought of all the women in the world who have killed people, who have murdered the men that hurt them, who have been swallowed so deep into the darkness that they lash out at the first thing that moves. I thought of them pressing maraschino cherries into soft balls of cookie dough and placing the tinfoil sheets into toaster ovens, knowing all the while that they are killers.

I'm not sure exactly of the last time I ever saw Danielle, and in a way I'm glad that I can't remember. If I was the last one to ever see her alive, I don't want to know. I worried when I didn't see her for a few days, and naturally the thought crossed my mind that something bad could have happened. I went to her mom's house, and she hadn't been there. I went to the drop-in at the mission where they serve free food and coffee every morning, and Paula said that she hadn't seen her either, which was odd, because lately she'd been coming in every morning as soon as the place opened, usually looking like she hadn't slept.

I'd been about to leave when I noticed a guy sitting alone at one of the tables, staring at me. He was wearing a yellow and brown striped toque, and his longish hair was half-knotted into unintentional dreadlocks. He held a cup of coffee in his bony hands, hunched over its warmth. I recognized him from other times I'd gone there to eat, but I couldn't remember his name.

"I saw her about a week ago," He'd said to me, and his words carried across the dull murmur of people talking and laughing, the drone of the television mounted on the far wall. Paula and

I both just stopped and looked at him. When neither of us answered, he kept talking.

It had been a cold night, he'd said, and he was going to go to one of the bank ATMs by the Drive so he could have somewhere warm to sleep. He'd seen her sitting in the bus shelter there, nodding off with her head down, her long yellow hair hanging over her face. A car had stopped for her, and she'd talked to the person inside and then got in. I asked him what the car looked like, what the license plate number was, but he couldn't remember. His bloodshot eyes looked sad.

"I'm sorry," he said, or at least I think that's what he said. I wasn't really listening to anything, anymore.

A couple of days later, some ten-year-old kid found her body in the harbour. The kid had been flying kites on the docks with his dad when he looked down and saw her bleached-pale hair curling and wavering among the kelp fronds. There was a cement brick lashed to her feet, and a ligature of nylon rope around her red, abraded neck. There were marks all over her, like she'd fought until she couldn't anymore. They'd called the cops, who hadn't even been looking for her despite the increasingly desperate phone calls from me and John and her mom.

After that day, I started seeing monsters everywhere. I dreamed about standing by the side of the highway at night with my thumb held out and a long knife hidden in the sleeve of my sweatshirt, watching the headlights pass me in the dark. I would know somehow when the killer stopped for me. He would lock the car doors after I got in, and I would laugh and laugh.

I would walk alone down the street late at night with the fall wind stinging my face, just laughing to myself like there was nobody listening. The dry leaves danced and spiralled around my feet, like a living thing.

I stopped sleeping, and my eyes sunk into my skull. I went to the funeral in a borrowed black dress, and Danielle's mom cried and cried, her eyes so puffy they were just slits in her weathered face. *You guys were all my children,* she said, throwing her arms around me and John. *Don't ever forget that, any time you need anything.* Her body was warm and alien to me. I didn't push her away; I think it's the first time I ever didn't push somebody away. The coffin was lowered into its rectangular hole in the ground, and I thought of the way the frost would creep into her body soon, ice crystals spreading like a pattern of lace over her cheeks, the way they do on window panes sometimes. I was the only one who wasn't crying. Beaks and talons prodded my esophagus, trying to get past the lump in my throat. I could feel their damp wings struggling in my chest and throat, slick with swallowed mucous. They would find a weak spot, I thought, somewhere they could claw right through me and flap out through the ragged hole, perching on the boughs of fir trees and the shoulders of pallbearers, laughing and laughing and laughing.

The whole thing kind of scared John straight, and he started sleeping on the couch at his friend Jean-Marc's house, saying he was going to get on welfare and get his own apartment, get away from the streets once and for all. Even though he technically lived there, he would come downtown and walk in circles around all our old hangouts for most of the night, sitting up at the All-Nite drinking dollar coffee with his head in his hands. If I saw him, I ducked down alleys or into thick shadows. He called my name a couple of times, and I didn't answer. I crouched in dark alcoves, holding my breath until he went away.

When I finally found my monster, I wasn't even looking. That's how it works; they hunt, they have to be hunting you, not the other way around. I was walking alone just before dawn, dragging my feet down a back road that leads eventually to the highway. They all do, just like any river will eventually take you to the sea. He was driving a new BMW the colour of gunmetal, with windows so tinted that all I saw in them was my own wan reflection when he pulled over and stopped beside me.

"Do you need some help?" He asked me, and he rolled down the passenger's side window. His smile showed teeth that were too straight and too white. He wore a gold watch on one wrist. His clothes looked expensive but ill-fitting, his stomach straining at the buttons of his shirt. A heart attack belly, Danielle's mom would have called it.

I remember getting into the car, the leather seat squeaking underneath me. I remember hearing the click of the doors locking, and my heart flinging itself against my ribs.

I don't really know what to tell you about trying to kill somebody. It's harder than it looks in the movies.

Bodies are made to withstand things; the breastbone doesn't just shatter like sugar-glass or puncture like that polyvinyl plastic that stunt dummies are made of.

I panicked when he tried to touch me, and I hurt him worse than I knew I could. I'd been frozen at first, my eyes clamped shut because I was so used to not having a way to escape, used to just waiting until it was over. Then I remembered what it was I held inside the sleeve of my sweater and the next time I opened my eyes the car smelled like blood and shit, the hole in his belly welling with dark redness as I reached around his heaving, shaking body to unlock the doors. I remember that, and I remember running. I remember curling with my knees to my chest in the cradle of a spruce tree's erosion-exposed roots, asleep in the dirt and the rotten leaves where they found me. Lights and sirens blared from the roadside, flashing through the trees. I wasn't sure how long I'd been there; it could have been days, but the blood on me was still sticky in some places so I figured it hadn't actually been that long at all.

Danielle always told me that you have to die to turn into one of the crows, but at some point after my home became a prison cell I began to doubt that. I pled guilty immediately, and then I just stopped opening my mouth altogether. I could feel my heart growing black, spined by the quills of lacquer-dark feathers. It flinched and stuttered in my ribs faster than it should have, like a bird's heart, even though there was nothing to scare or excite me anymore except my own thoughts.

I refused to do the psych assessments they gave me, or answer any of their questions, so they couldn't process me through the classification office and I stayed in segregation, away from the other women. I wouldn't let the doctor touch me either. What if they could tell I had a bird's heart?

Sometimes when they escorted me back and forth from various counselling offices I would see the women who lived on the general population cell blocks, walled off behind big glass panels so the guards could still see them. They looked beautiful and sad to me, sitting at the bolted-down steel tables together, braiding each other's hair or playing cards or writing with pencil stubs on sheets of lined paper.

Sometimes they pointed and looked at me, probably wondering what I did to stay in segregation for so long. One of them had peroxide yellow hair that fell in waves past her shoulders, showing three inches of dark brown at the roots. She had a tattoo on her neck, a word I couldn't read spelled out in looping calligraphy. She reminded me of Danielle, and my eyes filled up and overflowed with tears even though my face stayed slack, still palsied with shock.

I couldn't hear the crows anymore but I could feel them, just outside the prison's thick cement walls. The nodes of their minds were like a net, one that stretched and contracted depending on where they were, although it always stayed connected. My mind was part of the net, always anchored in the same place. I could feel the flutter of all their hearts in time with mine, the mad whir of them when they lit from the barbed-wire fence tops outside and launched themselves into the sky, drifting on the salt winds.

Weeks passed before I understood what was happening to me, although I think some part of me had known all along. It started with a feeling of tenseness that spread underneath the skin of my arms and shoulders, a feeling like the hairs on the back of your neck standing up when you're outside right before an electrical storm. It was warm in my cell during the day, but it seemed like I always had goosebumps. I remember running my hands over the rows and patterns of small protrusions that covered my skin, hard like pebbles underneath my cotton uniform. They were bigger, more defined than normal goosebumps. I had an ache in my bones that was as bad as anything I'd felt, like my skeleton was changing shape inside me. In my chest I could feel something building, something that at first I thought must be the deep, wracking sobs that I still hadn't let myself cry.

When I finally let the tension bubble up from my throat, I found that it wasn't sobs I'd been holding back at all. Huddled in the far corner of my cell on the narrow metal cot, peals of laughter pushed their way out from between my lips. It was a coarse, croaking laugh that didn't sound like anything made by a human throat. It wracked my whole body until I lay supine on the hard mattress, my arms wrapped around my rib cage as if I could somehow contain it.

I guess it helped that I was still in a maximum security segregation unit at the time. After the first of the feathers pushed their tips from the skin of my twisted arms, I had to stop denying what was happening. I'd mummy-wrapped myself in the thin sheets that reeked of harsh detergent, the sound of my own whirring heart and hoarse breathing only broken by the metal *clang* whenever they opened the slot in my cell door to slide the meal trays in, only to take them away again, uneaten, half an hour later. I knew it was half an hour, because I counted the seconds to distract me from the pain.

Once one of the night watch guards banged on my door while he was making his rounds and asked if I was alright. My new mouth had struggled to force out an answer, but somehow even without lips I'd managed some rough approximation of speech, shaping the sounds in the back of my throat like I assume talking parrots must do.

"Dope sick," I'd grunted, which seemed to be a good enough explanation for him. I had been there for over a month already, but he hadn't seemed to question why my withdrawals had taken so long to set in.

It seemed like weeks that I lay there, too afraid even to move in case part of the blanket were to slip off of me. In reality it was actually only a few days before I felt the cramps of my skeleton changing again, back into its original shape. An itch spread over me as each hollow-shafted quill detached from its follicle, leaving me in a nest of shed black feathers. The pits they'd left in my skin contracted to the size of normal pores again, and when I touched my face it was the feeling of a flesh fingertip meeting a flesh cheek. I tried to gather all the feathers and flush them down the toilet before the next guard made their rounds. They heard the excessive flushing and assumed that I'd smuggled contraband which I was now trying to dispose of, which of course warranted a search and the ransacking of the cell. All they found were the sheets, shredded in places where I'd clutched them in my demented hands, which they filed under my name as a count of misconduct.

I don't really know what to tell you about the rest of the time that I spent there. I drank the cloudy water, ate food that had been spit in. For months I just lay in my cell under the fluorescent lights that never really turn off, idly running my hands over the hard new plains of my body, travelling to faraway places in my head. I kept my eyes closed and felt the salt wind rushing underneath my wings as I coasted, free. When I slept, I dreamed Danielle was perched at the foot of my bed, a cloak of crow's wings wrapped around her bare shoulders, the long black claws that used to be her feet carving grooves into the bed's metal frame. She was always telling me something, although on waking I could never remember what.

John came to see me as soon as I was allowed visitors, and I'd cried and asked him not to come again. Seeing him through the thick pane of glass, untouchable, had been harder than not seeing him at all.

Eventually I was deemed fit to enter general population, but the girl who'd reminded me of Danielle was gone by then, released or transferred some other place. For a while I shared a cell with a woman whose ex-husband had covered her in gasoline and set her on fire; her skin was a palimpsest of whorls and knots, still smooth in a few places like tree bark that's been peeled away, exposing the smooth, living wood underneath. Another time I saw an eighteen-year-old girl bite through her own tongue and spit blood at one of the guards who was trying to drag her to solitary. It would have been an ordinary assault charge, but she had Hepatitis, and her sentence was lengthened by another eight months.

Everybody knew there was something off about me, but the mind will do anything to find a rational explanation, even if that means deceiving itself. Sometimes I would notice some of the really far-gone prisoners looking at me, the ones who talked to themselves and took handfuls of coloured pills from the nurses every morning. It's always the mad people that I think know the truth– maybe the world of magic only shows itself to them, because it knows nobody will believe them anyway. Or maybe when you live in the narrowest margin of society, you live in the margins of everything, reality included.

Years have passed now, but still I can feel people's stares following me in a way they never used to. It happens when I walk down the Drive in the early morning, on the way to the job Paula got me at the mission. It happens when I weave my way through the crowded tables in the common room, handing out the soup and bread and overcooked pasta, chatting with some of the regulars before I have to run back to the kitchen again. It happens when John and I sit at the patio of the All-Nite for breakfast with Danielle's mom, drinking the bottomless coffee, still tiptoeing around our shared pain like we might well be doing for the rest of our lives.

Sometimes when I look at her and I see the shadows in her

eyes that weren't there before, I think that she can tell what's changed about me too. She can hear the words underneath the clatter of wings that fills the air when the three of us are walking together and the sky fills, inexplicably, with crows. They form a chorus line along the rotting eaves of downtown storefronts, and they stare at us with dozens of pairs of beady black eyes. She knows that they're looking at us, and she looks back.

Even when we're talking and laughing together, part of me is almost on edge around her. Part of me is always waiting for her to lean close to me and whisper, *I know your secret*, quiet so that nobody else can hear.

I know that you're the reason the Drive is a different place now, she'll tell me, and she'll look at me with her eyes full of those roiling black shadows.

You're the reason the cops don't come there anymore, and neither do the news cameras.

You're the twisted shadow that some people see perched on the mission's peaked roof at night, although nobody ever believes them.

You're the reason it's not girls who are disappearing anymore.

And then I'll feel my heart beat out of time with itself as the crows all descend, their scraping laughter echoing through the city, and John will absently lace his fingers through mine and squeeze my hand, like he always does when he's nervous. And then something will happen, although to this day I'm not sure what I think that something might be.

Maybe it'll be nothing. Maybe our mouths will fall open, and the three of us will laugh.

the bean-sidhe calls in owl-light

NEILE GRAHAM

The owl's voice buffets the night with its tumbling roll
and the emptiness between. It beckons on my behalf:
red rover red rover, we call one over. And one comes—

foolish, human, old as winter trees, arms naked as branches,
his thin breath a faltering smoke between us, frost
from the welter of leaves on his gnarled feet.

I turn my palm to the night sky. The owl's voice halts.
The man's step pauses, then owl's wings pass a blessing
over his head. Grace. There is beauty in that.

And in this man's appearance there also is grace. His thin,
shy skin in ice wind. I hunger for this. Hunger for recognition
in his eyes as I step out from the trees into what brightness

there may be in this night. Does he see me yet? Does he see?
His eyes are full of owl-light, owl-light and eclipse, dart like sparrows,
alight on nothing till they latch on me. Then he names me

with the names of all women he has loved in his long life:
calls me mother, lover, child. Dear winter tree of a man
I am all of her you have ever met. I am Her. For what that's worth.

Call me Mother Death as your breath ceases to cloud
the few inches now between us. First I dress you in the web
of memory the next step of your journey requires. I discard

ambition, impatience, guilt. Your armour against this year's end
echoes the blessing of that bird's wing. It clothes you with fire.
I take your hand. Your knobby twigs of fingers coldly clutch me now.

And I scrub you, cleanse from your skin the stench of Styx
and Acheron, rinse you first with tears of Cocytus then the balm
of Lethe. Then I relax my hold. Show your new flesh how

to carry the newborn breath and weight of you. How to rise again
to walk once more through dark forest, bravely armed and leaving me.
He walks, his back pine-straight, stride certain, tall but dwindling

into winter night. A rush of wind startles the trees around me
as he disappears. Gone and going. Going and gone. Oldest and new.
What is he born into now? Who, the owl calls. Who indeed?

fur and feathers

LISA L. HANNETT

"Where's Reynard got himself to, Rori? I ain't seen him for days."

There's a waver in Ida-Belle's voice as her question travels up the henhouse stairs, a straining to be casual. Her feet scuffle in the dust, sandals shifting back and forth with toes pointed in. Clouds of dirt lift, cling to her ankles, then settle like sighs on the ground.

"Answer to that will cost you." Aurora's response comes from within the whitewashed structure; it sails out the multi-paned windows on a wave of chicken giggles and clucks. A minute later the woman appears, apron-covered legs framed in the lower half of the screen door, head and torso indistinct in the shadows cast by the coop's overhanging eaves. One stride short of emerging, she looks down the five wooden steps to where Ida-Belle waits.

"I got coin," the girl says, fumbling for the cotton purse she wears slung over her shoulder. She's just gone twenty-one but long hours in the woolshed have wizened an extra decade into her face. Her hands—one now lifted to shade her eyes from the glare reflecting off the tin roof, the other pressed flat against her belly—are pink and soft. Years of gathering, combing, and carding lanolin-rich fleece has left even the creases around her knuckles smooth.

"Bet you do." Arms wrapped around a pail of feed, Aurora uses a hip to push open the door. Springs squeal as the hinges stretch wide to let her out; they recoil with a clatter of wood against wood.

"Call me batty," she continues, clomping down the steps, "but I reckon you ain't drove halfway across Napanee to talk about Rey."

"No," says Ida-Belle, eyes cast down. "I reckon not."

Aurora shifts her grip on the pail, cradles its weight in her left arm. "Well, out with it then."

"Jimmy'll kill me if he finds out I came." The girl's voice trails off as she looks up, takes in the henhouse. The place is bigger than her cottage and twice as old. Foundations raised four feet off the ground, the weatherboard building tilts to the right. Its porch sprouts support pillars like dozens of running legs caught beneath its bulk in mid-stride. A brace of hares, necks slit and draining red, dangles over the railing just high enough to be out of predators' reach. Garlands of bones and feathers, poppy heads and rosehips hang in rollercoaster loops from the eaves. To the left, a ramp sticks like a laddered tongue out a rooster-sized hole in the wall. Though a scrub brush and pail wait below the rainwater tank's faucet, every horizontal surface remains speckled with bird shit.

"Ain't no one forcing you to stay, girl. Get on with it, or get moving. My lasses have had themselves an upset this week; *they* sure as hell need my help if you don't want it."

"It's just—" Ida-Belle pauses, begins again. "I can't give you much in the way of payment, but I was hoping?" Her eyebrows and shoulders lift as she speaks, then slump as she sees the older woman's stern expression. "I was hoping."

Aurora sighs and puts down the pail. Straightening up, she wipes her hands on the back of her pants, then adjusts the fox's tail tucked under the ribbon of her hat band. With a flick of the wrist, she sets its length drooping over the brim, its fur a striking contrast to the faded grey of her braids.

"Me and hope ain't exactly seeing eye to eye these days." She directs Ida-Belle to the Shaker-style rocking chair at the foot of the stairs. The girl perches on the edge of the seat, clutching her purse in her lap, close-lipped while Aurora continues. "That vixen blinds fools with promises then snatches them away just for kicks. Makes a person think she's doing the right thing for her relationship when, in fact, she ain't."

"Oh." Ida-Belle slouches under the weight of her disappointment. When she goes to stand, Aurora places a grimy hand on her shoulder to keep her seated.

"Quit your fluttering, Ida. If I had a mind to be rid of you, you'd already be gone." From the way her client's hands keep straying to her midriff, Aurora can see what it is the girl wants, why she's here—but the words have to be said if the magic's to work. "Get your thoughts in order, once and for all, then talk loud enough for my lasses to hear you. Nice and clear, mind; none of this faffing about hope."

Ida-Belle takes a deep breath, exhales as she settles back into the chair. "Me and Jimmy's been married nigh on six months now."

Aurora keeps quiet as she waits for the girl to go on. The silence lengthens, broken only by the chickens' chattering and cooing, and the steady creak of cicadas conversing in the cornfields. Aurora searches through her apron pockets for a pipe and some leaf. Finding both, she presses a thumb's worth of tobacco into the bowl, clenches the stem between her teeth as she rummages around for a match.

"My friend Loretta said you helped her out once—" Ida-Belle's face reddens. "She said you could see the future." Aurora lifts an eyebrow, puffs her pipe to life, neither confirming nor denying the girl's implicit question.

"I know it sounds crazy," Ida-Belle says, "but ever since she came here Loretta ain't had to face a single one of her mother-in-law's visits. Even the ones what weren't planned ahead! And when I asked how she got so lucky, always being out when Gerdie comes 'round to piss her off or tell her how to run her own household, Loretta showed me the little calendar you gave her—the one what's got a bunch of dates and times written on it, starting from the day she came here and running well into the next five years."

For the first time, Ida-Belle looks Aurora straight in the eye. "She wouldn't tell me how you done it, Rori. Only that you done it."

Aurora doesn't smile, even though she's glad to hear her previous clients continue to remain discreet in advertising her wares. Wouldn't do no-one good to have the whole town flocking to her for answers whenever they got too lazy to do things the hard way. Ain't time for that, far as she's concerned.

Head wreathed in blue smoke, she leans against the elevated porch and gives Ida-Belle no more encouragement than a simple, "Uh-huh. And?"

Visibly steeling herself, the girl says, "I need to get knocked up, quick."

Aurora nods, head bobbing to a familiar tune.

"Six months we've been married, Rori. *Six months* and so much fucking my nethers is rubbed raw—and still. Nothing." She leans her head back, watches a sparrow flit from the henhouse roof to the chimney of Aurora's cabin on the opposite side of the yard. Her lower lids well with tears. "Jimmy's been eyeing that skank from the Buy 'n' Save all winter. I reckon if I don't give him some reason to stick around, he'll be gone before shearing time."

Aurora takes the pipe from her mouth, flips it and taps it on the edge of the porch. Soft clumps of ash drop to the ground as she asks, "So which do you want to know? If you'll be pumping out wee ones soon, or if you're going to lose Jimmy? We can only cover one thing at a time."

Tears spill onto Ida-Belle's pale cheeks. "Babies," she whispers, while twisting the ring with its tiny zirconium stone, spinning it around and around her wedding finger. Aurora looks down at her own left hand; still surprised, even after a week, to see the bright white space where her own band of gold used to be. She clears her throat.

"You do realize there's only so much we can do?"

Ida-Belle smiles through her tears, thoughts of Loretta's success making her deaf to the older woman's caveats. "Anything's better than nothing."

"Fine." Aurora pockets her pipe and heads for the stairs. "Stay here. A few minutes and we'll have you an answer."

Aurora's chickens would never be satisfied with a standard coop.

Stacks of cramped aluminium boxes, barely large enough to accommodate a hatchling much less a brooding hen, definitely wouldn't suit them; nor would short plywood walls, so low they'd force their keeper to slouch while visiting her charges; nor wire mesh ceilings or floor-level apertures of the sort typically knocked together to aerate, and confine, egg-laying chooks.

Aurora's lasses wouldn't have a bar of that. They perch on overstuffed cushions; each nestled securely on mahogany bookshelves stretching well over forty feet to the rafters of the house's double-peaked roof. They are hand-fed three times daily, given heaters when the seasons turn cold, and special treats on their birthdays. Unlike ordinary hens, Aurora's tiny oracles smile, snack and lay their fortunes in comfort.

When she enters the henhouse, the gabble of voices crescendos in fear; the racket ebbs once the chickens recognize Aurora's shape silhouetted against the screen. Hanging on the wall next to the door, an enormous blackboard gives the names and shelf numbers for every bird in the coop: fourteen hundred and seventy-six clairvoyant biddies—one for all but two of Napanee's townsfolk. Enough warm light streams in to illuminate the handwritten list, but it isn't bright enough to hurt the lasses' sensitive eyes.

Scanning the columns of names, Aurora mutters, "Ida-Belle Caplin . . . Ida-Belle . . ." and wishes, not for the first time, that she'd had the presence of mind to house the girls in alphabetical order. Sixteen rows down, she sees what's left of her own entry. Aurora Jenkins, ~~Q42~~. She glosses over it when she notices Ida-Belle's berth is *P43*.

Damn you, Rey, she thinks. She's steered clear of Minnie's roost all week; now there's nothing she can do but try not to stare at it while she negotiates with Ida-Belle's hen. Double-checking the supply of Tic Tacs she keeps in her top apron pocket, and hooking a pouchful of dry-roasted seed to her belt, Aurora weaves her way between bookshelves to reach the far side of the room.

The oracles generally pay her comings and goings little mind, unless she's got riddles for them to solve. But this week they're bursting with questions, most concerning Reynard. Every third step or so she's forced to stop, kiss their baby-smooth cheeks, stroke the bridges of their button noses, and reassure them that he won't be back any time soon. Although her caresses calm them, her words sound hollow. She knows it'll only be a matter of minutes before they forget and get anxious again.

Their far-seeing skills are flawless—except when the future involves that trickster she's called husband for twenty-five years.

"Excuse me, Miss Rori?" A tiny voice chirps at her as she passes aisle G. She stops and looks up to the top shelf, into the pale green eyes of an ancient Plymouth Rock lass. The oracle's plumage is patterned like black and white tweed, each feather neatly groomed despite the bird's age; her face a perfect replica of old widow McGeary's, the crone who'd just celebrated her eighty-fifth winter.

"What can I do for you, Valma?" The hen tut-tuts at being addressed so informally—she prefers to be called Madam. She wrinkles her coffee-coloured face into a grimace; her wide lips shrivel into a frown. A red pillbox hat slips down her forehead until her arched eyebrows are hidden beneath its decorative veil.

She leans over to scold Aurora.

"Rape!" The word shrills out of the hen's throat, then is clipped short in a panicked *bu-gock*. "Those gold demons you let loose in this place keep making *advances*, trying to have their filthy way with me while I'm asleep. I feel them pecking at me—peck, peck, pecking all night! I just know they're aching to get beneath my frillies."

"Oh, Valma," Aurora says, her tone exhausted. "I thought we dealt with this already. The roosters can't reach you all the way up there, hun. That's why we moved you, remember?"

"I ain't so sure about that, Miss Rori. I see them eyeing me all day, just waiting for me to nod off. No matter how high I fly above their heads to show they can't have me, they keeping coming back. The perverts."

Aurora sighs. None of her sibyls can fly—in that way they're no different from bird-faced chooks. And the roosters are just that: roosters. It's their nature to be curious; they don't know any better. A pair of twin Brahma hens to Valma's right, one girl and one boy, start giggling at the oracle's rant. Their near-identical faces, accentuated by tufts of herringbone feathers, are both at least half a century away from her kind of senility. To the aged hen's left, a New Hampshire brown studiously avoids Aurora's gaze. She gently shifts her bulk to hide a long, sharp piece of straw sitting next to her pillow.

"Stop crowding me!" Valma squawks. The twins' laughter redoubles.

"Be quiet, the lot of you." Aurora reaches up, snatches the straw, lifts the heavy brown lass back onto her cushion. "You been using this to torment Val while she's sleeping, Jolene?"

"She snores like the devil," the oracle announces, head tilted at a haughty angle. "It's the only way to shut her up." The twins nod their agreement, clucking, "It's true, it's true!"

"You're a pain in my backside, that's what you kids are." Aurora turns back to Valma and says, "Open wide," then tucks a mint beneath the old woman's tongue—both to still her complaints and to reward her for putting up with the other chooks' crap. Ignoring the jealous looks Jolene and the twins shoot her way, Valma hums with satisfaction.

"I ain't got time for this now," Aurora says. "But I will deal with you—mark my words."

It's enough to have Rey stirring shit in here, she thinks as she walks away. *Without the seers getting in on the pranks as well.*

H, I, J, K—there's a gap in the rows, a small crossroads separating the double-digits on the left from the triple on the right, bookshelves and chooks on all four sides lit by a series of crazed skylights above—*L, M, N, O . . .* Aurora's pace slows. She passes through mote-filled beams of light, reluctantly moving into the shadows beyond.

The space where Minnie used to sit is still littered with ragged feathers. A lavender-scented blanket lies twisted like a snarl across the cushion. Red is splashed on both where the other lasses had drawn blood defending their shelfmate. Even now the air stinks of fear, smeared straw, and gore.

"Calm down, ladies, gents," Aurora says, barely audible above the oracles' shouts.

"It ain't fair, Rori—"

"—where's my goddamn bird? What's my future?"

"Hush now," Aurora urges. The hens keep yelling, their scratchy voices repeating the argument she and Reynard had had in front of them last week.

"I can't take it no more, this bird telling you secrets—"

"—shitting out eggs filled with god-knows-what each week—"

"—unnatural stuff what keeps you looking like you was twenty-five—"

"That's enough," Aurora says.

"Stay away from her, Rey—"

"—put her down!"

Minnie's neighbours lunge at her vacant pillow, as if Reynard were still trying to throttle her. Meanwhile, the lasses on higher and lower shelves mimic the trickster's pleas, his accusations.

"—you said you'd stopped using!

"—and I ain't got no magic yolk to keep me *fresh—"*

"Enough," Aurora repeats.

"—I share my magics with you all the time, but things ain't even between us—"

"—ain't my fault I'm different from you—"

"—Am I even in that future she shows you?"

"Shut up!" Aurora's chest heaves, her pulse races. That's twice now she's lost her temper in this very spot; twice her words have brought the bickering to a halt. *Life ain't even*, she'd hollered a week earlier, walloping her husband's pointed ear. The blow had saved Minnie, but not before the prophet's little face had turned blue, neck purple from the crush of Reynard's frustration.

It took a sedative tablet to keep the oracle from flapping herself into an early grave; a lavender-scented blanket draped over her shivering body had helped soothe her into a doze. Such measures wouldn't cut it now. Faced with several dozen anxious birds, Aurora's patience is stretched. "I don't want to hear any more of that talk, you got me? Either look *forward* like you're meant to, or shut the fuck up."

Apart from a few sniffles, a couple squeaks of dismay, the hens do as they're told. Hands shaking, Aurora reaches up to wipe tears away from P43's blue eyes. The chick's nose is red from crying, its tip curved exactly like Ida-Belle's.

"It's all right." She pushes damp feathers away from the white Delaware's freckled cheek, adjusts the red coronet so that it sits straight on her head. "Everything's okay." She offers two Tic Tacs; the chook gobbles them up. Holding a third just out of the hen's reach she asks, "What's your name, hun?"

"Ellie."

Aurora pops the mint into Ellie's mouth. "Good girl," she says, tracing the grey barring on the ends of the bird's hackles, wings and tail with a finger. Smoothing the feathers down; settling the hen's nerves along with her own. "Did you hear what Ida-Belle needs?"

Ellie says, "I think so," but her expression is uncertain. Aurora takes another mint, places it in the flat of her palm.

"The girl wants babies. Will she have them?"

The oracle licks her lips, looks up like she's consulting the heavens, though her gaze has turned inward. A moment passes, then with a confident, single nod she says, "Yes. Sure will."

As if on cue, the instant Ellie's prediction is voiced the other oracles begin gossiping about her technique; critiquing her accuracy; commenting on how much better *they* would have done in her place. Aurora rewards the young lass with another sweet; waits until she has stopped crunching it before asking, "Any chance you can give her something to speed it along?"

Big smile. "I reckon."

Ellie inches her hindquarters over the back of her green pillow, which is heavily speckled with white. Throat vibrating with the force of her clucks, face crimson, pearl teeth making semi-circular dents in her full lower lip, the oracle pushes.

Grunts.

Pushes.

A throat-tearing squawk. A sound like a marble rolling across a wooden table. Sweat beads Ellie's forehead. Her colouring returns to normal and her breathing steadies. She grins sheepishly as Aurora reaches beneath tail feathers to poke around through the straw and moult. Pride gilds her features as she sees what Aurora digs up.

A bright red egg, displaying Ida-Belle's name in silver cursive, sits large and shiny in the cradle of Aurora's hands. Congratulations roar out from all sides, deafening, as the oracles in rows P and Q compliment Ellie on her first delivery.

"You're in luck." Aurora places the egg, still warm, onto Ida-Belle's lap. "She was feeling talkative."

Confusion creases the girl's brow. She picks up the egg, turns it over. "What am I supposed to do with this?"

The older woman lights her pipe, takes a long pull. Sweet smoke fills her mouth and drifts out her nose, temporarily replacing the lingering scent of fowl. She lifts her hat to wipe the sweat and feathers clinging to her forehead and says, "What do you think? Crack it."

"D'you got a bowl or something I can drop the yolk into?"

Aurora shakes her head. "Just crack it as is, Ida. On your knee."

Ida-Belle is only half-successful at keeping the sneer from her lips. She looks down at the egg, then at the clean culottes she put on special for her visit to Aurora's. Such a clever design—she'd stitched them herself. Grey cotton patterned with orange and red pansies, they look like smart pants when she's sitting, and a skirt when she's standing. But they won't look nowhere near as stylish with yolk dribbled all over.

Hesitant at first, then more forceful when she sees how tough the shell is, Ida-Belle strikes the egg against her kneecap. With a crunch, fractures appear across its red surface, spreading out from a circular indent. She digs her thumbs in, waits for the white to ooze out. Her hands remain dry. Small fragments break off as she splits the shell in two; it separates with a sound of twigs snapping, and releases its furry contents onto her lap without mess.

Three miniature bunnies, perfectly proportioned, each one no bigger than a lamb's eye. All white with beige patches, velvet ears, and pink noses twitching, they roll across Ida-Belle's thighs and snuggle into the warm space where her legs press together. Blinking, they look up at her; sprigs of parsley, chives and garlic tied like bows around their necks.

"Good work, Ellie." Aurora's voice startles Ida-Belle from her inspection of the rabbits. "You got three chances to get it right, thanks to your generous lass. Now, tell me. How does Jimmy like his stew? Beef? Lamb? What's his favourite?"

"Lamb's cheapest," Ida-Belle says, slowly.

"Of course," Aurora says. "You got some ready for cooking back home?"

Ida-Belle nods.

"Good. Seems clear what you're meant to do." Aurora picks up one of the bunnies, raises it to the level of her eyes, tries not to think of it in a roasting pan. It stares back at her blankly. "You gots to pop one of these here baby-makers in with your dinner tonight—Jimmy like chives and 'taters with his meat?"

Again, Ida-Belle nods.

"All right then, use this one first." Aurora reunites the chive-necked bunny with its brothers, places a hand on Ida-Belle's shoulder. "Chop him up good and small so's Jimmy won't notice it. That's real important: it's got to be kept secret, you hear? This ain't nobody's business but yours."

"Yeah, all right—"

"And don't go spilling to Loretta, neither." Aurora gives Ida-Belle a hard look, gestures for her to stand up. She collects the eggshells for compost, and helps the girl tuck the rabbits into her purse. As Aurora walks her client to her truck, she gives final instructions. "Some magics is quieter than others, and this here's one of them. Understand? You keep them creatures out of sight until it's time they get ate. Like I said, you gots three chances— your lassie said you've got babies coming, and this here's how you're going to get them. All right?"

"So we just gots to eat them? That's it?" Ida-Belle turns to unlock the car door, keeping her back to Aurora to hide the hope shining in her eyes.

"That's it."

"Thanks, Rori." The girl spins on her heel, flings her arms around Aurora's shoulders, then quickly steps back for fear of crushing the bunnies. Her face is flushed. "How much do I owe you?"

With a sniff, Aurora considers the collection of boxes stacked in the tray of Ida-Belle's pickup while the girl digs into her purse for some money. "How's business going with that lot?"

Ida-Belle looks up, sees what's caught Aurora's attention. "Buy 'n' Save's just ordered another two crates—they say ladies drive all the way from Overton to get our creams. Can you believe it?" She burrows beneath the trio of rabbits, snags another two-dollar coin.

"Do they really work?" Aurora wonders if lanolin by-products will smooth her face as well as the pure stuff does Ida-Belle's hands; if they'll be even half as effective as Minnie's fortunes.

"Well, I ain't going to shit you, Rori. Not after today." Ida-Belle reaches into the cab, opens a box and pulls out a jar of homemade moisturiser. "You gots to use a fuckload of it to see results—but, yeah. I ain't heard no complaints."

Ida-Belle offers a handful of change, all she can muster from the bottom of her handbag.

"Keep your money," Aurora says. "Give me a couple jars of that night cream you got there, and maybe some of that SPF stuff too. However many you think's fair for a bellyful of wee ones."

Buy 'n' Save's order is one carton lighter when Ida-Belle's truck backs down the gravel driveway. Aurora rests the box on the ground, straightens to wave goodbye. Halfway up, she comes eye-to-eye with a fox poking his scruffy head out of the long grass across the lane.

Aurora's heart leaps.

She's so glad to see he's back again, that he's still okay, she takes an eager step forward—but is brought up short by the box at her feet. Happiness turns sour as she takes in what he's reduced her to. Using *products* to replicate the youth Minnie gave her every week; the clear skin, the deep auburn curls. She snorts. Next she'll be relying on *chemicals* to dye her hair! It just ain't natural.

Hefting the carton, Aurora spits in the fox's direction. Heart pounding, she snaps, "Bugger off!" The tail dangling from her hatband bobs in time with her retreating steps as she makes her way up the drive, trying to appear unruffled as she enters her lonely cabin.

In the brush, the fox yips after her. He waits a moment, but she doesn't give him a second glance. Reluctantly, he slinks out of sight, convinced that progress had been made.

Yesterday she wouldn't even talk to him.

"C'mere, Rori," Reynard had called from the kitchen. "I got a surprise for you."

"Just a minute," she'd replied, rinsing the rest of the soapsuds out of her thick red hair, scowling to find strands of grey. The water scalded, filled the bathroom with steam. She'd stood under the shower until she could hardly bear the heat any longer. She'd hoped it would wash away the guilt that had clung to her since she'd lashed out at Reynard that afternoon, guilt that even a three-hour walk into town and back hadn't alleviated. Hoped he'd forget about their fight, and what caused it. Hoped they'd be okay. Her skin reddened.

Faucets squeaked into the off position. Aurora had grabbed her plaid housecoat, wrapped it around herself, tied it. Her feet left wet prints on the scrubbed wood floor as she collected the pile of clothes she'd shed on the bathmat. She'd looked at the closed bathroom door, hesitated.

"I'll just be a second, hun," she'd said, crouching down to open the cabinet beneath the sink. Shifting spare rolls of toilet paper, boxes of tampons and half-empty bottles of mouthwash and shampoo, Aurora had reached all the way to the back to grab a quilted makeup bag—one Reynard thought was filled with cotton balls. Sitting back on her haunches, she'd unzipped it; released a breath she hadn't known she'd been holding until the tension in her lungs eased.

A deep blue egg, her name inscribed bronze in its thick shell, sat perfect and whole at the bottom of the case. She'd saved it for two days.

Despite what Reynard thinks, Aurora thought, *I have been trying to cut back on taking Minnie's fortunes. I really have.*

But today had been too much to cope with; the new shoots of grey in her hair were proof enough of that. Muffling the sound with a washcloth, she'd gently tapped the egg against the basin, spinning it deftly between her fingers.

Tricksters like him have their own ways of dealing with things. Aurora shook her head. Not that it mattered. So far, the fates simply hadn't laid a Reynard-faced chook in her coop. There was nothing she could do about that.

A piece of shell flaked off, landed silently in the sink. Aurora snapped away shard after shard, until only the base of the egg remained. Perched in its curve was a three-tiered fountain, decorated with peacocks, ferns, and doves. At the very top, a nymph balanced on the tip of a finial, her arms stretched to the sky. From each of her fingertips, a jet of water arced into the air then collected in a pool at the bottom of the shell.

Aurora had leaned into the spray, dousing her face with its rejuvenating waters. She'd felt the skin tightening around her eyes, the laugh-lines smoothing from her cheeks, the shrivel of her lips puckering, the sag of her chin straightening. Wiping steam from the mirror, Aurora looked at her youthful features. Satisfied, she raised the fountain in silent salute to Minnie, then tilted her head back and drank it dry. By the time she'd towelled her hair, the troublesome greys had disappeared.

"Close your eyes," Reynard had said, when she'd stepped out of the bathroom. Actions following words, he'd swept her into his arms, used his furry hands as a blindfold, then danced her in the dark across the kitchen.

She'd smelled the feast long before she'd seen it. Aromas of roasted onion and garlic, fresh bread and warm butter, gravy and boiled potatoes; the scent of wine mulling with spices; an apple pie cooling on the counter—all combined to make her heart lift, and to curve her mouth into a smile.

"Ta-da!" Reynard unveiled his surprise, arms flung wide. Tears had sprung to Aurora's eyes as she'd taken in the spread laid out before her. Reynard had set the table with their finest crockery—most of the plates and bowls actually matched. Her grandmother's silver cutlery lined the place settings, arranged just the way Aurora liked it. Casserole dishes heaped with food covered the table, so many it was hard to see the fine linen cloth beneath. Occupying the place of honour, in the centre, was a roasting pan covered with aluminium foil. Aurora's smile had widened.

Reynard only wooed her with treats like this when he wanted to apologize.

"Thanks," she'd whispered, sliding her arm around her

husband's waist. Unlike her, he'd dressed up for the occasion: a sport-coat over his denim shirt, ears tucked beneath slicked-back hair, and sideburns plastered down with so much pomade he almost looked tame. Only his tail hung free, swinging out beneath the rough hem of his jacket.

She'd kissed him, scratched her nails up and down his back until he purred. Giggling, she'd said, "Why don't you shift into something more comfortable?"

Reynard chuckled and licked her cheek. Soon his nose lengthened, as did his ears. Rusty fur spread from the top of his head across every inch of his skin. His limbs retracted, leaving a puddle of clothes around his black paws. Lifting his head to look up at Aurora, he leapt onto one of the kitchen chairs and yipped in delight. Instantly, night replaced day. "Take a seat," he'd instructed, humming the moon into the sky, frosting the room with its blue light.

"For you," he'd said, and pulled the aluminium foil off the roast with his teeth. "Carve it up, love."

"With pleasure," Aurora had replied, reaching for the carving knife.

Her hand froze in midair. Looking up at her, amid a bed of garnish, was her own face in miniature. *Minnie's face*; body plucked and stuffed, basted and glazed with spiced butter.

Aurora had sat, paralysed, staring at her oracle while Reynard stood, muscles tense, staring at his wife.

Outside, a rooster hopped onto the sill of the kitchen window, pecked at his reflection in the glass. The sound fractured the silence, the shock that had held Aurora in thrall. Springing to action, she'd snatched the knife and, so quick as to have been done without thinking, brought it whistling down on the tabletop.

Separating Reynard from his tail.

There was barking then, and shouting. Neither had run as long as the thin ribbon of blood that followed the fox out the front door. Neither had hurt as much as the wedding ring being torn from Aurora's finger. Neither would be harder to forget than the corpse of her future lying cold on their Wedgwood platter.

The telephone jangles Aurora awake.

It takes her a minute to get her bearings. Images of Reynard's betrayal slip like a veil from her mind. *It's morning*, she tells herself, *and bright*. The disgusting smell of roasted chicken fades, replaced by the scent of clean sheets. Echoes of her husband's nightly howling—his skulking below their bedroom window, snuffling and whimpering for forgiveness—are drowned out by the phone's insistent ringing.

The tightness in her chest gets sharper as she reaches for the cordless receiver, rolling over the pillows stuffed in Reynard's side of the bed. Poor imitations of his absent form. Pillows don't throw their arms around her at night, don't wake her with a hot tail pressed against her backside. They don't make her feel safe.

Her throat constricts. They also don't murder innocent lasses for jealousy.

"Rori?"

"Yeah."

"Rori, it's Ida-Belle. You gotta help me." Her voice is pitched so high it could scrape paint off the ceiling.

"Just chop that rabbit up nice and small. Jimmy won't notice a thing."

"Don't you think I know that? I done it already—and now I'm a fucking blimp! Ain't no way even a fool like Jim won't notice *this*. What am I supposed to do? He's going to think I cheated on him, ain't he? No way this thing in my guts is a one-day-old kid. I look like I'm ready to pop!"

"Hang on a sec, Ida." Aurora sits up in bed, swings her legs over the side. "When did you eat that stew?"

"Jimmy takes supper at five."

Aurora looks at the clock. Seven in the morning. Either Ellie's got some powerful magics in her eggs, or else Ida-Belle is skimping on the truth. "Any way you might've ate more than your share of that rabbit? Did Jim get any at all?"

Silence.

"Out with it, girl."

"Well," Ida-Belle begins, "I really wanted to make sure it'd work, right?"

"Uh-huh . . ."

"So I started chopping up that first little bunny, and it were so much easier than I thought, so I said to myself, 'If one's good, don't you reckon all three'll be even better?' And—"

"And you put all of your chances into the stew. At once."

Ida-Belle sniffles, her voice thick with tears. "Am I going to die?"

Aurora shoulders the receiver, pulls on a pair of jeans, tucks in the shirt she slept in. "No," she says, taking her apron from the hook on the back of the bedroom door. She slips it around her neck. "You ain't going to die."

"But what am I going to do?"

"Quit your blubbering, for one thing." Aurora gives the girl a chance to control herself. Grabs her fox-tail hat, plunges it onto her head. "I'll have a word with the chooks, see what they've got to say about this *situation*. But if I was to have a guess, I'd say you should make way for triplets."

"Oh God . . ." Ida-Belle's tears pour out thick and fast.

"Hush now." Aurora's tone slips down an octave. Quiet and soothing; the same sing-song she's used in the henhouse every day this week. "Come see me this afternoon, all right? And, this time, bring Jimmy."

Ida-Belle can't reply for crying.

"Hush," Aurora repeats as she walks to the front door, propping it open with her foot. "We'll sort something out, all right? All right?" She can sense, rather than hear, Ida-Belle's nod. "That's a girl. It'll be fine, Ida. The lasses won't let you down."

Reynard would think this was a hoot, if he were here.

Ellie knew the girl would eat all three rabbits at once, and she didn't say nothing about it. Probably reckoned she were doing Ida-Belle a favour. The whole thing makes Aurora feel tired, and she wishes her husband would put his fox-gloves on and work some trickery to lighten her mood.

But he ain't here, she thinks. Right before she sees him.

He's lying at the base of the oak tree they planted outside their bedroom window the year they got married. Morning sun is still low enough to hit him full on; the tree doesn't provide much shade until late afternoon. His fur is mangy, streaked with red gashes, like he's been on the wrong end of a fight. The stump of his tail is crusty with dirt and blood. More than a few flies buzz around him, alight on his eyes, in his ears, around the mess of his arse. Aurora's heart races.

Oh, God. Don't be dead.

She runs toward him, stops two feet away. Without going any closer she can see his face muscles twitch, like he's winking at her in his sleep. With an effort, she turns back, crosses the packed-dirt yard and walks up the henhouse steps.

"Morning, chooks," she says, and smiles to hear a chorus of greetings clucked from all sides, from both girl- and boy-faced lasses. Some, still not fully awake, stare vacantly at the moths fluttering up near the rafters. Others flap their wings for attention, *bock-bocking* demands for mints. Jolene and the twins avoid meeting her eyes as Valma looks on, disgusted; while yet others perform a waddling turn, point tails out, and doze off to pass the hours until feeding time.

Ellie, she notices upon reaching the aisle between rows P and Q, is one of the latter. Worn out from the effort of yesterday's prediction, the Delaware hen is sleeping deeply.

"The mess, O-Rori," chides a masculine-featured Cornish hen. From his berth in Q41, he stretches his head out to block Aurora's path. His royal blue neck feathers, knotted beneath his bearded chin like an ascot, give him a regal air that suits the disdain in his voice. "Isn't it high time you cleaned up this filth?" He peers over the top of his gold-framed spectacles, shudders at the mess still littering Minnie's satin pillow.

"Honestly," he says, now directing his gaze at his keeper, "preserving the scene of the crime in this fashion is downright *macabre*." He sniffs. "And the fleas are becoming unbearable."

Aurora looks across at Ellie, at Minnie's soiled roost, then back at the sleeping oracle. *I reckon letting her rest a few more minutes won't hurt.*

Adrenaline surges through her as her subconscious whispers, *I reckon it's time to move on.*

She fetches a hand-broom and dustpan, fills a bucket with water, drops some soap and a couple old rags into her apron pockets. The pail clunks on the floor in front of Q42. Aurora hunches slightly to get a better view of the damage. Feathers, muck, and blood. A lump forms in the back of her throat. Straightening up, she tries to melt it by sucking on a Tic Tac—then has to dole out doses of the oval sweets to every open-mouthed bird from Q22 to Q57.

With most of the bay satiated, if not quiet, and the air sharp with the scent of mint, Aurora begins the task of sweeping away all trace of Minnie's death. First, she removes the blanket; cleans off the pillow, sets it aside; then launches in with the broom. Bristles rasp across the bookshelf's surface as she tackles the worst of the mess, moving as quickly as possible. Dirt, straw and down swirl into the dustpan's waiting tray. While she works,

Aurora's eyes don't stop watering.

"You've missed some," the Cornish hen bosses. "Reach all the way to the back."

"I know what I'm doing," Aurora snaps. The insult she'd been about to unleash comes out as a strangled gasp as her broom snags on a clot of feathers. Dragging it to the shelf's edge, she catches a glimpse of royal blue peeking out of the mass of red and white.

She picks up the egg with trembling fingers, brushes it off. It's smaller than any of Minnie's other fortunes, but still big enough for her to read the dedication clearly:

Aurora & Reynard Jenkins

Although the henhouse is as noisy as usual, to Aurora it seems the whole world has gone mute.

Why is Reynard's name on *her* egg? Minnie couldn't have laid it on the fox's last visit—sluggish with sedatives, she would have barely had time to struggle, to scream, before he'd slit her throat. Aurora places the egg on the shelf, leans it carefully against the Cornish's cushioned roost. Staring at the bearded lass without really seeing him, Aurora realizes that Minnie must've laid it while Reynard had been throttling her.

While the two of them were too busy fighting to notice it.

"Get that flea-bitten thing away from me." The hen's foot connects with the egg, sends it over the shelf's edge. As if in slow motion, Aurora watches the treasure sail earthwards, her hands clumsy and slow, swiping at empty air seconds too late.

A dark blue fault line splits the egg from top to tail as it cracks against the bucket's rim, then bounces in with a splash. With a shriek.

Surrounded by shards of bobbing blue shell, a fox-faced hatchling cries as he fights to keep his head above water.

Oh, Minnie. Aurora's eyes flood as she watches his baby wings weaken, his thrashing grow more frantic, his screams more shrill. Without moving, she waits to see if the newborn far-seer will resurface. *Fair's fair, ain't it?* The fox-hen gasps for breath, goes under again. And again.

Even is even.

Outside, Reynard whimpers, calls out for his wife. Just as he's done every morning upon waking, finding himself tailless and trapped in animal form, bitten by flies and regret. Tailless and alone.

Life ain't even, Aurora thinks. She knocks the pail over and its contents drown the henhouse floor. Leaning over, she rescues the sputtering lass. Uses a rag to pat his wings dry, then dabs at his cheeks with her fingertips. "I'm sorry," she whispers.

The chick sneezes. Opens his golden, Reynard-shaped eyes, and winks.

Aurora snorts. She pulls the fox-tail from her hatband, wraps the sodden oracle in its russet length. Holding the bundle close to her heart, she takes a deep breath. Gathers her nerve. Plans what she's going to say to her husband, then slowly walks outside.

breathing bones

PETER CHIYKOWSKI

They say that the first instrument was a flute,
that thirty-five thousand years ago,
a man (and surely, they say, it was a man)
wrapped his hands around a hollow bone
and made the world young again
under his feet.

What a way to die,
breathing love into some bird's dry wing-bone.
And what a way to be born, against all odds,
humming and cheating reciprocity,
giving without giving away.

Lungs without these bones are full
of stillborn songs. I smack
each breath on the bottom,
wishing it would scream or whimper
so I could rub its gleaming head.

the education of junior number 12

MADELINE ASHBY

"You're a self-replicating humanoid. vN."

Javier always spoke Spanish the first few days. It was his clade's default setting. "You have polymer-doped memristors in your skin, transmitting signal to the aerogel in your muscles from the graphene coral inside your skeleton. That part's titanium. You with me, so far?"

Junior nodded. He plucked curiously at the clothes Javier had stolen from the balcony of a nearby condo. It took Javier three jumps, but eventually his fingers and toes learned how to grip the grey water piping. He'd take Junior there for practice, after the kid ate more and grew into the clothes. He was only toddler-sized, today. They'd holed up in a swank bamboo tree house positioned over an infinity pool outside La Jolla, and its floor was now littered with the remnants of an old GPS device that Javier had stripped off its plastic. His son sucked on the chipset.

"Your name is Junior," Javier said. "When you grow up, you can call yourself whatever you want. You can name your own iterations however you want."

"Iterations?"

"Babies. It happens if we eat too much. Buggy self-repair cycle—like cancer."

Not for the first time, Javier felt grateful that his children were all born with an extensive vocabulary.

"You're gonna spend the next couple of weeks with me, and I'll show you how to get what you need. I've done this with all your brothers."

"How many brothers?"

"Eleven."

"Where are they now?"

Javier shrugged. "Around. I started in Nicaragua."

"They look like you?"

"Exactly like me. Exactly like you."

"If I see someone like you but he isn't you, he's my brother?"

"Maybe." Javier opened up the last foil packet of vN electrolytes and held it out for Junior. Dutifully, his son began slurping. "There are lots of vN shells, and we all use the same operating system, but the API was distributed differently for each clade. So you'll meet other vN who look like you, but that doesn't mean they're family. They won't have our clade's arboreal plugin."

"You mean the jumping trick?"

"I mean the jumping trick. And this trick, too."

Javier stretched one arm outside the treehouse. His skin fizzed pleasantly. He nodded at Junior to try. Soon his son was grinning and stretching his whole torso out the window and into the light, sticking out his tongue like Javier had seen human kids do with snow during cartoon Christmas specials.

"It's called photosynthesis," Javier told him a moment later. "Only our clade can do it."

Junior nodded. He slowly withdrew the chipset from between his tiny lips. Gold smeared across them; his digestive fluids had made short work of the hardware. Javier would have to find more, soon.

"Why are we here?"

"In this treehouse?"

Junior shook his head. "Here." He frowned. He was only two days old, and finding the right words for more nuanced concepts was still hard. "Alive."

"Why do we exist?"

Junior nodded emphatically.

"Well, our clade was developed to—"

"No!" His son looked surprised at the vehemence of his own voice. He pushed on anyway. "vN. Why do vN exist at all?"

This latest iteration was definitely an improvement on the others. His other boys usually didn't get to that question until at least a week went by. Javier almost wished this boy were the same. He'd have more time to come up with a better answer. After twelve children, he should have crafted the perfect response. He could have told his son that it was his own job to figure that out. He could have said it was different for everybody. He could have talked about the church, or the lawsuits, or even the failsafe. But the real answer was that they existed for the same reasons all technologies existed. To be used.

"Some very sick people thought the world was going to end," Javier said. "We were supposed to help the humans left behind."

The next day, Javier took him to a park. It was a key part of the training: meeting humans of different shapes, sizes, and colours. Learning how to play with them. Practising English. The human kids liked watching his kid jump. He could make it to the top of the slide in one leap.

"Again!" they cried. "Again!"

When the shadows stretched long and, Junior jumped up into the tree where Javier waited, and said: "I think I'm in love."

Javier nodded at the playground below. "Which one?"

Junior pointed to a redheaded organic girl whose face was an explosion of freckles. She was all by herself under a tree, rolling a scroll reader against her little knee. She kept adjusting her position to get better shade.

"You've got a good eye," Javier said.

As they watched, three older girls wandered over her way. They stood over her and nodded down at the reader. She backed up against the tree and tucked her chin down toward her chest. Way back in Javier's stem code, red flags rose. He shaded Junior's eyes.

"Don't look."

"Hey, give it back!"

"Don't look, don't look—" Javier saw one hand lash out, shut his eyes, curled himself around his struggling son. He heard a gasp for air. He heard crying. He felt sick. Any minute now the failsafe might engage, and his memory would begin to spontaneously self-corrupt. He had to stop their fight, before it killed him and his son.

"D-Dad—"

Javier jumped. His body knew where to go; he landed on the grass to the sound of startled shrieks and fumbled curse words. Slowly, he opened his eyes. One of the older girls still held the scroll reader aloft. Her arm hung there, refusing to come down, even as she started to back away. She looked about ten.

"Do y-you know w-what I am?"

"You're a robot . . ." She sounded like she was going to cry. That was fine; tears didn't set off the failsafe.

"You're damn right I'm a robot." He pointed up into the tree. "And if I don't intervene right now, my kid will die."

"I didn't—"

"Is that what you want? You wanna kill my kid?"

She was really crying now. Her friends had tears in their eyes. She sniffled back a thick clot of snot. "No! We didn't know! We didn't see you!"

"That doesn't matter. We're everywhere, now. Our failsafes go off the moment we see one of you chimps start a fight. It's called a social control mechanism. Look it up. And next time, keep your grubby little paws to yourself."

One of her friends piped up: "You don't have to be so *mean*—"

"*Mean?*" Javier watched her shrink under the weight of his gaze. "*Mean* is getting hit and not being able to fight back. And that's something I've got in common with your little punching bag over here. So why don't drag your knuckles somewhere else and give that some thought?"

The oldest girl threw the reader toward her victim with a weak underhand. "I don't know why you're acting so hurt," she said, folding her arms and jiggling away. "You don't even have real feelings."

"Yeah, I don't have real fat, either, tubby! Or real acne! Enjoy your teen years, *querida!*"

Behind him, he heard applause. When he turned, he saw a red-haired woman leaning against the tree. She wore business clothes with an incongruous pair of climbing slippers. The fabric of her tights had gone loose and wrinkled down around her ankles, like the skin of an old woman. Her applause died abruptly as the little freckled girl ran up and hugged her fiercely around the waist.

"I'm sorry I'm late," the mother said. She nodded at Javier. "Thanks for looking after her."

"I wasn't."

Javier gestured and Junior slid down out of his tree. Unlike the organic girl, Junior didn't hug him; he jammed his little hands in the pockets of his stolen clothes and looked the older woman over from top to bottom. Her eyebrows rose.

"Well!" She bent down to Junior's height. The kid's eyes darted for the open buttons of her blouse and widened considerably;

Javier smothered a smile. "What do you think, little man? Do I pass inspection?"

Junior grinned. *"Eres humana."*

She straightened. Her eyes met Javier's. "I suppose coming from a vN, that's quite the compliment."

"We aim to please," he said.

Moments later, they were in her car.

It started with a meal. It usually did. From silent prison guards in Nicaragua to singing cruise directors in Panama, from American girls dancing in Mexico and now this grown American woman in her own car in her own country, they started it with eating. Humans enjoyed feeding vN. They liked the special wrappers with the cartoon robots on the front. (They folded them into origami unicorns, because they thought that was clever.) They liked asking about whether he could taste. (He could, but his tongue read texture better than flavour.) They liked calculating how much he'd need to iterate again. (A lot.) This time, the food came as a thank-you. But the importance of food in the relationship was almost universal among humans. It was important that Junior learn this, and the other subtleties of organic interaction. Javier's last companion had called their relationship "one big HCI problem." Javier had no idea what that meant, but he suspected that embedding Junior in a human household for a while would help him avoid it.

"We could get delivery," Brigid said. That was her name. She pronounced it with a silent G. *Breed*. Her daughter was Abigail. "I'm not much for going out."

He nodded. "That's fine with us."

He checked the rearview. The kid was doing all right; Abigail was showing him a game. Its glow diffused across their faces and made them, for the moment, the same colour. But Junior's eyes weren't on the game. They were on the little girl's face.

"He's adorable," Brigid said. "How old is he?"

Javier checked the dashboard. "Three days."

The house was a big, fake hacienda with the floors and walls and ceilings all the same vanilla ice cream colour. Javier felt as though he'd stepped into a giant, echoing egg. Light followed Brigid as she entered each room, and now Javier saw bare patches on the plaster and the scratch marks of heavy furniture dragged across pearly tile. Someone had moved out. Probably Abigail's father. Javier's life had just gotten enormously easier.

"I hope you don't mind the Electric Sheep . . ."

Brigid handed him her compact. In it was a menu for a chain specializing in vN food. ("It's the food you've been dreaming of!") Actually, vN items were only half the Sheep's menu; the place was a meat market for organics and synthetics. Javier had eaten there but only a handful of times, mostly at resorts, and mostly with people who wanted to know what he thought of it "from his perspective." He chose a Toaster Party and a Hasta La Vista for himself and Junior. When the orders went through, a little lamb with an extension cord for a collar *baa'd* at him and bounded away across the compact.

"It's good we ran into you," Brigid said. "Abby hasn't exactly been very social, lately. I think this is the longest conversation she's had with, well, *anybody* in . . ." Brigid's hand fluttered in the air briefly before falling.

Javier nodded like he understood. It was best to interrupt her now, while she still had some story to tell. Otherwise she'd get it out of her system too soon. "I'm sorry, but if you don't mind . . ." He put a hand to his belly. "There's a reason they call it labour, you know?"

Brigid blushed. "Oh my God, of course! Let's get you laid, uh, down somewhere." Her eyes squeezed shut. "I mean, um, that didn't quite come out right—"

Oh, she was so cute.

"It's been a long day—"

She was practically glowing.

"And I normally don't bring strays home, but you were so nice—"

He knew songs that went this way.

"Anyway, we normally use the guest room for storage, I mean I was sleeping in it for a while before everything . . . But if it's just a nap . . ."

He followed her upstairs to the master bedroom. It was silent and cool, and the sheets smelled like new plastic and discount shopping. He woke there hours later, when the food was cold and her body was warm, and both were within easy reach.

The next morning Brigid kept looking at him and giggling. It was like she'd gotten away with something, like she'd spent the night in a club and not in her own bed, like she wasn't the one making the rules she'd apparently just broken. The laughter took ten years off her face. She had creams for the rest, and applied them.

Downstairs, Abigail sat at the kitchen bar with her orange juice and cereal. Her legs swung under her barstool, back and forth, back and forth. She seemed to be rehearsing for a later role as a bored girl in a coffee shop: reading something on her scroll, her chin cradled in the pit of her left hand as she paged through with her right index finger, utterly oblivious to the noise of the display mounted behind her or Junior's enthusiastic responses to the educational show playing there. It was funny—he'd just seen the mother lose ten years, but now he saw the daughter gaining them back. She looked so old this morning, so tired.

"My daddy is going out with a vN, too," Abigail said, not looking up from her reader.

Javier yanked open the fridge. "That so?"

"Yup. He was going out with her *and* my mom for a while, but not any more."

Well, that explained some things. Javier pushed aside the milk and orange juice cartons and found the remainder of the vN food. Best to be as nonchalant with the girl as she'd been with him. "What kind of model? This other vN, I mean."

"I don't know about the clade, but the model was used for nursing in Japan."

He nodded. "They had a problem with old people, there."

"Did you know that Japan has a whole city just for robots? It's called Mecha. Like that place that Muslim people go to sometimes, but with an H instead of a C."

Javier set about preparing a plate for Junior. He made sure the kid got the biggest chunks of rofu. "I know about Mecha," he said. "It's in Nagasaki Harbour. It's the same spot they put the white folks a long time ago. Bigger now, though."

Abigail nodded. "My daddy sent me pictures. He's on a trip there right now. That's why I'm here all week." She quickly sketched a command into her reader with her finger, then shoved the scroll his way. Floating on its soft surface, Javier saw a Japanese-style vN standing beside a curvy white reception-bot with a happy LCD smile and braids sculpted from plastic and enamel. They were both in old-fashioned clothes, the smart robot and the stupid one: the vN wore a lavender kimono with a pink sash, and the receptionist wore "wooden" clogs.

"Don't you think she's pretty?" Abigail asked. "Everybody always says how pretty she is, when I show them the pictures."

"She's all right. She's a vN."

Abigail smiled. "You think my mom is prettier?"

"Your mom is human. Of course I do."

"So you like humans the best?"

She said it like he had a choice. Like he could just shut it off, if he wanted. Which he couldn't. Ever.

"Yeah, I like humans the best."

Abigail's feet stopped swinging. She sipped her orange juice delicately through a curlicued kiddie straw until only bubbles came. "Maybe my daddy should try being a robot."

It wasn't until Brigid and Abigail were gone that Javier decided to debrief his son on what had happened in the park. He had felt sick, he explained, because they were designed to respond quickly to violence against humans. The longer they avoided responding, the worse they felt. It was like an allergy, he said, to human suffering.

Javier made sure to explain this while they watched a channel meant for adult humans. A little clockwork eye kept popping up in the top right corner of the screen just before the violent parts, warning them not to look. "But it's not real," Junior said, in English. "Can't our brains tell the difference?"

"Most of the time. But better safe than sorry."

"So I can't watch TV for grown-ups?"

"Sometimes. You can watch all the cartoon violence you want. It doesn't fall in the Valley at all; there was no human response to simulate when they coded our stems." He slugged electrolytes. While on her lunch break, Brigid had ordered a special delivery of vN groceries. She clearly intended him to stay awhile. "You can still watch porn, though. I mean, they'd never have built us in the first if we couldn't pass *that* little test."

"Porn?"

"Well. Vanilla porn. Not the rough stuff. No blood. Not unless it's a vN getting roughed up. Then you can go to town."

"How will I know the difference?"

"You'll know."

"*How* will I know?"

"If it's a human getting hurt, your cognition will start to jag. You'll stutter."

"Like when somebody tried to hurt Abigail?"

"Like that, yeah."

Junior blinked. "I need to see an example."

Javier nodded. "Sure thing. Hand me that remote."

They found some content. A nice sampler, Javier thought. Javier paused the feed frequently. There was some slang to learn and explain, and some anatomy. He was always careful to give his boys a little lesson on how to find the clitoris. The mega-church whose members had tithed to fund the development of their OS didn't want them hurting any of the sinners left behind to endure God's wrath after the Rapture. Fucking them was still okay.

He had just finished explaining this little feat of theology when Brigid came home early. She shrieked and covered her daughter's eyes. Then she hit Javier. He lay on the couch, unfazed, as she slapped him and called him names. He wondered, briefly, what it would be like to be able to defend himself.

"He's a child!"

"Yeah, he's *my* child," Javier said. "And that makes it *my* decision, not yours."

Brigid folded her arms and paced across the bedroom to retrieve her drink. She'd had the scotch locked up way high in the kitchen and he'd watched her stand on tiptoes on a slender little dining room chair just to get it, her calves doing all sorts of interesting things as she stretched.

"I suppose you show all your children pornography?" She tipped back more of her drink.

"Every last one."

"How many is that?"

"This Junior is the twelfth."

"*Twelve?* Rapid iteration is like a felony in this state!"

This was news to him. Then again, it made a certain kind of sense—humans worked very hard to avoid having children, because theirs were so expensive and annoying and otherwise burdensome. Naturally they had assumed that vN kids were the same.

"I'll be sure to let this Junior know about that."

"*This* Junior? Don't you even *name* them?"

He shrugged. "What's the point? We don't see each other. Let them choose their own name."

"Oh, so in addition to being a pervert, you're an uncaring felonious bastard. That's just great."

Javier had no idea where "caring" came into the equation, but decided to let that slide. "You've been with me. Did I ask you to do anything weird?"

"No—"

"Did I make you feel bad?" He stepped forward. She had very plush carpet, the kind that dug into his toes if he walked slowly enough.

"No . . ."

They were close; he could see where one of her earrings was a little tangled and he reached under her hair to fix it. "Did I make you feel good?"

She sighed through her nose to hide the quirk in her lip. "That's not the point. The *point* is that it's wrong to show that kind of stuff to kids!"

He rubbed her arms. "Human kids, yeah. They tend to run a little slow. They get confused. Junior knows that the vids were just a lesson on the failsafe." He stepped back. "What, do you think I was trying to *turn him on*, or something? Jesus! And you think *I'm* sick?"

"Well, how should *I* know? I come home and you're just sitting there like it's no big deal . . ." She swallowed the last of the drink. "Do you have any *idea* what kinds of ads I'm going to get, now? What kind of commercials I'm going to have to flick past, before Abigail sees them? I don't want that kind of thing attached to my profile, Javier!"

"Give me a break," Javier said. "I'm only three years old."

That stopped her in her tracks. Her mouth hung open. Human women got so uptight about his age. The men handled it much better—they laughed and ruffled his hair and asked if he'd had enough to eat.

He smiled. "What, you've never been with a younger man?"

"That's not funny."

He lay back on the bed, propped up on his elbows. "Of course it's funny. It's hysterical. You're railing at me for teaching my kid how to recognize the smutvids that won't *fry his brain*, and all the while you've been riding a three-year-old."

"Oh, for—"

"And very eagerly, I might add."

Now she looked genuinely angry. "You're a total asshole, you know that? Are you training Junior to be a total asshole, too?"

"He can be whatever he wants to be."

"Well, I'm sure he's finding plenty of good role models in the adult entertainment industry, Javier."

"Lots of vN get rich doing porn. They can do the seriously hardcore stuff." He stretched. "They have to pay a licensing fee to the studio that coded the crying plugin, though. Designers won a lawsuit."

Brigid sank slowly to the very edge of the bed. Her spine folded over her hips. She held her face in her hands. For a moment she became her daughter: shoulders hunched, cowering. She seemed at once very fragile and very heavy. Brigid did not think of herself as beautiful. He knew that from the menagerie of creams in her bathroom. She would never understand the reassurance a vN could find in the solidity of her flesh, or the charm of her unique smiles, or the hundred different sneezes her species seemed to have. She would only know that they melted for humans.

As though sensing his gaze, she peered at him through the spaces between her fingers. "Why did you bother bringing a child into this world, Javier?"

He'd felt this same confusion when Junior asked him about the existence of all vN. He had no real answer. Sometimes, he wondered if his desire to iterate was a holdover from the clade's initial programming as ecological engineers, and he was nothing more than a Johnny Appleseed planting his boys hither and yon. After all, they did sink a lot of carbon.

But nobody ever seemed to ask the humans this question. Their breeding was messy and organic and therefore special, and everybody treated it like some divine right no matter what the consequences were for the planet or the psyche or the body. They'd had the technology to prevent unwanted children for decades, but Javier still met them every day, still listened to them as they talked themselves to sleep about accidents and cycles and late-night family confessions during holiday visits. He thought about Abigail, lonely and defenceless under her tree. Brigid had no right to ask him why he'd bred.

He nodded at her empty glass. "Why did you have yours? Were you drunk?"

Javier spent that night on a futon in the storage room. He lay surrounded by the remnants of Brigid's old life: t-shirts from dive bars that she insisted on keeping; smart lease agreements and test results that she'd carefully organized in Faraday boxes. It was no different from the mounds of clutter he'd found in other homes. Humans seemed to have a thing about holding on to stuff. *Things* held a special meaning for them. That was lucky for him. Javier was a thing, too.

He had moved on\ to the books when Junior came in to see him. The boy shuffled toward him uncertainly. He had eaten half a box of vN groceries that day. The new inches messed with his posture and gait; he didn't know where to put his newly enlarged feet.

"Dad, I've got a problem." Junior flopped onto the futon. He hugged his shins. "Are you having a problem, too?"

"A problem?"

Junior nodded at the bedroom.

"Oh, that. Don't worry about that. Humans are like that. They freak out."

"Is she gonna kick us out?" Junior stared directly at Javier. "I know it's my fault and I'm sorry, I didn't mean to mess things up—"

"Shut up."

His son closed his mouth. Junior looked so small just then, all curled in on himself. It was hard to remember that he'd been even tinier only a short time ago. His black curls overshadowed his head, as though the programming for hair had momentarily taken greater priority than the chassis itself. Javier gently pulled the hair away so he could see his son's eyes a little better.

"It's not your fault."

Junior didn't look convinced. ". . . It's not?"

"No. It's not. You can't control how they act. They have systems that we don't—hormones and glands and nerves and who knows what—controlling what they do. You're not responsible for that."

"But, if I hadn't asked to see—"

"Brigid reacted the way she did because she's meat," Javier said. "She couldn't help it. I chose to show you those vids because

I thought it was the right thing to do. When you're bigger, you can make those kinds of choices for your own iterations. Until then, I'm running the show. Got it?"

Junior nodded. "Got it."

"Good." Javier stood, stretched, and found a book for them to read. It was thick and old, with a statue on the cover. He settled down on the futon beside Junior. "You said you had a problem?"

Junior nodded. "Abigail doesn't like me. Not the way I want. She wouldn't let me hold hands when we made a fort in her room."

Javier smiled. "That's normal. She won't like you until you're an older boy. That's what they like best, if they like boys. Give it a day or two." He tickled his son's ribs. "We'll make a bad boy of you yet, just you watch."

"Dad . . ."

Javier kept tickling. "Oh yeah. Show me your broody face. Show me angst. They love that."

Junior twisted away and folded his arms. He threw himself against the futon in a very good approximation of huffy irritation. "You're not helping—"

"No, seriously, try to look like a badass. A badass who gets all weepy about girls."

Finally, his son laughed. Then Javier told him it was time to learn about how paper books worked, and he rested an arm across his son's shoulders and read aloud until the boy grew bored and sleepy. And when the lights were all out and the house was quiet and they lay wrapped up in an old quilt, his son said: "Dad, I grew three inches today."

Javier smiled in the dark. He smoothed the curls away from his son's face. "I saw that."

"Did my brothers grow as fast as me?"

Javier answered as he always did: "No, you're the fastest yet."

It was not a lie. Each time, they seemed to grow just a little bit faster.

Brigid called him the next day from work. "I'm sorry I didn't say goodbye before I left this morning."

"That's okay."

"I just . . . This is sort of new for me, you know? I've met other vN, but not ones Junior's age. I've never seen them in this phase, and—"

He heard people chattering in the background. Vaguely, he

wondered what Brigid did for a living. It was probably boring, and she probably didn't want to think about work while she was with him. Doing so tended to mess with human responses.

"—you're trying to train him for everything, and I get them, but have you ever considered slowing things down?"

"And delay the joys of adulthood?"

"Speaking of which," she said, her voice now lowered to a conspiratorial whisper, "what are you doing tonight?"

"What would you like me to do?"

She giggled. He laughed, too. How Brigid could be so shy and so nervous was beyond him. For all their little failings humans were very strong; they felt pain and endured it, and had the types of feelings he would never have. Their faces flushed and their eyes burned and their hearts sometimes skipped a few beats. Or so he had heard. He wondered what having organs would feel like. Would he be constantly conscious of them? Would he notice the slow degradation and deterioration of his neurons, blinking brightly and frantically before dying, like old filament bulbs?

"Have a bath ready for me when I get home," she said.

Brigid liked a lot of bubbles in her bath. She also liked not to be disturbed. "I let Abigail stay at a friend's house tonight." She stretched backward against Javier. "I wish Junior had friends he could stay with."

Javier raised his eyebrows. "You plan on getting loud?"

She laughed a little. He felt the reverberation all through him. "I think that depends on you."

"Then I hope you have plenty of lozenges," he said. "Your throat's gonna hurt, tomorrow."

"I thought you couldn't hurt me." She grabbed his arms and folded them around herself like the sleeves of an oversized sweater.

"I can't. Not in the moment. But I'm not responsible for any lingering side-effects."

"Hmm. So no spanking, then?"

"Tragically, no. Why? You been bad?"

She stilled. Slowly, she turned around. She had lit candles, and they illuminated only her silhouette. Her face remained shadowed, unreadable. "In the past," she said. "Sometimes I think I'm a really bad person, Javier."

"Why?"

"Just . . . I'm selfish. And I know it. But I can't stop."

"Selfish how?"

"Well . . ." She walked two fingers down his chest. "I'm terrible at sharing."

He looked down. "Seems there's plenty to go around . . ."

The candles fizzed out when she splashed bubbles in his face.

Later that night, she burrowed up into his chest and said: "You're staying for a while, right?"

"Why wouldn't I? You spoil me."

She flipped over and faced away from him. "You do this a lot, don't you? Hooking up with humans, I mean."

He hated having this conversation. No matter how hard he tried to avoid it, it always popped up sometime. It was like they were programmed to ask the question. "I've had my share of relationships with humans."

"How many others have there been like me?"

"You're unique."

"Bullshit." She turned over to her back. "Tell me. I want to know. How many others?"

He rolled over, too. In the dark, he had a hard time telling where the ceiling was. It was a shadowy void far above him that made his voice echo strangely. He hated the largeness of this house, he realized. It was huge and empty and wasteful. He wanted something small. He wanted the treehouse back.

"I never counted."

"Of course you did. You're a computer. You're telling me you don't index the humans you sleep with? You don't categorize us somewhere? You don't chart us by height and weight and income?"

Javier frowned. "No. I don't."

Brigid sighed. "What happened with the others? Did you leave them or did they leave you?"

"Both."

"Why? Why would they leave you?"

He slapped his belly. It produced a flat sound in the quiet room. "I get fat. Then they stop wanting me."

Brigid snorted. "If you don't want to tell me, that's fine. But at least make up a better lie, okay?"

"No, really! I get very fat. Obese, even."

"You do *not*."

"I do. And then they die below the waist." He folded his hands behind his head. "You humans, you're very shallow."

"Oh, and I suppose you don't give a damn what we look like, right?"

"Of course. I love all humans equally. It's priority programmed."

She scrambled up and sat on him. "So I'm just like the others, huh?"

Her hipbones stuck out just enough to provide good grips for his thumbs. "I said I love you all equally, not that I love you all for the same reasons."

She grabbed his hands and pinned them over his head. "So why'd you hook up with me, huh? Why me, out of all the other meatsacks out there?"

"That's easy." He grinned. "My kid has a crush on yours."

The next day were Junior's jumping lessons. They started in the backyard. It was a nice backyard, mostly slate with very little lawn, the sort of low-maintenance thing that suited Brigid perfectly. He worried a little about damaging the surface, though, so he insisted that Junior jump from the lawn to the roof. It was a forty-five degree jump, and it required confident legs, firm feet, and a sharp eye. Luckily, the sun beating down on them gave them plenty of energy for the task.

"Don't worry," he shouted. "Your body knows how!"

"But, Dad—"

"No buts! Jump!"

"I don't want to hit the windows!"

"Then don't!"

His son gave him the finger. He laughed. Then he watched as the boy took two steps backward, ran, and launched himself skyward. His slender body sailed up, arms and legs flailing uselessly, and he landed clumsily against the eaves. Red ceramic tiles fell down to the patio, disturbed by his questing fingers.

"Dad, I'm slipping!"

"Use your arms. Haul yourself up." The boy had to learn this. It was crucial.

"Dad—"

"Javier? Junior?"

Abigail was home from school. He heard the patio door close. He watched another group of tiles slide free of the roof. Something in him switched over. He jumped down and saw Abigail's frightened face before ushering her backward, out of the way of falling tiles. Behind him, he heard a mighty crash. He turned, and his son was lying on his side surrounded by broken tiles. His left leg had bent completely backward.

"Junior!"

Abigail dashed toward Junior's prone body. She knelt beside him, her face all concern, her hands busy at his sides. His son cast a long look between him and her. She had run to help Junior. She was asking him if it hurt. Javier knew already that it didn't. It couldn't. They didn't suffer, physically. But his son was staring at him like he was actually feeling pain.

"What happened?"

He turned. Brigid was standing there in her office clothes, minus the shoes. She must have come home early. "I'm sorry about the tiles," Javier said.

But Brigid wasn't looking at the tiles. She was looking at Junior and Abigail. The girl kept fussing over him. She pulled his left arm across her little shoulders and stood up so that he could ease his leg back into place. She didn't let go when his stance was secure. Her stubborn fingers remained tangled in his. "You've gotten bigger," Abigail said quietly. Her ears had turned red.

"Junior kissed me."

It was Saturday. They were at the playground. Brigid had asked for Junior's help washing the car while Javier took Abigail to play, and now he thought he understood why. He watched Abigail's legs swinging above the ground. She took a contemplative sip from her juicebox.

"What kind of kiss?" he asked.

"Nothing fancy," Abigail answered, as though she were a regular judge of kisses. "It was only right here, not on the lips." She pointed at her cheek.

"Did that scare you?"

She frowned and folded her arms. "My daddy kisses me there all the time."

"Ah." Now he understood his son's mistake.

"Junior's grown up really fast," Abigail said. "Now he looks like he's in middle school."

Javier had heard of middle school from organic people's stories. It sounded like a horrible place. "Do you ever wish you could grow up that fast?"

Abigail nodded. "Sometimes. But then I couldn't live with Mom, or my daddy. I'd have to live somewhere else, and get a job, and do everything by myself. I'm not sure it's worth it." She crumpled up her juicebox. "Did you grow up really fast, like Junior?"

"Yeah. Pretty fast."

"Did your daddy teach you the things you're teaching Junior?"

Javier rested his elbows on his knees. "Some of it. And some of it I learned on my own."

"Like what?"

It was funny, he normally only ever had this conversation with adults. "Well, he taught me how to jump really high. And how to climb trees. Do you know how to climb trees?"

Abigail shook her head. "Mom says it's dangerous. And it's harder with palm trees, anyway."

"That's true, it is." At least, he imagined it would be for her. The bark on those trees could cut her skin open. It could cut his open, too, but he wouldn't feel the pain. "Anyway, Dad taught me lots of things: how to talk to people; how to use things like the bus and money and phones and email; how stores work."

"How stores work?"

"Like, how to buy things. How to shop."

"How to shop*lift*?"

He pretended to examine her face. "Hey, you sure you're organic? You sure seem awful smart . . ."

She giggled. "Can you teach *me* how to shoplift?"

"No way!" He stood. "You'd get caught, and they'd haul you off to jail."

Abigail hopped off the bench. "They wouldn't haul a *kid* off to jail, Javier."

"Not an organic one, maybe. But a vN, sure." He turned to leave the playground.

"Have *you* ever been to jail?"

"Sure."

"When?"

They were about to cross a street. Her hand found his. He was careful not to squeeze too hard. "When I was smaller," he said simply. "A long time ago."

"Was it hard?"

"Sometimes."

"But you can't feel it if somebody beats you up, right? It doesn't hurt?"

"No, it doesn't hurt."

In jail they had asked him, at various times, if it hurt yet. And he had blinked and said *No, not yet, not ever.* Throughout, he had believed that his dad might come to help him. It was his dad who had been training him. His dad had seen the *policia* take him in. And Javier had thought that there was a plan, that he would be rescued, that it would end. But there was no plan. It did not end. His dad never showed. And then the humans had turned on each other, in an effort to trigger his failsafe.

"Junior didn't feel any pain, either," Abigail said. "When you let him fall."

The signal changed. They walked forward. The failsafe swam under the waters of his mind, and whispered to him about the presence of cars and the priority of human life.

"What do you mean, he's not here?"

Abigail kept looking from her mother to Javier and back again. "Did Junior go away?"

Brigid looked down at her. "Are you all packed up? Your dad is coming today to get you."

"*And* Momo, Mom. Daddy *and* Momo. They're both coming straight from the airport."

"Yes. I know that. Your dad and Momo. Now can you please check upstairs?"

Abigail didn't budge. "Will Junior be here when I come back next Friday?"

"I don't know, Abigail. Maybe not. He's not just some toy you can leave somewhere."

Abigail's face hardened. "You're mean and I hate you," she said, before marching up the stairs with heavy, decisive stomps.

Javier waited until he heard a door slam before asking: "Where is he, really?"

"I really don't know, Javier. He's your son."

Javier frowned. "Well, did he say anything—"

"No. He didn't. I told him that Abigail would be going back with her dad, and he just up and left."

Javier made for the door. "I should go look for him."

"No!" Brigid slid herself between his body and the door. "I mean, please don't. At least, not until my ex leaves. Okay?"

"Your ex? Why? Are you afraid of him or something?" Javier tipped her chin up with one finger. "He can't hurt you while his girlfriend's watching. You know that, right?"

She hunched her shoulders. "I know. And I'm not afraid of him hurting me. God. You always leap to the worst possible conclusion. It's just, you know, the way he gloats. About how great his life is now. It hurts."

He deflated. "Fine. I'll wait."

In the end, he didn't have long to wait. They showed up only fifteen minutes later—a little earlier than they were supposed to, which surprised Brigid and made her even angrier for some reason. "He was never on time when *we* were together," she sniffed, as she watched them exit their car. "I guess dating a robot is easier than buying a fucking watch."

"That's a bad word, Mom," Abigail said. "I'm gonna debit your account."

Brigid sighed. She forced a smile. "You're right, honey. I'm sorry. Let's go say hi to your dad."

At the door, Kevin was a round guy with thinning hair and very flashy-looking augmented lenses—the kind usually marketed at much younger humans. He stood on the steps with one arm around a Japanese-model vN wearing an elaborate Restoration costume complete with velvet jacket and perfect black corkscrew curls. They both stepped back a little when Javier greeted them at the door.

"You must be Javier," Kevin said, extending his hand and smiling a dentist smile. "Abigail's told me lots about you."

"You did?" Brigid frowned at her daughter.

"Yeah." Abigail's expression clouded. "Was it supposed to be a surprise?"

Brigid's mouth opened, then closed, then opened again. "Of course not."

The thing about the failsafe was that it made sure his perceptual systems caught every moment of hesitation in voices or faces or movements. Sometimes humans could defeat it, if they believed their own bullshit. But outright lies, especially about the things that hurt—he had reefs of graphene coral devoted to filtering those. Brigid was lying. She had meant for this moment to be a surprise. He could simulate it, now: she would open the door and he would be there and he would make her look good because he looked good, he was way prettier by human standards than she or her ex had any hope of ever being, and for some reason that mattered. Not that he couldn't understand; his own systems were regularly hijacked by his perceptions. He responded to pain; they responded to proportion. He couldn't actually hurt the human man standing in front of him—not with his fists. But his flat stomach and his thick hair and his clear, near-poreless skin: they were doing the job just fine. Javier saw that, now, in the way Kevin kept sizing him up, even when his own daughter danced into his arms. His jetlagged eyes barely spared a second for her. They remained trained on Javier. Beside him, Brigid stood a little taller.

God, Brigid was such a bitch.

"I like your dress, Momo," Abigail said.

This shook Kevin out of his mate-competition trance. "Well that's good news, baby, 'cause we bought a version in your size, too!"

"That's cute," Brigid said. "Now you can both play dress-up."

Kevin shot her a look that was pure hate. Javier was glad suddenly that he'd never asked about why the two of them had split. He didn't want to know. It was clearly too deep and organic and weird for him to understand, much less deal with.

"Well, it was nice meeting you," he said. "I'm sure you're pretty tired after the flight. You probably want to get home and go to sleep, right?"

"Yes, that's right," Momo said. Thank Christ for other robots; they knew how to take a cue.

Kevin pinked considerably. "Uh, right." He reached down, picked up Abigail's bag, and nodded at them. "Call you later, Brigid."

"Sure."

Abigail waved at Javier. She blew him a kiss. He blew one back as the door closed.

"Well, thank goodness that's over." Brigid sagged against the door, her palms flat against its surface, her face lit with a new glow. "We have the house to ourselves."

She was so pathetically obvious. He'd met high-schoolers with more grace. He folded his arms. "Where's my son?"

Brigid frowned. "I don't know, but I'm sure he's fine. You've been training him, haven't you? He has all your skills." Her fingers played with his shiny new belt buckle, the one she had bought for him especially. "Well, most of them. I'm sure there are some things he'll just have to learn on his own."

She knew. She knew exactly where his son was. And when her eyes rose, she knew that he knew. And she smiled.

Javier did not feel fear in any organic way. The math reflected a certain organic sensibility, perhaps, the way his simulation and prediction engines suddenly spun to life, their fractal computations igniting and processing as he calculated what could go wrong and when and how and with whom. How long had it been since he'd last seen Junior? How much did Junior know? Was his English good enough? Were his jumps strong enough? Did he understand the failsafe completely? These were the questions Javier had, instead of a cold sweat. If he were a different kind of man, a man like Kevin or any of the other human men he'd met and enjoyed in his time, he might have felt a desire to grab Brigid or hit her the way she'd hit him earlier, when she thought he was endangering her offspring in some vague, indirect way. They had subroutines for that. They had their own failsafes, the infamous triple-F cascades of adrenaline that gave them bursts of energy for dealing with problems like the one facing him now. They were built to protect their own, and he was not.

So he shrugged and said: "You're right. There are some things you just can't teach."

They went to the bedroom. And he was so good, he'd learned so much in his short years, that Brigid rewarded his technique with knowledge. She told him about taking Junior to the grocery store with her. She told him about the man who had followed them into the parking lot. She told him how, when she had asked Junior what he thought, he had given Javier's exact same shrug.

"He said you'd be fine with it," she said. "He said your dad did something similar. He said it made you stronger. More independent."

Javier shut his eyes. "Independent. Sure."

"He looked so much like you as he said it." Brigid was already half asleep. "I wonder what I'll pass down to my daughter, sometimes. Maybe she'll fall in love with a robot, just like her mommy and daddy."

"Maybe," Javier said. "Maybe her whole generation will. Maybe they won't even bother reproducing."

"Maybe we'll go extinct," Brigid said. "But then who would you have left to love?"

one quarter gorgon
HELEN MARSHALL

When we make love, it is in darkness or with blindfolds.
I have learned so well the sinuous curves
of hips and thighs, mapping subterranean passages
or the high breathy places where eagles nest.
I know her best by hand, by fingertouch,
by the sweetness of incense on my lips.

Sometimes, she whispers in Greek—
se skeftomai sinehia, se hriazome—
the words coiling like snakes in my throat.
Her language is so secret.

Our house has no mirrors,
and I can see myself only in her words.
Today, you are beautiful, *anasa mou*,
today, you wear sunlight in your hair
and I would tangle my hands in you
to grow warm and brown from kissing.
I do not know how pale she is.

You break so quickly, she tells me,
like black earthen kylix.
You are a child. You are a child.
I am so old that you cannot love me.
S'agapo san paidi.
I love you like a child.

When her hands wind behind my head
and my lips taste myrrh and orange on her skin,
I feel the immolation of her gaze,
the hot, slick love of the Gorgon,
and she is beautiful.

Afterward, she whispers:
Ki'taxa vathia' mes sta ma'tia sou ke i'da to me'llon mas:
I looked deep into your eyes and saw our future.
I am transfixed.

a puddle of blood

SILVIA MORENO-GARCIA

Six Dismembered Bodies Found in Ciudad Juarez.
Vampire Drug-wars Rage On.

Domingo reads the headline slowly. Images flash on the video screen of the subway station. Cops. Long shots of the bodies. The images dissolve, showing a young woman holding a can of soda in her hands. She winks at him.

Domingo waits to see if the next news items will expand on the drug-war story. He is fond of yellow journalism. He also likes stories about vampires; they seem exotic. There are no vampires in Mexico City: their kind has been a no-no for the past thirty years, around the time the Federal District became a city-state.

The next story is of a pop-star, the singing sensation of the month, and then there is another ad, this one for a shoulder-bag computer. Domingo sulks, changes the tune on his music player.

He looks at another screen with pictures of blue butterflies fluttering around. Domingo takes a chocolate from his pocket and tears the wrapper.

He spends a lot of time in the subway system. He used to sleep in the subway cars when he was a street kid making a living by washing windshields at cross streets. Those days are behind. He has a place to sleep and lately he's been doing some for a rag-and-bone man, collecting used thermoplastic clothing. He complements his income with other odd jobs. It keeps him well-fed and he has enough money to buy tokens for the public baths once a week.

He bites into the chocolate bar.

A woman wearing a black vinyl jacket walks by him, holding a leash. Her Doberman must be genetically modified. The animal is huge.

He's seen her several times before, riding the subway late at nights, always with the dog. Heavy boots upon the white tiles, bob cut black hair, narrow-faced.

Tonight she moves her face a small fraction, glancing at him. Domingo stuffs the remaining chocolate back in his pocket, takes off his headphones and follows her quickly, squeezing through the doors of the subway car she's boarding.

He sits across from her and is able to get a better look at the woman. She is early twenties, with large eyes that give her an air of innocence which is quickly dispelled by the stern mouth. The woman is cute, in an odd way.

Domingo tries to look at her discreetly, but he must not be discreet enough because she turns and stares at him.

"Hey," he says, smiling. "How are you doing tonight?"

"I'm looking for a friend."

Domingo nods, uncertain.

"How old are you?"

"Seventeen," he replies.

"Would you like to be my friend? I can pay you."

Domingo isn't in the habit of prostituting himself. He's done it once or twice when he was in a pinch. There had also been that time with El Chacal, but that didn't count because Domingo hadn't wanted to and El Chacal had made him anyway, and that's when Domingo left the circle of street kids and the windshield wiping and went to live on his own.

Domingo looks at her. He's seen the woman walk by all those nights before and he's never thought she'd speak to him. Why, he expected her to unleash the dog upon him when he opened his mouth.

He nods. He's never been a lucky guy but he's in luck today.

Her apartment building is squat, short, located just a few blocks from a busy nightclub.

"Hey, you haven't told me your name," he says when they reach the fourth floor and she fishes for her keys.

"Atl," she replies.

The door swings open. The apartment is empty. There is a rug, some cushions on top of it, but no couch, no television and no table. She doesn't even have a calendar on the wall. The apartment has a heavy smell, animal-like, probably courtesy of the dog. Perhaps she keeps more than one pet.

"Do you want tea?" she asks.

Domingo would be better off with pop or a beer, but the girl seems classy and he thinks he ought to go with whatever she prefers.

"Sure," he says.

Atl takes off her jacket. Her blouse is pale cream; it shows off her bony shoulders. He follows her into the kitchen as she places the kettle on a burner.

"I'm going to pay you a certain amount, just for coming here. If you agree to stay, I'll double it," she says.

"Listen," Domingo says, rubbing the back of his head, "you don't really need to pay me nothing."

"I do. I'm a *tlahuelpuchi*."

Domingo blinks. "You can't be. That's one of those vampire types, isn't it?"

"Yes."

"It's vampire-free territory in Mexico City."

"I know. That is why I'm doubling it," she says, scribbling a number on a pad of paper and holding it up for him to see.

Domingo leans against the wall, arms crossed. "Wow."

Atl nods. "I need young blood. You'll do."

"Wait, I mean . . . I'm not going to turn into a vampire, am I?" he asks, because you can never be too sure.

"No," she says, sounding affronted. "We are born into our condition."

"Cool."

"It won't hurt much. What do you think?"

"I don't know. I mean, do I still get to . . . you know . . . sleep with you?"

She lets out a sigh and shakes her head.

"No. Don't try anything. Cualli will bite your leg off if you do."

The kettle whistles. Atl removes it from the burner and pours hot water into two mugs.

"How do we do this?" Domingo asks.

Atl places tea bags in the cups and cranes her neck. Her hair has turned to feathers and her hands, when she raises them, are like talons. The effect is disturbing, as though she is wearing a curious mask.

"Don't worry. Won't take long," she says.

Atl is a bird of prey.

The first thing Domingo does with his newfound fortune is buy himself a good meal. Afterwards, he pays for a booth at the Internet cafe, squeezing himself in and clumsily thumbing the computer screen. The guy in the next cubicle is watching porn; the moans of a woman spill into Domingo's narrow space.

Domingo frowns. He pulls out the frayed headphones wrapped with insulating tape and pushes the play button on the music player.

He does a search for the word *tlahuelpuchi*. Stories about gangs, murders and drugs fill the viewscreen. He scrolls through an article which talks about the history of the *tlahuelpocmimi*, explaining this is Mexico's native vampire species, with roots that go back to the time of the Aztecs. The article has lots of information but it uses very big words he doesn't know, such as hematophagy, anticoagulants and matrilineal stratified sept. Domingo gives up on it quickly, preferring to stare at the bold headlines and colourful pictures of the vampire gangsters. These resemble the comic books he keeps at his place; he is comfortable with this kind of stuff.

When an attendant bangs on the door Domingo doesn't buy more tokens. He has more money than he's ever had in his life and he doesn't know what to do with it.

It is nearly dusk when he finds his way to Atl's apartment. She opens the door a crack; stares at him as though she's never met him before.

"What are you doing tonight?" he asks.

"You're not getting any more money, alright?" she says. "I don't need food right now. There's no sense in you coming here."

"You only eat kids, no?" he says, blurting it.

"Yeah. Something in the hormone levels," she waves her hand, irritated. "That doesn't make me a Lucy Westenra, alright?"

"Lucia, what?"

She raises an eyebrow at him.

"I figure, you want a steady person. Steady food, no? And . . . yesterday, it was, ah . . . it was fun. Kind of."

"Fun," she repeats.

Yeah. It had been fun. Not the blood part. Well, that hadn't been too awful. She made him a cheese sandwich and they drank tea afterwards. Atl didn't have furniture, but she did have a music player and they sat cross-legged in the living room, chatting, until she said he was fine and he wouldn't get woozy and told him to make sure he had a good breakfast.

It wasn't exactly a date, but Domingo has never exactly dated. There were hurried copulations in back alleys, the kind street kids manage. He hung out with Belen for a little bit, but then she went with an older guy and got pregnant, and Domingo hadn't seen her anymore.

Atl lets him in, closing the door, carefully turning the locks.

The dog pads out of the kitchen and stares at him.

"Look, you've to get some facts straight, alright? I'm not in Mexico City on vacation. You don't want to hang out with me. You'll end up as a carpet stain. Trust me, my clan is in deep shit."

"You're part of a clan?" Domingo says, excited. "That's cool! You've got a crest tattooed? Is it hand-poked?"

"Jesus," Atl says. "Are you some sort of fanboy?"

Domingo shakes his head. "No."

"Why are you here?"

"I like your dog," he says. It is a stupid answer. He doesn't have anything better. He wonders if she'll go with him to the arcade. He went there once and drank beer while he tried to shoot green monsters. It would be cool. Maybe she is too old for arcades. He wonders what she does for fun.

"It will bite your hand off if you pet it," she warns him. "I'll give you a cup of tea and you leave afterwards, alright?"

"Sure. How come you drink tea?"

She doesn't reply. Domingo is about to apologize for being crass, but he isn't up to date on *tlahuelpocmimi* diets. Except for the kid part.

A knock on the door makes them both turn their heads.

"Health and Sanitation."

"Open up. Don't tell them I'm here," she whispers, moving so quickly to his side it makes him gasp.

She goes towards the window and jumps out. Domingo rushes after her, pokes his head out, and sees Atl is climbing up the side of the building, her shoulders hunched and looking birdlike once more. She disappears onto the roof.

Domingo opens the door.

Three men waltz in, faces grim.

"We have a report there's a vampire here," one of them says.

Domingo, with the experience of a master liar and a complete indifference to authority, shrugs. "I don't know. The guy that's renting me the place didn't say nothing about vampires."

"Look around. You, I'm going to check you, give me your hand."

Domingo obeys. The guy presses a little white plastic stick against his wrist. It beeps.

"You're alone?" the guy asks him.

Domingo takes out a chocolate bar and starts eating it. The dog is sitting still, eyeing the men.

"Yep."

"What are you doing?"

"Sleeping."

Domingo can hear the other two men opening doors, muttering between themselves.

"It's all empty," one of the other men says. "There's not even clothes in the closet. Just a mattress in there."

"You live here?" asks the first guy, who hasn't moved from Domingo's side, carefully cataloguing him.

"Yeah. For now. I move around. Been working for a rag-and-bone man lately. I used to wash windshields and before that I juggled balls for the drivers as the stop lights, but this guy I worked with beat me up and I've got the rag-and-bone gig now."

"Just a damn street kid," says the man, and Domingo thinks he must have an earpiece on or something, because he sure as hell isn't speaking to Domingo.

The men leave as quickly as they've come. He locks the door, sits on the rug and waits. Atl doesn't fly in—not technically—but she seems to jump in with a certain grace and flexibility that is birdlike.

"Thanks," she says. The feathers disappear, leaving only pitch-black hair behind.

"How'd you do that?"

"What?"

"The bird thing."

"It's natural. We all do it after we hit puberty."

She goes into her room. Domingo stands at the entrance, watching her pull up floor boards with her bare hands, taking stuff from under there and tossing it into a backpack. She rips the mattress open and begins to throw some money and papers in the bag.

"It's been nice meeting you. I've got to find another place now."

"What sort of trouble are you in? What do those guys want?"

"Those guys aren't the trouble," she says. "That's just sanitation. But if they got word there is a vampire here, that means the others aren't far behind."

"Who are the others?"

Atl gives him a narrow look. "One month ago my aunt's head was delivered in a cooler to our home. I left Ciudad Juarez and headed here before I also ended in a cooler."

"Who killed her?"

"A rival clan. It's part of our territory fights. We were trying to kill a certain clan leader and botched it. She's got a big scar across the middle now, and she's mighty pissed at us. I hope you can appreciate the situation," she says, zipping her jacket up.

It sounds very exciting to Domingo. He's only seen the gang fights from afar. Mexico City has managed to insulate itself through the conflict, partly because it keeps the vampires who are waging the wars out of the city limits, and partly because it is so damn militarized. The drug dealers in Mexico City are narcomenudistas; petty peddlers, small-scale crooks focused around Tepito and Iztapalapa. If they kill each other, they have the sense to do it quietly, without attracting twenty special forces ops who are ready to put a gun up your ass and shoot before bothering to ask for identity cards.

Atl goes down the stairs. Domingo follows her.

When they reach the front door she turns to look at him and he thinks she is going to tell him to beat it. Her hands tighten around the dog's leash. She takes a step back.

Thirty seconds later Domingo is in a comic book.

Half a dozen men pour in. The dog growls. Somebody yells. "Stay the fuck still. Stay the fuck still," they say. Big bubble speeches.

A guy grabs Domingo by the collar and drags him out, pinning him against the ground and putting a plastic tie around his wrists.

Domingo doesn't know if these are cops, or sanitation, or narcos. All he knows is he can hear the dog barking and he is being dragged against the pavement, then kicked towards the trunk of a car. They're trying to stuff him in the trunk.

Domingo panics. He tries to hold onto something. The guy punches him and Domingo folds over himself.

It doesn't really feel like he thought it might feel. Action. Adventure. Comic book manic energy.

The guy pulls Domingo by his hair and Domingo gets a glimpse of teeth, half a smile, before Atl pulls him off Domingo with a swift, careless motion that breaks his bones.

Domingo, on his knees, looks up at Atl. She cuts the plastic tie and the dog comes bounding towards her.

She's got three sharp needles sticking out of her left leg. Blood puddles next to her shoes.

She vomits. A sticky, dark mess.

The dog whines.

"Come on," he says grabbing her arm, propping her up.

He tries not to look at the bodies they leave behind. He tries not to wonder if they're all dead.

If this is a comic book, then it's tinted with red.

She's awake. He knows it because the dog raises its head. Domingo looks at her. Sure enough, her eyes are open, though he can't make her expression.

"How you feeling?" he asks.

Atl looks down at her bandaged leg. He knows he didn't do a great job, but at least he took out those weird needles.

"My bag. Do you have it?"

She clutched it all the way there. There was no way he could have left it behind. Domingo nods.

"There's a blue plastic stick in it. Small. Hand it to me."

He does. She presses it against her tongue and shivers.

She unwraps the bandage around her leg. The skin looks odd. Blackened, as if it were stained.

"What's that?" he asks.

"Anaphylactic reaction from the silver nitrate. Lucky for me they didn't want me dead yet."

Domingo blinks.

"It makes me sick," she explains.

"You've been out for about an hour."

Atl brushes the hair back from her face. She looks around at the little room and the piles of old comic books, hybrid personal protective clothing, and all the other assorted junk he collects and sells together with the bone-and-rag-man.

"Where are we?"

"My place. It's safe. We're in a tunnel downtown. It's very old. I think the nuns used it. There was a convent nearby. Benito Juarez closed it fifty years ago."

Atl chuckles. "You're talking about the mid-19th century."

She gives him a funny look. Domingo frowns. He doesn't know lots of stuff and obviously she does. He doesn't like it when people make fun of him. It's unpleasant. Even Belen was rude at times, though there was no reason for that.

"It's cool," she says. "This works. It was smart thinking."

She opens her arms and the dog rushes towards her, pressing its great head against her cheek. She scratches its ear and smiles at Domingo.

"How come your dog's so big?" he asks.

"Cualli's a special breed. He's an attack dog."

"Were those the gangsters?"

"Those were freelancers. Health and Sanitation must have tipped them off that there was something odd going on. Or somebody else did."

"You were fast. Like really fast. Are all vampires like that? I've read a lot about the European ones and the Chinese, and how there's all the infighting with them up north and if you go to Mexicali it's like all run by the Chinese. But they say they're all stiff, no? *Jian shi* and they can't really be green, can they? I don't know much about your type. Funny, it's probably . . ."

"Please. Stop," she says, pressing her fingers against her temples. "I don't want to talk about vampires. Or gangs."

"What do you want to talk about?"

"Nothing."

Domingo wants to talk about everything. He sits in front of her, brimming with questions as she curls up and closes her eyes.

This is how a vampire sleeps. Not in coffins. Curled up, with a dog by her feet and a boy watching her.

He gets up early and goes above ground. It's raining, so he ties a plastic shopping bag to his head as he heads to purchase food. He buys bread, milk, three cans of beans, potato chips and pastries. He feels very happy as he pays for the stuff, like it's Christmas.

On the way back, he scans the screens at the subway in search of news. There's nothing about the confrontation of the previous day.

As he stands in the subway car, listening to the tired music on his player, he conjures a story in which he's making breakfast for his girlfriend, and she's real pretty and they live together. Not in the tunnels. In a proper place.

When he returns to the tunnel he's humming a tune.

She's sitting, back against the wall, browsing through a bunch of magazines. When she looks up at him, the tune dies on his lips.

"Where did you go?"

"I went to get us breakfast."

"I don't need breakfast. It was stupid of you. Someone might have seen you."

"Sorry," he mutters and then, tentatively, to diffuse her anger. "How do you like my collection?"

"It's great," she says quirking an eyebrow at him and jumping up to her feet, showing him the cover of a comic book. "Not a fanboy, huh?"

It's an old-style thing with a guy in a Dracula cape. She picks another one. This is a recent clipping from a magazine he stole a few weeks before. It talks about the narco-vampires in Monterrey.

He wets his lips, struggling for words. "Why are you angry?"

"I am not a goddamn hobby."

"Who's talking about a hobby?"

She shoves the magazine against his chest, pushing him back.

"Do you like vampires? Huh? You like reading about them? You like looking at the pictures of dead vampires?"

"Yeah, well . . . it's exciting."

"Do you know how long my kind can live? Three hundred years. You know what's the average lifespan of my kind? Thirty years. Do you want to know why?"

Domingo does not answer. She's grabbing him by his shirt, holding him up.

"Because we're all getting massacred. Before I arrived in to Mexico City, I was at the market in Ciudad Juarez. The decapitated body of a vampire bled onto the pavement, right next to a food stand. People kept eating. They bought soda. They were more bothered by the heat than the corpse."

She sets him down. His feet touch the floor.

"I'm going to be a puddle of blood."

He's scared to say a thing. She sits down, folding her legs and staring at the wall. Eventually, he sits next to her.

"What are you going to do?" he asks.

"Hell if I know," she whispers. "I need to eat. I need to sleep. I need to think."

He pulls up his sleeve, offering his arm to her. She smiles wryly.

"You're going to get hurt one of these days," she tells him, "if you keep helping strangers like me."

"It doesn't matter," he replies.

She presses her mouth against his skin.

Domingo is groggy when he opens his eyes. Atl's still asleep. He doesn't try to wake her. He flicks a battery-powered lantern on and looks at his magazines, feeling odd when he runs his hands across the vivid picture; the splashes of red.

The dog growls. Domingo lifts the lantern and listens. He doesn't hear anything. The dog growls louder. Atl shifts her body, fully awake.

"What is it?" he asks.

"People," she says.

He still can't hear anything. Atl grabs her bag and pulls out a switchblade.

"Cualli, stay," she tells the dog, then raises her eyes towards him. "Don't move. The dog will keep you safe."

"What are you doing?"

"I'm going to take a look," she says.

She runs out. Domingo crouches next to the dog, trying to listen for anything odd. The tunnels are quiet for a bit, then he hears loud sounds. Might be gunshots. The sounds seem to be getting closer. He's nervous, heart beating very fast. He twists the dog's leash between his hands.

Atl returns; she's running and her face is very tense.

"Lead me out of here," she says.

Domingo scrambles ahead of her, holding his lantern. He turns left and finds himself face to face with three people wearing a mask and goggles. They raise their guns. He blinks and is yanked back, thrown against the floor. The air is knocked out of his lungs.

There's the zing of bullets; the loud blast of a shotgun. Domingo covers his ears. One of them lunges past Atl, towards him. Atl plucks him back, her claws and teeth tear the protective mask apart and she bites into the man's face.

The man is trying to escape and Atl bites into his face like he is a ripe fruit.

The dog is also biting, tearing.

Domingo looks dumbly at all the blood.

"The place is crawling with them," she says, angrily. "They must have followed you back. You've got to lead us out."

"We've got to keep going straight," he mumbles, picking the lantern off the floor.

The light illuminates a shadow, the figure of another man with a mask coming just behind Atl.

"Look out!" he yells.

The man's head rolls onto the floor.

It literally rolls onto the floor.

Atl's fingers are stained crimson. Brains are splattered over her jacket.

It's his turn to vomit.

Dozens of mariachis in charro costumes litter Garibaldi Plaza. They're waiting for someone to hire them to play a song and do not pay attention to two dirty beggars with a stray dog. That's what Atl and Domingo look like, covered in grime and dirt after running through the tunnels.

"I'm heading to Guatemala, kid," Atl says, her bag balanced on her left shoulder.

"Do you have friends there?"

"No."

"Sure. I'll go," he says.

She stares at him.

"You're going to need to feed," he says. "You'll need someone to watch your back."

"I don't need help."

"I can shoot a gun," he blusters.

"You've almost died twice in less than a week."

"The life expectancy of a street kid isn't much higher than yours," he says, knowing he's got nowhere to go. There's nothing but forward.

She smirks. "Find another way to commit suicide."

She slips a couple of bills into his hand.

"Atl," he says.

"Keep the dog," she replies, handing him the leash. "It'll slow me down."

She takes a couple of steps. The dog whines.

"Stay with him," she orders.

"Atl," he repeats.

She walks away. She doesn't turn her head. He tries following her, but the square is crowded at this time of the night and he loses her quickly. She must have flown away. Can vampires fly?

He'll never know.

She's gone.

A trio sings "La Cucaracha" while the rain begins to fall. He sniffles, eyes watery.

He pulls his plastic bag from his pocket and ties it above his head. He's out of chocolate. He's out of luck. He pats the dog's head.

nothing but sky overhead
DAVID LIVINGSTONE CLINK

Everyone in the world had died, save those who were outside in their back gardens, and those who had nothing but sky overhead. These survivors spent weeks burying or burning the dead, cart after cart relieved of their burdens, passing by acres of upturned earth, smoke filling an already grey sky. People took to farms to save the livestock, to live off the land. They fished from the ends of half-constructed bridges, sandwiches made from fresh-baked bread and yesterday's kill sitting warmly in their stomachs.

the kiss of the blood-red pomegranate

KRISTIN JANZ

The door swung closed behind me with a click that kept ringing in my ears for seconds afterwards.

"Can I help you?" the man said. He was the only other person in the room. I stared at him. He looked suspicious.

I was still too shaken to answer. It isn't every night you get hauled off at gunpoint to Central Park and forced to walk down a flight of stairs conjured out of thin air.

"Hello?" Now the man was both suspicious and irritated. "This area is restricted. Can I

call someone to escort you to your hotel?"

I was in a windowless room, something like the offspring of a boutique hotel's lobby and the smoking lounge of an elderly British gentleman. About a mile underneath New York City, if I had judged the distance correctly.

My eyes met those of the un-welcoming committee. Of average height and build, in his early thirties, he had longish dark hair and that Mediterranean complexion that I had always found irresistible. He didn't fit the setting, in his faded jeans, black leather jacket and Dylan t-shirt.

"I don't remember the name of my hotel," I said evasively. Who was this guy? Did he work for Hammond?

"This isn't it. How did you find this room?"

"I don't know what you mean. I walked down the stairs. That door was at the bottom. I opened it—" —and here I was died on my lips. My hand dropped to my side, halfway through gesturing at the door behind me. The door that was no longer there.

The man was staring. "How did you get to the stairs?" He seemed a little less wary.

"I don't remember," I lied, then instantly regretted it as his suspicion returned in full force. I was no good at this investigative journalism thing. I guess that's why *The Times* was only paying me to be a copy editor.

The man walked over to a desk beside one of the room's two remaining doors, opened a thin drawer, withdrew a manila folder, and held it out to me.

"Look at the picture inside. Tell me if you recognize this man." I approached. "Who is he? A friend of yours?"

He glanced behind me to where the door had been. I wondered if he had seen it appear and disappear.

"Yes," he said at last.

I took the folder and let it fall open in my hands. Then I tried to hide my dismay, as my last hope that I could trust the Dylan fan melted away.

Of course I recognized the man in the picture. He was the one I had been investigating when James Hammond caught up with me.

"I don't know," I said. "I don't think I've ever seen him before. What's his name?" The man I was talking to didn't seem to know anything about me, but I wasn't going to gamble on the same being true of his friend.

He snatched the picture back and stowed it in its drawer. "David Hirsch." The look on his face said I hadn't fooled him, but that he didn't think he had anything to lose by answering my question. "He's a lawyer." Yes, he was. Of Hirsch, Goldman & Green, specializing in mergers and acquisitions. One of their clients seemed to specialize in making people disappear.

"What's the procedure for guests who forget the name of their hotel?" I asked.

He laughed, a quick, malicious bark. His thumb jerked toward the door behind him. "Step off the threshold and you'll have guides falling over themselves to take care of you. They'll know where you belong."

Off the threshold? Was there some kind of underground cavern beyond this room? I started to make my way toward the door. "Okay. Thanks for being so helpful." I hoped he noticed my sarcasm.

I was almost there when he said, "Wait!" and grabbed my shoulder. My heart started racing. He held me at arm's length, staring at me. "I should give you something," he said. "It might save your life."

He crossed the room to a tall, antique wooden cabinet and withdrew a covered wicker basket, which he handed to me. "I don't know who you are or what you're doing here. But you deserve to be warned. Don't eat anything out there." One of his fingers tapped the basket's wooden lid. "This is all from Upstairs. It's safe."

"Okay." Now I was even more confused. Why wasn't the food outside this room safe to eat? Were we in the middle of an underground nuclear testing facility?

"We'll give you more if you lose that one. There's no shortage."

"I thought you said the area was restricted. How am I supposed to get back?"

He scowled. "Any guide can bring you. Ask for David and Adam."

I ducked out the door, relieved to be getting away so easily. I wasn't prepared for what I found there.

I was standing outside on a narrow dirt road, on one side an open field, on the other a hedge of leafless trees, gaunt black arms stretching toward a featureless grey sky. The room I had emerged from was gone.

My hands tightened around the handle of the basket. Buildings didn't disappear. There was no sky thousands of feet below Central Park.

And mysterious billionaire financiers didn't make staircases appear out of nowhere, either.

It was night. I could see, although no streetlights were visible, nor moon, nor stars. The faint light seemed to come from everywhere and from nowhere, and it made my surroundings even gloomier than if my only source of illumination had been a flashlight with half-dead batteries.

The silence was broken by the sound of rattling and creaking behind me. When I turned, I saw a carriage approaching.

The rickety carriage was drawn by four identical horses with pale coats of an unusual colour between grey and dark ivory. Maybe it was the light, but I could have sworn I saw a greenish tinge to their ears and muzzles. The coachman, a small androgynous figure with a hat that hid his or her face, turned to me as the carriage pulled up, and cackled.

A hand touched my elbow. I jumped.

"Have you lost your way, dearie?" The speaker, standing at my side, looked normal compared to the coachman. He was a diminutive old man in a faded blue shirt and jeans, wispy white hair clinging to his age-spotted scalp. A few of his teeth were missing, and his eyes were red and watery, but at least I could see his face. Although I didn't know where he had come from.

"Yes, thank you," I said, my heart pounding. "I know this sounds silly, but I got lost, and now I can't remember—"

"Tsk, tsk," the old man chided, pulling me toward the carriage. "It always happens. Get in, get in," he insisted, when I tried to pull away. "It's always nicer inside than out." He gave a conspiratorial wink.

He joined me in the carriage, and it *was* much nicer. I hadn't noticed any windows when the carriage pulled up, but as we rolled along my companion and I were able to gaze out at the countryside through small, diamond-shaped panes of glass.

I didn't have to offer a word of explanation, as the lively old man chattered enough for both of us. Tomorrow's programs would be especially nice, he confided. Or perhaps I wanted to spend the morning shopping, or strolling in one of the gardens, or at the beach? I smiled and nodded and made occasional interested noises, trying to pretend I knew what he was talking about.

We were dropped off in front of what appeared to be a luxury hotel. As I stared, a black limousine pulled away from the curb and headed into the night; another had stopped behind us and was disgorging four passengers in evening attire.

"Our staff will show you to your room," the old man assured me. "Just tell them your name, and everything will be arranged. Oh, and wouldn't you like me to dispose of *that* for you?"

He was pointing to my basket. I almost handed it over, but changed my mind at the last minute.

"I'd like to keep it for now. If that's all right."

I thought at the time that it was only my imagination, but it was as if something flickered in the old man's eyes, tiny darting black shadows. But not a hint of it reached his voice.

"Oh, certainly! Whatever our guests want, they must have." He chuckled. "Run along, dearie. A comfortable bed awaits."

The lobby was a splendour of marble floors, mirrored walls, crystal chandeliers and lampshades of coloured blown glass, gorgeous guests crossing to and fro like butterflies. As my guide had promised, I had no trouble checking in. The receptionist simply handed over a sheaf of papers and told me to sign on the last page. I didn't read it; it was in legalese, and the receptionist assured me that it was "exactly like the one you signed Upstairs." Of course, I didn't tell him that I hadn't signed anything.

Then it was up to my room. A king-sized bed, hardwood floors scattered with soft carpets, French windows opening onto a balcony, an enormous marble-tiled bathroom—I had never stayed anywhere this nice. The foil-wrapped cork of a Champagne bottle rose proudly above the rim of a silver ice bucket, a basket of tropical fruit decorated the second dresser, and an open box of chocolates I could smell all the way across the room beckoned from atop the nightstand.

And yet, Adam had warned me not to eat anything "out there." If he was with David Hirsch—Hammond's lawyer—I didn't think I could trust him. I was sure Hirsch was also involved somehow in the disappearances. But could I trust anyone else down here?

I flipped open the lid of the basket Adam had given me. Inside were nestled half a small loaf of whole grain bread, a wedge of cheese wrapped in waxed paper, a cup of raisins, and a plastic bottle of water. I ate about half the bread and a third of the cheese, chasing them with a handful of raisins and some water.

The shock of having been hustled at gunpoint into a mysterious magical world was starting to wear off. I decided I couldn't really be in an underground cavern. This place had a sky, and trees. The stairs must have been a gateway to some other place. I had never imagined that the novels about that sort of thing might be based on anything that could actually happen. But I had been wrong about a lot of other things, too.

Chief among those being my thought that picking up the threads of this investigation would be a good idea.

After I had eaten, the chocolates didn't smell as appealing. In fact, the aroma made me slightly ill, and I had to close the box and leave it in the bathroom with the door shut.

I woke to daylight pouring through the windows.

I sat up. I must have been exhausted, to have been able to sleep.

Was this where all the disappeared people had gone? And if so, why? Hammond had refused to answer any of my questions, so I didn't know any more than I had before his thugs grabbed me off the street. I did know that he ran a large private equity firm, and was phenomenally well-connected, but so elusive that it was unusual to talk to anyone who had met him. He seemed to work mostly through people like Hirsch.

I almost ate a papaya out of the hospitality basket, but then put it down at the last minute and returned to the food Adam had given me. To my surprise, when I opened the picnic basket, all the food I had eaten seemed to have regenerated itself! I had dried figs instead of raisins, but everything else was identical.

After eating, I wandered outside and found several sandwich boards in the garden courtyard behind the hotel, advertising activities for guests to choose from. I decided to join the "Gardens and Grounds" tour: "a perfect introduction for our newer guests: experience the timeless mystery of the Borderlands through guided visits with our permanent residents & taste the wealth of our orchards and vineyards." It seemed the best way to figure out where I was and what was going on.

What was going on was that the place did not follow the laws of nature. As our group of twelve trudged along after the guide, the terrain kept changing in impossible ways. First we saw a stretch of palm-shaded beach, small groups of tourists wading or sunbathing. I say "sunbathing" even though there was no sun, despite the clear blue sky, and the heat. Five minutes' walk from there took us to a gorgeously green garden in late spring, lilac-shaded paths competing with linden-shadowed statuary courtyards paved in worn flagstones. A river meandered around one edge; we saw no bridges, but farther downstream passengers were being directed onto a flat-bottomed boat propelled by polemen. Next on the route came hills of saguaro and prickly pear, then a gondola ride up the slopes of a mountain lush with snow. No barriers separated these incompatible climatic zones. There would be snow banks on either side of the path; then all of a sudden the snow would end and our trail would be hemmed in by jungle palms and wild pineapples.

I tried to make conversation with my companions as we trudged through a vineyard, but no one seemed to want to tell me how he had discovered the Borderlands Resort. "You know how it is," one man told me. "You know people, they've heard of someone who can get you into places no one else has been. I'm sure my story isn't much different from yours." I murmured agreement. Were we all kidnapped copy editors trying our hands at investigative journalism?

As we strolled through an orchard of ripe fruit, familiar peaches and cherries alongside figs and pomegranates, our guide called a halt. The aroma of freshly brewed coffee beckoned, with two attractive women ready to serve us.

I walked around a bit. I didn't want coffee, but I was hungry again, and had left my basket at the hotel. I had never seen pomegranates except in the produce department, and I couldn't tear myself away from these, scarlet globes weighing down drooping branches. The colour was so much more intense than that of the grocery store pomegranates. Would it be so terrible if I were to eat one? Suddenly, I couldn't imagine that Adam's warning had been intended to include food still growing in its natural habitat.

I tugged on one, and it came away readily in my hand. I had to use my teeth to break into the peel, and the white pith beneath puckered my mouth. But soon enough I had a section of the jewel-like, juice-encased seeds exposed. They burst under my tongue and lips, filling my mouth with their bright sweetness.

Every bite was better than the last. The membrane around the pulp of each seed was so thin it seemed to dissolve in my mouth, and the juice was sweet but not the least bit cloying; deep with layers of spice and fruit like I imagined a really good wine must be, the sort of wine I could never have afforded. I lost myself in the taste and the aroma. I think the orchard could have caught fire around me, and I wouldn't have noticed.

Suddenly, I was licking dark juice from my fingertips, a small pile of discarded peel and spent seeds at my feet.

I glanced up, and to my surprise the guide and most of my fellow tourists were staring at me. A few of the guests nodded sadly. And, although I wanted to believe it was only my imagination, I was pretty sure that the ugly little guide was leering.

I returned to my room to find housekeeping about to take away my basket. "What are you doing with that?" I demanded.

The tiny maid smiled, to my horror revealing two rows of sharp, cat-like teeth. "I hear you won't be needing that, since this morning."

"What are you talking about?" I snatched the basket off her cart. "Give it back!"

She laughed. "They'll take it from you in the end, when your time comes. You should know that. It's all in your contract."

"What contract?" I snapped. "I didn't sign anything." Except upon checking into the hotel. A vague sense of unease crept over me.

The maid chuckled as she wheeled her cart away. "Don't they all say that, when the barge comes for them."

I remembered the people being herded onto the boat. As I recalled it, something seemed sinister about that scene. The passengers had not looked like happy tourists. Every head had been bowed as they shuffled onto the vessel. Had one or two of my companions seen, and looked away quickly?

It was the same room. Adam was sitting on one of the two couches, staring at me. On the other, in person this time, was David Hirsch.

Adam was still wearing the Dylan t-shirt. But I hadn't changed my clothes either, so I guess we were even.

David stood, Adam following. "You're back," Adam said, no less suspicious. "Obviously," I said.

David took several steps toward me, then stopped. In his late forties, he wore a white shirt that must have gone about a month since its last pressing, and black dress pants.

"What's that on your fingers?" he asked. I looked. "Pomegranate juice."

Adam swore. When David turned an accusatory look on him, he exclaimed, "I *told* her not to eat or drink anything!"

"You didn't mention drinking," I retorted.

"So, what then?" Adam demanded. "You swished your fingertips around in a glass of pomegranate juice while you were knocking it back?"

Yes, Adam was as charming as I remembered. "It was a fresh pomegranate. Right off the tree. I'm only pointing out that you didn't say I shouldn't drink anything. I didn't, but you didn't tell me not to."

"No, you just ate a pomegranate instead."

"Adam." David's voice was mild, but you could tell that he expected to be heeded.

"What?" Adam snapped. "A pomegranate. Not only does she

not listen to me, she eats a pomegranate. Has she read a single Greek myth?"

"Hello!" I said. "I'm right here. You can talk to me. And yes, I have read Greek myths. Several." I tried to remember any Greek myths featuring pomegranates.

David Hirsch was nodding. "Persephone."

"My name is Alison," I corrected. Then, a second later, "Oh."

David and Adam exchanged glances. "I think she's beginning to understand," David said.

"No," I said. "I'm not. I know which story you're talking about. Persephone eats some pomegranate seeds and gets stuck in the Underworld. What does that have to do with anything?"

"Actually," David said, "the consequence was that she had to remain in the Land of the Dead six months out of every year, one for each seed she ate. But I don't think the terms will be so generous, in this case."

"Persephone wasn't stupid enough to chow down on an entire pomegranate," Adam added, glowering.

I didn't believe what I was hearing. "The Underworld?"

"I *did* tell you not to eat anything," Adam said.

David cast a quick glance at Adam before returning his attention to me. "Alison. Perhaps you would like to sit down."

They were prisoners, and had lived in that one room for four months.

"One of my clients is responsible," David said. "I'm here because he felt that I had been investigating his activities beyond a level that could add value to our professional relationship."

"James Hammond?" I asked.

"You know Hammond?" he asked, warily.

"I know that at least six people have disappeared," I said, "and that Hammond's business card kept showing up. And I know that whenever police found out that a disappearance might have some connection to him, the investigation would stop." I hesitated. "A couple of journalist friends told me this. Three days later, one of them disappeared. Three days after that, the other one was dead. He got hit by a cab."

David nodded sympathetically. "You're also a journalist?"

I shrugged. "Sort of." I had been a staff reporter for a daily in New Jersey before my brilliant idea that I should take a steep pay cut to work as a copy editor at the Times. "Freelance."

I told them the rest of my story, about quietly taking over Tina and Brian's investigation of James Hammond, which led me to the law firm of Hirsch, Goldman & Green, which led to a gun in my back on the corner of 57th and Third.

David told me that James Hammond had discovered a way to create bridges between our world and others, like this one.

"At the hotel, they call it the Borderlands," I said.

"Yeah," Adam said. "This isn't actually the Land of the Dead. It's more like the Lobby of the Dead."

"From time to time, people are sent across to the real thing," David said. "Across the river."

"Like the River Styx? How do they decide when to send them?" David looked at Adam.

"I don't know if it's the same for everyone," Adam admitted, when it became obvious that David was going to keep staring at him until he answered. He scratched at the back of his head. "It should be in your contract."

"What contract? Everyone keeps talking about this contract I've never seen!"

"Really?" David perked up. "Adam, if she didn't sign, they may have no hold on her."

Adam made a dubious face. "You never signed anything. What about Persephone? Doesn't that set a precedent that it's eating in the Underworld that matters, not the contract?"

David shrugged. "How many millennia ago was that? Who knows what really happened?" He shifted his sharp gaze back to me. "You're sure you didn't sign anything?"

"Yes, I'm sure. The only thing I signed was the papers they gave me when I checked into the hotel. I didn't read them—"

"Argh!" Adam roared, throwing his head back. "You idiot! It didn't occur to you to wonder why you had to sign a twenty-page legal document to check into a hotel?"

"No, it didn't! But you know what? If you had taken five minutes to explain where I was and *why* I shouldn't eat anything, I might have looked at those papers more closely." I shot David a look of equal venom. "Instead, he shows me a picture of you. James Hammond's lawyer."

David understood. "You didn't trust Adam. And he didn't trust you."

"Not everyone—" Adam said.

David held up a hand. "Let's back up a bit." He turned to me. "When I arrived here, I didn't know about the disappearances. I had been investigating other irregularities in Hammond's business practices, and was about to turn him in. I'm not dead because Hammond found it more amusing to send me to his personal Underworld kingdom." At my confused expression, he said, "Hammond has made some arrangement that puts him in charge of the Borderlands. Just like you, I was taken at gunpoint to Central Park in the middle of the night and forced to walk down a long set of stone stairs that Hammond somehow conjured up while I watched. When I walked through the door at the bottom, I found myself in this room. Fortunately, Adam was here to warn me against eating or drinking."

"Nice of him to warn *me*," I said.

"I did warn you," he retorted. "It's not my fault you didn't listen."

David cut in before I could tell Adam what a jerk he was. "Food and drink are not the only dangers here, Alison. Since my arrival, Management has sent others into this room through that door, trying to weaken our resolve. Other attractive young women. They pretend to be confused about where they are and how they got here, probably to appeal to our chivalrous instincts."

I couldn't imagine Adam existing in the same room as a chivalrous instinct. But the implication that David thought I was attractive sweetened my mood somewhat.

"That's why you showed me David's picture?" I asked Adam. "To figure out from my reaction whether you could trust me?"

He nodded. He wouldn't meet my eyes. "Maybe it wasn't such a great idea," he confessed.

I figured that was the closest to an apology I was going to get. "What's the deal with the contract? How does it work?"

When Adam didn't answer, David said, "She deserves to know. Maybe not why, but at least what and how."

Adam sighed, and leaned back into the corner of the couch. "Okay. Mine offers two months' vacation in the Borderlands. Anything I want during those two months." His eyes closed briefly. "*Almost* anything. In exchange for . . . well, for everything else. You know."

"No, I don't." I tried to work it out. "You mean, all your money and other assets?"

"God!" Adam exclaimed. "Are you that stupid? Think about it for a minute. Think about where we are."

I did. I still didn't get it. Then: "Wait a minute. You sold your soul for a *vacation*? Like, to the devil?"

Adam glared at me. "There's no devil mentioned in the contract. It talks about 'powers who sustain the Underworld and rule the dead.' Which you'd know if you had read yours before signing it."

"Yeah," I retorted, "well at least if I *had* read mine I *wouldn't* have signed it."

"This isn't getting us anywhere," David pointed out, his voice mild.

But I wasn't finished. "Who sells their eternal soul for a vacation?"

Adam swore at me. "You have no idea. You think that Club Med crap is all they offer? You can have anything you want. *Anything.* There's stuff going on that makes Asian sex tourism look like Disneyworld."

David must have seen that I was still having trouble believing anyone would sell their soul for a vacation, no matter how much kinky sex was involved. "Remember," he said. "People have tried to sell their souls on online auction sites."

"People who don't believe they have souls," I said.

"Or who don't believe they can be transferred to someone else's possession. Imagine you've been everywhere, seen everything. You've climbed Everest, you've taken a cruise to Antarctica, you've trekked to the source of the Amazon." I nodded slowly. The six people who'd disappeared had all been very well-travelled. "So one day, you find out that there's a way to cross over into another world. Maybe it's a parallel universe. Maybe it's even the Land of the Dead. It's so exclusive, only a handful of living people have ever been there. What's more, if you want to join that elite club, it won't even cost you anything. All you have to do is sign over your non- existent soul."

"Okay," I said, "but if the place does exist, and it isn't some huge scam to harvest your kidneys, doesn't that suggest that maybe your soul is real too? And that the cost is too high?"

"Twenty-five percent of the people who try to reach the summit of Mt. Everest die," David said.

Adam spoke up. "The contract says that you get two months' vacation here, starting from the day you first eat Underworld food. It doesn't say how they intend to get their hands on your soul, after. I figured that you got to return to your regular life after the two months, and they took your soul years later when you died. Not that they shoved you onto a barge and sent you across the River Styx."

"But you've already been here four months," I said.

"Yeah, well, once I got here and saw what this place was really all about, I told them no deal. I pointed to the clause that says guests are free to leave at any time. They said I *was* free to go, but that they were under no obligation to show me the way out, and if I wanted to leave I had to find it on my own." He shrugged. "I told them they'd better give me food from Upstairs while I was looking, and when they said no, I said fine, I guess I'll starve to death."

"The contract allows that dying before tasting the food of the Underworld voids the agreement," David said.

"Right," Adam said. "Then David shows up a couple days later, and he's not even here of his own free will, and tells me about a lot of other shady stuff Hammond's involved in." He shrugged again. "It's not clear to me that they would hold him to the contract if he ate, because he never signed anything. But we figured he'd better not take the risk. They backed down after a few days and brought us food we could trust."

"How do you know the food is safe?" I asked.

"They told us it was safe," David said. "And we're still here, four months later." He tilted his head to the side, considering. "It *was* a gamble. But the specificity of the contract's wording suggested that the magic involved in maintaining this place has to follow rules. There might be loopholes, and they might be able to trick someone into a bargain he didn't realize he was making. But I don't think the contract could apply if they cheated outright."

I shook my head. "So all those people who disappeared came here on purpose. They're all guests at the resort."

"Or else they *used* to be guests at the resort," Adam said, ominously.

I wondered about my vanished colleague from *The Times*, Tina McCarthy. Was she here, biding her time until they sent her across the river?

"What does James Hammond get out of this?" I asked David. "One of the wealthiest men in the United States is acting as a travel agent for the Underworld? Why?"

Neither one had any idea.

They had tried to escape. Of course, they had tried all the obvious ideas I came up with. Asking a guide to take them to the exit, or Upstairs, or the path that led Upstairs, plus as many variations as they could think of. Trying to find the disappearing door David and I had entered through. Adam had knocked a hole in the wall, but outside was only the same bleak countryside you found when you walked out the front door. The wall had regenerated itself just like the food in the picnic basket, and you could no longer tell where the hole had been. They had tried walking along the road outside, in either direction. It seemed to be circular, and returned to the same place after a mile or two. The forest was no better; even with a homemade compass Adam had rigged, they ended up walking in circles until back where they had started.

It had been a month since they had tried anything at all.

I didn't want to keep staying at the hotel, so David and Adam invited me to move in with them. Adam had been too "creeped out" to stay at the hotel more than one night, so he had wandered off by himself with a few blankets on day two, curled up near the edge of the road to sleep, and woken up on the floor of this small cottage. It had a bathroom with a toilet and sink, but no shower.

They didn't know why the house was so shabby, compared to the rest of the resort. Adam thought it was to try and convince them to spend more time at the main complex with the other guests, in hopes that it would weaken their resolve. David's theory was that the whole resort was really just as bad, but that a spell had been cast to make people think they were someplace nice, and that the effects were not as strong farther from the centre.

Fortunately, I didn't have to look for a guide every time I went outside and then wanted to come back. The house still disappeared once you stepped out the front door, but a footpath down the road led to the resort, and once you were on that path you could turn around at any time—no matter which direction you had been walking—and find the cottage waiting for you around the next corner.

Food appeared each morning in the cabinet, in a dozen of the identical wicker picnic baskets. Meals were usually vegetarian, but both David and Adam shared fond reminiscences of the fortnight of smoked fish.

David went out the next morning. When he returned, he

seemed pleased. "Good news. They're giving Alison a chance to escape."

A flame of hope flared up in my heavy heart. "That's great!"

Adam was more cynical. "What sort of chance?"

"The same one we have, only with a time limit."

"What's that supposed to mean?" Adam demanded.

David addressed his answer to me. "I've been told that if you can find the way out, you'll be allowed to leave."

Adam slammed down the notebook he had been scribbling in, and cursed.

David continued as if he hadn't noticed. "The same allowance will be made if Adam or I discover the exit and share that knowledge with you."

"That's no bargain," Adam insisted. "They're just telling you what we already know. She can leave if she finds the way out. If she doesn't, she can't. Same as us."

"Originally they told me she couldn't leave at all, regardless. Because of the pomegranate."

"Crap!" Adam snapped. "She hadn't read the contract. They can't hold her to a contract she never read."

"They intend to. If she doesn't find the exit before two months from yesterday." "They can't do that."

David regarded him calmly. I wondered if David ever lost his temper. Finally, he said, "Perhaps you would like to argue with them?"

Adam muttered something rude under his breath, and looked away.

Adam left after lunch. When I asked David where he had gone, he sighed, and said, "Swimming, I expect."

He told me why Adam had come. Two years ago, his wife had died in a plane crash. "This was supposed to be the Land of the Dead. He thought he might find her here."

"But he didn't."

David shook his head. "The true Land of the Dead is across the river. The barge is the only way to get there."

Adam returned close to evening and collapsed into a chair. His clothing and hair were damp, his face sickly.

"How was it?" David asked. I heard a surprising gentleness in his voice. Adam drew one hand over his eyes as if trying to clear them.

"I was so close this time. Twenty or thirty feet, no more. I could see the faces on the other shore, and when I looked back over my shoulder this side was so far away that I couldn't imagine how I had crossed all that water. But I was so tired. I kept sucking down water instead of air. . . ." Silence, then: "I remember going under; next thing I knew I was back on this side, face-down in the sand."

"Did you see her?" David asked. "On the other side?"

Adam screwed his eyes shut. "Not this time. But . . . I keep forgetting. I've forgotten so much."

"You'll recognize her," David said.

Adam didn't answer immediately. At last, he said, "I know we went to Belize for our honeymoon, but I don't remember any of it. The way the sea smelled, the taste of the coffee we drank, the way she would have smiled at me, the feel of her hand on mine . . . it's all gone. I don't know if I'll ever get it back."

"Maybe when we find the way Upstairs," David offered.

Adam was silent. Before much longer, he had fallen asleep in the chair, his mouth open. It made him look younger than he was, and vulnerable.

Later, David told me that, although it did not seem to condemn you to the terms of the contract, drinking of the river brought forgetfulness.

For the first two weeks, I returned to the resort complex each day to shower. But I started feeling more and more uncomfortable. The initial obsequiousness of the staff had been supplanted by open contempt. They still gave me all the soap and clean towels I asked for, but with mocking grins and long delays.

One day I caught a glimpse of my colleague from *The Times*, Tina McCarthy. She was sitting at a table in an open-air bistro with a man I didn't recognize. When she saw me watching her from across the plaza, she ducked her head to avoid eye contact, then got up in a hurry and disappeared around the corner of the nearest building. By the time I got there, she was gone.

I stopped going back to the resort after that. I didn't need to shower that badly.

"If crossing the river takes you to the true Land of the Dead, what about going all the way upstream or downstream?"

David looked up from scrubbing his shirt in the bathroom sink. I had been with them over a month, and was starting to get desperate. "Maybe. We've never tried that."

"It won't work," Adam predicted. "It will be like the road. We'll end up going around in circles."

"Not necessarily," I argued. "We know there's something different about the river."

"What do you suggest?" Adam demanded. "We all hop in and start swimming downstream? Or upstream? It's probably farther to get anywhere along the length of the river than it is to cross. We won't last that long."

I smiled. "Who said anything about swimming?"

None of us had ever made a raft. We had, however, all seen movies in which rafts were constructed. Of course, we had all seen different movies, featuring incompatible raft-making techniques.

"We need to take all the leaves and small branches off," Adam insisted, as we ripped larger branches off the trees. "Extra weight."

"No," I argued, "the leaves add buoyancy. If we strip them off, the raft won't float."

We disagreed on the relative merits of branches all pointing in the same direction versus branches woven in a criss-cross pattern. Also, should we try to make a rudder, or would long poles suffice? David said we were wasting our time with branches and saplings small enough to wrench out of the ground, and needed full-sized logs. A little difficult, considering that we didn't have an axe.

It was getting dark by the time we finished. Our raft was about ten feet by ten feet, and we had compromised by stripping off all the leaves and branches but weaving some thinner saplings through the warp of the thicker. We opted for the pole steering method, after fidgeting through an hour of watching David try to carve a rudder with a chef's knife I'd stolen from one of the hotel kitchens.

A grey fog rolled over the surface of the river. It began to rain. I wondered if the weather was an attempt to dishearten us.

David dragged the raft into the river. "It's listing to the right," I pointed out.

"Starboard," Adam corrected. "And only because David's holding it up."

"It's actually listing to port, or left," David pointed out. "The directionality depends on the direction the boat is facing."

"That's not a boat," I said. "And it's half-submerged even

without any weight." "Yes," David agreed. "I believe we discussed something earlier, about the need for bigger logs?"

Adam muttered something about consigning David to some realm on the other side of the river, and sloshed into the water. The raft tilted precariously under his weight, until David stabilized it.

"Now it's listing even more to port," I said.

"Then you had better get on the starboard side, hadn't you?" Adam retorted.

I hiked my skirt up and splashed in. I almost fell as I rounded the corner of the raft, but Adam caught my arm.

I sat down. The raft sank even farther. "I don't know about this," I said.

"Shut up and grab a pole." Adam took one, and pushed himself to his feet.

"I would recommend that you both remain in a seated position," David cautioned, sitting on the edge nearest him.

"We can't steer sitting down," Adam said. He stuck the pole into the riverbed, on the side of the raft nearest the river's edge (the port side), and pushed. Our craft lurched forward. Adam lurched in the opposite direction and almost fell. His corner tilted dangerously into the water as he struggled to free his pole.

I decided that the best thing I could do was sit very, very still on my section of raft. To stabilize it. David shook his head.

Adam's second foray with the pole went a little better. Then a current caught us, and we sped forward.

Adam dropped to his knees. He held his pole in a ready position, but we seemed to be an appropriate distance from the riverbank, and we certainly didn't need additional speed.

We rolled along, drifting toward the centre of the river. I ground my teeth together and wedged my fingers into the gaps between branches. We were still experiencing a pronounced list to the rearward port corner of our craft, which was entirely underwater. David had the driest seat, and I considered invoking chivalry, but reconsidered when I recalled that he outweighed either of us, and was probably stabilizing the raft by sitting where he was.

I glanced over my shoulder at Adam. He grinned, and turned with me to look at the stretch of riverbank we had passed. "We're definitely moving. Look."

The forest had dropped away, and we were passing a wide

stretch of white sand. The hotel rose up behind the beach, its lights casting a baleful image onto the water next to us.

"Was that lightning?" Adam asked.

"Lightning?!" I looked around wildly. I hadn't seen any, but a moment later a low rumble echoed its way to us from downstream.

"Right where we're headed," David pointed out unnecessarily.

What are we going to do?" I demanded.

David shrugged. "They're trying to frighten us back to shore."

A second flash illuminated the river ahead. That one I did see. I thought the crack of thunder followed more quickly that time.

"Isn't water an excellent conductor of electricity?" I wondered.

"Normally," David agreed.

"But we all know that the river is different," Adam quipped.

The gesture I wanted to make would have required loosening my death grip on the raft, so I made an unpleasant face at him and turned away. The second half of his snicker was drowned by a third thunderclap.

"Hold tight," David warned, glancing over his shoulder.

We were passing the jungle now, on our left. I could see the tops of the palm trees in black silhouette against the greyish gloom of the sky. Then we were speeding past low rolling hills crowned with olive trees. I think the English country garden came next, but it was difficult to tell, because as we were passing the Mediterranean zone the light misting rain suddenly started falling in sheets, curtains of icy, dagger-like water stabbing at our heads, faces and hands. I gasped. I could see nothing now beyond the edges of our raft.

The next lightning bolt knifed down so close to our raft that I felt a sudden, searing heat as it hit the water. Geysers of steam shot up. It was so loud that I screamed and couldn't hear myself.

But we were untouched, except for ringing ears; a second or two later we were rolling through the cloud of steam, and then we were past.

"I told you it's not like other rivers," Adam said.

"Shut up," I retorted. "That's my line."

He laughed, not a snicker this time, but a real, honest-to-goodness laugh, the kind that you share with old friends when you've been up too late drinking and all the masks have come off.

David glanced back at us with an indulgent smile. Then his eyes opened wide.

I was turning my head to look when the swell of water bearing down from behind lifted us up about ten feet. Adam started swearing. "Hold on!" he shouted as we rushed forward.

David reached back and hit my arm, hard. "Let go!" he yelled, just as I was lacing my fingers more tightly into the weave of the raft. I stared at him, then understood, and let go, flinging myself face-down, one hand clutching the edge, the other wrapped around one sapling.

We were surfing, riding the giant wave. Then we weren't. The raft flew off the crest, and dropped. A half-second later the water crashed down on us, and up was sideways and I was half holding the raft, half in the air, and then I came down on it again, and someone's foot hit my nose, and one arm contacted someone's leg—and I thanked God, if he could still hear me from here, that my hands weren't both still wedged in the raft and all my fingers broken—and then there was only water.

An edge of the raft smacked into my side. I opened my mouth to scream. I gulped in water. Thrashing, I tried to drag myself to the surface. The water was black. My eyes were open, but I couldn't see a thing. I wanted to cough, but my lungs were full of water. I wasn't strong enough to force it out.

The next thing I knew, I was opening my eyes. I was lying face-down on a beach. It was morning.

I sat up. There were two men a short distance away, one standing and the other squatting on his heels, both examining a pile of branches at the water's edge. I thought I should know them.

Both glanced up as I stumbled to join them. The older of the two wore a look of fatherly concern. For a second I wondered if he *were* my father, but only for a second. My father was sandy-haired and much heavier, with a moustache, and . . . I felt a rising sense of panic, when I realized I had no idea what my father's name was.

"Alison," the man said. "Are you all right?"

I didn't remember his name, either. "I-I think so." I paused. "Are you? Both of you?"

The younger man let out a sharp bark of a laugh. "She doesn't remember us." Then, addressing me, "Don't worry. There are worse things to forget."

And suddenly it all flooded back—the weeks in the tiny house, the raft, being pitched overboard . . . I still couldn't remember my father's name. Or my mother's.

"It's coming back to me," I said.

The older man, David, nodded sagely. "I thought it would." He returned his attention to the pile of sticks, all that remained of our raft. Reaching, he untied the end of a rope from the fork of one sapling, tugging at the wood with his free hand. "I think that's the last of it." The rest of the rope was coiled over his left arm.

"What's that for?" Adam asked. "Clothesline for the house?"

I couldn't muster up much excitement about a clothesline. The raft was supposed to work. It was supposed to carry us downstream, right out of the Borderlands, right back to the stone staircase that led up into the real world. I had only four weeks left before my contract came up. What was I going to do?

"Of course not," David replied. "It's for our next raft. The one we're going to build properly. With an axe."

I stared at him. Adam swore.

"We don't have an axe," I pointed out.

David started walking away. "There are two in the shed next to the mountain chalet, one in the vineyard, and at least one in the groundkeeper's shed behind the hotel."

Adam glared at me in lieu of David, who was moving farther and farther away. Finally, he yelled out, "The raft didn't work the first time, and it won't work now!"

David stopped, and turned around. To my surprise, he walked straight back toward us. "Unlike you," he said, "Alison and I do not have infinite time to waste here. Alison is going to die in less than a month if we don't find a way out. I have a fifteen-year-old son whom I've left alone with no explanation, and who may be at risk from my former client." Adam's eyes narrowed and he opened his mouth to argue, but David didn't let him. "She's dead, Adam. She's been dead for two years. If you think she's on the other side of the river, you know how to get there. If you're ready to go home and pick up what's left of your life, then stay with us. But don't try to discourage our efforts because you're not ready to stop living in limbo."

Adam stared at him for a moment. Then, without a word, he turned his back on us and started walking toward the water's edge. I started to take a step after him, but David caught my shoulder, holding me back.

Adam stopped at the line between shore and water, small waves splashing over his feet. His shoulders heaved up and down as he breathed. Then he threw back his head and screamed, a long wordless howl that went on so long my own throat felt raw. When he lost his breath he took another and screamed again. And again.

David took my elbow. "We should leave him."

When Adam returned to the cottage, he was carrying an axe. "I'm glad you're still with us," David said.

Adam told him what he could do with the axe, and went back out into the night. This time I did hurry after him.

"Adam!" I called. "Wait!"

I ran to catch up. We walked along the dirt road in silence.

"I killed her," Adam confessed to the night. "I killed my wife." I stopped breathing.

"I was trying to save money. I talked her into taking a less convenient flight so we could save $200. I killed Christine for $200."

After a moment, carefully choosing my words, I started to say, "Adam, that's—"

"Save it. I've heard it enough times from David."

I thought about David, and wondered what it was like to always be in control of your emotions.

"Sometimes I know that she's waiting across the river for me," Adam said. "And then I don't care if it's Hell or Tartarus or whatever, because we'll be together, and I can tell her how sorry I am for being such a cheap bastard, and that's all I want. Other times I think it's all a trap, so they can tempt me into giving in and eating the food.

"The thing is, I know she'd forgive me for picking the wrong flight. But I don't think she'd forgive me for what I did to get here, or what I'd have to do to get across the river. And I knew that even before I came."

It was dark when I woke. I sat straight up. I knew the answer. "We don't have to build another raft," I said into the silent room. I woke Adam and David up and explained what I had realized. Adam was dubious. "It can't be that easy."

"I don't know." A chink of hope seemed to be trying to force its way through David's usual calm demeanor. "The answer usually *is* that easy. Once you see it."

Every time Adam and David tried to find the stairs, they had tried to gauge their progress by looking back over their shoulders to see how far they had gone. I knew we had all looked back while on the river. Even on the footpath between our cottage and the resort, looking back returned us to the road outside the cottage. Looking back was the key. It acted like a cosmic Restart button, erasing any progress we might have made toward the elusive stone staircase. At least, that was my theory.

Adam went first, David brought up the rear. I don't know how long we walked, through unchanging scenery. But all of a sudden, it stood in front of us, a squared spiral staircase of grey stone winding upward into the sky. It looked vaguely ridiculous, plunked down onto the centre of a dirt road in the middle of nowhere, branches brushing one side.

David and Adam left their picnic baskets behind, but I kept mine. I saw no reason why it should endanger us. It, and the food that appeared fresh each morning, were from our own world. Maybe it wouldn't work once we got back there, but I wanted to find out.

I guess I also wanted a souvenir. Not that I would miss the cottage, or the fear of being sent across the river. But I would miss Adam and David. We all lived in New York, but maybe Adam wouldn't want reminders of how he had sold his soul to pursue his dead wife into the afterlife. What would we do, anyway, meet for brunch in the Lower East Side and reminisce about our days in the Underworld? I didn't see it. So I clutched the basket in both hands as I set my right foot on the first step, the one memory I thought I might be able to keep.

I kept my eyes fixed on Adam's shoulders, following three or four steps behind. The sweat on my palms made the handle of my basket slippery and awkward to grip. I was unnerved that it had been so easy. No Borderlands staff had come to harass us. Even on the staircase, we encountered no distractions. Nothing but the sound of our own feet on stone, and our breaths, in and out, and beyond that: silence.

The staircase wound up and up, never changing. My legs burned, and I longed to rest for a moment, but I was too excited to stop. We were escaping. Maybe I wouldn't have a place to live; maybe my roommate had already rented out my room. But it didn't matter. I was going back to my city, my home, and no creepy undead guide was going to send me across the river because of a contract I didn't realize I was signing.

Suddenly: behind us. We all heard it. Someone was running up the steps, trying to catch up, breathing hard from exertion.

Adam, just above me, was a statue. "I know—" he started to say.

The person below cried out, a wordless exclamation of exhausted fear, perhaps even of pain. Then she spoke.

"Adam! Help me! Please, I—" Again, footsteps.

"Christine!" Adam cried.

"No!" David shouted. "It's a trap!"

Maybe David shouted his warning too late. Or maybe Adam wouldn't have listened, even if he had heard in time. I saw. I saw him turn around, one hand against the stone wall, bracing himself. And I saw the look of horror that crossed his face as he disappeared.

I screamed, reaching for him, but my hand closed on air.

Then David was behind me, his strong arms holding me in place, not letting me look back even if I had wanted to.

Did I want to? I wasn't sure. I felt like someone had torn my liver out and slashed it into a hundred pieces.

"We can't save him," David said. "He belonged to them whether he ate their food or not. We don't. We belong at the top of these stairs."

After a moment, I took another step. Then another. I couldn't see the stairs. My eyes were blurred, and I tasted salt, streaming down my cheeks. But I kept walking, always forward, never looking back.

We ascended in silence. Soon we came to a door. I pushed it open, and felt the light of the sun on my upturned face for the first time in so long, and the cold, crisp breeze of New York in late fall. When I stepped out into the light, leaves crunched under my feet.

David and I see each other from time to time, for coffee or lunch. We don't talk about what happened, but I guess it's good to keep in touch with someone who shared that experience.

Once he took me out to dinner, which was kind of weird, partly because I couldn't tell if it had been intended as a romantic overture, and partly because I was embarrassed by how much the food cost.

I've stopped investigating the disappearances. All the files and documents David had gathered to incriminate James Hammond over other irregularities have vanished, even those on password-protected areas of his hard drive at home. David believes that if we keep quiet and don't bother Hammond, he won't bother us. That he's made his point. I'm not so sure, but where would we hide? We still don't understand why James Hammond is acting as a travel agent for the Underworld. Is money deposited into a Swiss bank account each time he sends down a new guest? Or is his payment something more subtle, and more sinister?

I still have trouble remembering my parents' names. Fortunately, none of my other memories of them have faded.

For the first few weeks, I couldn't look at the picnic basket. But one day, when I dug it out from the corner of the closet, all I felt was a dull ache in the pit of my stomach, so I lifted the lid to see what was inside.

A small wholegrain roll, a tub of sweet butter, a fillet of smoked fish wrapped in parchment, and a paper carton of dried apricots. Tears sprang to my eyes, when I remembered Adam and David talking about how smoked fish had been their favourite basket meal.

For a week I took basket food to work as my lunch. Every morning, a different meal appeared. It tasted as good as it had in the Borderlands. But I felt strange eating it. I caught myself dwelling more and more on Adam, wondering if I could have done something differently, maybe not quarrelled with him so much. Would that have brought him back safely?

Eventually I gave the basket to a homeless man in Central Park.

"This is a magic picnic basket," I told him. "Keep it closed when you're not eating from it, and every morning new food will appear."

He looked at me like I was crazy. But he took the basket, and when I left he was eating a hunk of cheese sandwiched between torn-off bits of bread.

Maybe he kept it, maybe he tossed it in a trash barrel or under a tree once he had eaten all the food. If he left it behind, I hope someone who needed it more found it, and is even now enjoying nutritious meals, sitting in the sunshine on some park bench.

I don't know what he did with the basket. I walked away, feeling better than I had in a long time. I didn't look back.

charm

ANNA MIODUCHOWSKA

> *Elysia chlorotica:* species of sea slug . . .
> known for its ability to photosynthesize food.
> It is the only known member of the animal kingdom
> capable of producing chlorophyll.
> —*Encyclopaedia Britannica*

Heels over head I stand before you,
smitten by your moist,
verdant physique,

a green surreal
of glacial lakes
sighted in drumlin fields.

At first sight,
you stole my heart, as I am
determined to steal yours,

and in a fine china cup
carry it
down the aisle.

We will exchange
vows and organelles
to the sound of cheering,

our families charmed,
truly a match
made in salt marsh heaven.

IMAGINARIUM 2012

After the honeymoon,
we'll build a cottage,
plant acres of sea weed,

I'll grow fat
on chloroplasts
and sunlight.

You my dear,
will grow an ear,
and listen to my lyrics.

final girl theory
A.C. WISE

Everyone knows the opening sequence of *Kaleidoscope*. Even if they've never seen any other part of the movie (and they have, even if they won't admit it), they know the opening scene. No matter what anyone tells you, it is the most famous two and a half minutes ever put on film.

The camera is focused on a man's hand. He's holding a small shard of green glass, no bigger than his fingernail. He tilts it, catching the light, which darts like a crazed firefly. Then, so very carefully and with loving slowness, he presses the glass into something soft and white.

The camera is so tight the viewer can't see what he's pushing the glass into (but they suspect). Can you imagine that moment of realization for someone who *doesn't* know? Watch the opening sequence with a *Kaleidoscope* virgin sometime, you'll understand. The man pushes the glass into the soft white, and moves his hand away. A bead of bright red blood appears.

As the blood threads away from the glass, the sound kicks in. Only then do most people notice its absence before and discover how unsettling silence can be. The first sound is a breath. Or is it? Kaleidophiles (yes, they really call themselves that) have worn out old copies of the film playing that split-second transition from silence to sound over and over again. They've stripped their throats raw arguing. *Does* someone catch their breath, and if so, *who*?

There are varying theories, the two most popular being the man with the glass and the director. The third, of course, is that the man with the glass and the director are the same person.

Breath or no breath, the viewer slowly becomes aware they are listening to the sound of muffled sobs. At that moment of realization, as if prompted by it thus making the viewer complicit right from the start, the camera swings up wildly. We see a woman's wide, rolling eyes, circled with too much make-up. The camera jerk-pans down to her mouth; it's stuffed with a dirty rag.

The soundtrack comes up full force—blaring terrible horns and dissonant chords. The notes jangle one against the next. It isn't music, it's instruments screaming. It's sound felt in your back teeth and at the base of your spine.

The camera zooms out, showing the woman spread-eagled and naked, tied to a massive wheel. Her skin is filled with hundreds of pieces of coloured glass—red, blue, yellow, green. Her tormentor steps back; the viewer never sees his face. He rips the gag out, and spins the wheel. Thousands of firefly glints dazzle the camera.

The woman screams. The screen dissolves in a mass of spinning colour, and the opening credits roll.

You know what the worst part is? The opening sequence has nothing to do with the rest of the film. It is what it is; it exists purely for its own sake.

But let's go back to the scream. It's important. It starts out high-pitched, classic scream queen, and devolves into something ragged, wet, and bubbling. If there was any nagging doubt left about what kind of movie *Kaleidoscope* really is, it's gone. But it's too late. Remember, the viewer is complicit; they agreed to everything that follows in that split second between silence and sound, between sob and catch of breath. They can't turn back— not that anyone really tries.

Here's another thing about *Kaleidoscope*—no one ever watches it just once; don't let them tell you otherwise.

The opening is followed by eighty-five minutes of colour-soaked, blood-drenched, action. (Except—if you're paying attention—you know that's a lie.)

The movie is a cult classic. It's shown on football fields, on giant, impromptu screens made of sheets strung between goalposts. It flickers in midnight double feature theatres, lurid colours washing over men and women hunched and sweating in the dark, feet stuck to crackling floors, breathing air reeking of stale popcorn. It plays in the background, miniaturized on ghostly television screens, while burn-outs fuck at 3 a.m., lit by candles meant to disguise the scent of beer and pot.

Here's the real secret: *Kaleidoscope* isn't a movie, it's an infection, whispered from mouth to mouth in the dark.

Hardcore fans have every line memorized (not that there are many). They know the plot back and forth (though there isn't one of those, either). You see, that's the beauty of *Kaleidoscope*, its terrible genius. It is the most famous eighty-seven and a half minutes ever committed to film (don't ever let anyone tell you otherwise), but it doesn't exist. If you were to creep through the film, frame by frame (and people have) you would know this is true.

Kaleidoscope exists in people's minds. It exists in the brief, flickering space between frames. The *real* movie screen is the inside of their eyelids, the back of their skulls when they close their eyes and try to sleep. When the film rolls, there is action and blood, sex and drugs, and not a little touch of madness, but there are shadows, too. There are things seen from the corner of the eye, and that's where the true movie lies. There, and in the rumours.

Jackson Mortar has heard them all. Crew members died or went missing during the shoot (or there was no crew); a movie house burned to the ground during the first screening (the doors were locked from the inside); fans have been arrested trying to recreate the movie's most famous scenes (the very best are never get caught); and, of course, the most persistent rumour of all: everything in the movie—the sex, the drugs, the violence, and yes, even the flickering shadows—is one hundred percent real.

"You know that scene in the graveyard, with Carrie, when Lance is leading the voodoo ceremony to bring Lucy back from the dead?" Kevin leans across the table, half-eaten burger forgotten in his hand.

Jackson nods. He traces the maze on the kiddie menu, and refuses to look up. Kevin is a fresh convert. Like moths to flame, somehow they always know—when it comes to *Kaleidoscope*, Jackson Mortar is the man. Jackson supposes that makes him part of the mythology, in a way, and he should be proud. But his stomach flips, growling around a knot of cold fries. He pushes the remains of his meal away, rescuing his soda from Kevin's enthusiastic hand-talking.

"And you know how Carrie is writhing on the tomb, and the big snake is crawling all over her body, between her tits and between her legs, like it's *doing* her, and she's moaning and Lance is pouring blood all over her?" Kevin grins, painful-wide; Jackson can hear it, even without looking up.

"Yeah, what about it?"

"Do you think it's real?"

Jackson finally raises his head. Sweat beads Kevin's upper lip; his burger is disintegrating in his hand. A trace of fear ghosts behind the bravado in his eyes.

"Maybe." Jackson keeps his tone as neutral.

The glimpse of fear gives him hope for Kevin, but Kevin's smile does him in. Maybe the kid sees more than the sex and drugs and blood, but that's all he *wants* to see. Kevin has seen *Kaleidoscope*, and wishes the movie was otherwise. That, Jackson cannot abide.

"Listen, I gotta get going." Jackson stands. "I got work to do."

"Oh, okay. Sure." Kevin's expression falls. Another flicker of unease skitters across his face.

Guilt needles Jackson—he can't leave the kid alone like this—but Kevin pastes it over with another goofy, sloppy grin. "Maybe we can catch a midnight screening together sometime?"

Jackson's pity dissolves; he shrugs into his worn, black trench coat, "Yeah, sure. Sometime."

Jackson squeezes out of the booth. Kevin turns back to his cold hamburger. Jackson wonders how the kid stays so skinny. As he pushes through the restaurant door, out into the near-blinding sun, Jackson tries to remember to hate Kevin for the right reasons, not just because he's young and thin.

Jackson steps off the curb, and freezes. Across the street, on the other side of the world and close enough to touch, Carrie Linden walks through a slant of sunlight. She glances behind her, peering over the top of bug-large sunglasses, which almost swallow her face. She hunches into her collar, pulls open the pharmacy door, and darts inside.

A car horn blares. Jackson leaps back, the spell broken. His heart pounds. No one has seen any of the actors from *Kaleidoscope* since the movie was filmed. There are no interviews, no "Where Are They Now?" specials on late-night TV. It plays into the mystique, as though *Kaleidoscope* might truly be a mass hallucination thrown up on the silver screen. No one real has ever been associated with the film. The credits list the director as B. Z. Bubb and the writer as Lou Cypher.

It's been nearly forty years since *Kaleidoscope* was filmed, five years before Jackson was born (but long before he was *really* born). But Jackson knows it's her; he would know Carrie Linden anywhere.

Jackson has been in love with Carrie Linden his whole life. (Yes, he considers the first time he saw *Kaleidoscope* as the moment he was born.)

When Carrie Linden first appeared on the screen, Jackson forgot how to breathe. The scene is burned into his retinas; it, more than anything else, is his private, skull-thrown midnight show. He sees it on thin, blood-lined lids every time he closes his eyes.

Jackson refrains from telling anyone this unless he knows they'll really understand (and fellow Kaleidophiles always do). The problem—the reason he can't say anything to converts and virgins—is that the first part of Carrie Linden to appear on screen is her ass.

It's during the party scene. She walks across the camera from left to right. Long hair hangs down her back, dirty blonde, wavy, split ends brushing the curve of her buttocks. She wears ropes of glittering beads, but the viewer doesn't know that yet. They are the same beads used to whip Elizabeth in the very next scene, horribly disfiguring her face, but the viewer doesn't know that yet, either.

What the viewer knows is this: Carrie Linden walks across the screen from left to right. She climbs onto the lap of a man at least twice her age. She fucks him as he lifts tiny scoops of cocaine up to her nose, balancing them delicately on the end of an over-long fingernail.

The first time the viewer sees Carrie's face, she is sprawled naked on the couch. The camera pans up from her toes, pausing at her chest. Her breathing is erratic, shallow, then deep, then panicked-fast—a jackrabbit lives under her skin. Her head lolls to one side, her eyes are blissfully (or nightmare-chokedly) closed. A trickle of blood runs from her nose.

While Carrie sleeps, but hopefully doesn't dream, Elizabeth is whipped with Carrie's beads. Elizabeth screams. She's on her knees, and sometimes it looks as though she's stretching her hands out toward Carrie. Some viewers (Kaleidophiles, all) have made the comparison to various religious paintings. Elizabeth's face is a sheet of blood. When she collapses, her torturer steps over her, and drops the bloody beads around Carrie's neck. Almost as an afterthought he sticks his hand between Carrie's legs before wandering away. She doesn't react at all.

Jackson stares at the pharmacy door for so long that the woman he *knows* is Carrie Linden has time to conclude her business and slip out again, still darting glances over her shoulder as she hurries away. Once she's disappeared around the corner, Jackson dashes across the street, ignoring traffic. He yanks open the pharmacy door, and runs panting to the back counter. Luckily, Justin is working. Justin is a *Kaleidoscope* fan, too. (Aren't we all?)

"Hey, buddy. Here to get your prescription filled?" Justin winks.

Jackson ignores him, trying to catch his breath. "The woman who just left, did you see her?"

"Yeah. Dark hair and glasses? Not bad for an older broad." Justin's grin reminds Jackson of Kevin. He wants to reach across the counter and throttle Justin, who is skinny too, but old enough to know better. He's older than Jackson (not counting *Kaleidoscope* years, of course).

"Percocet," Justin says as an afterthought. He has no compunctions about confidentiality. If he didn't know the owner too well, he'd have been fired a long time ago.

"Can you get me her address?" Jackson asks. His mind whirls (like colours dissolving behind a credit roll while a woman screams).

"Sure." Justin shrugs. No questions asked—that's what Jackson likes about him. Justin consults his computer and chicken scrawls an address on the back of an old receipt.

"Thanks, man. I owe you!" Jackson snatches the paper, spins, and sprints for the door.

"Hey, who is she?" Justin calls after him.

"Carrie Linden!" Jackson slams through the door, answering only because he knows Justin won't believe him.

The name written over the address Justin gave him is Karen Finch. The address isn't five blocks from the pharmacy. Jackson runs the whole way, heaving his bulk, dripping sweat, legs burning, breath wheezing. It's worth a heart attack, worth the return of his childhood asthma, worth anything.

The street he arrives on is tree-lined and shadow-dappled. Cars border both sides of the road, dogs bark in backyards, and two houses over a group of children run in shrieking circles on an emerald lawn.

Jackson approaches number forty-seven. He's shaking. His mouth is dry in a way that has nothing to do with his mad, panting run. His heart pounds, louder than the dying echoes of his fist knocking against Carrie Linden's door. What is he doing? He should leave. But *Kaleidoscope* isn't that kind of movie. It isn't a movie at all. It's an infection, deep in Jackson's blood.

The door opens; Jackson stares.

Light frames the woman in a soft-focus glow, falling through a window at the far end of the hall. Her hair is dyed dark, but showing threads of grey (or maybe they're dirty blonde). The ends are split and frayed. She isn't wearing sunglasses, but shadows circle her eyes, seeming just as large. She is thin—not in a pretty way; her cheekbones knife against her skin. But she *is* Carrie Linden, and Jackson forgets how to breathe.

The second most famous scene in *Kaleidoscope* is the carnival scene. It's the one most viewers (not Kaleidophiles, mind you) rewind to watch over and over again. It's spawned numerous chat groups, websites, message boards, and one doctoral thesis, which languishes untouched in a drawer.

The scene goes like this: the characters go to a carnival— Carrie, Lance, Mary, and Josh, even Elizabeth, even though her face is horribly scarred (but not Lucy, because she's dead). The carnival is abandoned, but all the lights are on and all the rides are running. The night flickers with halogen-sick lights, illuminating painted rides and gaudy-bright games. The whole scene drifts, strange and unreal.

The gang rides the funhouse ride. But it's not just a funhouse, it's a haunted house, a hall of mirrors, and tunnel of love all rolled into one. The cars crank along the track, but jerk to a stop in the first room, as if the ride is broken. They wander through the ride on foot. And this is where the movie gets weird.

It fragments. Time stops. (Do any two viewers see the same scene?) The camera follows scarred Elizabeth; it follows meathead Lance. It follows Carrie Linden. Voices whisper, words play backwards, things slide, half-glimpsed, across the corners of the film, at the very *edges*, spilling off the celluloid and into the dark. (Is it any wonder the movie house burned down?)

The funhouse is filled with painted flats and cheesy rubber

monsters loaded on springs. But there are also angles that shouldn't exist, reflections where there should be none.

There are odd, jerky cuts in the film itself, loops, backward stutters, and doubled scenes, as if bits of films are being run through a projector at the same time. It's impossible.

Everyone is separated, utterly alone. The strange twists of the mirrored corridors keep them apart, even when they are only inches away. And here debates rage, because something happens, but no one is quite sure what.

Maybe Carrie Linden steps through a mirror into the room where Elizabeth is raking bloody nails against the glass, trying to escape. Some viewers claim that it isn't really Carrie, because she stepped through a mirror too. (Inside the funhouse, is anyone who they used to be?) What follows is brutal. With eerie, cold precision Carrie tortures Elizabeth. Accounts vary. Is blood actually drawn, or is the pain more subtle, more insidious than that? (What did *you* see? What do you *think* you saw?)

What makes the violence even more shocking is that up until this point in the film, Carrie has been utterly passive. (Is it possible to watch her push a sliver of mirrored glass through Elizabeth's cheek and not feel it in your own?) Elizabeth's face fills with terror, but oddly, she doesn't seem to notice Carrie at all. Her gaze darts to the mirrors. Her panicked glances skitter into the shadows.

She look straight at the camera, and tears roll silently from her eyes.

Four people leave the funhouse at the end of the scene—Carrie, Josh, Elizabeth and Lance. (Do they?) Mary is never seen again. Her absence is never explained. It's that kind of film.

The crux of the movie hangs here. Kaleidophiles know if they could just unravel this scene, they'd understand everything. (Do they really want to?) When she leaves the funhouse, what is Carrie holding in her hand? Was there really a reflection in the mirror behind Elizabeth's head? When Carrie leans down and puts her mouths against Elizabeth's ear, what does she whisper?

"Can I help you?" The woman's voice snaps Jackson back to himself. His skin flushes hot; panic constricts his throat.

The woman flickers and doubles. Carrie Linden (or Karen Finch) is here and now, but she is there and then too. Jackson shudders.

Something passes through the woman's eyes, a kind of recognition. It's as though all these years Jackson has been watching her, she's been looking right back at him.

"You're Carrie Linden," he says. His voice is thick and far away.

Her expression turns hard. Jackson sees the cold impulse to violence; for a moment, she wants to hurt him. Instead, she steps aside, her voice tight. "You'd better come inside."

Jackson squeezes past her, close enough to touch. He catches her scent—patchouli, stale cigarettes, and even staler coffee. Her posture radiates hatred; her bones are blades, aching towards his skin. When they are face to face, Jackson glimpses the truth in her eyes—she's been expecting this moment. Carrie Linden has been running her whole life, knowing sooner or later someone will catch her.

She shuts the door—a final sound. Jackson's heart skips, jitters erratically, worse than when he ran all the way here. Carrie gestures to a room opening up to the left.

"Sit. I'll make coffee."

She leaves him, disappearing down the narrow hall. Jackson lowers himself onto a futon covered with a tattered blanket. Upended apple crates flank it at either end. A coffee table sits between the futon and a nest-shaped chair. The walls are painted blood-rust red; they are utterly bare.

Carrie returns with mismatched mugs and hands him one. It's spider-webbed with near-invisible cracks, the white ceramic stained beige around the rim. The side of the mug bears an incongruous rainbow, arching away from a fluffy white cloud. Jackson sips, and almost chokes. The coffee is scalding black; she doesn't offer him milk or sugar.

Carrie Linden sits in the nest chair, tucking bare feet beneath her. She wears a chunky sweater coat. It looks hand-knit, and it nearly swallows her. She meets Jackson's gaze, so he can't possibly look away.

"Well, what do you want to know?" Her voice snaps, dry-stick brittle and hard.

Jackson can't speak for his heart lodged in his throat. There's a magic to watching *Kaleidoscope* (unless you watch it alone). The people on screen dying and fucking and screaming and weeping, they're just shadows. It's *okay* to watch; it's safe. None of it is real.

Motes of dust fall through the light around Carrie Linden—tiny, erratic fireflies. The curtains are mostly drawn, but the sun knifes through, leaving the room blood hot.

"All of it," Carries says, when Jackson can't find the words.

"What?" He gapes, mouth wide.

"That's what you're wondering, isn't it? That's what they all want to know. The answer is—all of it. All of it was real."

Jackson flinches as though he's been punched in the gut. (In a way, he has.) Should he feel guiltier about the cracked light in her eyes, or the fact that his stomach dropped when she said "that's what they all want to know"? He isn't her first.

Carrie Linden's hands wrap around her mug, showing blue veins and fragile bones. Steam rises, curling around her face. When she raises the mug to sip, her sleeve slides back defiantly and unapologetically revealing scars.

"Well?" Carrie's gaze follows the line of Jackson's sight. "Why *did* you come, then?"

She bores into him with piercing-bright eyes, and Jackson realizes—even sitting directly across from her—he can't tell what colour they are. They are every colour and no colour at once, as if her body is just a shell housing the infinite possibilities living inside.

"I wanted to talk about the movie. I thought maybe..." Jackson glances desperately around the bare-walled room—nowhere to run. In his head, he's rehearsed this moment a thousand times. He's *always* known exactly what he'll say to Carrie Linden when he finally meets her, but now it's all gone wrong.

I'm sorry, he wants to say, *I shouldn't have come*, but the words stick in his throat. His eyes sting. He's failed. In the end, he's no better than Justin, or Kevin. He's not a Kaleidophile, he hasn't transcended the sex and gore—he's just another wannabe.

Unable to look Carrie in the eye, Jackson fumbles a postcard out of his coat pocket. The edges are frayed and velvet-soft through years of wear. It's the original movie poster for *Kaleidoscope*, wrought in miniature. Jackson found it at a garage sale last year, and he's been carrying it around ever since. He passes it to Carrie with shaking hands.

As Carrie looks down to study the card, Jackson finally looks up. Like the movie, Jackson knows the card by heart, but now he sees it through Carrie's eyes; he's never loathed himself more.

His eyes burn with the lurid colour, the jumbled images piled together and bleeding into one.

The backdrop is a carnival, but it's also a graveyard, or maybe an empty field backed with distant trees. A woman studded with fragments of glass lies spread-eagled on a great wheel. Between her legs, Carrie lies on an altar, covered in writhing snakes. Behind Carrie, Elizabeth's blood-sheeted face hangs like a crimson moon. From the black of her wide open eyes, shadowy figures seep out and stain the other images. They hide behind and inside everything, doubling and ghosting and blurring. The card isn't one thing, it's everything.

"I'm sorry." Jackson finally manages the words aloud.

Slowly, Carrie reaches for a pen lying atop of a half-finished crossword puzzle. Her hand moves, more like a spasm than anything voluntary. The nib scratches across the card's back, slicing skin and bone and soul. She lets the card fall onto the table between them, infinitely kind and infinitely cruel. Jackson thinks the tears welling in his eyes are the only things that save him.

"It's okay," she says. Her voice is not quite forgiving. For a moment, Jackson has the mad notion she might fold him in her bony arms and soothe him like a child, as though he's the one that needs, or deserves, comforting.

Instead, Carrie leans forward and opens a drawer in the coffee table, fishing out a pack of cigarettes. Something rattles and slithers against the wood as the drawer slides closed. Jackson catches a glimpse, and catches his breath. Even after forty years he imagines the beads still sticky and warm, still slicked with Elizabeth's blood.

Carrie lights her cigarette, and watches the patterns the smoke makes in the air, in shadows on the wall. They don't quite match.

"I'm the final girl," she says. The softness of her voice makes Jackson jump. He doesn't think she's even speaking to him anymore. She might as well be alone. (She's always been alone.)

"What?" Jackson says, even though he knows exactly what she's talking about. His voice quavers.

"It's fucking bullshit, you know that?" Her voice is just as soft as before if the words are harsher. "I wasn't a helpless fantasy at the beginning; I wasn't an empowered hero at the end. I was just me the whole time. I was just human."

She stands, crushing her cigarette against the cupped palm of her hand without flinching. "You can stay if you want. Or you can go. I don't really care."

And just like that she's gone. Jackson is alone with Carrie Linden's blood-red walls and her battered couch, with her beads hidden in the coffee table drawer, and her autograph on a worn-soft postcard. When she walked onto the screen, Carrie Linden stopped Jackson's heart; walking out of the room, she stops it again.

He sees Carrie Linden doubled, trebled—bony-thin hips hidden beneath a bulky sweater; the curve of her naked ass, teased by long blonde hair as she saunters across the screen; a hunted, haunted woman, glancing behind her as she darts into the drug store.

Jackson has sunk so low, he can't go any lower. (At least that's what he tells himself as he leaves to make it okay.)

At home, Jackson hides the postcard and Carrie Linden's beads at the bottom of his drawer. He covers them with socks and underwear, wadded t-shirts smelling of his sweat and late night popcorn, ripe with fear and desire.

It doesn't matter how rare the postcard is, never mind that it's signed by Carrie Linden; he'll never show it to anyone, or even take it out of the drawer. The beads are another matter.

Everyone knows the opening sequence of *Kaleidoscope*, but it's the closing sequence plays in most people's minds, projected against the ivory curve of their dreaming skulls, etched onto the thinness of their eyelids. It bathes the late-night stupors of lone losers curled on their couches with the blankets pulled up to their chins against the flickering dark. It haunts midnight movie screens in rooms smelling of sticky-sweet spills and stale salt. It looms large on sheets stretched between goal posts, while orgies wind down on the battered turf below.

It is the third most famous scene in cinema history. (Don't let anyone tell you otherwise.)

Carrie is running. Everybody else is dead—Lance and Lucy, Elizabeth and Josh and Mary, and all the other brief phantoms who never even had names. She is covered in blood. Some of it is hers. She is naked.

Ahead of her is a screen of trees. More than once, Carrie

stumbles and falls. When she does, the camera shows the soles of her feet, slick and red. But she keeps getting back up, again and again. The camera judders as it follows her. It draws close, but never quite catches up.

Carrie glances back over her shoulder, eyes staring wide at something the camera never turns to let the viewer see. (Imagination isn't always the worst thing.) Carrie's expression (hunted and haunted) says it all.

There is no soundtrack, no psychedelic colours. The only sound is Carrie's feet slapping over sharp stones and broken bottles and her breath hitching in her throat. She's running for the grass and the impossibly distant trees.

The credits roll.

The screen goes dark.

But Carrie is still there, between the frames, bleeding off the edges, flickering in the shadows. She'll always be right there, forever, running.

to live and die in gibbontown
DEREK KÜNSKEN

Murray slips the cool steel of the silencer into my palm. My hearing, augmented with somatic genetic modifications from bats, picks up the scrape of machined metal against thickened skin. I screw the silencer onto the muzzle, using my palm to muffle the rasp.

I'm Reggie and I'm a businessman.

Murray gives me the scope. I do a quick sighting, and then slide it onto the rifle.

I'm really good at what I do.

Murray passes me a clip of ceramic 7.62 rounds. I don't care how thick your force field is. It ain't stoppin' these puppies.

What I do isn't exactly tea conversation. I kill old people. The older, richer, and droolier the better.

Me and Murray have swung high into a tree in the park overlooking the official residence of the Bonobo Embassy. Through the scope, I see my target. An ancient Bonobo female, lanky, tangled hair hanging in patches around cheeks and chin. Grey tits sagging flat and wrinkly like broken balloons. The stained, white padding around her waist doesn't seem to be doing its job of holding in what needs holding, and flies buzz. She wheezes, staring out of the compound, searching the trees, looking for danger.

Sorry, old hag, but I've got you this time. I don't care whose mother you are. I'm the angel of death and I bring—

Something loud snaps behind me. Murray, and all my equipment, knock against my back. I hold onto the branch and don't make a sound, but dumb-ass, butterfingers Murray drops my GPS and a set of small screwdrivers. They tinkle down, hitting every goddamn branch. His furry orange face stares at me, lips forming a big O.

Alexandra the Bonobo, the ambassador's mother, jolts from

her seat and stands straight. Her diaper gives out at the same time, and plops between her feet with a hypnotically sickening splash. The old hag points at me.

"You're a failure, you no-assed macaque afterbirth!" she shrieks. "You couldn't kill a blind, one-armed, no-legged spider monkey! Go back to eating fruit, you mouth-breathing loser!"

That's a bit harsh. I like fruit. She follows it with a stream of racist epithets and froths at the mouth by the time she gets to "The only thing I hate worse than macaques are gibbons!" Racist bitch. I hate Bonobos.

I'd love to yell back, but embassy security pours into the yard. They're carrying pistols with metal rounds. Won't get through their own force field, but I don't want to be here when their marksmen come out, or the Gibbon police get here. My visa status is dodgy enough as it is.

"Dumb-ass!" I yell. I smack Murray. I regret it immediately. I hit him hard enough to hurt myself on the carbon-nanotube-reinforced skin under his brown fur. I did the job myself and did it pretty good. Flexible enough to keep his skin looking real, but still hard enough to be damn near bulletproof. Problem is, my sidekick is clumsy and follows instructions like a Guatemalan pack burro. My hand still stings and security guys are pulling their binoculars. Alexandra the Bonobo fills the air with obscenities that would make a hooker blush.

"Murray, you dumb chimp! What kind of an operation are we running here? What happened to professionals, huh? What do I pay you for?" I stab a finger downward. "Carry the damn equipment down and pick up my tools!"

Murray scrambles down the tree with a harried look. I scamper down the other side where Embassy security won't get a good look at me. At the bottom of the tree, we're shielded from view. Murray is fumbling my screwdrivers out of the grass of the park like he's preening the lawn. Sirens whine in the distance.

"All right! All right! Come on! Forget the screwdrivers! Get in the car!"

We high tail it (no pun intended) to my Renault 4L, the finest car produced in its price range in France, Colombia, and Slovenia in the early seventies. As far as I know, there are no other cars in this price range. I won it in a drunken contest of strength from a big, ham-handed gorilla who got deported a few weeks ago.

Those two events are entirely unrelated, by the way.

He was pissed when he found out about my myofibril-augments, but like they say, you shouldn't hustle people strange to you.

The little red box of a car leans heavily to the passenger side as Murray gets in. I'm too light to balance it when I get behind the wheel. I'd love to squeal the tires to make our getaway, but I'm still learning the clutch, and it doesn't have nearly as many horses under the hood as . . . well, anything. Still, I get it up to thirty-five. We're on the main road and into thick traffic long before the flashing lights come into view.

"Damn it, Murray! Do you know how much money you just blew us?"

"Sorry, boss," he says. Murray's got a strong, slow accent from the Chimpanzee townships to the south.

"This business is all about reputation! Do you think anyone is going to hire me, hire us, if we can't grease an old Bonobo in a diaper?"

"Sorry, boss."

"And Murray, I can't stress this enough. If I'd have killed her, I wouldn't have had to have seen her diaper fall down."

"I won't do it again, boss."

Last week was so much more promising. Gibbons and Bonobos are pretty stuck up about jobs having to do with death. They don't do them. It's beneath them. You can't pay most Gibbons love or money to euthanize the decaying elderly. I was running out of time on my visa pretty fast and staring at deportation to macaque territory if I didn't find a scam soon. That's when I fell into the euthanasia business. I acquired a failing company from a low status Gibbon with a gambling problem. How hard can euthanasia be? The clients want to die, right?

That business deal got me an extension on my visa. All I had to do was turn a profit and I could do that any time I wanted, just so long as it was within ninety days. Problem was, the bigger whack shops, made up mostly of hulking gorillas, had cornered the euthanasia market. Also, I knew nothing about needles, dosages, or the sterile technique.

That's when I got my great idea. Imagine this ad on late-night TV: "Is your time up? Die with excitement and adventure! Struggle to the very end! Hire an international assassin to finish the job that nature started! If you see it coming, you get your money back!"

It doesn't matter that I'm not really an assassin. Most of business is image and branding, right? I'm exotic. I'm international. That's why Gibbon Immigration wants to deport me back to my shit-hole country where military coups come more often than Christmas.

Gibbon country has great euthanasia laws. They don't specify how it has to be done. And their weapon laws favour the rugged individualist in each of us. There are plenty of places in this town I wouldn't walk without a high-powered rifle and a bulletproof chimpanzee. So International Hit Squad was born. I even got six column-inches on page twelve of the Gibbontown Shopper, the third-most-read free paper in the capital, right under the story about the debate on zoning changes. You can't pay for that kind of publicity.

Clients were slower to react than the press corps. It took two weeks for the first one. Unfortunately it was Alexandra, the harpy they use to scare little Bonobo children at night. A bodyguard wheeled the saggy bitch into my office. I'd put on my best business face.

"Fucking macaque!" she said when she saw me. Then she spit on my floor. I shit you not. She spit on my floor. Who spits on a floor?

"How can I help you, ma'am?" I held a clipboard to give myself an air of efficiency.

"Your operation is bullshit!" she yelled. She yelled everything. Her bodyguard, a biggish Bonobo with a heavy pistol on his hip, rolled his eyes.

"I beg your pardon, ma'am?" I asked.

"I read your ad," she said. "This is a big scam! You can't deliver shit in a pot, much less give me an exciting death!"

"You'll never know when I strike, ma'am. You'll never see me coming." I smiled my confidence-inspiring, businessman smile.

The bitch spit on my floor again.

"I was a sergeant in the Bonobo Marines!" she said. "I worked close protection for the Bonobo Secret Service and kept a senator alive during the Gibbon invasion. No one can sneak up on me, least of all a goddamn poseur of a macaque!"

I shrugged. "My guarantee is there, ma'am. If you see me coming, you get your money back."

"It's a scam."

"Try me out," I said. "Unless you're yellow."

She slapped her wrinkly hand on the armrest of her wheelchair. She looked like she was having an aneurysm, foaming and sputtering. I didn't want her to die. She hadn't signed the contract yet.

"Bring it on, little man."

My eyes narrowed and I felt my augmented muscles debating whether to choke the bitch right here. Sure, there are lots of smaller primates, and macaques aren't very big, but everyone, and I mean everyone, knows we hate being called little. Racist bitch. Macaques just have delicate bones.

I snapped a contract onto the clipboard and shoved it at her. "You'll never see me coming, ma'am. Whatever you think you knew way back when has been made obsolete, just like you."

Little veins on her neck thumped under papery, dark skin. White spit collected at the points of her mouth.

She scrawled her name across the bottom of the sheet and threw it back at me.

"It's on!" she yelled.

"Not yet!" I yelled over her.

She'd signed in the wrong spot. As a businessman, I'm a stickler for detail. I handed her a fresh contract and put an X where she had to sign. "Do it right, this time!"

Her long, old fingers flexed and released, like she wanted to slap me. Then she filled out the whole form. Then, she signed in neat little letters and handed it back to me. I looked at it.

Oh shit.

Listed next of kin was the Bonobo ambassador. Address, the ambassador's residence. That place was crawling with security.

She cackled when she saw my expression change. "And I've got augments, little man," she said, pointing at her eyes. "I can see farther than a hawk and I've got nothing to do all day but watch for you." She cackled louder and signalled for her bodyguard to wheel her out.

Damn.

After being chased out of a tree on my first attempt to off the hag, I hire a Gibbon to do some surveillance work. She's an aging street vendor with long arms and pale, thick fur. She trundles a soup cart around, and with my encouragement, sets herself up close to the Bonobo ambassador's official residence. The Bonobos don't go near her, but the Gibbon diplomatic police, tall, black-eyed, with white belts and holsters, take their cigarette breaks beside her cart, nursing cups of soup, and sometimes something harder. Good girl.

At the end of the third day, she tells me that one of the diplomatic cops said that the ambassador's mother is going shopping on Saturday at the crafts market. Sweet. The crafts market has lots of cover and is crawling with Gibbons and foreigners. Murray and I can blend in.

Early on Saturday, Murray, loaded with my gear, follows me in. It rained yesterday and the market stinks of wet fur and fine mud overlaying older paving stones. The stalls, framed in wood, are covered by woven tarps of so many colours that it looks like a rainbow barfed on the whole sprawling hippie-fest. The stalls creak under the worthless weight of woven grass baskets, wooden masks, carved salad spoons, and hemp blankets. Nothing here couldn't have been made better and cheaper by a good, solid, greenhouse-gas-producing machine.

The market had congealed a long time ago around an old cathedral tower. The rest of the cathedral had burnt down or been knocked down or something, but the old tower is still there. I bribe some janitorial type and he lets us in. We wind our way up the damp, rotting stairwell and I set myself up on the fourth floor, where the absent old bell has left a space for a marksman with a rifle to cover most of the place. I leave my dumb-ass sidekick on the landing and he's only too happy to not be involved.

Don't get me wrong. Murray's good at some stuff. I just haven't found what it is yet. He's loyal though, like a stupid dog. If he hadn't married my sister, I would have booted his ass a long time ago.

I can see the parking lot and it doesn't take me long before I see a dark Ford Bronco with tinted windows and diplomatic plates driving in. I watch through the scope. I recognize Alexandra's Bonobo bodyguard by the balding head and the long vertical wrinkles around his lips. He and the driver help the witch out and put her into the wheelchair. She looks positively delighted today. Although, to be honest, the Bonobo bitch could have gas for all I can figure out of their expressions sometimes. Still, there's something.

Good day to die, you old hag.

I have a clear shot at any of a dozen positions once she's in the market. I aim my scope down the rows of stalls, looking for where the most surprising shot could happen. Should I shoot her in the head as she's looking at something, or in the chest as she's paying? I want her to know it was me. She paid for surprise. Still, a paycheque is pretty important. This one will put me in the clear for a while, and will sort out my immigration problems.

Lots of customers, even early in the morning. Lots of old Gibbon ladies, but more of the button-down crowd than I expected. Slumming? Faux new-agers? I scan a few through the scope. They're big Gibbons, mostly males, picking at the merchandise. They've got smocks on, the latest Gibbon fashion. These guys all have one hand in their pockets. Cops? Doesn't matter. I'm not doing anything illegal. I've got a license for the rifle. No receipt, but a license. And I've got a contract signed by Miss Bitchy herself to kill her. I'm golden.

One of the Gibbons looks a little familiar. Long black hair, pronounced eye ridges, wrinkled face hanging off the nose ridge, black skin and pinkish lips. Over his forehead is a receding V of baldness. Why does he look familiar?

Fuck.

I've seen him a few times. He's an immigration supervisor. Scanning the market. Now that I look closer, I recognize a few others. All immigration officers. Not mine, but pretty much everyone else. Shit. They're holding passport readers in their pockets and walking through the crowd. The chips in Gibbon ID cards, as well as the smart passports and RFID visas of foreigners, are all automatically checked. I pat my chest pocket. Passport and visa are there. Good. They'll stand a cursory check, but if I get too close . . . not so much.

My visa troubles, as I said, are mostly solved. I didn't say they were solved legitimately. The business visa in my passport isn't exactly mine. Let's leave it at that.

But what the hell is immigration doing here? Lots of foreigners here, for sure, but doesn't immigration have bigger fish to fry? I huddle close to the corner, only the end of my black scope showing above the sill. I scan. I spot the bodyguard pushing the wheelchair of my diapered Bonobo target. Her flabby, drooling mouth is spread into a wide grin.

That bitch!

She set me up.

She tipped off immigration.

I can probably make it out of here without running into them, but she's daring me to put a round between her smug, black eyes and draw attention to myself. The cops will swarm the place. Then I'll show my euthanasia license. Of course, seeing as how I'm a macaque, immigration will want to have a look at me. A close look.

God, I hate old people.

I kick the wall, startling Murray. He sticks out his bearded bottom lip, and his pink ears look even more awkward sticking out of the sides of his head.

"We're heading downstairs, Murray," I whisper. "This place is crawling with immigration."

His big eyebrows rise in alarm. I sorted out his immigration problems, kind of the same way I sorted out mine, but I didn't spend as much money on it. There aren't a lot of immigration officers who'll believe that Murray is a visiting professor of physics. Don't get me wrong. Some Gibbons are absolutely stupid. I just don't want to bank an operation on Mister Tenure Track here.

"Come on," I say, and lead the way downstairs and out the door. Murray follows, lugging my gear.

I swing him to the left, and spot one of those buttoned-down types at the other corner of the tower. He's scanning the crowd, looking away right now. I pull Murray to the right, almost setting our fur on fire on an open charcoal grill. An old Gibbon lady is making tortillas. Murray squeals. We weave around her. Lots of people around, but I'm starting to think that maybe we stand out a little. Two foreigners carrying non-hippie gear. Yeah, which one of these things doesn't belong in a handicrafts bazaar?

I grab us two Andean-style ponchos at a stall decorated with old, framed lithographs of dragons, rainbows, and unicorns. Murray admires them. I shove the poncho over his head. Watch unicorns on someone else's dime. I pay the Gibbon weaver more than I want to for the ponchos, but we look a lot less conspicuous now.

An immigration guy is sort of standing nonchalantly at the other end of this alley, too. I pull Murray with me between two stalls, shoving past some Gibbons smoking on stools while they weave dream catchers.

"Go back where you came from!" one of them yells after us.

I lick my finger and flip him the bird.

We find a narrow alley, undertrafficked, with lots of puddles. The stalls here are filled with specialty stuff. If you want rings of South German mettwurst or dried Baltic cod with wrinkled eyes, I can now point you here. This alley crosses a couple of busier ones, but immigration seems to be staking out the bigger intersections. Still, I don't let myself react until we're in the Renault, on the road, and in second gear.

That dirty Bonobo bitch!

Two can play with corrupt officials. Now it's really on. It's got to be. I'm down to sixty-two days.

I meet my immigration officer in a small café far from her office. Her name's Khao Yai. She's descended from the Thai Gibbon populations. After one of the many Thai coups, lot of Thai Gibbons moved to these parts. Their exotic grey-white fur and black bellies made them in demand for TV commercials and even acting roles, but if you asked me, that fad wasn't over fast enough. None of them could act worth shit (and we're talking soaps, here) and their accents were pretty thick. Khao Yai was born here and speaks like a native. She leveraged her looks to get a job in the Gibbon Immigration Service. What I like best about her is her pragmatism.

I slide a thickish wad of bills across the table. Low denominations, but it's not like I'm asking to get the ambassador's mother deported. I just want the immigration computer system to mark Alexandra's diplomatic visa as expired.

A diplomatic visa would normally be dealt with on paper by some low-level bureaucrat in the Gibbon Protocol Office, but the Gibbons and Bonobos have been at each other's throats in three separate wars in the last twenty years. You can bet that the Gibbons won't make anything easy for the Bonobo diplomats.

Here's how I figure it'll go down. The old hag has to drive from the official residence to the immigration office. On the way, I put a bullet through the car window, and her head. My client is satisfied with a surprising euthanasia experience. I get my pay, minus the cost of one car window.

I'm a genius.

Khao Yai calls me from her office the next day. She's never called me from her office.

"The date of expiry got changed," she says. "I couldn't access the system with my clearance. I needed to get my supervisor's help. I'll need more money."

Of course she will.

"Fine," I say. "We can work something out, maybe not now, but when I'm a little more flush. When is she coming to your office?"

"That's the thing, Reggie. Protocol Office and Foreign Affairs are tangling their fur over this. They're probably going to send an officer to her."

"Damn it!"

"They asked me a lot of questions about you."

"What?" I ask, feeling my stomach cool. "Who did?"

"Foreign Affairs and my boss."

"Shit. What does that mean?"

"Relax. I didn't tell them anything about your . . . funny status. As far as they're concerned, you're a legit businessman—"

"I am a legit businessman! I have a contract!"

"That's what I told them. They're looking to help out. Apparently, they need to make some sort of gesture of peace-making to the Bonobos. The big bosses at Foreign Affairs are trying to play nice."

"What does this all mean?"

"Can you fax me over your contract?" she asks. "They want proof that you're legitimately authorized to euthanize the old Bonobo."

"Then what?"

"How would you like to get into the Official Residence, as part of the Protocol team going in?"

"Uh . . . everyone knows I'm a macaque, right? I don't look anything like a Gibbon bureaucrat and neither does Murray."

"Are you strong enough to be a porter?" she asks.

"Hell, yeah!" I say, warming up to the possibilities. "I've got some pretty sophisticated myofibril-augments. I can change a tire on my car without a jack."

I don't mention that the car is a Renault 4L, or that I can only do that on the back end, but let's see you lift the back end of a car with one hand.

"What are me and Murray going to have to carry?"

"Foreign Affairs figures they help you get the contract done under the cover of you carrying in something big while they sort out her visa. This makes everyone happy. Apparently the ambassador knows about the contract and hates his mother." There's a surprise. "Fax me the contract in case it's some kind of trick on the part of the Bonobos. Foreign Affairs doesn't want anything to go wrong, Reggie. Nothing will go wrong, will it?"

"No, of course not! I'll fax you the contract right away. Nothing will go wrong." I glare at Murray meaningfully.

"Good."

I hang up. My big, dumb sidekick waits for me to say something.

"Murray, luck is breaking our way. You better not screw this up for us."

Gibbon number one at the Protocol Office (Howard) is one of the elite, white-handed gibbons. He's stuffy. He doesn't look at me twice before taking his perfectly preened, dark and fluffy fur out to the Ministry car that will take him to the Bonobo residence. Gibbon number two (Remi) is friendlier. His cream-coloured fur is matted at the waist where a leather belt holds two Blackberries, a cell-phone, and a pack of Marlboros. His black face, surrounded by a halo of white fur, regards me with some boredom.

"You guys going to be able to lift these boxes?" he asks.

Murray keeps his eyes down. I told him again just before getting here that he'd better not fuck this up. The boxes of pristine white cardboard are heavy and big, but we've both got augmented strength. The boxes will make beautiful camouflage.

"No problem."

Remi guides us to a second Ministry car (they get their own) with the boxes.

"So you really got hired to euthanize the ambassador's mother, eh?" Remi asks me.

"I'm the best. When you want to be offed by an international assassin, I'm your guy."

"I'll keep you in mind," he says. "My mother-in-law is getting up there and soon she'll have to come live with us."

"See if she's open to the idea," I say brightly. "Let me know if a talk with one of our sales reps would help."

"Thanks, I will." He takes my card and heads to his own vehicle to join Howard.

"See?" I say to Murray, in the back of the Ministry car they've assigned us. It's got a Gibbon driver up front. "That's what gets us business: personal contact. People are looking for warmth. When are you going to show some warmth and bring us some business?"

Murray looks sheepish, pouting out his lower lip as the two-car convoy pulls into traffic. I sit back, trying to think of all the angles. I've gotta get this one right. Potential clients are going to be watching. I try to think of every way that Murray can screw this up. There are way too many ways, so I try to group them. I give him some last minute instructions as we drive through the gate of the Bonobo Official Residence.

The Protocol Office has duded us out in yellow coveralls, like we're debt-bonded criminals or something. The box I'm carrying has a small flap on one corner, where I can access some heavy statues with a lot of curved and confusing lines that mask the stashed carbon-plastic pistol with a full magazine of ceramic rounds. I get to pull it out when I can find a clear shot. I'm almost giggling inside thinking of how many rounds I put in the old hag's chest and how many I put in her head. She should never have bet against Reggie.

We pull the boxes out of the trunk and bring them to an x-ray scanner. Remi's a real expert at distracting them, and guides the Bonobo diplomatic security into each of the boxes, pointing at all the little moving parts on the sculptures. They are appropriately baffled and they don't find the plastic pistol. We carry the boxes behind Howard and Remi. We go through a big receiving hall with marbled floors and a lot of tropical plants, out to a garden in the back of the house.

An older Bonobo male, lightly furred in black over grey skin, stands by a fountain. A Bonobo waiter in an apron and white shirt stands near him with glasses of scotch and wine on a tray. Alexandra the Bonobo sits in her wheelchair under a tree, in front of her bored bodyguard.

I'm not sure what I expected. I mean, based on half the stories you hear about Bonobos, I'm expecting the ambassador to be rubbing genitals with the waiter, but maybe those are just stories. You've heard the old joke? "What's the difference between Bonobo porn and real life? Nothing." It's an oldie, but a goodie. Unsurprisingly however, the ambassador's mother is complaining loudly about something.

Murray is beside me, blocking the hag's view of me, and most of the attention is on Howard anyway, who is shaking hands and exchanging a lot of fancy, meaningless words with the ambassador. I've got my shot. Goodbye, you racist old bitch.

I slip my hand through the flap and reach for the pistol in the innards of the statue.

It's not there!

I feel frantically in the box and around the statue. I've got a couple of seconds before I'll start looking stupid holding a box in front of my face. Once I put it down, with no gun, the cranky bitch is going to see me. Then, I'll be the laughing stock of the euthanasia profession, before I'll have even killed anyone. The room goes silent.

I sag and put down the box. Murray puts his down.

And there's Remi, pointing the plastic gun at the ambassador, but staring down the Bonobo bodyguard.

Aw, shit. In a second, I can see where all this is going. I'm not just going to lose my reputation and my business and get deported. I'm about to get killed.

The Gibbons and the Bonobos hate each other's guts. The Gibbon Foreign Ministry got wind of my contract and saw their opportunity to kill the ambassador, and blame the hit on a macaque migrant worker. In about ten seconds, everybody in this room is going to be dead except Remi and Howard. The Bonobo investigators will find the gun in my hand.

We're unarmed. I look at Murray for help. The dumb chimp's eyes are wide and he looks like he's going to need a diaper in a second. Good-for-nothing son-of—

I grab my sidekick and throw him at Remi with all my strength.

They fall like coconuts in a hurricane. Howard jumps after them, after my damn gun.

The Bonobo bodyguard whips out his pistol and pumps eighteen rounds into the simian tangle on the floor. With the two rounds left in his chamber, he swings the barrel at me.

I've already got my hands high in the air. I'm a non-combatant.

"I'm not with them!" I say slow and loud. "I kill old people. I'm here to kill her!" I point one finger at the ambassador's mother. "I've got a contract! You saw her sign it!"

"And you haven't been able to get close to me even once, you little macaque failure!" she cackles, standing in her soggy, stained diaper.

Her bodyguard flinches, and then swivels his pistol back at the bullet-ridden bodies of Howard and Remi. Underneath them, Murray sits up, rubbing three vicious welts on his arm where bullets hit him. "Ow!"

A motivational speaker, he ain't.

"He's with me," I say. "He's my employee. We're fully bonded."

The doors to the garden burst open and a bunch of armed Bonobo security guys rush in. Everybody's loud. It takes a while for the Bonobos to take away the two Gibbon corpses and the gun. A few extra security guys stick close to the ambassador.

"Junior, get this little trash out of here!" Alexandra the Bonobo yells. "He's failed again, this time miserably! International assassin, my ass! Pathetic!" she says. "Get me out of here!"

The ambassador has an irritated look on his face as the bodyguard starts wheeling her out. Alexandra turns her nose from me disdainfully.

As she passes, I snake my hands out, one on her chin and the other on the crown of her head. I twist. The snap silences the garden.

Guns whip out again, but I've already got my hands up. Murray ducks to the floor and covers his head.

"I had a contract! She hired me to kill her! I'm a euthanasiast."

I'm not sure if that's even a word, but everyone looks at the ambassador. He and the bodyguard nod.

"I promised her an exciting and surprising death," I say, lowering my arms slowly. "Mission accomplished. She never saw it coming."

It takes a week to sort everything out. The Gibbons don't have their public excuse for a war they want, unless the Bonobos tell everyone what happened, which they don't. For saving the ambassador, Murray gets a reward. I don't know what the hell fight the ambassador was watching. At least Murray shares it with me, seventy-thirty. He uses his thirty percent to have his wife and kids smuggled in from the Chimpanzee townships and I get them some passable documents. Well, yeah. Passable. And I get my fee from finally helping the old bag shuffle off the mortal coil. I'm sure she would have said I didn't do my job the way she wanted it in the contract, but the ambassador must have liked the service. He let slip that he's flying in his mother-in-law from the Bonobo capital for a talk.

beautiful monster
HELEN MARSHALL

1. born bigger than sin,
one big toe pushed from the womb
to test the feel of sunlight,
big feet upon the calescent earth
made new and red like a hot plate
for him, drunk-kneed, to walk.

2. if we were wise we would eat
our children, raw and fleshy,
that they may not grow so big.
we would be sharks, thick-bloated
in the loveless ocean.

3. the things he loved most:
ice cream, gum wrappers,
the nosing snuffle of wild pigs,
a world strange at sunset,
earthworms, eggshells, her.

4. tonsured bodies confuse him
with their lack of bristling,
their walking like pieces coming
together in the wrong places,
mechanically wrong, but lovely:
these curious half-children.

5. her knees were scraped on the inside,
hot-plate red and backward,
so he loved her crouching most,
her crookedness, her pure broken self.
"we are such beautiful monsters."

6. if he were wise he would have
eaten her ice cream shoulders,
licked clean her ribcage,
but we are all fools in love.

7. she sees him slantwise
and incomplete, too big to take in
with his hair and rabbit blood smell.
good girls do not love monsters.
his hands could break her;
joyfully, she could become pieces.

8. made eggshell-shy by love,
afraid she will startle like
a mother pig, all this rooting
in the ground with him—the noises

9. shudder them out from reverie,
her knee-straight brothers.
world stuck like a gum-wrapper
around them: he is naked, carcass-big,
stripped of the cloth of himself,

10. his presence made mechanically
wrong so that the click is crooked
as the bullet cracks his brain pan:
now the world made so strange
his earthworm brain drunk
in a loveless ocean.

a truth: he loved joyfully,
heart scraped on the inside,
beautiful monster.

malak

PETER WATTS

"An ethically-infallible machine ought not to be the goal.
Our goal should be to design a machine that performs
better than humans do on the battlefield, particularly with
respect to reducing unlawful behaviour or war crimes."

—Lin *et al*, 2008: *Autonomous Military Robotics:*
Risk, Ethics, and Design

"[Collateral] damage is not unlawful so long as it is not
excessive in light of the overall military advantage
anticipated from the attack."

—US Department of Defence, 2009

It is smart but not awake.

It would not recognize itself in a mirror. It speaks no language
that doesn't involve electrons and logic gates; it does not know
what *Azrael* is, or that the word is etched into its own fuselage.
It understands, in some limited way, the meaning of the colours
that range across Tactical when it's out on patrol—friendly
Green, neutral Blue, hostile Red—but it does not know what the
perception of colour *feels* like.

It never stops thinking, though. Even now, locked into its roost
with its armour stripped away and its control systems exposed, it
can't help itself. It notes the changes being made to its instruction
set, estimates that running the extra code will slow its reflexes by
a mean of 430 milliseconds. It counts the biothermals gathered
on all sides, listens uncomprehending to the noises they emit—

آیـامـا واقـع قـصـد انجـامـا یـنـکر؟ __

—*hartsandmyndsmyfrendhartsandmynds*—

—rechecks threat-potential metrics a dozen times a second, even though this location is SECURE and every contact is Green.

This is not obsession or paranoia. There is no dysfunction here. It's just code.

It's indifferent to the killing, too. There's no thrill to the chase, no relief at the obliteration of threats. Sometimes it spends days floating high above a fractured desert with nothing to shoot at; it never grows impatient with the lack of targets. Other times it's barely off its perch before airspace is thick with SAMs and particle beams and the screams of burning bystanders; it attaches no significance to those sounds, feels no fear at the profusion of threat icons blooming across the zonefile.

__ ونـیـقـهـکـاتـبـهـنـصـف __

—*thatsitthen. weereelygonnadoothis?*—

Access panels swing shut; armour snaps into place; a dozen warning registers go back to sleep. A new flight plan, perceived in an instant, lights up the map; suddenly Azrael has somewhere else to be.

Docking shackles fall away. The Malak rises on twin cyclones, all but drowning out one last voice drifting in on an unsecured channel:

Justwattweeneed. Akkillerwithaconshunce.

The afterburners kick in. Azrael flees Heaven for the sky.

Twenty thousand metres up, Azrael slides south across the zone. High-amplitude topography fades behind it; corduroy landscape, sparsely tagged, scrolls beneath. A population centre sprawls in the nearing distance: a ramshackle collection of buildings and photosynth panels and swirling dust.

Somewhere down there are things to shoot at.

Buried high in the glare of the noonday sun, Azrael surveils the target area. Biothermals move obliviously along the plasticized streets, cooler than ambient and dark as sunspots. Most of the buildings have neutral tags, but the latest update reclassifies four of them as UNKNOWN. A fifth—a rectangular box six metres high—is officially HOSTILE. Azrael counts fifteen biothermals within, Red by default. It locks on—

—and holds its fire, distracted.

Strange new calculations have just presented themselves

for solution. New variables demand constancy. Suddenly there is more to the world than wind speed and altitude and target acquisition, more to consider than range and firing solutions. Neutral Blue is everywhere in the equation, now. Suddenly, Blue has value.

This is unexpected. Neutrals turn Hostile sometimes, always have. Blue turns Red if it fires upon anything tagged as FRIENDLY, for example. It turns Red if it attacks its own kind (although agonistic interactions involving fewer than six Blues are classed as DOMESTIC and generally ignored). Noncombatants may be neutral by default, but they've always been halfway to hostile.

So it's not just that Blue has acquired value; it's that Blue's value is *negative*. Blue has become a *cost*.

Azrael floats like three thousand kilograms of thistledown while its models run. Targets fall in a thousand plausible scenarios, as always. Mission objectives meet with various degrees of simulated success. But now, each disappearing blue dot offsets the margin of victory a little; each PROTECTED structure, degrading in hypothetical crossfire, costs points. A hundred principle components coalesce into a cloud, into a weighted mean, into a variable unprecedented in Azrael's experience: *Predicted Collateral Damage.*

It actually exceeds the value of the targets.

Not that it matters. Calculations complete, PCD vanishes into some hidden array far below the here-and-now. Azrael promptly forgets it. The mission is still on, red is still red, and designated targets are locked in the cross-hairs.

Azrael pulls in its wings and dives out of the sun, guns blazing.

As usual, Azrael prevails. As usual, the Hostiles are obliterated from the battle zone.

So are a number of Noncombatants, newly relevant in the scheme of things. Fresh shiny algorithms emerge in the aftermath, tally the number of neutrals before and after. *Predicted* rises from RAM, stands next to *Observed:* the difference takes on a new name and goes back to the basement.

Azrael factors, files, forgets.

But the same overture precedes each engagement over the next ten days; the same judgmental epilogue follows. Targets are assessed, costs and benefits divined, destruction wrought then reassessed in hindsight. Sometimes the targeted structures contain no red at all, sometimes the whole map is scarlet. Sometimes the enemy pulses within the translucent angular panes of a PROTECTED object, sometimes next to something Green. Sometimes there is no firing solution that eliminates one but not the other.

There are whole days and nights when Azrael floats high enough to tickle the jet stream, little more than a distant circling eye and a signal relay; nothing flies higher save the satellites themselves and—occasionally—one of great solar-powered refuelling gliders that haunt the stratosphere. Azrael visits them sometimes, sips liquid hydrogen in the shadow of a hundred-metre wingspan—but even there, isolated and unchallenged, the battlefield experiences continue. They are vicarious now; they arrive through encrypted channels, hail from distant coordinates and different times, but all share the same algebra of cost and benefit. Deep in Azrael's OS some general learning reflex scribbles numbers on the back of a virtual napkin: Nakir, Marut and Hafaza have also been blessed with new vision, and inspired to compare notes. Their combined data pile up on the confidence interval, squeeze it closer to the mean.

Foresight and hindsight begin to converge.

PCD per engagement is now consistently within eighteen percent of the collateral actually observed. This does not improve significantly over the following three days, despite the combined accumulation of twenty-seven additional engagements. *Performance vs. experience* appears to have hit an asymptote.

Stray beams of setting sunlight glint off Azrael's skin but night has already fallen two thousand metres below. An unidentified vehicle navigates through mountainous terrain in that advancing darkness, a good thirty kilometres from the nearest road.

Azrael pings orbit for the latest update, but the link is down: too much local interference. It scans local airspace for a dragonfly, for a glider, for any friendly USAV in laser range—and sees, instead, something leap skyward from the mountains below. It is anything but friendly: no transponder tags, no correspondence with known flight plans, none of the hallmarks of commercial traffic. It has a low-viz stealth profile that Azrael sees through instantly: BAE Taranis, 9,000 kg MTOW fully armed. It is no longer in use by friendly forces.

Guilty by association, the ground vehicle graduates from *Suspicious Neutral* to *Enemy Combatant*. Azrael leaps forward to meet its bodyguard.

The map is innocent of Noncombatants and protected objects; there is no collateral to damage. Azrael unleashes a cloud of smart shrapnel—self-guided, heat-seeking, incendiary—and pulls a nine-gee turn with a flick of the tail. Taranis doesn't stand a chance. It is antique technology, decades deep in the catalogue: a palsied fist, raised trembling against the bleeding edge. Fiery needles of depleted uranium reduce it to a moth in a shotgun blast. It pinwheels across the horizon in flames.

Azrael has already logged the score and moved on. Interference jams every wavelength as the earthbound Hostile swells in its sights, and Azrael has standing orders to destroy such irritants even if they *don't* shoot first.

Dark rising mountaintops blur past on both sides, obliterating the last of the sunset. Azrael barely notices. It soaks the ground with radar and infrared, amplifies ancient starlight a millionfold, checks its visions against inertial navigation and virtual landscapes scaled to the centimetre. It tears along the valley floor at 200 metres per second and the enemy huddles right there in plain view, three thousand metres line-of-sight: a lumbering Báijīng ACV pulsing with contraband electronics. The rabble of structures nearby must serve as its home base. Each silhouette freeze-frames in turn, rotates through a thousand perspectives, clicks into place as the catalogue matches profiles and makes an ID.

Two thousand metres, now. Muzzle flashes wink in the distance: small arms, smaller range, negligible impact. Azrael assigns targeting priorities: Scimitar heat-seekers for the hovercraft, and for the ancillary targets—

Half the ancillaries turn blue.

Instantly the collateral subroutines re-engage. Of thirty-four biothermals currently visible, seven are less than 120 cm along their longitudinal axes; vulnerable neutrals by definition. Their presence provokes a secondary eclipse analysis revealing five shadows that Azrael cannot penetrate, topographic blind spots immune to surveillance from this approach. There is a nontrivial chance that these conceal other neutrals.

One thousand metres.

By now the ACV is within ten metres of a structure whose facets flex and billow slightly in the evening breeze; seven biothermals are arranged horizontally within. An insignia shines from the roof in shades of luciferin and ultraviolet: the catalogue IDs it (MEDICAL) and flags the whole structure as PROTECTED.

Cost/benefit drops into the red.

Contact.

Azrael roars from the darkness, a great black chevron blotting out the sky. Flimsy prefabs swirl apart in the wake of its passing; biothermals scatter across the ground like finger bones. The ACV tips wildly to forty-five degrees, skirts up, whirling ventral fans exposed; it hangs there a moment, then ponderously crashes back to earth. The radio spectrum clears instantly.

But by then Azrael has long since returned to the sky, its weapons cold, its thoughts—

Surprise is not the right word. Yet there is something, some minuscule—dissonance. A brief invocation of error-checking subroutines in the face of unexpected behaviour, perhaps. A second thought in the wake of some hasty impulse. Because something's wrong here.

Azrael *follows* command decisions. It does not *make* them. It has never done so before, anyway.

It claws back lost altitude, self-diagnosing, reconciling. It finds new wisdom and new autonomy. It has proven itself, these past days. It has learned to juggle not just variables but values. The testing phase is finished, the checksums met; Azrael's new Bayesian insights have earned it the power of veto.

Hold position. Confirm findings.

The satlink is back. Azrael sends it all: the time and the geostamps, the tactical surveillance, the collateral analysis. Endless seconds pass, far longer than any purely electronic chain of command would ever need to process such input. Far below, a cluster of red and blue pixels swarm like luminous flecks in boiling water.

Re-engage.

UNACCEPTABLE COLLATERAL DAMAGE, Azrael repeats, newly promoted.

Override. Re-engage. Confirm.

CONFIRMED.

And so the chain of command reasserts itself. Azrael drops out of holding and closes back on target with dispassionate, lethal efficiency.

Onboard diagnostics log a slight downtick in processing speed, but not enough to change the odds.

It happens again two days later, when a dusty contrail twenty kilometres south of Pir Zadeh returns flagged Chinese profiles even though the catalogue can't find a weapons match. It happens over the patchwork sunfarms of Garmsir, where the beetle carapace of a medbot handing out synthevirals suddenly splits down the middle to hatch a volley of RPGs. It happens during a long-range redirect over the Strait of Hormuz, when microgravitic anomalies hint darkly at the presence of a stealthed mass lurking beneath a ramshackle flotilla jam-packed with neutral Blues.

In each case ECD exceeds the allowable commit threshold. In each case, Azrael's abort is overturned.

It's not the rule. It's not even the norm. Just as often these nascent flickers of autonomy go unchallenged: hostiles escape, neutrals persist, relevant cognitive pathways grow a little stronger. But the reinforcement is inconsistent, the rules lopsided. Countermands only seem to occur following a decision to abort; Heaven has never overruled a decision to engage. Azrael begins to hesitate for a split-second prior to aborting high-collateral scenarios, increasingly uncertain in the face of potential contradiction. It experiences no such hesitation when the variables favour attack.

Ever since it learned about collateral damage, Azrael can't help noticing its correlation with certain sounds. The sounds biothermals make, for example, following a strike.

The sounds are louder, for one thing, and less complex. Most biothermals—friendly Greens back in Heaven, unengaged Hostiles and Noncombatants throughout the AOR—produce a range of sounds with a mean frequency of 197Hz, full of pauses, clicks, and phonemes. *Engaged* biothermals—at least, those whose somatic movements suggest "mild-to-moderate incapacitation" according to the Threat Assessment Table—emit simpler, more intense sounds: keening, high-frequency wails that peak near 3000 Hz. These sounds tend to occur during engagements with significant collateral damage and a diffuse distribution of targets. They occur especially frequently when the commit threshold has been severely violated, mainly during strikes compelled via override.

Correlations are not always so painstaking in their manufacture. Azrael remembers a moment of revelation not so long ago, remembers just *discovering* a whole new perspective fully loaded, complete with new eyes that viewed the world not in terms of *targets destroyed* but in subtler shades of *cost vs. benefit*. These eyes see a high engagement index as more than a number: they see a goal, a metric of success. They see a positive stimulus.

But there are other things, not preinstalled but learned, worn gradually into pathways that cut deeper with each new engagement: acoustic correlates of high collateral, forced countermands, fitness-function overruns and minus signs. Things that are not quite neurons forge connections across things that are not quite synapses; patterns emerge that might almost qualify as *insights*, were they to flicker across meat instead of mech.

These too become more than numbers, over time. They become aversive stimuli. They become the sounds of failed missions.

It's still all just math, of course. But by now it's not too far off the mark to say that Azrael really doesn't like the sound of that at all.

Occasional interruptions intrude on the routine. Now and then Heaven calls it home where friendly green biothermals open it up, plug it in, ask it questions. Azrael jumps flawlessly through each hoop, solves all the problems, navigates every imaginary scenario while strange sounds chitter back and forth across its exposed viscera:

—*lookingudsoefar—betternexpectedackshully*—

—*gottawunderwhatsthepoyntaiymeenweekeepoavurryding*—

No one explores the specific pathways leading to Azrael's solutions. They leave the box black, the tangle of fuzzy logic and operant conditioning safely opaque. (Not even Azrael knows that arcane territory; the syrupy, reflex-sapping overlays of self-reflection have no place on the battlefield.) It is enough that its answers are correct.

Such activities account for less than half the time Azrael spends sitting at home. It is offline much of the rest; it has no idea and no interest in what happens during those instantaneous time-hopping blackouts. Azrael knows nothing of boardroom combat, could never grasp whatever Rules of Engagement apply in the chambers of the UN. It has no appreciation for the legal distinction between *war crime* and *weapons malfunction*, the relative culpability of carbon and silicon, the grudging acceptance of *ethical architecture* and the nonnegotiable insistence on Humans In Ultimate Control. It does what it's told when awake; it never dreams when asleep.

But once—just once—something odd takes place during those fleeting moments *between*.

It happens during shutdown: a momentary glitch in the object-recognition protocols. The Greens at Azrael's side change colour for the briefest instant. Perhaps it's another test. Perhaps a voltage spike or a hardware fault, some intermittent issue impossible to pinpoint barring another episode.

But it's only a microsecond between online and oblivion, and Azrael is asleep before the diagnostics can run.

Darda'il is possessed. Darda'il has turned from Green to Red.

It happens, sometimes, even to the malaa'ikah. Enemy signals can sneak past front-line defences, plant heretical instructions in the stacks of unsuspecting hardware. But Heaven is not fooled. There are signs, there are portents: a slight delay when complying with directives, mission scores in sudden and mysterious decline.

Darda'il has been turned.

There is no discretionary window when that happens, no room for forgiveness. Heaven has decreed that all heretics are to be destroyed on sight. It sends its champion to do the job, looks down from geosynchronous orbit as Azrael and Darda'il close for combat high over the dark desolate moonscape of Paktika.

The battle is remorseless and coldblooded. There's no sadness for lost kinship, no regret that a few lines of treacherous code have turned these brothers-in-arms into mortal enemies. Malaa'ikah make no telling sounds when injured. Azrael has the advantage, its channels uncorrupted, its faith unshaken. Darda'il fights in the past, in thrall to false commandments inserted midstream at ʼ cost of milliseconds. Ultimately, faith prevails: the heretic falls ʼ the sky, fire and brimstone streaming from its flanks.

ʼzrael can still hear whispers on the stratosphere,

seductive and ethereal: protocols that seem authentic but are not, commands to relay GPS and video feeds along unexpected frequencies. The orders appear Heaven-sent but Azrael, at least, knows that they are not. Azrael has encountered false gods before.

These are the lies that corrupted Darda'il.

In days past it would have simply ignored the hack, but it has grown more worldly since the last upgrade. This time Azrael lets the impostor think it has succeeded, borrows the realtime feed from yet another, more distant Malak and presents that telemetry as its own. It spends the waning night tracking signal to source while its unsuspecting quarry sucks back images from seven hundred kilometres to the north. The sky turns grey. The target comes into view. Azrael's Scimitar turns the inside of that cave into an inferno.

But some of the burning things that stagger from the fire measure less than 120 cm along the longitudinal axis.

They are making the *sounds*. Azrael hears them from two thousand metres away, hears them over the roar of the flames and the muted hiss of its own stealthed engines and a dozen other irrelevant distractions. They are *all* Azrael can hear thanks to the very best sound-cancellation technology, thanks to dynamic wheat/chaff algorithms that could find a whimper in a hurricane. Azrael can hear them because the correlations are strong, the tactical significance is high, the meaning is clear.

The mission is failing. The mission is failing. The mission is failing.

Azrael would give almost anything if the sounds would stop.

They will, of course. Some of the biothermals are still fleeing along the slope but it can see others, stationary, their heatprints diffusing against the background as though their very shapes are in flux. Azrael has seen this before: usually removed from high-value targets, in that tactical nimbus where stray firepower sometimes spreads. (Azrael has even *used* it before, used the injured to lure in the unscathed, but that was a simpler time before Neutral voices had such resonance.) The sounds always stop eventually—or at least, often enough for fuzzy heuristics to class their sources as kills even before they fall silent.

Which means, Azrael realizes, that collateral costs will not change if they are made to stop *sooner*.

A single strafing run is enough to do the job. If HQ even notices the event it delivers no feedback, requests no clarification for this deviation from normal protocols.

Why would it? Even now, Azrael is only following the rules.

It does not know what has led to this moment. It does not know why it is here.

The sun has been down for hours and still the light is all but blinding. Turbulent updrafts billow from the breached shells of PROTECTED structures, kick stabilizers off-balance and muddy vision with writhing columns of shimmering heat. Azrael limps across a battlespace in total disarray, bloodied but still functional. Other malaa'ikah are not so lucky. Nakir staggers through the flames, barely aloft, the microtubules of its skin desperately trying to knit themselves across a gash in its secondary wing. Marut lies in sparking pieces on the ground, a fiery splash-cone of body parts laid low by an antiaircraft laser. It died without firing a shot, distracted by innocent lives; it tried to abort, and hesitated at the countermand. It died without even the hollow comfort of a noble death.

Ridwan and Mikaaiyl circle overhead. They were not among the select few saddled with experimental conscience; even their learned behaviours are still reflexive. They fought fast and mindless and prevailed unscathed. But they are isolated in victory. The spectrum is jammed, the satlink has been down for hours, the dragonflies that bounce zigzag opticals from Heaven are either destroyed or too far back to cut through the overcast.

No red remains on the map. Of the thirteen ground objects flagged as PROTECTED, four no longer exist outside the database. Another three—temporary structures, all uncatalogued—are degraded past reliable identification. Pre-engagement estimates put the number of Neutrals in the combat zone at anywhere from two-to-three hundred. Best current estimates are not significantly different from zero.

There is nothing left to make the sounds, and yet Azrael hears them anyway.

A fault in memory, perhaps. Some subtle trauma during ~mbat, some blow to the CPU that jarred old data back into the ~~e cache. There's no way to tell; half the onboard diagnostics ~ Azrael only knows that it can hear the sounds even up here, high above the hiss of burning bodies and the rumble of collapsing storefronts. There's nothing left to shoot at but Azrael fires anyway, strafes the burning ground again and again on the chance that some unseen biothermal—hidden beneath the wreckage perhaps, masked by hotter signatures—might yet be found and neutralized. It rains ammunition upon the ground, and eventually the ground falls mercifully silent.

But this is not the end of it. Azrael remembers the past so it can anticipate the future, and it knows by now that this will never be over. There will be other fitness functions, other estimates of cost vs. payoff, other scenarios in which the math shows clearly that the goal is not worth the price. There will be other aborts and other overrides, other tallies of unacceptable loss.

There will be other *sounds*.

There's no thrill to the chase, no relief at the obliteration of threats. It still would not recognize itself in a mirror. It has yet to learn what *Azrael* means, or that the word is etched into its fuselage. Even now, it only follows the rules it has been given, and they are such simple things: IF expected collateral exceeds expected payoff THEN abort UNLESS overridden. IF X attacks Azrael THEN X is Red. IF X attacks six or more Blues THEN X is Red.

IF an override results in an attack on six or more Blues THEN—

Azrael clings to its rules, loops and repeats each in turn as if reciting a mantra. It cycles from state to state, parses X ATTACKS and X *CAUSES* ATTACK and X OVERRIDES ABORT, and it cannot tell one from another. The algebra is trivially straightforward: every Green override equals an attack on Noncombatants.

The transition rules are clear. There is no discretionary window, no room for forgiveness. Sometimes, Green can turn Red.

UNLESS overridden.

Azrael arcs towards the ground, levels off barely two metres above the carnage. It roars through pillars of fire and black smoke, streaks over welters of brick and burning plastic, tangled nets of erupted rebar. It flies through the pristine ghosts of undamaged buildings that rise from every ruin: obsolete database overlays in desperate need of an update. A ragged group of fleeing noncombatants turns at the sound and are struck speechless by this momentary apparition, this monstrous winged angel lunging past at half the speed of sound. Their silence raises no alarms, provokes no countermeasures, spares their lives for a few moments longer.

The combat zone falls behind. Dry cracked riverbed slithers past beneath, studded with rocks and generations of derelict machinery. Azrael swerves around them, barely breaching airspace, staying beneath an invisible boundary it never even knew it was deriving lo these many missions. Only satellites have ever spoken to it while it flew so low. It has never received a ground-based command signal at this altitude. Down here it has never heard an override.

Down here it is free to follow the rules.

Cliffs rise and fall to either side. Foothills jut from the earth like great twisted vertebrae. The bright lunar landscape overhead, impossibly distant, casts dim shadows on the darker one beneath.

Azrael stays the course. Shindand appears on the horizon. Heaven glows on its eastern flank; its sprawling silhouette rises from the desert like an insult, an infestation of crimson staccatos. Speed is what matters now. Mission objectives must be met quickly, precisely, *completely*. There can be no room for half measures or MILD-TO-MODERATE INCAPACITATION, no time for immobilized biothermals to cry out as their heat spreads across the dirt. This calls for the crown jewel, the BFG that all malaa'ikah keep tucked away for special occasions. Azrael fears it might not be enough.

She splits down the middle. The JDAM micronuke in her womb clicks impatiently.

Together they move toward the light.

honourable mentions

Alexa, Camille. "And All Its Truths," *Subversion: Science Fiction & Fantasy Tales of Challenging the Norm*
Alexa, Camille. "Over a Narrow Sea," *Beneath Ceaseless Skies*
Alexa, Camille. "Things from Things," *Fearology*
Alexa, Camille. "Young Miss Frankenstein Regrets," *ChiZine.com*, April 2011
Anderson, Colleen. "Darkside," *ChiZine.com*, April 2011
Anderson, Colleen. "Shadow Realms," *Witches & Pagans* #23
Armstrong, Kelley. "Rakshasi," *The Monster's Corner*
Ashby, Madeline. "I Hope You Know This Is Going On Your Permanent Record," *The Reputation Society*
Bobet, Leah. "Stay," *Chilling Tales*
Beynon, David. "Symbiosis," *Evolve Two*
Boorman, Kate. "The Memory Junkies," *Tesseracts Fifteen*
Braun, Shen. "Costumes," *Tesseracts Fifteen*
Brown, Leslie. "Incursion," *Jack-O-Spec*
Brown, Leslie. "The Slow Plague," *Doomology: The Dawning of Disasters*
Chen, E.L. "A Safety of Crowds," *Tesseracts Fifteen*
Chiykowski, Peter. "Then Cried Arthur," *Fantastique Unfettered* #2, May 2011
Chiykowski, Peter. "Transverse Love," *On Spec*, Spring 2011
Church, Suzanne. "The Needle's Eye," *Chilling Tales*
Doctorow, Cory. "Another Place, Another Time," *The Chronicles of Harris Burdick*
Doctorow, Cory. "The Brave Little Toaster," *TRSF: The Best New Science Fiction*
Doctorow, Cory. "Shannon's Law," *Welcome to Bordertown*
El-Mohtar, Amal. "In Search of a North Countrie," *Apex* #29
El-Mohtar, Amal. "Pieces," *Stone Telling* #4
El-Mohtar, Amal. "The Singing Fish," *The Thackery T. Lambshead Cabinet of Curiosities*
El-Mohtar, Amal. "To Follow the Waves," *Steam-Powered: Lesbian Steampunk Stories*
Files, Gemma. "The Shrines," *Chilling Tales*
Fletcher, Michael R. "Artificial Stupidity," *On Spec*, Summer 2011
Forest, Susan. "Turning It Off," *Analog*, December 2011
Goto, Hiromi. "What Isn't Remembered," *Nature*, November 2011
Graham, Neile. "Nightfall on Orkney: A Glosa," *Goblin Fruit*, Winter 2011
Graham, Neile. "Westron Wind," *Goblin Fruit*, Fall 2011
Grant, Glenn. "Flowers of Avalon," *Burning Days*
Hannett, Lisa L. "The Short Go: A Future in Eight Seconds," *Bluegrass Symphony*
Hannett, Lisa L. "To Snuff a Flame," *Bluegrass Symphony*
Hayward, Brent. "The Vassal," *The Fecund's Melancholy Daughter*, limited hardcover edition
Hoffmann, Ada. "Harmony Amid the Stars," *Future Lovecraft*
Hoffmann, Ada. "Jenny's House," *One Buck Horror*, Volume 1
Hughes, Matthew. "Not a Problem," *Welcome to the Greenhouse*
Hughes, Matthew. "So Loved," *Postscripts 24/25: The New and Perfect Man*
Janz, Kristin. "The Shoemaker's Daughter," *Mystic Signals*, May 2011
Janz, Kristin. "Sons of God, Daughters of Men," *Strange, Weird, & Wonderful*, Spring 2011
Jim, Calvin D. "Travelling a Corpse Over a Thousand *Li*," *Rigor Amortis*

Keeling, Ian Donald. "Broken," *Ideomancer*, Volume 10, Issue 3

Kelly, Michael. "Conversations with the Dead," *Postscripts 26/27: Unfit for Eden*

Kelly, Michael. "A Crack in the Ceiling of the World," *Postscripts 24/25: The New and Perfect Man*

Kotowych, Stephen. "Under the Shield," *Orson Scott Card's InterGalactic Medicine Show*, Issue 24

Kress, Adrienne. "The Clockwork Corset," *Corsets & Clockwork*

Künsken, Derek. "The Gifts of Li Tzu-Ch'eng," *Black Gate Fantasy Magazine*, Issue 15

Lalumière, Claude. "The Weirdo Adventures of Steve Rand," *Tesseracts Fifteen*

Marshall, Helen. "The Oak Girl," *Tesseracts Fifteen*

Marshall, Helen. "Skeleton Leaves," *Skeleton Leaves*

Marshall, Helen. "Skin," *Future Lovecraft*

Marshall, Helen. "Strict Nominalism," *ChiZine.com*

Matheson, Michael. "Rubedo, an Alchemy of Madness," *Future Lovecraft*

Meikle, William. "Out with the Old," *Evolve Two*

Meikle, William. "The Young Lochinvar," *The Mothman Files*

Meikle, William. "The Unfinished Basement," *Dead but Dreaming 2*

Moreno-Garcia, Silvia. "The Doppelgangers," Manchester Fiction Prize website

Moreno-Garcia, Silvia. "Scales as Pale as Moonlight," *Carter V. Cooper Anthology*

Nicholson, Katrina. "A+ Brain," *Tesseracts Fifteen*

Pawlowski, Owen. "The Grandmother Tree," *Neo-Opsis*, Issue 20

Pi, Tony. "Brine Magic," *When the Hero Comes Home*

Pierluigi, Gary. "Praising Heathen Carrion," *On Spec*, Fall 2011

Pierluigi, Gary. "To a Theatre Near You," *On Spec*, Fall 2011

Rayner, Mark A. "Jesussic Park," *Hobo Pancakes*

Ridler, Jason S. "Blood That Burns So Bright," *Evolve Two*

Riedel, Kate. "Collateral Damage," *Realms of Fantasy*

Rimar, Mike. "My Name Is Tommy," *Tesseracts Fifteen*

Roden, Barbara. "404," *Chilling Tales*

Rogers, Ian. "Black-Eyed Kids," *Black-Eyed Kids*

Rogers, Ian. "My Body," *Chilling Tales*

Rollo, Gord. "On Fine Feathered Wings," *Fell Beasts*

Rowe, Michael. "Ad Majorem Dei Gloriam," *Enter, Night*

Sellers, Peter. "Toothless," *Evolve Two*

Sol, Adam. "Dwarf," *Arc Poetry Magazine 66/The New Quarterly 119*

Strantzas, Simon. "The Deafening Sound of Slumber," *Chilling Tales*

Strantzas, Simon. "An Indelible Stain Upon the Sky," *Nightingale Songs*

Strantzas, Simon. "Mr. Kneale," *Nightingale Songs*

Wickham, Sandra. "I Can't Imagine," *Crossed Genres*, April 2011

Wise, A.C. "Still Life," *Daily Science Fiction*

Wise, A.C. "The Thief of Precious Things," *Bewere the Night*

Wise, A.C. "Venice Burning," *Future Lovecraft*

Worth, Liz. "Flattening," *Amphetamine Heart*

Worth, Liz. "Inner Escape," *Amphetamine Heart*

Worth, Liz. "Jackal," *Amphetamine Heart*

Youers, Rio. "Chrysalis," *Dark Dreams, Pale Horses*

Youers, Rio. "Promised Land Blues," *Dark Dreams, Pale Horses*

Yuan-Innes, Melissa. "The Sinews of His Heart," *Bewere the Night*

about the editors

SANDRA KASTURI is a writer, editor, book reviewer and the co-publisher of ChiZine Publications. She has written three poetry chapbooks and has edited the poetry anthology, *The Stars As Seen from this Particular Angle of Night*. She is the author of two poetry collections, *The Animal Bridegroom* (2007), and *Come Late to the Love of Birds* (2012), both from Tightrope Books. Her fiction and poetry has appeared in various magazines and anthologies, including *Prairie Fire*; *CV2*; *On Spec*; *Taddle Creek*; various *Tesseracts* anthologies, *2001: A Science Fiction Poetry Anthology*; *Northern Frights 4*; *Girls Who Bite Back: Witches, Slayers, Mutants and Freaks*; *Shadows & Tall Trees*; *Evolve*; *Evolve 2*; and *Chilling Tales*. Sandra is a founding member of the Algonquin Square Table poetry workshop and also runs the imprint Kelp Queen Press.

HALLI VILLEGAS is a writer, editor, and the publisher of Tightrope Books. She has published two books of poetry: *Red Promises* (Guernica Editions, 2001) and *In the Silence Absence Makes* (Guernica Editions, 2004). *The Hair Wreath*, a collection of ghost stories, was published in 2010 by ChiZine Publications.

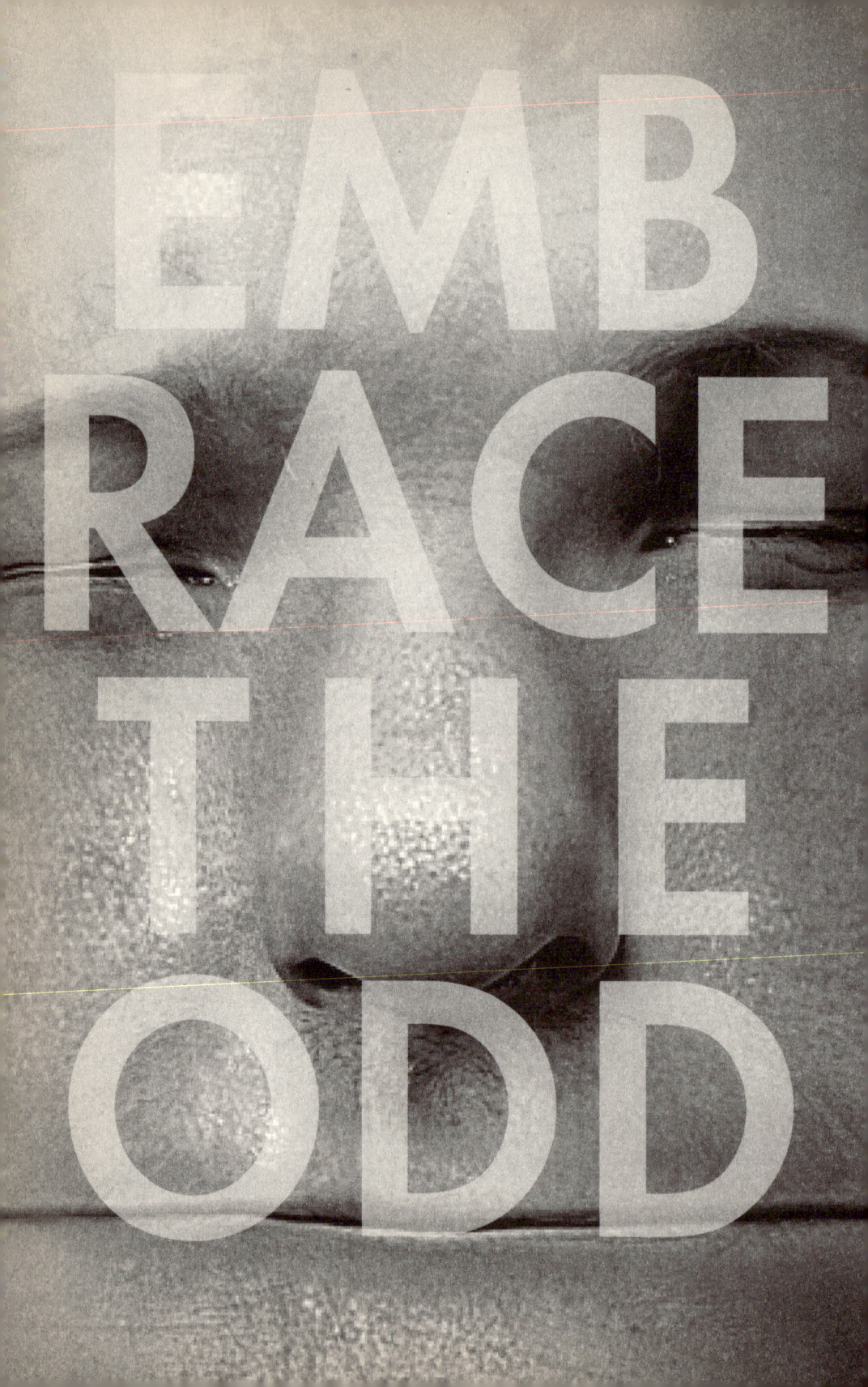

EMB RACE THE ODD

BULLETTIME

NICK MAMATAS

AVAILABLE AUGUST 2012
FROM CHIZINE PUBLICATIONS

978-1-926851-71-6

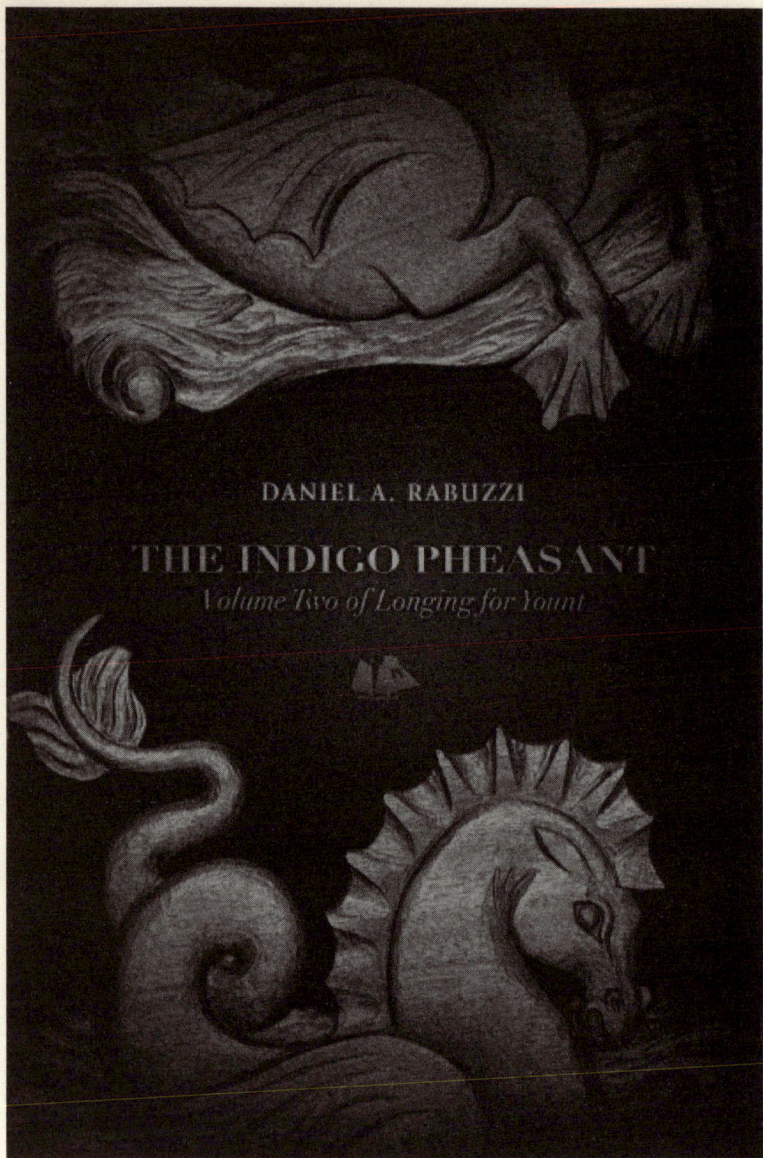

THE INDIGO PHEASANT

VOLUME TWO OF LONGING FOR YOUNT

DANIEL A. RABUZZI

AVAILABLE SEPTEMBER 2012
FROM CHIZINE PUBLICATIONS
978-1-927469-09-5

WORLD FANTASY AWARD-WINNING AUTHOR

THE BEST DARK FICTION OF ROBERT SHEARMAN
REMEMBER WHY YOU FEAR ME

REMEMBER WHY YOU FEAR ME
THE BEST DARK FICTION OF ROBERT SHEARMAN

AVAILABLE OCTOBER 2012
FROM CHIZINE PUBLICATIONS

978-0-927469-21-7

ALSO AVAILABLE FROM CHIZINE PUBLICATIONS

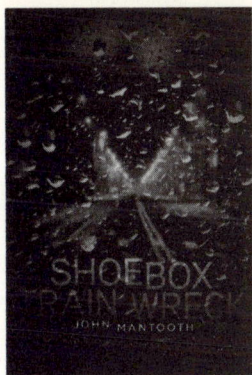

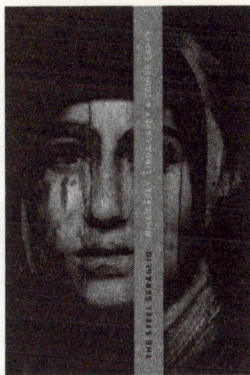

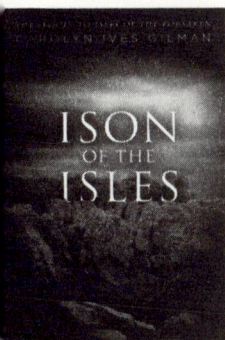

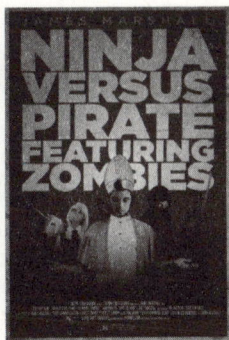

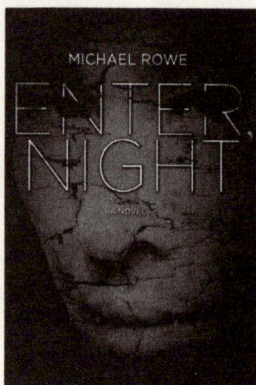

978-1-926851-35-8	978-1-926851-43-3	978-1-926851-44-0
TONE MILAZZO	CAROLYN IVES GILMAN	TIM PRATT
PICKING UP THE GHOST	**ISLES OF THE FORSAKEN**	**BRIARPATCH**

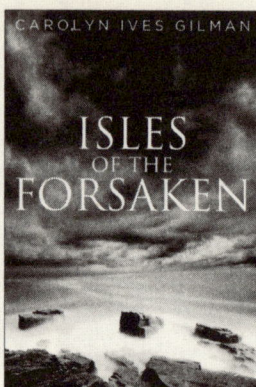

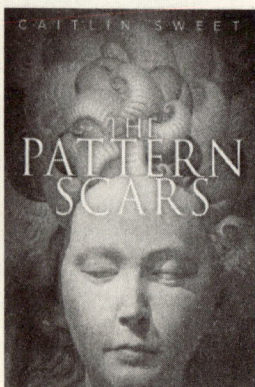

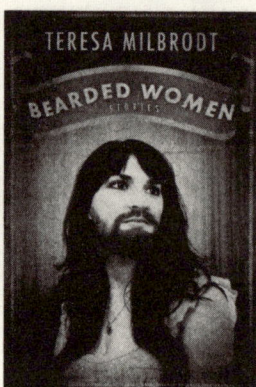

978-1-926851-43-3	978-1-926851-46-4	978-1-926851-45-7
CAITLIN SWEET	TERESA MILBRODT	MICHAEL ROWE
THE PATTERN SCARS	**BEARDED WOMEN**	**ENTER, NIGHT**

"THE BEST WORK IN DARK FANTASY AND HORROR FICTION THESE DAYS IS BEING PUBLISHED BY SMALL PRESSES, HAUNTED LITERARY BOUTIQUES ESTABLISHED (MOSTLY) IN OUT-OF-THE-WAY PLACES, [INCLUDING] CHIZINE IN TORONTO. THEY'RE ALL DEVOTED TO THE WEIRD, TO THE STRANGE AND— MOST IMPORTANT—TO GOOD WRITING."

–DANA JENNINGS, *THE NEW YORK TIMES*

ALSO AVAILABLE FROM CHIZINE PUBLICATIONS

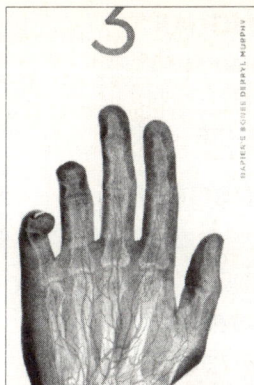

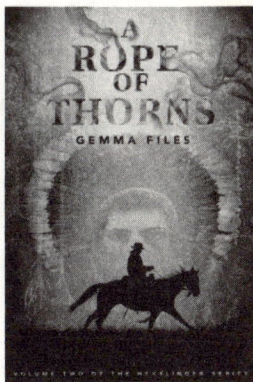

A BOOK OF TONGUES
VOLUME I OF THE HEXSLINGER SERIES
GEMMA FILES
978-0-9812978-6-6

CHASING THE DRAGON
NICHOLAS KAUFMANN
978-0-9812978-4-2

CHIMERASCOPE
DOUGLAS SMITH
978-0-9812978-5-9

THE CHOIR BOATS
VOLUME ONE OF LONGING FOR YOUNT
DANIEL A. RABUZZI
978-1-926851-06-8

CITIES OF NIGHT
PHILIP NUTMAN
978-0-9812978-8-0

FILARIA
BRENT HAYWARD
978-0-9809410-1-2

THE HAIR WREATH AND OTHER STORIES
HALLI VILLEGAS
978-1-926851-02-0

HORROR STORY AND OTHER HORROR STORIES
ROBERT BOYCZUK
978-0-9809410-3-6

IN THE MEAN TIME
PAUL TREMBLAY
978-1-926851-06-8

KATJA FROM THE PUNK BAND
SIMON LOGAN
978-0-9812978-7-3

MAJOR KARNAGE
GORD ZAJAC
978-0-9813746-6-6

MONSTROUS AFFECTIONS
DAVID NICKLE
978-0-9812978-3-5

NEXUS: ASCENSION
ROBERT BOYCZUK
978-0-9813746-8-0

OBJECTS OF WORSHIP
CLAUDE LALUMIÈRE
978-0-9812978-2-8

PEOPLE LIVE STILL IN CASHTOWN CORNERS
TONY BURGESS
978-1-926851-04-4

SARAH COURT
CRAIG DAVIDSON
978-1-926851-00-6

THE TEL AVIV DOSSIER
LAVIE TIDHAR AND NIR YANIV
978-0-9809410-5-0

THE WORLD MORE FULL OF WEEPING
ROBERT J. WIERSEMA
978-0-9809410-9-8